The Short Path to Becoming Heroes

Book 1 of Becoming Heroes Trilogy

By

Major Ursa

Burlington, Vermont

Onion River Press
47 Maple Street, Suite 214
Burlington, VT 05401
info@onionriver.com
www.onionriver.com

ISBN: 978-1-957184-52-4 Paperback
ISBN: 978-1-957184-53-1 eBook
Library of Congress Control Number: 2024903914

Acknowledgement

This book is for all the heroes in my own life. For my Great Grandfather who never let his blindness or the occasional telephone pole stop him from living or being happy. For all the times he stirred my ketchup with his finger to make it taste better. For my father who served his country with honor. He faced bout after bout of cancer with courage. They were incredible role models for a young boy and alter as a man. They were not the only heroes in my life, but their impact is beyond measure.

Thanks again GD for all your hard work.

Author's Note

We live in a strange and often confusing world. Instead of celebrating the sacrifices of great men and women, we are being told that there is no such thing as a hero. Isn't the world a hard enough place without taking heroes away from our children? People need heroes. Not characters from a book or movie or even from the sports teams. We need the real heroes that have and will change our world for the better.

For those who do not believe in heroes, I have news for you. Heroes are real. They abound in our history and they are changing our world each and every day. Heroes are the people who do the hard things, the right things, even when there is a cost. They understand sacrifice. Heroes are not perfect people. Their lives are filled with mistakes and regrets. Despite their faults and fears, they give of themselves when and where there is a need.

Who are these heroes? There are so many if you just look. A general who repeatedly rode a white horse into battle to inspire his troops knowing he would be the target of every enemy soldier who saw him. A woman who goes onto a battlefield armed with only a pitcher of water to comfort injured soldiers. A pilot who dies taking his A-10 into the same fight over and over to rescue his countrymen from an ambush. A young pilot on his first solo flight that refuses to eject from a burning plane because he cannot let that jet crash into the homes of people he does not even know. A policewoman who responds to a midnight call for help knowing that each call might be an ambush. A fireman who disobeys orders, entering a burning building to save a trapped child. And sometimes, it is simply a teacher who refuses to give up on a child that does not even realize they are crying for help.

Finding heroes is not hard. They are all around us every day of our lives. All it takes is looking with your heart and not your head. The much more difficult task is finding the hero within ourselves. Not just finding them, but allowing them to act. Can we find the courage to be that hero that our world so disparately needs? Can we do it every day of our lives? Being a hero is never easy, it usually comes at a cost. A wise man once said "Without sacrifice, there can be no love." I hope we can all have the courage to love that way.

CONTENTS

Prolog

Annah sat at the dining room table sipping the glass of juice that Althea had just brought her. This place, Stormhold Keep, was so different from where she had spent the last six years of her life. Her home back in Sanctuary only had four rooms. It had seemed so large for just three of them. Stormhold was large and confusing, especially for a person who was blind.

It was not just the size that made her new home seem so daunting. It was also the number of people. Someone was always rushing around on an important errand. Back at the grove, the only person she had ever had to worry about getting run over by was her little sister, Meerah. Mama had always sent her outside when she was in the mood to dart around the house.

Here in Shorty's home, there were at least a dozen adults moving about plus Althea's three young children. Everyone moved too fast and with such purpose. Auras kept darting in, out, and around the room. She was almost afraid to get out of her chair. So, she sat and listened.

There were always several discussions going on at the same time. She wondered if this room was the center of activity for the entire Keep. People discussed everything from planting crops to building new homes for the refugees. Everyone had a job or several jobs. Everyone except her. Even the other people Shorty had rescued from the slave market had something to occupy their time. They were planning a return to their old homes or finding a place to fit in here at Stormhold. Annah felt lost. She did not even have her garden to work in anymore.

Annah realized that she was lonely. It was an absurd thought with so many people around her, but they were busy and she had no one to talk to. Even Shorty had been called away to meet with the dwarves that built homes for the newcomers to Stormhold. She smiled as she realized that included a home for Mama and Meerah. They would arrive in a couple days.

Annah sipped more of the juice as she thought about all of the new people she was coming to know. She would never be lonely again. She had never lived in a community this size. So many people, and so much loss. All of them were refugees of one kind or another. Now they all worked so hard to make a future for themselves. Could she do any less? As she placed the glass back on the table, a strong, callused hand came to rest on her shoulder. "Hello, Annah. May I join you?"

Annah turned her head to see an aura filled with gold and silver hovering right behind her. "Kisa. Yes, please. Everyone seems so busy and I do not want to get in their way."

Annah heard a chair slide closer to her and Kisa's aura settled beside her. Kisa's voice was as soothing as her aura. "They have not forgotten you, Annah. They just have so many new people to care for that it is a little chaotic at the moment."

"I know Kisa, but I do not know how to help or even how to fit in."

Kisa leaned in and whispered softly, "Give yourself time, Annah. You will find your place among them. When things settle down, they will seek you out."

Annah smiled. "I know. It is just hard right now. Too many changes all at once. So, what are you up to today?"

Annah watched the golden color grow brighter in Kisa's aura. "Roiland and I are going home this afternoon. The Arch Mage has agreed to take us."

Annah blurted out. "You have to leave so soon?" She hated how needy her voice sounded even to herself.

Kisa placed a hand on her arm. "I have two energetic young boys and a small daughter waiting for me to return. They are being watched by a grumpy dwarf and a very pregnant young woman. So yes, we need to head home in a few hours."

Annah looked down at her own lap. "I am sorry. I just wanted to talk and everyone here is too busy. Even Shorty. There is so much I want to know."

She heard Kisa's soft laugh. "We have some time now, Annah. I doubt Dualis will be ready any time soon. Let me get some food and we can talk while I eat. You need to eat too. How about one of Althea's muffins?" Annah nodded and Kisa rose from her chair. "Think about what you want to ask. I will be right back."

As Kisa walked away, Annah thought about all of the things she wanted to know. She had so many questions. So many whos and whats and whys. She hardly knew where to begin.

Kisa returned and set a small plate in front of her. Annah heard a larger plate being placed in front of Kisa's chair. Kisa sat. "So where would you like to start Annah? I will warn you. I spent too many years adventuring. I will talk with my mouth full sometimes. These eggs are incredible."

Annah thought for a moment. "I think I want to start at the beginning. How did you meet Shorty? He said you were afraid of him when you first met. What happened that made you afraid?"

Kisa began to laugh and almost choked. "I almost died is what happened. No, before you ask, it was not Shorty's fault. But it was not easy to tell who was a friend or an enemy that night."

Annah turned her chair to towards Kisa's aura. "Who tried to kill you?"

Annah heard Kisa's fork scrape across the plate. "It is a long story. Are you sure you want to sit that long?"

Annah nodded and Kisa continued. "That had to be one of the worst storms I ever got caught in. I was miles from anywhere that I knew…"

Part 1
Choosing Who to Be

"Bestus tings eber – New Friend an Squirrels"

Chapter 1
Out of the Rain

Kisa slipped quietly into the small village and paused to look around. The rain was still heavy and she was cold. Worse, her long braid seemed to be absorbing all the rain despite her heavy cloak and hood. The back of her head felt twenty pounds heavier.

The main road through the place was an even mix of large puddles and mud. She needed to get out of the storm. There were about a dozen small buildings, most of which were already dark despite the early hour. She guessed the simple farm folk were smarter than she was and they had just called it a day. A warm bed was preferable to being drowned by the storm.

There was one building near the village center that showed signs of life. Light leaked out from the storm shutters on several windows along its front. As she looked up into the grey sky, she could just make out smoke rising from a large chimney and a smaller one. The idea of a warm fire really appealed to her.

Kisa began picking her way through the mud and the puddles. She managed to avoid the deeper sinkholes as she made her way towards what she assumed was an inn. As she got closer, it became apparent just how old and rundown the place really was. But it was her only option other than backtracking nearly ten miles to the port town along the trade river.

She reached a small hitching post and moved past it to the steps leading up to a covered porch that stretched from one end of the building to the other. She climbed the stairs and stepped out of the rain. Even that small comfort felt wonderful. Kisa placed a hand on a support column while she took a long breath that didn't contain more water than air. The column beneath her hand was old and smooth. She wondered how many hands it had taken to wear away so much of the grain.

Kisa noticed a sign beside a sturdy wooden door. She moved forward and traced her fingers over the letters in the dim light. She stifled a giggle and then shook her head. She wondered what kind of innkeeper would name an inn "The Leaky Bucket"? She sent a silent prayer to her Goddess that it really did not leak. But leaky or not, it has to be drier than on the road. She braced herself, pushed the heavy door open with both hands, and stepped inside.

The heat and warmth of the room hit her as she closed the door against the cold, damp air. She stood dripping as she waited for her eyes to adjust to the light. Her nose began to tell her about the room long before her eyes could see through the light of the many lanterns. The room was filled with the mingled scents of old smoke, stew, fresh bread, and unwashed bodies. The smells of the occupants were far from appealing, but the smell of food made her stomach growl anyway.

Thankfully, the room was dry, warm, and relatively clean. The main room was larger than it looked from the outside. The inn was also crowded. There were at least a dozen tables, all full, crowded into the space. On the right side near the back was a small platform, raised about a hand's height off the main floor. She assumed it was for entertainers. Along the far wall was a long oak bar polished and shinning in the lamplight. There were eight sturdy stools along its front. She could see a doorway behind the bar. A young girl carrying a tray of food and drinks came through the doorway, so she guessed it led into the kitchen.

Most of the seats at the bar were full. One empty barstool was in the center and a second was down on the right side near the raised platform. She headed for the one near the platform. She was not comfortable having strangers on both sides of her.

The stool was not that tall and once on it, Kisa found that the bar was about chest height to her. She turned her back to the bar and slipped off her backpack and rested it on the floor beside her. She hesitated a moment and then pulled off the hooded cloak as well and lay that over the backpack to dry.

Kisa began to squeeze the water out of her long braid as she studied the patrons. The crowd seemed to be a normal mix of locals and travelers. The group seemed to be composed of about half humans with a good mix of halflings among them. There was a table of dwarves as well as a lone dwarf sitting at the far end of the bar. She also spotted a lone elf sitting at a small table back near the door. As her eyes returned to the center of the room, Kisa sucked in her breath as she realized that two of the center tables were occupied by orcs.

Kisa forced her eyes to move on as she continued to squeeze water out of her hair. She saw a large shape sitting on the floor on the backside of the raised platform. Its face was in the shadows of a support column so she could not make out its race, but it was huge. As she tried to make out a face, the sound of breaking pottery followed by loud shouting erupted from the center of the room. Kisa's gaze darted back to the tables where the orcs sat. Two of them were standing and yelling at each other. There was a broken bowl and a lumpy puddle of stew on the floor between them.

Kisa frowned and began to count the orcs. She figured there were at least ten of them controlling the center of the room. As she continued to stare, she realized several were half human and the largest of those was a mix of orc, human. and something she did not recognize. Whatever mix of races he was, he was much larger than the rest and was obviously their leader. Kisa wondered if her decision to enter this place was such a good idea after all.

Kisa jumped as a bar towel thumped into the back of her head and fell to the floor. She spun around on the stool as a soft male voice came from the other side of the bar. "That lot will take your stares as an insult or as an invitation. Neither will go well for you, girl. Best look elsewhere. And try wiping that water off my floor before someone slips and I have a fight in my inn."

Kisa slid off the stool and soaked up the water from her hair into the towel. When most of the puddle on the floor was gone, she got back onto the stool. She faced the bar this time and tossed the wet towel back. "Thanks for the warning. They just caught me by surprise."

The innkeeper caught the wet towel and placed it under the bar. He slid another dry one across to her. "Finishing drying your hair before it makes another puddle." Kisa nodded her thanks and began to run the towel down her braid.

The serving girl came out of the kitchen with another tray of food. The smell of it hit Kisa and her mouth began to water. She stared at the food as the tray disappeared into the crowd. She turned back around again catching the scent of fresh bread. She realized just how hungry she was.

Her attention returned to the man behind the bar who was now smiling at her. He was an older man of about fifty years. He wiped his hands on the apron he wore and held out a hand. "Welcome to the Bucket. She is not much to look at, but she is all mine. My name is Leaky." He paused for a second and waited until Kisa finally reached up to grasp his hand. He gave it a quick shake before letting go. He winked at her. "And no, cannot rightly say why my Ma stuck me with that one. But, twas probably fair since she got stuck raising me. What can I do for you, traveler?"

Kisa glanced down at her cloak. It took her a second to process it all. She was not used to talking as she had traveled alone the past week. She had been avoiding people since she had headed west from the coast. After a moment she met his eyes. "Can you make the rain stop? Short of that, something hot to eat and some of that incredible smelling bread. And maybe some water to drink if its clean."

Leaky chuckled and stepped through the door into the kitchen. He returned a moment later to place a steaming ceramic mug in front of Kisa. "The water is not always safe unless it is boiled these days." He glanced quickly at the tables with the orcs. "Our new neighbors have camped upstream from here and they do not seem concerned about the water supply." He gestured at the mug. "That is a good root tea my wife makes. It has a bit of a kick and it will warm your insides."

Kisa nodded and took a sip. It was a little bitter but the sudden heat in her middle did help immensely. A young girl slipped out the kitchen doorway and placed a bowl of stew, a spoon, and a small loaf of bread in front of her. The girl quickly disappeared back into the kitchen. Kisa relaxed a little. Things were looking up.

She thanked Leaky and picked up the spoon. She stared at it for a
moment and then put it back on the bar. She reached into a pouch
on her belt and pulled out her own spoon. Then she took a bite,
being careful not to burn her mouth. The stew had a thick broth with
potatoes, mushrooms, carrots, and surprisingly large pieces of meat.
She took another bite and mumbled around a full mouth, "Very good.
Thanks."

Leaky grinned at her and whispered conspiratorially, "You must be
really hungry. It is not that good, but it is the only meal my wife knows
how to cook. After a couple hundred bowls of it… well you get the
idea. But I'll tell the wife you said so." He grinned and then added,
"We got us a wandering bard in town. Music is not half bad but his
news is depressing. He should start in a bit. Enjoy the music but if he
sets to preaching, just try to stay out of the way."

Kisa asked, "Out of the way of what?" But Leaky was already moving
to the far end of the bar where the lone dwarf was sitting with a large
mug. She studied the dwarf for a moment as she ate. He seemed young,
but his arms were corded with muscle and the large axe leaning against
the bar next to him looked dangerous. Kisa went back to her food but
kept an eye on her backpack and cloak.

As Kisa was finishing her stew, an older man with a limp clambered
up onto the platform and began to play a lute. His clothing was worn
but clean. His short beard was gray, and well groomed. There was a
rapier hanging on his belt. The hilt was simple and functional. It was
obviously not just for decoration. He began to sing in a rich baritone.

The music was soothing and Kisa relaxed into the melody and the
food. Leaky was right, the stew really was not that good unless you
had not eaten all day. The spices tended to build and after the first
couple bites you could not taste much anymore. The bread was to die
for though and Kisa wished for more.

Kisa picked up the now cooler mug and turned her back to the bar. She
studied the room over the lip of the mug. As she glanced around, she
again noticed the figure on the floor behind the platform. He was easily
the largest humanoid she had ever seen. Sitting on the floor, he was
taller than she was on the stool. She had no idea what his origins were.

Kisa watched as he sat and bounced a small ball up and down on the floor. He had a simple and honest look on his face. He seemed to be trying unsuccessfully to bounce the ball to the rhythm of the music. Kisa decided he was not a risk to her but was not sure why she felt sure of it.

Kisa had finished her tea and was debating whether to ask about a room when the man's song came to an end. Although he no longer sang, his fingers continued to stroke the strings of the lute in a new pattern. His playing grew softer and the old man began to speak in a surprisingly powerful voice. His words seemed to carry to every corner of the room. His cadence blended with the melody. Kisa finally recognized the music as an old hero ballad. This was no ordinary minstrel. Kisa, like most of the other patrons, was drawn into the magic of his words.

> *"It has been nearly two thousand years since the Great Change when mortals nearly destroyed our world with their search for power. We were lucky to survive our own madness. There were many changes not the least of which was the birth of the races of dwarf, elf, halfling, and many others. Magic was also born to our world. Since that time, the Elves and the Druids have done much to restore and heal this land. That is especially true here in the North near the Lake Country.*
>
> *Now the races once again face a crossroads. Evil again threatens our world. But instead of banding together, the races squabble amongst themselves. Each is seeking dominance over its neighbors. Individuals again seek power and attempt to use that power to subjugate all. And we watch. You waste precious time drinking and gossiping in a seedy tavern such as this."*

Leaky yelled out, "Watch it, old man!" But the attempt at humor fell flat and many in the room begin to look nervously towards the door. The orcs who had been loud and obnoxious, were now still and quiet.

The old man continued.

"You waste time and pretend that all is well while your friends and family are being enslaved right under your noses. You do nothing. How many children must be taken before you listen? Before you see what is before your eyes?"

The bard fell silent and stared around the room accusingly.

The silence was shattered by the sound of chair legs scraping across the floor and the sudden clatter of a chair toppling. Kisa jumped at the sound and turned to see the tall half-orc surge to his feet and spin to face the bard. His face was pockmarked and scarred and one incisor was noticeably longer. Kisa held her breath as he snarled and pulled an incredibly large sword from over his shoulder. "Shut up, you old fool. I have warned you to keep your tales to yourself. The music is bad enough without your lies thrown in. Now it is time to pay for your insolence."

The bard set aside his lute and placed a hand on his rapier's hilt. "I do not care about your threats or your warnings. If the truth bothers you so much, either crawl back to your caves or come and see if these old bones are as fragile as you think they are." The old man stood straighter and motioned the half-orc forward.

The half-orc grasped his sword hilt with both hands. "I am not so stupid fool! This is no duel where you can catch me off guard. It is simply time for you to die. Kill him!"

At his order, Kisa heard the twang of bowstrings come from behind the bar near the entrance to the kitchen. She hissed as two sets of fletching appeared in the bard's stomach. Kisa glanced back to see two more orcs with crossbows standing behind the bar. Kisa cursed herself. "Stupid to lose track of your surroundings. Going to get yourself killed one of these days."

The half-orc turned and raised his sword over his head. Then he bellowed over the rising panic of the patrons trying to exit the inn. "Any other fools want to open their mouths and spread lies?" The rest of the orcs rose and began to pull out their own weapons.

Chapter 2
The Fog of Battle

Kisa watched the half-orc turn to face the door, laughing at the panicked people trying to flee. There were several screams as someone fell on the way towards the exit. Once the half-orc's back was to her, Kisa quietly slipped to the floor to examine the bard. The two bolts had gone in deep and there was a lot of blood. She had no idea if her magic was strong enough to save him, but she had to try.

Kisa reached inside her shirt and drew out a silver chain. At its end was a beautifully carved sheaf of wheat. It was carved from hardwood and the painting was as detailed as the woodwork. Each stalk and piece of grain seemed lifelike in its detail.

Kisa clutched the Holy Symbol tightly in her right hand and placed the other near the bolt in the center of the bard's stomach. She stared at the wheat in her hand. Her eyes lost their focus as she prayed, "Mother of All, Great Akka, please grant heal..."

At that moment, blinding pain erupted below Kisa's right armpit. Her focus and spell were lost along with her ability to breath. She felt her ribs give as she rolled to her side in the Bard's blood. Through the haze of pain, she saw the half-orc standing over her with a large iron-toed boot extended from the brutal kick.

The half-orc glared down at her. "I said he dies. Fool, your pain will be as great as his. It just will not last as long. Die now, Priestess, and be a good example to this town on why they should mind their own business." He raised his huge sword over Kisa's head and laughed.

Kisa stared up at the giant sword still trying to breathe through the pain in her chest. She realized she was about to be cut in half. Oh, Mother Goddess, she thought. To come so far just to die in a stupid tavern brawl. Kisa looked into the brute's eyes defiantly, unwilling to give it the satisfaction of seeing her fear.

Kisa saw the blade rise high into the air. Then two huge hands came from behind the half-orc to grasp the sides of its head. The hands gave a sharp twist to the side and there was a sickening crack. Suddenly the half-orc was staring behind himself and the large sword clattered to the floor before Kisa.

Kisa blinked in confusion as the half-orc seemed to stand there staring backwards with two extra hands raised to its head. Then the body fell sideways to lie on its stomach with its empty eyes staring up at the ceiling. Kisa looked back up to see that her attacker had been replaced by a large form that had to be nearly eight feet tall.

Kisa gripped her side as she coughed. Through her tears, she swore she saw a broad face smiling down at her. She shook her head and the image slowly cleared. It was the figure from behind the platform. He had a wide nose centered in a plain-looking face. The eyes that stared back at her were the palest green that she had ever seen.

He continued to smile and then his large mouth opened to reveal tusk-like incisors. Kisa gasped and then the figure spoke. "Hullo, Lady. I be Shorty. Hopes no bees too bad hurt. Sorry me so slow. Drops ball."

Kisa grunted as she rolled back to her knees. "Shorty? I must have hit my head. Leaky inns and giants named Shorty." Kisa began to laugh and then realized how much laughing hurt. She hissed and clutched her side near her broken ribs.

Shorty shook his head, "No giant. Ogre wid peoples inside. Me little ogre."

Her confusion growing, Kisa stared up at him. "You ate people?"

The large shook its head violently. "Yucky. No eats people. Mama say taste bery bad. Horse muches betterer."

Kisa watched as the ogre's attention shifted to the shiny sword at his feet. He crouched and picked it up. He lifted it easily in his left hand and gave it a practice swing. "Bery nice sword. Me keeps. Orc no needs. Him bery muches dead."

Kisa groaned as the discussion took another unexpected turn. She shook her head again, wondering if it was all a bad dream. She glanced past Shorty to see what was happening in the rest of the inn. She noticed three more orcs closing in on her rescuer. She gasped out softly, "Be… Behind you." Then she slid her left hand down to the belt pouch and pulled out a small vial filled with a dark green liquid. Kisa could not manage two hands on the vial, so she used her teeth to remove the wax seal from the vial.

At her warning, the ogre rose and spun to see the three orcs spreading out to attack him. Kisa heard him mutter, "Dis maybeso gonna hurts." Then he stepped forward to meet them drawing a second equally large sword from over his shoulder.

———————————

Thorn sat on his stool and nursed a large pewter tankard of dark ale. Not bad for a human brew, he thought as he took another swallow. He listened idly as the bard sang. The village and inn were as comfortable as anything he had found since leaving his home near Deephole. He wondered if the village had a smith already. If not, it might be a good place to stay until spring. Well, if the innkeeper had enough of this ale to last that long.

He caught a foul scent and sighed. It would be a nice place to winter except for the smell of orc. Thorn looked again at the two tables of orcs and grimaced in disgust. "Stupid humans ought to get rid of the vermin."

The music got quieter and Thorn began to pay attention to the words of the bard. He shook his head. "Damned fool ought to know where this will lead." Thorn reached down and slid his axe from against the bar to between his knees. Best to be ready. He figured it would not be long now. Fighting was one of his favorite pastimes. Killing orcs was even better. He just hoped he could have another ale afterwards.

As Thorn took another sip of the ale, he carefully watched as two more orcs came out of the kitchen. They both carried loaded crossbows. The closer of the two was just out of axe reach. Damn cowards he thought as heard a chair fall over behind him. "Stupid minstrel. And I be the bigger fool for sticking my arse in the middle of it."

He heard the large orc leader yell, "Kill him" and watched the two behind the bar raise their crossbows and fire. Thorn glanced at the Innkeeper to gauge his reactions. Leaky shook his head and lowered a large war hammer back under the bar. Thorn grunted and then lifted his tankard to throw it. He shook his head and lifted it to his lips and quickly downed the remainder of the ale. Before either of the two orcs behind the bar had looked up from their target, Thorn leaned back and hurled the heavy tankard at the closer of the two orcs.

The tankard covered the short distance in the blink of an eye, connecting with the orc's head. There was a meaty thunk and the whine of bending metal.

Thorn watched the orc slump over the bar. There was a large dent in its head and blood trickled from its ear.

Thorn glanced down as the tankard clattered to the floor. He watched as it slowly stopped spinning. One side of it was caved in. Thorn grinned to himself. "Hard head I guess." Then he glanced over at the innkeeper who had a look of concern on his face. Thorn winked at him. "Oops. Good news is, I did not waste a drop of your fine ale. No spill to clean up."

Thorn spun around on his stool and took his axe into his hand. "Maybe it would have been more impressive if I was drunk." Thorn shrugged and eyed the room. He watched the big one snap the half-orc's neck. "Nice move. Need to keep an eye on that one. Might take some chopping to bring him down." Thorn noted that the room had dissolved into chaos. The patrons were pressing for the door and the orcs seemed to enjoy adding to the panic.

One of the orcs was staring at him and Thorn grinned back at it. He raised his voice and shouted, "I can smell you from here, you ugly piece of cave rat dung!" The particularly ugly specimen began to move towards Thorn with a mace in one hand.

Thorn grinned. "Guess he liked my compliment." He slipped from his stool and raised his axe to rest on his shoulder. There was no time to unstrap the shield from his back so he slid the stool up beside his other hand. It would stop at least one blow before splintering. He hoped he had enough coin to pay for the broken stool and more ale.

The orc eyed Thorn's axe and paused. It began to mutter and gestured as it cast a spell. The orc raised its voice and hissed. "Freeze Dwarf!"

Thorn's body went perfectly still. His axe still rested on his shoulder. His body was rigid and not a muscle moved anywhere. He did not even blink as the orc moved closer.

The orc grinned as it came to stand before Thorn. It leaned in so close its breath stirred the hairs on Thorn's beard. It whispered, "Dwarves are not so tough. Dark One's magic fixed you good. Gonna kill you and make a cloak from your hide so all will know my power. It will be a pleasure skinning you."

The orc raised its mace and Thorn suddenly whispered, "Maybe, maybe not, midden breath."

The orc's mouth fell open at the same instant Thorn's axe buried itself in its chest. Thorn watched its eyes glazed over and muttered. "Stupid orc. Spells and dwarves do not go together. Any fool knows that. Slaying you was a mercy killing. Yer breath stinks like you died a long time ago."

Thorn tried to pull his axe free, but it was stuck. He shook it hard and the dead orc just flopped around on the blade. He sighed in exasperation and lowered the blade and kicked the body until it came off. "Stupid orc."

Thorn glanced back to see Leaky staring at him in shock. Thorn shrugged. "Axe is a little harder to use with the damn thing flopping around like that. At least the look on its face when I hit it was pretty funny." Thorn turned back to find another orc to play with.

H'aor sat drinking his wine reviewing his instructions from the Elven Council. He was waiting for the bard to finish before making contact.

He just wished he knew who the representative from the Druids was. Telling him his contact was somewhat unique didn't help much. He hoped the bard's information was worth the risks of this mission. H'aor glanced nervously at the orcs in the center of the room. He really did not want to be noticed by them.

H'aor sat alone at a table along the wall near the door. Only one table sat between him and the open night. He had 'accidentally' put out the lantern closest to his seat, but he still felt exposed in the well-lit inn. He glanced at the elderly halfling couple sitting at the table closest to the door. They were not likely to be an issue if things went badly tonight.

He began spinning a coin on the table as he waited for the bard to finish. He did not like waiting and his hands needed something to do. H'aor slowly slid his chair away from his table when the bard began to speak. The coin settled to the middle of the table, forgotten. Why was the fool stirring up the orcs? The bard was supposed to gather information, not start a war between the humans and the orcs.

H'aor glanced at the door making sure the way was still clear. His orders were clear. He was not to involve the Elven Nation in this fight. The Council had not decided whether to participate in the war they saw coming here in the south.

The fighting started before H'aor had decided what to do next. His contact was lying on the floor with a pair of crossbow bolts in him. He considered slipping out before things got out of control, but he still needed to find out who the Druid's agent was.

The brawl began to escalate. Several of the orcs went down quickly including their leader. A human female was on the floor and several other patrons had been attacked as they fled. H'aor glanced towards the door and noticed that several of the orcs had shoved their way to it and were blocking the exit. H'aor cursed himself and looked for another way out. The only other exit was through the kitchen past the remaining orc with a crossbow.

One of the orcs blocking the door nudged his partner and then stepped toward the table the two elderly halflings now hid behind. Before H'aor could react, the orc stabbed his sword through the male's chest.

The orc pulled the sword free and raised it over his head to strike the female down.

Without thinking, H'aor stood and barked out a harsh phrase in the language of the Arcane, "shEH laKH!" He raised a hand towards the attacking orc and two sapphire bolts of energy shot forward, striking the orc in the chest. It dropped its bloody sword as it stared down at the two blackened holes. Then it collapsed on the table the halflings had been using. The table groaned and then the legs buckled. The orc and the tabletop hit the floor with a loud slap of wood on wood. The halfling woman reached below her skirt and pulled out a dagger. She nodded to H'aor and started to move cautiously towards the door.

As H'aor watched, the tiny woman moved to the wall and began to slide along it towards the door. The orc there was threatening anyone who came near the door with a large rusty axe. It did not appear to notice the halfling. She moved quietly but quickly until she stood with her back to the door and the oblivious orc before her. She watched his movements for several breaths and then brought her dagger up. Without warning, she stabbed it into the orc's back in the kidney area. The orc dropped the axe as it arched its back in pain. Several patrons grabbed it and pulled it to the ground. The halfling woman slipped out the door.

H'aor drew a slender longsword in his left hand. He looked around again trying to decide what options he had left. He glanced at the orc he had killed and wondered how he would explain this mistake to his father and the Council.

Kisa swallowed the contents of the vial and sighed in relief as the pain in her ribs subsided. She took a deep breath and muttered. "What a blessed waste. My only healing draft gone. Second time this night I lost track of my surroundings. Next time will be the death of me."

She glanced up to see her rescuer facing bad odds. She reached for her mace but then stopped. She had no idea how to help him with those two huge blades weaving around him. Instead, she reached for the Holy Symbol hanging from its chain around her neck. She was trying to choose a target for her magic when she caught movement in the

corner of her eye. Kisa looked back towards the bar. One of the two
orcs who had shot the bard was there with his crossbow reloaded. She
realized he had a great view of her rescuer's back.

Kisa looked down at her Holy Symbol and began to pray as the orc
leaned against the bar and aimed for the very large back of the being
who saved her life. She intoned, "Akka, Earth Mother, lend me your
weapon to save him."

The orc settled both elbows on the bar and took aim at the ogre's back
as the ogre slashed left and right trying to keep all three opponents at
bay. Unnoticed by the orc aiming his crossbow, a glowing white light
formed over its head and quickly resolved into the shape of a hammer.
As the orc placed his finger on the trigger, the hammer came down fast
striking the orc on its shoulder.

The crossbow went off as the hammer struck, but the bolt went high
and wide. It penetrated the far wall and hung there vibrating. The orc
swung around rapidly trying to use the crossbow as a club. But there
was nothing behind him except several bottles on a shelf that shattered
on impact.

The orc looked puzzled, but the hammer came down again. This time
it stuck the orc on the back just below his neck. The orc staggered and
fell to a knee. Kisa focused and the hammer descended one more time.
The orc fell to the floor unmoving.

Kisa glanced at the ogre who still managed to hold off his opponents.
She had no other battle spell available this day, he would have to
manage on his own. Then she turned back to the dying bard to see if
she could save him.

––––––––––––––––––––

Joachim looked out from under the table where he was hiding. This
was a terrible place for a young thief to be. Tavern brawls like this
were one of the big reasons he had left Island Town. Well, that and the
very large price on his head. Who would have thought that picking one
pocket would be worth so much gold? Joachim watched the fighting
nervously. These villagers were nuts. This was not just letting off

steam. This fight was about killing and he did not like the feel of it at all.

His attention shifted back to the gigantic warrior. He was badly outnumbered but so far had managed to use the length of his two swords to keep all three orcs from hurting him. Joachim did not know much about sword fights, but even he could see it would not continue much longer. The orc to the big guy's left was getting around behind him. The other two orcs were faster than the big guy. It was only a matter of time before one of them got through.

Joachim wasn't the only one who jumped when the huge warrior missed a parry and took a sword thrust into his right thigh. It did not appear to be deep, but there was blood dripping from the leather covering that leg.

Sensing victory, the three pressed their attack on their lone opponent. Joachim figured it was over. The behemoth had tried, but three on one was tough odds. Suddenly the huge warrior lunged at the center orc with the sword in his left hand. The orc stumbled backwards, but the strike had been a ruse. The warrior followed the lunge with a viscous slash of the right blade at the orc on that side. It too backed away.

The orc to the left realized it opponent could not bring either blade around that far. It came rushing in on the undefended side with its sword raised for a killing blow. Joachim's mouth fell open as the warrior punched out with his left hand driving the hilt of the sword into the orc's face. The power of the blow crushed bone with a crack that could be heard above the other sounds of battle. Its nose erupted with blood spraying everywhere. Joachim watched in fascination as several teeth bounced across the floor. The orc flew backwards to slide across into a table spilling the two drinks resting on top of it. The orc did not get back up.

The remaining two orcs resumed their attack. The one to the right made another quick move and the warrior took another cut. This one on his upper arm. The orc that had been in the middle began shifting to the warrior's left trying to keep him from bunching them up. As it moved around, it came closer to the tables where Joachim hid.

Joachim was enjoying the show but was not at all happy to be closer to the action. He was considering slipping away when he noticed a large pouch hanging from the orc's belt. He swore he could hear the coins moving around inside it. Joachim glanced at the bar. Both orcs there were down. It was a way out if he was fast. And Joachim knew he was very fast.

But he was going to need coins to move on. The money in that pouch was calling his name. He knew this was a bad idea, but he needed a way to pay for food and supplies. Besides, none of these townsfolk were likely to complain if he stole from one of the orcs. Joachim unconsciously began to slide from under the table. He crept under another table that was just behind the orc. His right hand slid behind his back and pulled forth his prized knife. This was the reason he had left his home. Maybe it could make him some money now.

Joachim began to carefully watch the pattern of the orc's attacks.

———————————————

Shorty felt the blood seeping down his leg into his boot. The wound did not hurt too badly, but the blood loss would slow him. That was bad. The orcs were already faster than he was. The cut on his arm was more serious as it limited his reach on that side.

He started to look for a way to end the fight. The problem was these two orcs seemed to work well together. Two orcs were better than the three he started with, but he knew he was in trouble. The only option Shorty saw was to run. But the woman and the old man who made pretty music needed him. He would protect them.

Shorty was beginning to consider doing something foolish. But he could not think of anything that would not get them all killed. Then a he spotted the young human hiding beneath the table. Shorty had no idea if he would help or just hide there. Seeing no other option, Shorty attempted to force the orc closer to the boy's hiding spot.

Shorty smiled when the young human darted out and buried his knife into the back of the orc to Shorty's left. But instead of turning to face their remaining opponent, the boy bent over the fallen orc as if his tiny blade was stuck.

The last orc turned on the new threat and quickly closed the gap between them. The boy looked up in fear as he saw death coming for him. He fumbled for his knife, but it was still in the back of the dead orc. The boy froze as the remaining orc raised its sword to slash down at him.

Shorty began to step forward, but he was too far to reach the boy in time with his injured leg. Shorty took the only option he had left. He threw the new sword with his uninjured left arm. It flew straight through the air, passing close to the young boy.

The sword tip penetrated the orc's upper leg. But it was a shallow wound and the weight of the blade pulled it out. The sword clattered to the floor near the boy. The move distracted the orc and before it could strike the boy, Shorty was there to block its swing. The orc turned on Shorty, but the Shorty was tired of the game. He punched the orc in the stomach with his left fist. As it doubled over from the blow, Shorty droved his sword into the junction of its neck and shoulder. Blood spurted on the blade and on the boy crouched beside the orc. The orc dropped to the floor. Shorty looked down to see fear in the boy's eyes. "Bees kay. Orc dead."

Shorty bent over gingerly and picked out his new blade. He examined it for a moment and then smiled down at the boy. "Good sword. Me keep." He pointed at the orc the boy was kneeling over and added, "Muches tank youse. Good poke."

The boy just looked at him and then at the sword. "Nobody throws a sword! It could have hit me. What were you thinking?"

Shorty shook his head and grinned. "Little bit missed youse." Then Shorty gazed around absorbing what was left of the fight. There were three orcs still up and they were scurrying out the door. Something small and hairy was chasing them. As the first one swept the door open, the last one in line stumbled to the floor. Shorty looked closer and saw a muscular body with a long red beard wrapped around its legs. The form crawled up the orc until it could reach its head. Shorty watched the figure grab a handful of hair and use it to pound the orc's head into the floor over and over.

Shorty looked down at the boy and whispered, "Fuzzface bery, bery scary. Neber makes dem bees mad."

The second orc made it out the door and disappeared into the rain.

Chapter 3
Into the Rain Once More

The main room of the tavern remained a place of confusion long after
the orcs disappeared. Leaky met briefly with most of the locals before
sending them to their homes. Soon after the last had departed, the
halfling woman who had killed the orc by the door returned with an
elderly man wearing a nightshirt over his trousers.

She directed him first to the male halfling she had been sitting with.
He knelt to examine the body. After a moment he looked up at her with
sorrow etched on his face and shook his head. He tried to reach out and
pat her arm but she slapped his hand away. He moved on to the next
victim as she slumped to the floor and placed her hand on the dead
halflings face.

H'aor watched as the nightshirt-clad man moved around the room to
the four other locals that had fallen or been cut down by the orcs. He
noted the man who was obviously a cleric ignored the orc bodies as if
they did not matter. He paused and cast spells over three of the victims
and H'aor saw that they were able to get up and move slowly to the
door. The final body was that of a woman who lay in a large pool of
blood. The cleric simple stared down at her with a pained look on his
face.

He took a moment to figure out who was who from the fight. It
appeared that those who had fought the orcs were what he would call
adventures, people who sought out trouble for a profit. He was not sure
about the Priestess or the boy, but the big warrior and the dwarf were

definitely brawlers. Most of the locals including the innkeeper had stayed out of the fighting. He figured that made sense as they had to live here after this was over. Those like him could move on to avoid the orc's revenge. H'aor figured that five of them had killed or run off a dozen orcs. The big warrior and the dwarf had done the most damage, but he, the cleric and the boy had done well. His participation would be a problem if either of the orcs remembered the elf and his magic.

H'aor realized that he needed to check on the bard and began to move that way. The large warrior was moving slowly that way. He seemed to be favoring his injured leg. The young boy was hanging back near back at the orc he killed. H'aor watched with a grin as the boy removed a large pouch and slid it inside his cloak.

The dwarf stomped back from the door. He stopped at a table where there were two upright tankards that had somehow not been spilled. H'aor watched as the dwarf grabbed one and took a mouthful. He seemed to hold it in his mouth for a second and then spit it back out. Then he downed the rest. He grinned over at H'aor and winked. "Next time I will remember not to bite the damn things. Taste horrible. But I did not like the dagger in his hand. Seemed like a good idea at the time." The dwarf grabbed the second tankard and joined H'aor in his walk towards the bard and cleric.

They walked together to the small platform. H'aor sheathed his sword as he went. The dwarf paused to pick up his axe along the way. They arrived as the large warrior asked, "Music man lib or dies?"

Kisa examined the bard as she knelt at his side. She ignored the voice of her rescuer as she tried to slow the flow of blood from the bard's wounds. She was concerned that the blood had a strange tint to it.

She placed her Holy Symbol over his stomach between the two bolts and prepared to once again call upon the Goddess to save the old man. Kisa focused on the Holy Symbol swinging gently before her. Before she began the spell, she took a good look around. The orcs appeared to be all down or fled. The ogre saw her scan the room and whispered to her in a loud voice. "Youse safe. Me protect"

Kisa returned her focus to the dying bard. She slid the bard's shirt up until she could see the wound beneath it. The skin there looked pale except at the edge of where the bolt had pierced his flesh. The wound had blackened and the skin around the bolt looked dead. The blood seeping out around the shaft also was not the bright red of healthy blood.

Kisa placed her hand near the first bolt and began to focus her magic. A clean emerald glow encased her hand. As the glow grew brighter, she grasped the embedded bolt and began to ease if from the wound. The emerald glow flowed down the shaft and into the wound as she pulled. The bolt came free and a blackish stream ran down the bard's side to the floor. Kisa turned her head to the side. The smell of rot rising from the drainage made her gag.

An older man in nightshirt and trousers knelt on the opposite side of the bard from Kisa. She looked up to see him shaking his head. "I have never seen or smelled anything like that. Even a wound gone bad does not smell so. And these wounds are fresh."

Kisa looked across at him. "Can you do more for him?"

He shook his head, "No, Priestess. I am a simple village cleric. I heal farm injuries and minor sickness. What healing I had this day was used to help my friends and neighbors. My duty was to them first and the bard had your help. I can only offer advice and I fear that I know little that will be much help to him or you."

Kisa turned her gaze back to the bard and reached for the second bolt. She had one spell left and she needed to hurry if she was to have any chance of saving him. She jumped when an ice-cold hand came up and grasped her wrist. She turned her eyes to the bard's face. He coughed and there was blood on his lips.

The old man looked at her with gratitude. "My thanks for your efforts, but save your spells. It is my time."

Kisa began to argue. "If we can get the other bolt out…"

The bard squeezed her wrist gently. "Hush, child. The bolts were poisoned. I feel the burning in my gut. The half-breed made sure he was rid of me this time."

Kisa looked at the other cleric but he refused to meet her gaze. "I have nothing for poison, Priestess. "

Kisa grew angry. "There must be something we can do." Her eyes traveled around the group gathered near the dying bard. A dwarf, elf, and young human boy stood watching her. The innkeeper, Leaky, stood to the side. None of them looked hopeful. She returned her eyes to the bard's gaze. "I am sorry, old one. I have no knowledge of poisons." Kisa felt another gentle squeeze on her arm. She looked into his eyes. "How can I serve you then, old one?"

The old man patted her hand before releasing it. "Nothing, Priestess. Well, maybe keep an eye on the half-ogre. He needs, well, a guide around other people. He is worth the trouble." Kisa just nodded.

The bard turned his gaze up towards the elf. Pain flickered across the old man's face. "Elf, you owe me. Your Council asked me to come here. I could have been back protecting my daughter. Instead, I traveled the land trying to prepare the people for war. You and your Council owe me."

H'aor dropped to a knee. He stared into the old man's eyes. Then he nodded. "I am H'aor dit Järvi-Suomi, third son of the Warden of the Western Lakes. I acknowledge the debt owed you Herald. What would you have of me and mine?"

The old man reached his right hand to his left wrist and slowly pushed up the sleeve. Something shined there. He fumbled there for a second and there was the soft snap of metal releasing. His hand came away with something large that shined like the purest silver.

The dwarf let out a whistle. "That is mithral. And old."

H'aor reached over and gently took it from the old man. He held it into the light. An intricately engraved bracer rested on his palm. The engraving was faded but seemed to be that of a figure surrounded by wings. H'aor ran his finger across the image and the runes around it. "The script is unknown to me. Herald. I assume it is important. What would you have me do with it?"

Thorn leaned in. "Not dwarven. Whoever crafted it was very skilled."

The old bard's body spasmed briefly. "Take that to my daughter. Tell her despite all, I found the other half." The old man began to cough bringing up more fouled blood. "She lives in the mountain beside the lake. Three days west… Long Lake. Protect her, Elf, in my stead. She knows the…"

He lay silent and his eyes closed. His body began to tremble. As the shaking came to an end, his eyes shot wide open. "She knows…. the orcs… orcs… west... death…" The bard's body shuddered one more time and went still, staring upward. Thorn bent and gently closed the bard's eyes.

H'aor looked down at the old man and sighed. This mission, his mission, was getting complicated. So much for something easy for a new agent to accomplish. H'aor raised his eyes to see the Innkeeper glaring at him. "What? You cannot blame me for this mess."

Leaky turned his glare on all of them except for the cleric who was moving quickly towards the door. Leaky's voice was a sharp rebuke. "I blame the five of you. The old fool knew the risk he took. By getting involved, you have given this entire town an enemy we cannot beat. Look around at the results of your meddling."

Kisa rose to her feet with anger in her eyes. "I am Kisa, sworn to serve the Goddess Akka. What would you have had me do? Let him die without even trying to save him? And would you have had them let me die as well?"

Leaky suddenly deflated, his anger spent. "Maybe, Priestess. I do not know. Was one old man worth the destruction of an entire village? Your actions killed a lot of orcs this night. More importantly, you killed their leader. He was important somehow. The others feared him." Leaky gestured around the room. "There will be a price for this. You can all run, but this is our home. At least it will be until they burn it down."

The room grew still as each studied the death that surrounded them. The silence was shattered as the dwarf slammed his axe head against the floor. "Not if they have someone else to blame. And if that someone else runs far from here and they have to chase'em, maybe your town and people will survive."

The group all turned to stare at the dwarf. Kisa looked puzzled. "Like who? Those orcs that got away know who did this."

Thorn grinned. "Do they? What do they know, Priestess? We are not locals or they would have seen us before. They will not dare report a bunch of soft villagers whooped their arses. It was that bunch of crazy adventurers that did the arse kicking. They will tell about this huge warrior that snapped their champion's neck like a twig. They know of a crazy dwarf and a nosey elf. They might or might not remember a woman and a boy, but three of us are definitely not from this village."

Thorn looked around the room. "We just need to act the part. We start by stripping the bodies of anything remotely valuable. And then we run. If they are as angry as the Innkeeper things, then they will come hunting for us. Especially if a certain innkeeper can whine and sound helpless enough."

Leaky raised an eyebrow and studied the dwarf. "Might work. Means I have to be damned convincing."

H'aor chuckled. "Not like you have much choice. Unless you want to come along."

Leaky shook his head. "I am not fool enough to travel with the lot of you. I outgrew that nonsense several decades ago." Then he headed back into the kitchen. His voice could be heard ordering everyone in the kitchen to go home.

H'aor raised his voice to be heard in the kitchen. "The escaping fugitives need to steal some travel food and a couple of empty sacks. If you really want to get rid of them that is." He then turned to the boy. "Strip the bodies of coins, pouches, rings, anything that might be valuable. Pile it up on the bar." The boy grinned and began to move away when H'aor added. "I expect to see the heavy one you lifted from that orc you stabbed on the bar too." The boy gave him a dirty look before moving to the Leader's body. He stared at the head facing the wrong direction and then shot a worried look at the large warrior.

Thorn looked at the bodies. "I will check the weapons and armor. If it is in good shape, it comes too. No self-respecting adventurer leaves good gear behind. Everyone knows adventurers are just common thieves." There was a grumble from the boy but Thorn just laughed.

Kisa turned to thank her rescuer when she noticed the blood on his arm and leg. She stepped closer and examined both wounds carefully while the others were busy. She smiled up at him. "You said your name was Shorty?" At his nod, she continued. "Thank you for your help tonight, Shorty. The half-orc planned to killed me." Shorty grinned as she used her water bottle to clean the blood from the two sword wounds. "Neither is that bad, my large friend, but I can only heal one at the moment. Which would you like me to heal for you?"

Shorty just looked confused. "What bees heal?"

H'aor grinned at her and whispered, "Small words."

Kisa shot him a dirty look and patiently explained. "I use magic to make the cuts go away. We call that healing."

Shorty thought for a moment. "Mama tell new word afore. Den Mama bees dead. Heal be make ouch go way? Maybe so?"

Kisa nodded and pointed at each of his wounds. "Pick one."

Shorty glanced over at the elf. "Run muches? Long way?"

At the elf's nod, Shorty pointed to his leg. Kisa gathered her magic and once again the emerald glow encased her hand once more. As the glow began to flow into Shorty's leg, he tried to reach down and touch it. "Bery purtty." The cut on Shorty's leg closed over and it bled no more. He grinned. "Muches tanks you."

Kisa smiled up at him. "You are most welcome, Shorty."

Leaky returned to the room with a large sack which he dropped on the bar. He threw two empty potatoes sacks on top of it. "Bag has bread, cheese, apples, some hard biscuits and jerky. Guess that was all those thieves could find without my help."

H'aor nodded his thanks and grabbed the two empty sacks. He tossed one to Thorn who began to stuff armor and weapons into it. The second, H'aor opened and scooped all the loose coins into. Next, he began to drop some of the belt pouches into to it. Every third one, he slid down the bar to land in front of Leaky.

The boy wandered over with several more pouches and watched the distribution. He leaned in, hissing in complained. "Hey, we almost died for those. Why are you giving them away? And so many?"

H'aor took the last three pouches from the boy. He tossed one of them to Leaky and dropped the others two in the bag. "Listen, boy."

The boy interrupted. "My name is Joachim. Not boy. I am sixteen. I am not a boy anymore."

H'aor turned on the boy with a look of annoyance. "Then don't act like a boy deprived of his toys Joachim. Two of them did die. And more may lose their homes. They have already lost more than we have. If you need a better reason, call it paying for the right to come back this way some day."

Joachim shook his head but sat down out of the way ripping some bread off a loaf still sitting on a nearby table.

Thorn returned with a heavy sack. "Some of it is junk, but it will make it look like we grabbed everything we could before we ran off." He handed the sack to Shorty and asked, "Think you can handle this load?"

Shorty picked it up and wander over behind the platform to tie it on his own large backpack. "Small. Me do."

Joachim whispered to no one in particular. "That is not small."

H'aor dumped some of the food into the bag of pouches and stuffed that bag into his own backpack. He held the bag of remaining food out to Kisa. "If you do not mind, Priestess." Kisa took it to put into her own backpack.

The five gathered around donning cloaks and packs. H'aor turned again to Leaky. "Anything you can tell us to make this run a little easier?"

Leaky grunted. "A bit. There were about forty of them in a camp about half an hour upstream. That would be north of here. Figure you got about half an hour before they bring the rest of that bunch back here. They got some scary big wolves too. Best I can suggest is to take the trail west out of town. If you can, stay ahead of them, you should be able to turn towards the north or northwest around sunrise."

Leaky paused and gestured towards the dead half-orc whose head was still facing the wrong way. "Rumor has it that this one was the son of some big leader among the orcs. You have more enemies now than you might like. The orcs have been raiding pretty much everything east of the mountains since the spring. Finding his daughter is going to take you into the thick of it."

"Thank you for that." H'aor replied and turned towards the door. Leaky cleared his throat and H'aor paused. "Something else?"

Leaky walked over to the broken table and picks up one of the legs. He stared at the group for a bit and then tossed the leg to Thorn. "The way I see it, if I am standing here all dumb and happy, they are not going to buy my story. I need to look like you stole that food if this is going to work. Think you can knock me out without the large dent you left in my tankard?"

Thorn hefted the table leg and walked behind Leaky with a wide grin. "My pleasure, Innkeeper. Always willing to do my part to make everyone happy. Nighty night." Thorn's swing caught Leaky on the back of the head. Thorn dropped the table leg and caught Leaky before he hit the floor.

Thorn lowered him amidst the broken pieces of table. Kisa checked the wound and nodded. A deep voice from the back of the group muttered. "No so nice. Fuzzface bery scary."

There were several chuckles as the group headed out into the heavy rain.

H'aor stood in the road and pointed off to the left. "That way is west. If we are lucky, they will lose us in the rain." With that he took the lead at a fast jog somehow avoiding the worst of the muck.

Kisa and Joachim took off after him, splashing through the mud and rain. Thorn looked back at Shorty. "Me or you at the back?"

Shorty shook his head vigorously. "No youse ahind me. Scary."

Thorn laughed and began to run. Shorty, drew his great sword from over his shoulder and began to trot behind the dwarf.

The five fugitives alternated jogging and walking through the night. The rain held at a steady rate throughout the dark hours. It finally began to dissipate near dawn. The land was beginning to rise into low hills as they traveled further west. H'aor called a halt just after sunrise. It was clear that everyone except the half-ogre was reaching the limits of their endurance. H'aor looked around. "We need to get a little rest, but not in the open. I don't know this area. Any chance one of you has been out this way?"

Thorn gazed off towards the mountains to the west. "Deephole has some mines up in those mountains. Sometimes it is easier to haul the ore down to the river to send it south than it is to bring it back through the tunnels. I have played guard once or twice." He turned and wandered up a small rise and the others followed behind. Thorn took a long look around. "We traveled near here when we came down from the mountains. If I can find it, there is a small cave not far from here. We will be out of sight and dry there."

Kisa gave him a grateful look. "Drying out sounds really good right now. And some food would be nice too." Joachim nodded his agreement.

Thorn turned southwest and his short legs set a grueling pace for about an hour. Thorn turned west at that point and headed for a stand of oak trees visible on a hillside. He moved cautiously in between the trees, heading deeper into the grove. The dwarf motioned the others to follow as he headed towards the hilltop that was now obscured by the foliage.

After a short distance, the group could see two tall oaks on the edge of a small clearing. Thorn slipped between them and pointed across the clearing to a crevice in the side of the hill, partially blocked by a large boulder. The boulder was taller than the ogre. A smile lit the dwarf's face as he headed for the boulder. "Cave entrance is just around here."

As Thorn stepped around the tall rock, he seemed to disappear. As the others came around it, they could see a narrow cleft leading into the hillside. Thorn's voice came from the darkness ahead and H'aor led the others into the darkness of the cleft. The channel only went back a dozen feet before taking a sharp right into total darkness. Thorn was humming happily to himself as he moved around in the dark. Kisa and Joachim followed slowly, stopping just inside. Kisa spoke to the darkness, "Friend Dwarf, this may work for you, but some of us don't see so well in without light."

Thorn chuckled and pulled a small pouch from his pocket. He shook out a coin that glowed brightly, lighting the entire cave. There was not much to see but it was dry and large enough for the whole group. Leaves were piled near the walls with the middle area of clear, hard-packed earth.

Once Kisa and Joachim had moved deeper into the cave, H'aor moved back to the entrance to wave Shorty in. The half-ogre had to remove his pack and turn sideways to fit through the cleft. Shorty felt overhead before entering the cave. He noted the low ceiling and crouched just inside the entrance.

Joachim sighed and pulled off his wet cloak and shook the moisture from it. Kisa dropped her pack and lay down placing her head upon it. "Goddess I am tired."

Joachim and H'aor moved across the cave from Kisa and sat. Thorn grinned at the group from the back of the cave. "We should be safe to rest for a few hours at least. But this would not be a good place to be trapped."

Joachim replied, "You really think they can track us through that rain? It came down hard."

H'aor nodded. "If they have wolves then probably. If they have a Shaman too then definitely."

Thorn shrugged. "They have one less shaman for certain but I would feel better moving on in a few hours.

Shorty looked at his companions and said, "Me watch. Me rest town fer day. Me protect."

Thorn nodded. "Wake us when the sun is high big guy. Understand?"

Shorty nodded and took up a position facing the entrance as everyone else settled in. Thorn pulled out a white cloth which he placed over the shining coin to mute the light. Except for Shorty, they all lay down and closed their eyes. Soon, the sound of heavy breathing filled the cave.

————————————

Shorty turned to watch his companions settle down to sleep. Being underground again felt familiar, but not really safe. Too many bad things had happened in the Ogre Caverns. He really did not miss the underground of his youth. Outside had many more fun things to do. Shorty did miss his family though. Mama and Papa were lost to him, but he sometimes wondered if his uncle had survived after the new Chief had been chosen.

Shorty eyes wandered around the small cave. The elf and the boy were interesting. They might be fun to have as friends. He would like to have friends. He did not have many that were not squirrels. His gaze moved on to the fuzzface at the back of the cave. He seemed to be asleep and that was good. He was scary. But he did fight good. That would help if the orcs found them. Shorty was never sure about the fuzzfaces. He had only met one before and that one had been scary too. But it had helped him and his uncle escape from the grey fuzzfaces. Those were even scarier.

Shorty finally focused on the woman. She was brave and smart. He thought for a minute. Kisa Lady. That was her name. Kisa Lady reminded him of Mama. She could make ouches be gone and she gave him a new word just like Mama did. He liked her. He would keep her safe. He had not been able to keep Mama safe, but he would protect Kisa Lady.

Shorty looked at the glowing piece of metal under a thin white cloth. He remembered another round piece of metal that glowed in the chambers of his Mama and Papa long ago. In his mind, a much younger Shorty stood before his Mama as she sat on her rock.

"Remember, my son, being bigger and or stronger just means you have a bigger job to do. You must protect. Protect all who are smaller than you. Do not be mean like those who hurt you. Use your strength to help others." Then she hugged him.

Shorty's eyes leaked water as her memory slipped away. He muttered "Yes, Mama. Me protect." He turned back to the crevice and listened for danger.

Thorn lay at the back of the cave and watched the half-ogre through half-closed eyes. He couldn't make out the soft words the big warrior spoke. He had been taught that ogres were trouble, but he saw something different in this one's eyes. He did not think it was any great wisdom he saw in those pale green eyes, but this one had heart. The ogre seemed to care and that was more than a little unexpected.

Thorn thought about what he knew of ogre-kin. He had to admit that he had little to go on besides the stories of his grand sire. And knowing which stories were true and which were just for entertaining pesky young dwarves was always the problem. The old dwarf had always had a tale to tell right up until the day he had died at the venerable age of 212. Thorn had loved the old soul. Grand sire was one of the few in the clan that understood Thorn's love of adventure and battle. Both of them were okay at the forge, but swinging an axe was their real love.

Thorn thought back. It had to be about a decade or so ago that he had listened to the ogre stories while working on his shield. He had not really believed that a dwarf in his third century was out fighting in the tunnels, but one never knew with the old ones, especially his Grand Sire.

That day, the old dwarf had sat on a rock occasionally pumping the bellows as he taught young Thorn the best way to layer the steel on a shield. His Grand Sire had sat there with his old pipe in his mouth telling tales occasionally acting out the battles with hand gestures. Grand Sire's hands had left the bellows to stroke his grey beard. He exhaled a large cloud of smoke which made Thorn's eyes water. "Remember pup. Ogres are the worst of them. Big hulking brutes that are mostly brainless. But they can hit hard enough to dent even good steel."

He paused for a moment and pointed to where he wanted Thorn to fix a small defect. "Only good news is that they be slow and they got sensitive feet. I remember one that I chased off. Took off the front of one foot with me axe and smashed the other foot with me hammer. Never seen nothin so funny as a three toed ogre running and screaming into the dark."

Grand sire had gotten a funny look on his face then. "Strange that one was. Met him again not that long ago. I got captured by a Drow slaving team not long after your Grand Dame passed away. I was angry and wandering places I should not have gone alone. I found something to take my anger out on, but it was more that I could handle on my own. They also caught the ogre and one of his young kin. If we had not been in separate cages, we might have killed each other instead of the Drow. Young one finally shamed us into working together to get away from the dark elves. Little ogre was incredibly strong. Broke the chains with his bare hands. Old one saved my life, damn him. Had to give him a nice spear and name him dwarf friend. Embarrassing it was. But he had courage."

Thorn shook his head at the memory and relaxed. He judged that this ogre was different somehow too. Then he allowed himself to sleep.

Chapter 4
In the Light of a New Day

Joachim woke with the feeling that something was not right. Well, something more than being on the run from a band of bloodthirsty orcs. Something more than needing to count on others for survival, especially people he had only met the night before. He lay on his side against the cave wall so he opened one eye and scanned his surroundings. It was safer not to give away that he was awake if there was danger.

The light coming from the covered coin was enough to make out the details of the cave. Now there was also light coming in from the only exit. The soft breathing of his sleeping companions was comforting as he lay there. Joachim turned his head to check out the big warrior that scared him. The guy was just huge and deadly. He still was not sure what had scared him more last night, the orc that had been about to cut him down or the huge sword that had come flying through the air to catch the orc in the leg.

Joachim focused on the exit from the cave and the crevice beyond. It was empty. No one was guarding the only way out. Joachim sat up to see better. The dwarf, elf, and priestess were all still asleep. Joachim began to panic and his words were much louder than he intended. "He is gone. The big coward just left us."

The others sat up and stared around. The dwarf already had his axe in hand. The elf rose to his feet and moved towards the exit from the cave. He stood listening and motioned the others to silence. He had a puzzled look on his face.

Joachim whispered, "Did he just take off or is he selling us out to the orcs?"

Kisa glanced at Thorn before replying softly, "I do not think he is the type to run away or to betray us. "

The dwarf held a finger to his lips as he eased past to join the elf at the exit. He motioned forward and the two began to creep up the passage. Joachim drew his knife and followed. The priestess was close on his heels.

The dwarf moved through the short passage with confidence and emerged into the afternoon sun behind the large boulder. As the elf came up beside him, they paused to listen. There was a soft muttering from the far side of the boulder, but the few words made little sense and were frequently interrupted by a high-pitched chittering noise. The sound of a crackling fire was drowned out when a deep voice began to hum tunelessly. The smell of roasting meat filled the air.

At the smell of fresh food, the dwarf stepped around the rock and into the clearing. The others followed him one by one out into the bright sun. A small cook fire was burning in a shallow pit with two rabbits hanging on a spit over it. There were a half dozen large gray squirrels running around the fire chasing each other or eating acorns that had been cracked and laid out on a large flat rock on the far side of the fire. Their ogre companion sat, occasionally rotating the spit with a large dagger. He seemed to be talking happily with another large gray squirrel that sat upon his shoulder.

Kisa put her hand over her mouth, but the sound of her giggles slipped out. The squirrels immediately scampered up the trees and were lost to sight. The last to leave was the one on the ogre's shoulder. It seemed to scold them for interrupting before it too disappeared into the trees. The ogre looked over at them and smiled. "Hullo. Hungries?" He pointed to some fresh apples resting on the ground near the front side of the boulder. "Bunny bees cook bery soon."

Kisa pushed past the others and walked over to place a hand on Shorty's shoulder. "You have been very busy today, my friend. Thank you."

Shorty beamed up at her and then turned to pull the spits off the fire. He slid the rabbits onto the flat rock next to the nuts and he began to cut them up.

Kisa moved over and grabbed a piece of fruit before going to stand beside one of the trees. She pulled her Holy Symbol from inside her shirt and sat down, crossing her legs and closing her eyes. She sat quietly for a time ignoring all that went on around her.

H'aor ducked back into the cave and returned with a small book. He took some of the rabbit, thanking Shorty before sitting down and opening his book.

Joachim approached the ogre slowly. He looked embarrassed as he mumbled his thanks and took some of the meat. Then he retreated back near the rock on the far side of the fire from the ogre. He sat and stared at the ogre as he ate.

Thorn came and sat beside Shorty. He ate some of the rabbit as he stared thoughtfully through the trees. "You did good this morning Shorty. Everyone needed the rest and this food. Thank you." Shorty smiled as he finished a large piece of the rabbit and reached for more. After a moment, Thorn continued. "How far have you looked around my, big friend?"

Shorty swallowed his bite and lost his cheerful look. "No goes bery far. Bunny catches close. No sees no orc. No sure ifn safe. Find water fer drink."

Thorn sat quietly as he chewed. "You are good out in the forest. Think you can stay at the back and pay attention? Warn us if something is coming?"

Shorty grinned and nodded. He finished the rabbit he was eating and moved the flat rock over near the boulder. Then he began to scoop out a hole using the dirt to put out the cook fire. When it was out, he used his large boot to push the coals into the hole burying the evidence of their fire.

Kisa finished her meditations and came over to squat beside the remains of the rabbit. She carefully nibbled on the hot meat. When she finished, she moved over to Shorty and gestured towards his arm.

The ogre grinned at her. "Heals?"

Kisa nodded and motioned for Shorty to sit. "I am glad you remember the word." She held the Holy Symbol over his arm and began her spell.

Shorty watched happily as the emerald glow began to sink into his wound. "Muches tank you, Kisa Lady."

Thorn stood. "Best eat quickly. We need to move out soon. And our next meal is going to be a long run from now." Kisa nodded and went back to picking at the meat.

Thorn wandered over to stand over the mage. H'aor closed his book as Thorn crouched beside him. The two chatted quietly, occasionally pointing off into the distance. Shorty found some larger oak leaves and began to wrap the leftover meat in them. Joachim and Kisa moved back into the cave to get their backpacks and cloaks.

Kisa stood in the low light of the covered stone and adjusted the straps on her backpack. Without turning she spoke softly. "Joachim, can I ask you something important?"

His voice came from behind her. "Sure, Lady. What is on your mind?"

Kisa paused for a moment. "What is with you and Shorty? Why are you always looking for trouble from him? I have seen you staring at him. It is like you expect him to try and eat you or something."

Joachim was silent for a long time. "He could have killed me. Throwing that sword so close to me was dangerous and stupid."

Kisa turned and stared at him. "The orc would have killed you. You know that right?"

Joachim nodded. "Yeah, but that sword sticks in my mind a lot more that the orc does. It is so big and it came so close."

Kisa whispered. "He saved me too in that fight. It was scary to look up and see something so big. But he did not hurt me. Not exactly what one would expect of an ogre or even a half-ogre."

Joachim stood very still, staring down at his feet. "I am kind of small. Not much food when I was young. But I am really fast. I survived in Island Town by staying ahead of trouble. Trouble was basically anyone bigger or stronger than I was. That was pretty much everyone." He paused and blew out a breath. "He is even bigger than those who ruled the street gangs. The big ones hurt people like me. They were all bullies. I keep expecting him to turn into one of them. And now I might need to depend on him to stay alive. I do not like that idea very much."

Kisa slung her pack over her shoulder. "Maybe not all the big, strong types are bullies, Joachim. Just like maybe some thieves can be trusted. Something to think about while you run today." With that, Kisa headed back out into the sunlight leaving Joachim to his thoughts. He was still standing there thinking when the elf and dwarf came in and grabbed their things. The dwarf returned the coin to its bag and the cave went dark. Joachim followed them out.

Within moments, the group was on the move. Shorty led his new friends to a small stream where everyone drank and refilled their water skins. H'aor looked around the group. "Keep the same order as yesterday. We will not push as hard today. We should be well into the hills by nightfall. There will be more cover in the hills so we will not be as exposed. If we do not see any sign of orcs today, we can get a good night's rest tonight. As best I can figure, we have three or four days of travel to get to the lake the old bard mentioned. From there we can each choose our own roads. Agreed?"

At the chorus of agreement, H'aor led the way out of the stand of trees and turned northwest, racing the sun towards the hills and mountains beyond.

The five near-strangers began to jog at an easy pace. The travel was easier in the daylight than it had been in the dark with the heavy rain coming down. H'aor often ranged far ahead and Shorty sometimes disappeared to the rear, but neither was out of sight for long. That left the three in the middle to chat.

Thorn seemed to struggle a bit more that day and Kisa asked if he was alright. Thorn laughed. "Call it a combination of short legs and too much time working a forge. I have arm muscles to spare, but my legs were not meant for running through the woods. I am a bit sore after last night. Besides, that blasted elf thinks we are all mountain goats the way he keeps scampering off."

Kisa and Joachim laughed. Joachim's curiosity got the better of him. "You are quite a way from Deephole, the trip here did not improve your running any?"

Thorn shrugged. "That was mostly walking or riding in a wagon. Chasing an elf like this is a whole nuther thing."

Joachim paused for a minute. "Dwarves know about ogres, right?" At Thorn's inquisitive glance, he continued. "I am just curious. Our ogre is huge, but he says his name is Shorty? What is with that?

Kisa listened in with curiosity as Thorn's face grew thoughtful. "Male ogres can run up to about ten feet tall. Among his kind, he would qualify as a runt. That must have made his life hell."

Kisa glanced at Joachim and then asked, "How so?"

Thorn sounded thoughtful as he answered, "Ogres are big on dominance and power. The biggest and strongest make the rules. Makes most street gangs look like friendly old women gossiping. Being that much smaller must have made him the target for just about every young ogre in his tribe. Surprising he survived at all. Either he is very smart or very strong. I am betting on strong."

Joachim looked away as he simply said, "Oh."

The terrain continued to rise as they forged further west. By late afternoon, the group climbed up to a lightly-wooded plateau stretching off to the north. The plateau was less than a mile wide and there was a visible ridge line rising above the western edge. The plateau was adorned by a mix of spruce and pine trees intermingled with stands of maple.

H'aor was waiting at the edge of the wooded area as Kisa, Joachim, and Thorn caught up. The dwarf was breathing heavily and he shot the elf a dirty look. Everyone except Thorn had caught their breath by the time Shorty jogged up to join them. H'aor waved his hand back behind him. "I found a faerie ring up ahead. It is old, but the magic might provide a little protection for us tonight. It is about the best we can hope for until we get into the mountains proper."

Thorn stared into the trees. "Are we going to have any issues with the little folk? We all need a good night of sleep, not one filled with little troublemakers picking on the big folk."

H'aor shrugged. "The ring is old and overgrown. I see no sign that it has been used in a long time. We should be able to rest there until the orcs catch up to us."

"Catches up?" Kisa blurted out. "We must have lost them by now. Right?"

Thorn motioned towards Shorty. "In case you did not notice, our big friend kept dropping out of view this afternoon. I doubt he was disappearing without cause."

Shorty turns back to study their trail. "Sees big wolf four time." Shorty held up three fingers to emphasize his point. "Trys ta throw rock last times. Misses."

Thorn sighed. "Sometime tomorrow then. We fight on our terms or theirs. Rest and food and maybe some fresh water."

H'aor led them into the trees. About a quarter mile in there was a perfect circle of maple trees. There were twelve trees around the perimeter and they were all twenty feet in height. The ring was almost twenty feet across and it was heavily shaded by the trees. The interior of the ring was filled with tall, soft grasses. It radiated a sense of peace.

H'aor entered and turned to face them. "I would like to share out the work here if no one objects." He focused first on Shorty. "You did well this morning. Any chance you can find us some food? "

Shorty nodded and pointed to his nose. "Me try smells sumtin." He dropped his pack and pulls out some leather strips before moving off into the woods.

H'aor looked next at Joachim. "Joachim, can you find us some wood for a small fire? The more the better, so we can keep it going all night.

And dry if it is possible with all this rain the other night. Not green either please. We don't want a lot of smoke to show where we are."

He then looked at Kisa. "Kisa, can you find water? We will need drinking water soon. I would prefer you and Joachim stay close to each other. Neither of you seems to have much experience in the wild." Kisa and Joachim dropped their packs and wandered into the trees talking softly.

H'aor pulled off his pack and rummaged around in it for some of the dry biscuit from the inn. He placed it on a maple leaf and set in under the tree on the eastern edge of the ring.

Thorn watched and asked, "Thought you said this place was old."

The elf shrugged. "It is, but why take chances? It is a small enough sacrifice to prevent problems." Thorn just grunted in response. H'aor stood and turned to see Thorn standing there with a wide grin on his face. "Find something funny?"

Thorn looked in the direction that the ogre had taken. "Mighty sad day when the elf asks an ogre to hunt in the woods. Your elf skills lacking?"

H'aor ignored the barb. "He has his skills and I have my magic. The wilderness was never as appealing to me as my spell books were. So yes, he can find something good to eat and all I can feed you is paper and ink."

Thorn grinned. "Fair enough. You are not as full of yourself as most elves. Makes me feel a little better. What did you want me to do?"

H'aor studied the woods for a moment. "This area was once glacier land. Should be a lot of old rock scattered around. I am hoping you can find us a place to make a stand. Anything that might even the odds. The wolves have our scent so it is only a matter of time before they catch us. Nothing evil should be able to penetrate the ring tonight if there is any moonlight. But come daylight, the magic of this place will not aide us."

Thorn scanned the area. "That ridge line might work. No promises, but I will see what I can find."

Thorn returned just before dusk to find Kisa, H'aor, and Joachim sitting around a small fire laid out in a pit that had been dug in the center of the ring. He sat down and leaned forward, idly drawing on the ground in the cleared space near the fire.

H'aor studied the dwarf and the lines he was tracing in the dirt. "Find anything useful?"

Thorn raised his head from his tracing. "Maybe. That ridge is high in places. It has a dried-up streambed running along the base. Not very many good places to climb it that I could see. I found one way up that is not too far away. There is a spot where the ridge wall collapsed. It forms a ramp of sorts. Lots of loose gravel and rock. Really poor footing. It can be climbed if you are careful. Might not be so easy if someone is on top waiting to cut you down."

H'aor nodded. "No easy way to get behind us?"

Thorn shook his head. "Not that I could find in the time I had."

H'aor smiled. "Better than I had hoped for. Hopefully they want us bad enough to come up after us. I am tired of running from orcs"

Thorn looked around. "Now where is that blasted ogre with dinner? I am hungry from all that running. Too blasted much of it the last couple days. I need food to fight on tomorrow."

Shorty returned just after dark with a small boar in one hand and his helm full of nuts in the other. He had a number of long sticks tucked under one arm. The sticks had been peeled of bark exposing fresh, green wood. Shorty crouched down and began to lay out the results of his hunt.

Thorn looked puzzled as he examined the boar. "You snared something that big ground in with a couple strips of leather?"

Shorty shook his head as he pulled out a large dagger and began slicing away the skin. "No. Has ta kills wid rock. Feeds nut ta squirrel. Pig sneak up me. It mad cuz me steal him nut. Me grab rock. Throw."

Shorty lifted the boar's head and pointed with his dagger at a large dent in the side of the boar's head.

Thorn looked at the dead boar checking the size of the dent in its head. "How big a rock did you grab?"

Shorty scratched his head. "Small." Shorty pointed with the dagger at his large helm full of nuts. "Dat big maybeso. Only one bees close."

They all watched as Kisa reached over and lifted the helm. She needed both hands to lift it up beside her head. It was easily twice the size of her head. Joachim leaned close to Thorn and whispered, "Just how strong is he?"

Thorn chuckled and replied, "You really do not want to find out."

Joachim shook his head and then looked up sharply. "Wait! Did you say you were feeding squirrels again?"

Shorty began to cut long strips of meat. "Me picks too manys nut in tree. No ken takes all. Share."

Joachim's eyes seemed to lose focus as he struggled for words. He finally managed to mutter, "But, why?"

Shorty shrugged as he began to push strips of meat onto the green sticks and hand them to his companions. "Dem hungries. Me too." As soon as everyone had meat, Shorty stuck two into the fire for himself.

Joachim watched his own meat cooking over the fire and looked again at Shorty. "What is it with you and squirrels? It is kind of creepy."

Shorty rotated his own meat and smiled as he watched it cook. "All good tings come wid squirrel. Like pig."

Before Joachim could ask anything else, Thorn gently nudged him with an elbow. "Give it up. It will just make your head hurt even more." As Joachim sighed, the others laughed. Shorty was oblivious to it all as he pulled the meat from the fire and began to eat. As people finished a portion, Shorty would slice off more strips.

The meal was eaten mostly in silence. More of the pig was cooked and set aside for the morning. Shorty took the remains of the boar off and buried it well away from their camp. When he returned, H'aor cleared his throat. "I think it is time we get to know a little more about each other. It would be nice to know who we are fighting beside before things get ugly tomorrow."

Chapter 5
Telling Tales

Four of the companions sat in silence around the fire. They were lost in their own thoughts and none seemed interested in being the first to speak. The ogre sat trying to stack nuts on top of each other. His efforts seemed to fail frequently, but he would just begin again humming happily. The sounds of the forest blended into a peaceful rhythm with the deep rumble and the clatter of falling nuts.

At length the elf stood. "Since it was my idea to get to know each other, it is only fair that I start this out. As you may have guessed from my conversation with the bard, my family is well known among the elves. My father and uncle both sit upon the Elven Council. Though I am only a third son, it was deemed appropriate that I take my turn in service to the Council. After what now seems an insufficient amount of training, I was sent on my first mission. I was to gather information about the apparent invasion of these lands by orcs. It sounded rather simple, meet the agent who was already working here and get his report. Then meet with the representative of the Druids to learn what they intended to do."

As H'aor paused for a moment. Joachim used the break to ask, "Does that make you like royalty or something? Is your family really rich and powerful?"

H'aor shook his head. "My people do not view things in quite the same way that humans do. It is not an easy concept, but I will try to explain. Humans believe that they can own the land. Humans also believe that they can rule both land and people. Elves believe that the land is eternal. It has existed and will continue to exist independent of the elves or any of the mortal races. We do not rule the land or the people who inhabit it. The land belongs to no one. We exist in harmony with the land and the people may come and go as they please."

H'aor studied the trees beyond the fire. "Elves owe service to the land that sustains us. We have responsibilities to each other and to the land. The more that we have been given in this life, the greater our responsibilities. The Council and the heads of the Elven Houses have the greatest responsibilities of all. They must serve all. And we must serve the world itself."

Thorn looked up to meet H'aor's gaze. "Noble ideas elf, but how does it work? Your family controls a large portion of the western lake region. Sounds powerful to me."

H'aor sighed. "We do not really control it, Thorn. Any may move in or move out by their own choice. If those who come nurture the land, we welcome them. If they harm the land, then we move to protect it. It has led to some conflicts with dwarven miners, I admit. But the lands my family protects do not belong to us. Not as humans or dwarves own land. We do not collect taxes or tithes. You might say that we belong to the land and not it to us."

H'aor sat down and stared into the fire. "For our purposes and our survival tomorrow, my family or status has little meaning. I am simply H'aor. I am a fighter and a mage. My skill with the blade is not great, but I can do my part in our defense. I am no master of the Arcane, but I am proficient in spells of the Second Circle. Considering the other warriors in our group, I suspect that my spells may be my greatest contribution."

His face grew grim. "Lastly, you should understand that there is more to what we face than just a rouge band of orcs threatening a few villages. Some new force of evil seeks a foothold in our world. It seeks those who will aid it willingly or unwillingly. And somehow, the people of this land must stop it or we are all doomed. What we see and learn must get back to those who can fight this power. No matter how the fight goes tomorrow, someone must get word of what we learn to the Councils of the Elves and the Druids. The knowledge must get to the leaders of the dwarves and the humans. We must learn all that we can. I have no right to order any of you to help my mission, but I do ask your aid."

There was a silent nod of heads and a tension seemed to leak out of the elf. "Thank you. I have pushed us on our travel out of necessity. But I have little battle experience. Another might be better suited to lead tomorrow. Know that I am happy to fight beside all of you." He went silent and placed another log into the fire.

Joachim turned to stare at H'aor. "Your world and mine could not be further apart. I have no family, no friends really, no lands, and definitely no responsibilities. I come from Island Town. I grew up in the streets. My folks died before I was nine and I have kept myself alive ever since. I don't know how to be part of a group like this. I know only how to take care of myself. The gangs, the guild, and even the supposedly nice people who say they just want to help… they always wanted to change me or own me. I would not be controlled by them. I saw what it did to others and it was not going to happen to me."

Kisa whispered softly into the darkness, "It sounds lonely and frightening."

Joachim just stared at her. "Have you ever seen what happens to young orphans in the big towns? It starts with telling them what is best for them. The call it helping them or teaching them or my favorite, saving them. But it is about changing them, changing how they think. It ends with them being little more than slaves. Instead of thinking for themselves, they can only repeat the garbage they were fed along the way. I wanted to think for myself. So, I did. I was faster and smarter than those who were bigger than me. I stayed ahead of them until the day I messed up. Then I ran. Now I am in a bigger mess and I am running once more."

Kisa asked quietly, "What happened to you, Joachim?"

Joachim looked down into the flames. "I messed up. I got angry. Worse, I got involved." He raised his eyes defiantly. "There was this rich merchant that ran a crew of younglings. He worked them hard and fed them little. But it was all they knew. They thought they had it good.

One day a little girl held back on him. She kept a few coppers of what she stole for him. He caught her though. As punishment, he pulled out a knife and sliced off her little finger. It cut so fast. I knew the knife was special. So, while he was explaining to those kids why he had to punish her, I slipped in behind him and stole that knife."

Joachim reached behind him and pulled out a blade. "This knife. I slipped away and was gone before he even knew it was missing. Did not help the girl or any of them, but it made me feel good to take it from him."

H'aor nodded. "So why did you have to run?"

Joachim began to laugh. "Turns out it is magic. Powerful magic. The old goat offered a big reward for information. Turns out the girl he cut saw me lift it. She sold me out. Don't know if she got the reward or not. I left Island Town that night. It was not a good place, but it was my town. I never really had a home, but I had a place at least. Now that is gone too."

Joachim idly plucked a blade of grass and laid it gently across the edge of the knife. He stared as the weight of the small piece of grass was enough to allow the knife to slice it in half. Each piece fluttered to the ground. Joachim lay the knife on his palm and it seemed to just disappear from sight.

He looked back into the fire. "I traveled hard till I ended up in that inn. And I got involved again. Worse, I killed that night. Never did that before. I did not like it. And now you say I might need to do it again. I do not like that either. But I will not let them hurt me. I will use my knife again before I let that happen. I will listen to you during the fight tomorrow. But I want no part of your war. I will find a place to belong. Somewhere."

Joachim inched back into the darkness where his face was no longer visible in the firelight.

Shorty stared intently at the young boy. He did not understand all the words, but he did understand the pain in the boy's voice. He had felt it himself. "Boy done good. Protect good."

Joachim hissed back at him from the shadows, "I am not a boy. I am sixteen years old and I have a name. Stop calling me boy. And I did not protect anyone. I got greedy for a fat purse. Taking care of others gets you hurt."

Shorty's eyes did not lose their intensity. "No bees mad me. No gots many word. Me lib cause youse sticked orc. Orc not hurts nobodies no more. Kill be bad. Maybe so. No kills badder. Youse pick good."

Kisa's voice came quietly from beside Shorty. "Maybe it would hurt less if you did not try to convince yourself that it was all about greed Joachim. You took a knife so it could not be used on others. And you probably saved Shorty. Getting involved makes you vulnerable and I think that scares you."

Joachim stopped arguing, lost in his own thoughts.

———————————————

Shorty looked around the group and then touched his chest. "Me bees Shorty. Bees ogre. Bees people. Bees both dem. Lib under mountain wid Mama an Papa an Tribe. Mama keeps safe. Hab many rule. Den Mama bees dead. Gets way. Go outside. Me like outside bery muches. Many games ta plays dere."

Shorty looked up at the night sky. "Outside good. Nobodies try hurt. Nobodies makes do bad tings. Meet man when feed squirrel. He say me gots tential. Me say no jus nut. Him bees Big Drud. Takes meet Elf Lard. Elf Lard gib home an teach sword like Papa. Now me help Big Drud too. He tell bout Lady. Maybe Lady talk me ifn do good."

H'aor came up on one knee. "Big Drud? The High Druid? You are my contact?" H'aor flashed a sign with his right hand.

Shorty stared at his hand and shook his head. "Not know what dat bees. Me ken do birdie." Shorty proceeds to put his two hands together and make his fingers wiggle.

H'aor groaned and muttered, "Father, what did you get me into?"

———————————————

Thorn chuckled at the look of horror on the elf's face. "Cheer up lad. At least he can throw you to safety if needs be."

H'aor shook his head in disbelief. "So, you were to help me gather information?"

Shorty got a confused look on his face. "Big Drud no say dat. He sat protect Music Man. Big Drud say jus bees Shorty. Dat makes all better." A look of sadness comes over Shorty's face. "No do good protect. Orc kilt Music Man. Now me gots ta fix."

H'aor sat back down shaking his head. "Not sure how we can do that, Shorty."

Shorty smiled back at H'aor. "Wait ta see what broke. Den hits broke bery hard. Fix it good."

Kisa, Thorn, and Joachim began to laugh softly at the simple logic of it all.

As the laughter died down, Thorn cleared his throat. "Guess it is my turn now. I am Thorn of Rockwood. That is a small dwarven settlement near the entrance to Deephole. I give no family or clan name. Bit of a scamp I was. I was a thorn in my family's side so it is the name I gave myself. Only one that would have really missed me is my Grand Sire and he has moved on now."

Thorn cracked a devilish smile. "I like to fight and I like to drink. I love to do both at the same time. But climbing through tunnels looking for some stupid rock is as boring as I can imagine. I am a fair hand at the forge, but I would rather use the weapons than make them. My parents eventually suggested that maybe I should try adventuring until I could learn to be a more proper dwarf. I do not see that happening any time soon, if ever."

Thorn tapped his large axe and shield. "Made these myself. Even the haft of the axe. No magic in them, but the steel is good and the axe is sharp. More important, I know how to use them. I have even been known to throw a wicked hammer on occasion."

H'aor chimed in with a smile. "Pretty good at biting orcs too, or so I have heard."

Thorn made a gagging motion then grinned. "Do not forget throwing empty tankards. As for the fight tomorrow, I for one am looking forward to it. I am sick of this running and hiding. Time to stand and make them run away or better yet, die."

He turned his head then to examine Shorty. "There be no love lost between your kin and mine ogre. But by every dwarven god's beard, I do like you Shorty. Fighting beside you will be a pleasure."

Shorty smiled nervously. "Dat good. Fuzzface still bery scary."

Thorn laughed and turned to look at Kisa.

Kisa sat silently for a long time fidgeting with her Holy Symbol.

Thorn whispered gently, "It is alright Priestess. No need to spill any dark secrets, tell only what you want."

Kisa looked up and stared at him. "I am not afraid. I just want no ties to my past. I was traveling that night to get away from it. This telling brings it all back. But it is necessary."

Kisa looked up and then dropped the Holy Symbol to hang from the chain around her neck. "I was raised in Boat Town. My parents were merchants and fairly prosperous. Money was their god and influence was the alter they worshiped at. People were tools to be used to achieve their ambitions. This was especially true of my mother. She married down when she met my father, but he had the money she needed to live the life she wanted."

Kisa stared at her hands. "I wanted to do things. Things that had meaning. But my lot was to be the perfect daughter. Look pretty and bring in a husband that would make my parents more powerful. They were already looking for a husband for me. They wanted me to marry some old man who had a seat on the council. They wanted to control his vote. I was to be the coin they paid him."

She smiled then. "I used to sneak out from time to time and walk around down near the docks. I liked to help people. There were so many poor and in need. I met an old woman. She taught me about Akka, Goddess of the Earth. I found something I could believe in. But then my parents began planning my betrothal. I ran away and found the old woman. She was a Priestess at the Temple. She took me there and helped me to hide. I studied for two years. But my parents finally got word of where I was and sent the watch to bring me home. I ran away again. I am a Priestess now, not their tool. I will not go back to being their puppet again."

She held up the beautifully carved and painted sheath of wheat. "One of my first healings was an old man in the market place. He had been cut while being robbed. He had no money, but Akka still healed him. He gave me this a few days later in thanks. This has more value to me than all the riches of my family."

Kisa picked up her mace from among her things. "I have not had a lot of practice with this, but I will fight evil. I can heal and I have a few battle spells. I will do what I can tomorrow."

Kisa put the mace down and turned her head to Joachim. "Is that knife as sharp as you believe it to be?"

Joachim slid back into the firelight and brought the knife out again. "Cuts through just about everything. Why?"

Kisa let go of the Holy Symbol again. She reached back behind her head and pulled the long braid forward. She began to untie it pulling her hair loose. Despite the rain and their travels, her long brown hair gleamed in the firelight. "This is one of the chains that holds me to my past. It is time to break it. One less risk in battle as well."

Kisa gathered her hair together in her two hands just above her shoulders. "I want you to cut it off. One clean cut."

Joachim stared at her. "Lady, you are nuts."

Kisa met his gaze in anger. "Will you do it or do I have to ask Shorty to use that big sword of his?"

Joachim got up and walked softly over to stand behind her. "Fine, but I still say you are nuts." He grabbed a handful of hair and paused. "Last chance."

Kisa snapped at him, "Do it!" Joachim brough the knife to her hair slicing easily through the first handful. He grabbed the rest and cut it at the same point. The large pile of hair fell to rest in Kisa's lap. There was a high-pitched squeal from the tree branches above them. As all eyes scanned the tree, H'aor asked, "What was that?"

Shorty's finger traced an arc through the air and away from the camp. "Bery big bug."

As the noise faded, all eyes returned to Kisa. She began to gather her hair and piled it beside her backpack. She did not smile and Joachim slipped back into his place by the fire. The group went silent as the darkness seemed to close in.

———————————————

Thorn watched his companions. There was a tension in the group that he did not like. There were too many issues from the past that the sharing had stirred up. None of it could not be solved in the near future. But all of them could interfere with their teamwork in the coming battle. If he had enough strong ale, he would just get them all drunk to take the edge off. Hell fire, he did not have any to take his own edge off. Maybe, he thought, they could just have a little fun.

With that thought, he turned to Shorty. "Still have that bag of gear I gave you at the inn?"

Shorty turned to his backpack and untied the bag from it. He turned and placed the heavy bag before the dwarf. He watched with interest to see what Thorn had planned.

Thorns opened the bag and dumped out a collection of weapons and armor. He motioned towards H'aor's backpack. "The pouches?" H'aor pulled another bag from his own backpack. After setting aside the food from Leaky, he poured an assortment of pouches and loose coins into a second pile.

Thorn began tossing pouches to each of them. "Coins in front of Joachim, anything else over here in the pile including any gems or jewelry. Time to learn what we got out of that fight besides a bunch of smelly orcs on our tails."

Joachim looked up with a wide smile. "I get all the money?"

Thorn shook his head. "No, nimble fingers, you get to count all the money. Now everyone will learn if your brain can keep up with those fingers." They all began to laugh and opened the pouches. There were groans and cheers as some held gold and some simply copper. But everyone seemed in a better mood as they focused on the present instead of old troubles.

By the time everything was opened, there was a nice sized pile of coins in front of Joachim that he was happily sorting and stacking. The group had also found a pair of rings, three gems, a vial of a green liquid sealed with wax, and two rolled-up parchments.

Thorn spread out the items so that none were touching each other. "I suspect most of this is useless, but you never know. Kisa and H'aor, by chance do either of you have the ability to detect magic tonight?" H'aor shook his head. "Not memorized right now." But Kisa nodded yes.

Thorn sat back from the pile. "Then you are in charge, Kisa."

Kisa looked at all of their loot and then around the group. "This is a pretty basic spell. Anything magic within the area of the spell will glow, including items that you may have on you. I was taught that there is a way to get the spell to reveal more information than just whether items are enchanted or not. Items with greater magical power glow brighter. The key is to have something for comparison."

Kisa looked around the group. "Does anyone beside Joachim have a magic item?"

Only Shorty responded as he excitedly dug into his backpack pulling out his brown rubber ball. He held it up proudly for Kisa to see. "Ball bees bery magic."

Kisa looked at it and smiled. "What does it do, Shorty?"

Shorty laughed happily, "It bounce bery high. Muches good fun."

Joachim looked on incredulously. "That is utterly re…" At this point, H'aor's elbow caught him sharply in the ribs. With a cough, he continued, "remarkable, Shorty."

Kisa smiled at Shorty. "That may be too powerful for my spell Shorty. Why not put it away for now?"

Shorty tucked the ball away again. "Dis bery fun game."

Kisa's gaze returned to Joachim. "What do you know about your knife Joachim? It might help us a little as we proceed."

Joachim shrugged. "A mage offered to buy it once. Apparently, mine was more powerful than the one he used. He offered a lot, but I could not part with it. What was I going to do with that much gold anyway? Probably would have just gotten me killed."

Kisa nodded. "That at least tells us that the magic on your knife is powerful. We can use that as a guide. Would you mind leaving it out with the other items please?"

Joachim placed his knife near the other items but within his reach.

Kisa lifted her Holy Symbol above the pile, but then H'aor held up a hand. "I think there is one more item we need to check as well. Shorty may be good, but that sword throw was almost too accurate."

Joachim flinched at the mention of the sword.

H'aor looked to Shorty. "Would you mind placing your new sword out here as well, Shorty?"

Shorty reached behind him and grabbed the half-orc's blade. Then he also grabbed his own blade and laid them both in the treasure pile. "Maybeso Papa sword gots magics too."

Thorn reaches out and rearranges things so the swords did not touch any other items, then H'aor lowered his hand.

Kisa bowed her head and began chanting softly to herself as she let the Holy Symbol hang from its chain near the collection of items. She rose to her knees, extending her chain out over the equipment. The golden sheaf of wheat began to swing back and forth changing direction at random intervals. They all watched as a golden glow much like that of ripened wheat encompassed the Holy Symbol. As it began to move faster, the light began to drip downward spreading to some of the objects lying on the ground. They too began to glow with the golden light.

The two items that seemed to attract the most of the dripping light were Joachim's knife and the half-orc's sword. The sword was possibly a little brighter, but it was hard to be sure as the color seemed somewhat different. To a lesser degree, the glow also emanated from one of the rings, the vial, and both rolled parchments. The only other piece of equipment that appeared to be magical was the mace and that was not nearly as bright as the other two weapons.

Thorn quickly removed the items that did not glow from the spells area of effect. Most he just tossed behind him. The non-magical ring landed in front of Joachim and it was added to the treasure pile. As Thorn sat back, Shorty point to the cleared area closest to H'aor. "Light make snake in grass."

A line of golden light began where Shorty had pointed and ran across the ground towards H'aor's backpack. As they watched, the line seemed to straighten and thicken, growing ever brighter. Thorn looked at the pack puzzled. "Forget something in there?"

H'aor carefully reopened the pack and shifted aside the cheese, jerky, and hard biscuits to reveal an almost blinding glow. The elf reached in an removed the bracer the bard had given him. The golden glow emanating from it light the entire faerie ring like a noon day sun.

Shorty muttered, "Purty."

Thorn spoke softly. "Let it go, Priestess, before it will show every orc within a hundred miles where we are." Kisa stopped her chanting and sat back.

As the glows faded away, H'aor placed the bracer carefully back in his pack. "I hope the bard's daughter knows what that is. Magic on that level is dangerous to use without a good understanding of it."

Thorn turned back to the items from the orcs. "Not our problem at the moment. That piece is for delivery. We should concentrate on what is before us. I hope something here might help us." Each of the companions stared down at the items that remained. Shorty picked up his Papa's sword with a look of sadness and placed it back in its sheath. He left the magic sword on the ground where Thorn had positioned it.

As H'aor tied his pack closed again, they soon turned their attention back to the remaining magic items. Their stares showed excitement and curiosity. Thorn lifted the two parchments and placed them closer to Kisa. "Those came from the shaman that thought he was so smart."

H'aor stared at the magical items. "Normally I would be concerned about cursed items. But most of this was being used by the orcs. I think the risk is minimal. Especially the sword since Shorty has already used it in battle."

Kisa reached out and touched the mace. There was dirt and grime caked on the head of the weapon. Despite the obvious lack of care the weapon had endured, there was no sign of rust or damage. Just a lot of dirt and old blood. "I think I am the only one who uses a mace. So, if there are no objections, I would like to try it. The magic isn't that strong, but then neither are my combat skills. Anything is bound to help." She sat released the weapon and sat back waiting for a decision.

Thorn pushed the mace in front of her. "We may need every edge we can get tomorrow. Its previous owner was none to kind to it. May it serve you well."

Kisa looked at Shorty. "I need to be sure about the mace. I am going to pick it up. If I do anything unusual, please take it away from me."

Shorty nodded and Kisa grasped the mace. She lifted it and began to clean some of the grime off of it. "It has good balance. Too bad the orc did not take better care of it."

H'aor pointed at the great sword that still lay before Shorty. "Shorty's new sword is at least as powerful as the dagger. The greenish tint to the magic is interesting. It would be nice to know what it meant. Keep it Shorty. No one else is strong enough to use it except Thorn and he seems to prefer the axe."

Shorty nodded and placed the sword beside his other blade.

Thorn shoved the parchments towards Kisa. "My guess is that these are clerical in nature. You know the risk of reading them. It is your call."

Kisa stared at them and shrugged. "The shaman obviously intended to use them. And as you said, any edge might help." She picked up the first parchment and unrolled it. After a few seconds of scanning it, she hissed and tossed it into the flames of their fire. Joachim yelped in protest, but his complaints died away as the flames turned black and sizzled loudly. The ashes of the parchment rose and drifted away and the flames return to their normal color. The odor of rotten eggs emanated from the fire.

Kisa shuddered. "That was foul magic. It was meant to inflict wounds, not heal them. I will not use such corruption." Before anyone could protest further, she unrolled the second parchment. She scanned it and rolled it back up placing it on the ground before her. "That contains but a single spell I recognize. It is a spell to hold up to three people immobile. It might help tomorrow."

Thorn grunted. "Same spell that fool orc tried to cast at me."

H'aor waved his hand at the ring and vial. "I can probably identify their magic given a day and the right spell components. Till then, I would not recommend handling them."

Joachim looked at the coins piled before him. "In Island Town, this would have been a poor haul."

Thorn grinned at him. "What did you expect? They were orcs. Probably spent everything they stole buying ale at the inn." Thorn tossed Joachim one of the larger pouches they had emptied. "Store it in there and feel free to amaze us with your counting skills."

Joachim began to scoop the coins into the pouch. "Sixteen gold, twelve silver, and thirty-five copper. We are definitely not rich. The ring that was not magic is not even gold. It is brass. Might get a couple silver for it."

H'aor placed the magic ring and vial into one of the pouches. "We can share out the gold and other coins if we survive the battle tomorrow. Now I suggest we get some sleep.

Thorn stood and stared around the group. "Faerie ring or not, we need watches tonight. The mage and cleric need to rest to get their spells back in the morning, so they are not options. And Shorty has been up for over a day. That leaves you and me Joachim. You want first or second watch?"

Joachim stared up at him. "I am wide awake now. Counting money gets my blood moving. Get some sleep, Thorn."

Thorn nodded and turned towards his bedroll.

Chapter 6
Things That Go Buzz in the Night

Joachim watched as his companions rolled out their blankets around the fire and settled down for the night. The big ogre was the first to fall asleep. His soft snores rose above the sounds of the insects in the night. The ogre still scared him, but learning that he had also been small and bullied had given Joachim something to think about. He was having a hard time thinking of the big guy as small and vulnerable though.

The firelight was not helping his night vision and the sounds of his companions made it hard to hear, so Joachim walked slowly into the darkness beyond the ring of trees. He squatted in the darkness facing back along their trail. After his eyes adjusted, he could see reasonably well in the light of the half-moon. Good thing I am used to working alone at night he thought. Otherwise, this would be a long watch after all the uphill running and hiking.

The night was peaceful and mostly quiet. It almost felt safe. The only sound he heard was a buzzing noise that drifted in and out of the trees. He grinned as he thought of Shorty's comment earlier in the evening. Big bug indeed. "Just hope you do not bite," he murmured to himself.

———————————

Thorn woke in the dark. His instincts were pretty good and he knew he had watch this night. But the boy had not come to wake him. Thorn's gut told him that he had slept longer than he should have. He cracked his eyes open and looked around without moving.

The moon had moved quite far across the sky while he slept. Too much time had passed while he slept off the previous day's run. Thorn guessed the boy should have woken him over an hour ago. Thorn also realized the firelight was much too dim. He turned his head to see that there were few coals still glowing red. The fire was almost out.

Thorn slid his hand slowly and quietly towards his axe. He felt better when his hand closed around the hardened wood of the haft. He gripped it tightly as he listened carefully to the sounds around him. Shorty's breathing was easy to pick out. He thought the elf was there as well. He heard nothing from where Kisa had settled her bedroll. He rose silently to one knee searching around him for signs of danger. Keeping his voice low, Thorn murmured, "Ware. Trouble."

The sound of Shorty's deep breathing quieted instantly. Thorn thought he heard H'aor crawling from his bedroll towards the nearby trees. The low hanging moon was suddenly blocked by a large figure rising silently from where the ogre had been sleeping. Thorn could just make out the glint of an impossibly long blade in the figures hand. He shook his head. Nothing that big should move so quietly.

H'aor whispered from off to the side, "What is going on, Thorn?"

Thorn eased over to Kisa's blankets, verifying that she was missing before answering, "Joachim never woke me. It is well past the start of my watch and the Priestess is missing."

The deep voice of the ogre came softly. "No smell orc."

H'aor moved softly across the camp and out into the open. His voice came clearly from outside the ring. "The boy is out here."

Thorn and Shorty moved to join him. As they left the ring of trees, they could see a warm body crumpled on the ground. Joachim was lying on his stomach with his knees curled tightly into his chest. Shorty slipped past the boy's prone form to a guard position. He whispered. "Him dead?"

Thorn moved closer and then cursed softly. "No, he's breathing. Just fell asleep on watch. Fool city dweller!"

H'aor bent closer and studied Joachim. "No, Thorn. I think he had help." H'aor reached out and plucked something from the back of Joachim's neck. He held up a small arrow about an inch long.

Shorty reached out a finger to brush the tiny object. "Bug bite?"

H'aor shook his head. "Not a bug. Sprites."

Thorn turned back to examine the ring of trees. "Is the damned ring still active then? You left them food. Why, elf?"

"This really does not make any sense," H'aor mused. "If we had angered the local Faerie, we would have had more trouble than this. And Joachim was outside the ring when he was attacked. More importantly, why take Kisa?"

Thorn turned back to face the sleeping boy and the tempting target before him. He pulled back his boot and smiled down at Joachim. "I have really wanted to do this several times since the fight at the inn. Sometimes even when things are bad, life has its special moments." Then Thorn kicked out catching Joachim in the seat of his pants, rolling him heals overhead across the ground.

As Joachim flopped over on his back, he looked up in surprise. "What? I did not fall asleep. I swear it."

Thorn laughed. "Are you really sure about that?"

H'aor gave Thorn a shove back towards the camp. "Leave him alone. Dwarves may be immune to sprite magic, but the rest of us are not." Instead of getting him all riled up, maybe you should see if you can find Kisa's trail while I study my spell book."

Joachim rolled to his feet. "Where is Kisa? Last I saw she was sleeping in camp. I never heard her move."

Thorn pointed to her empty bedroll. "That is the problem, you were not watching. She was gone when we woke up. I suspect whoever put you to sleep has a pretty good idea where she went."

Shorty ignored their argument and reentered the ring. He moved to Kisa's blankets and lifted them to his nose. Shorty began to sniff at the blankets. Then he moved out into the darkness and began to circle around the camp in widening arcs. He spent a lot of time on his hands and knees.

Thorn pulled out his continual light coin and tossed it to H'aor who held it in his hand over the small spell book. He sat silently studying the book while the others began to search for clues. It was not long before Shorty grunted and began to move off. Thorn called him back. "Wait, Shorty. We go together. H'aor will be finished soon enough."

Shorty reluctantly returned to the camp and began to strap on his other weapons and equipment. As soon as he had everything packed and loaded, he moved to the point where he picked up the scent.

Thorn looked at him curiously. "Can you keep her trail that way, Shorty?"

Shorty nodded his head as H'aor rose and tucked the book into his cloak. He handed the light back to Thorn who tucked it away. Darkness returned and they turned to follow Shorty.

As H'aor buckled on his sword, Thorn gave Shorty a wave to move out. The four moved into the darkness to find their missing friend.

Kisa woke slowly. Her head felt a little fuzzy and she was cold. She could not understand why her blankets were missing. The fire that had been so warm earlier in the evening gave off no heat. She placed her hand at her side and felt soft grasses piled beneath her. The realization that something was wrong finally pierced the fog in her head.

Kisa lay still, listening to the sounds around her. She could not hear her companions at all. Even Shorty's soft snores had been replaced by the sounds of night birds and insects. She opened one eye, but there was only the dim light of the moon to see by. Her hand moved slowly to where her armor and weapons should be, but she only felt more grass and dirt.

Kisa felt a moment of panic, but fought it back down. Fear was not going to help her. She was not bound, so she was not a prisoner, at least not yet. She brought her hand slowly back to her chest and was relieved to find her Holy Symbol was still hanging from its chain around her neck. She still had her magic, but even that needed to be restored.

Kisa took a slow, deep breath to calm herself. She placed her finger tips lightly on her link to Akka and began to pray. She thought of her current predicament and of the battle to come as she asked her Goddess to restore her spells.

When she finished her meditation, Kisa opened her eyes. She rose slowly to a sitting position and stared around her. She sat in a small circle of rocks. Most of the rocks were larger than she was so she could not see much of the surrounding area.

As she tried to understand how she got into this situation, she heard a buzzing noise coming from somewhere off to her left. The noise grew louder and closer. Unsure if this was a danger or not, Kisa prepared to cast a spell. Suddenly from above her, she heard a voice exclaim, "Hello, Pretty One! You are awake at last. Welcome, my guest."

Kisa glanced up and her eyes grew wide with wonder. Suspended in the air above the rocks was a tiny winged man not much bigger than the size of her open hand. His wings beat furiously as they kept not only his own body aloft, but also a small net filled with some kind of berry. Without realizing she spoke the words, she heard her own voice utter, "What? Who are you?"

The tiny figure darted in and dropped the net of fruit in her lap before returning to his previous position. "I am Skreee!" The tiny figure began to fly in circles around her. The buzzing noise grew louder and louder as its speed increased. His voice came out as a tiny shout. "Skreee, Mighty Warrior, has saved Pretty One from the Evil One who hurt her!" The tiny man came to a rest on the rock directly in front of Kisa.

Kisa stared at him in puzzlement. "I do not understand. Um, Skreee, is it? No one attacked me. I was not hurt. I was safe with my friends. Now I am lost I fear."

Skreee beamed with pleasure. "Not lost, Pretty One. This is my home. You are safe here. The Evil One will not find you. His magic blade will not cut you again. The Mighty Warrior Skreee will protect Pretty One."

Comprehension began to dawn on Kisa. "Oh,, Skreee, he did not attack me. I asked him to cut my hair." As she spoke, her hand rose to the hair on the back of her head. Instead of the recently cut hair she expected to find, her fingers sank into the familiar weight of her long waist length hair. It was back. How was that even possible? Again, words slipped from her lips unbidden. "Oh my."

Skreee leapt into the air again. His tiny figure began to do cartwheels in the air above her head. His voice proudly proclaimed, "Skreee the Magnificent healed Pretty One! Forest magic mended what the Evil One defiled. We have defeated the Evil One's wicked plan and now the Evil One must die."

Kisa's confusion turned to anger over the return of her hair and then to fear at the words of the tiny figure. "Did you kill my friends?"

Skreee came to rest on the rock again. "He is not a friend, Pretty One! Sadly, the Evil One still lives. Skreee did not kill him yet. Only put to sleep. No time to kill him yet. I had to rescue Pretty One. Now eat. You are my guest."

Kisa shook her head, but picked up one of the small berries and placed it in her mouth. It was sweet and juicy. As she tried to marshal her thoughts, Kisa's hands moved to her hair and began to weave it into its familiar braid. Her hands moved without thought as Kisa weighed her options. She had no idea where she was or how to get back to her friends. She had no way to force this small forest creature to do anything. She had to be smarter that he was if she was going to get back to her friends before the orcs attacked.

Kisa did her best to relax and hide her frustration. She tried to find the soothing tones she would use with an injured patient. "Skreee, I really need to return to my friends. They need my help. The orcs are coming and I must aid them in the fight."

Skreee rose and flew around the circle of stones before landing again. "Pretty One does not need to fight orcs. Skreee will hide you. The orcs cannot find you here in the ring of stone. Evil One cannot hurt you either. Skreee will protect you!"

Kisa's anger got the better of her. "You little idiot! He is not some evil villain." But she regained control of herself as Skreee crossed his arms over his chest and stared at her defiantly. She sighed in frustration and started again using a different approach. "My friend the elf needs my magic to help him." But she paused when she heard the sound of something large crashing through the brush.

Skreee looked up in alarm at the sound and drew a small bow from behind his back. He took a tiny arrow from a quiver at his side and set it to the string of the bow.

———————————————

Shorty continued moving through the trees at a rapid pace. The scent of the woman came and went. It was almost like she was jumping from place to place. The path was fairly straight though and after the first couple of times he lost the scent, Shorty was able to find it again quickly. He began to run as his confidence grew. He did not understand how Kisa Lady could jump around this way, but he knew which way she was headed.

Shorty and his companions were moving fast as they came to a small stream. Shorty splashed across and headed along his original path. But the scent was gone again. This time it did not return as before. Shorty began to move in circles, sniffing to pick the trail back up again.

Thorn moved up beside him and whispered, "What is wrong, Shorty?"

Shorty growled in frustration, "No smells no more."

H'aor suddenly hissed at them. "Quiet! Listen!"

As they all stood, they could suddenly hear what the elf's sharp ears had detected. The sound of Kisa arguing with someone carried through the trees from up the stream on the far side. Shorty forced his way through the underbrush towards the sound of Kisa's voice and the others moved quickly to follow.

They came to a large clearing after several hundred yards. In the center of the clearing was a perfect circle of boulders. Thorn looked to H'aor. "Another faerie ring?"

H'aor examined it with all of his senses. "Yes. And it is active. But it is weak. I have never seen one made with stone before."

Shorty ignored the discussion and drew his sword. He moved forward to the circle of rocks without any subtlety. Thorn sputtered, "No, wait." but it was too late. Shorty came up behind one of the large boulders. The tall warrior leaned over one of the rocks and stared into the interior of the ring.

————————————————

Kisa looked up to see a large and very angry face lean in over one of the boulders. At that instant, Skreee released his shot and the tiny arrow suddenly appeared at the end of the intruder's nose. Skreee yelled in triumph, "Sleep now, monster!"

Kisa recognized Shorty as he reached up and pulled the small missile from his nose, snapping it between his large fingers. She smiled as his deep, reassuring voice rumbled, "Bad bug! Bites gin an me squishes."

Skreee stared up at the angry ogre, dumbstruck that his tiny missile had no effect. Kisa began to giggle. Skreee reached for another arrow, but Shorty's giant hand shot forward. Skreee squealed and tried to launch himself into the air, but the huge fingers closed about his legs and feet. Shorty gave his hand a hard shake until the small bow fell from Skreee's grasp. Kisa managed to speak between her giggles. "Please do not hurt him, Shorty."

The ogre held the tiny figure up before his eyes and the two glared at each other. Thorn's voice came from the other side of the rock. "You alright, Kisa?"

Kisa rose to her feet. "I am now."

H'aor slipped between two of the rocks and joined Kisa. Moments later, Thorn and Joachim entered as well. As the young thief came into view, Skreee wailed in frustration. "No, the Evil One has invaded my home. Betrayed by an elf. I am undone. Kill me monstrous one."

Kisa began to laugh as her companions stared at the sprite in confusion. H'aor reached out and took the sprite from Shorty's hand. Shorty released it and shook his head. "Me tink me broked it. Maybeso shakes too hard."

H'aor glanced down at the sprite. "He could have killed you winged warrior. You began this fight. To the ogre you owe a life debt. Do the Faerie still have honor? Do you acknowledge the debt?"

Skreee's mouth opened and closed without sound. H'aor repeated his question. Skreee's head dropped in shame. "Skreee gives up. I owe you, elf."

H'aor shook his head. "No, your debt is to the ogre. You attacked him and he spared you. Agreed?"

At the sprite's nod, H'aor released him and turned to Shorty. "I will explain later, Shorty."

Kisa turned to her friends. "How did you find me?"

Thorn pointed to Shorty. "Seems that big nose of his is good for something besides snoring. He followed you most of the way here. Lost your scent a little way back. Nice job arguing with that bug. We followed your voice that last bit. Smart girl."

Kisa shook her head. "I wish that were true. I was just trying to get the stubborn fool to take me back."

H'aor stared at the sprite hovering miserably over the stone ring. Skreee was checking the bow he had recovered from the ground. H'aor ignored the sprite and asked Kisa, "Can you explain what this is all about? Why would a lone sprite attack a group this large?"

The sprite shot up above even the grasp of Shorty. "Skreee the Mighty Warrior is not afraid."

Kisa's lips twitched in the beginning of a smile. "Apparently, the 'Mighty Warrior'", she paused to gesture towards Skreee and then towards Joachim, "saw the Evil One attack me with his magic knife in camp."

Joachim stared at her. "Me, the Evil One? What did I do to hurt you?"

Kisa giggled again. "You cut my hair with your magic knife." Kisa held up a hand at Joachim's protest. "Yes, at my request. But Skreee did not understand. He decided to save me."

H'aor also began to laugh. "We do seem to get ourselves into a lot of unintended trouble. Now Joachim has an enemy for life. Beware Evil One." Everyone began to chuckle except for Joachim and Skreee.

H'aor paused and studied Kisa. "Speaking of the attack on your hair, it seems to have made a remarkable recovery."

Kisa gave the sprite a dirty look. "Apparently the mighty warrior knows some forest magic and was able to heal the damaged. For now, it can stay. We have other issues to deal with."

Thorn grew solemn. "We need to get back to camp and move to the spot I picked out. Dawn is not far off and we need to be prepared for the orcs.

As they began their trek back to their campsite, Skreee flew in to settle on Kisa's shoulder. Kisa whispered softly, "Now what, Skreee?" The sprite did not respond but simply turned to glare at Joachim.

H'aor fell into step beside Shorty. "The sprite owes you for not killing him. Chose well what you ask him to do."

Shorty growled softly. "No needs bug. Maybeso ask go way?"

H'aor looked over at the sprite. "No, Shorty. He is proud. He must do something he feels has value since you spared his life. He may be small, but he could be useful."

Shorty snorted but did not argue. He led the way back at a fast jog.

Chapter 7
Preparing for Battle

The companions plus one arrived back at their camp just as dawn was breaking. Shorty moved to bury the fire while his friends began packing up. Kisa shooed Skreee from her shoulder and began to put her chainmail back on. Her old mace went into her pack. Once the backpack was on her shoulders, she picked up her shield and hung the new mace from her belt.

Kisa looked up to see that Joachim and Thorn were ready to move out. H'aor still had his backpack open laying out some of the cheese and hard biscuits from Leaky to supplement the leftover boar meat. Everyone eagerly grabbed food to eat as they moved out.

As everyone was ready to move, Thorn pointed deeper into the trees to the west. "The ridge is that way." The dwarf took the lead setting a brisk pace with his short legs. Kisa and H'aor fell into step behind him. Skreee flew from the tree branch where he had watched to Kisa's shoulder. He sat facing backwards, keeping a watchful eye on Joachim. Joachim just shook his head and fell well behind Kisa and her angry passenger. Shorty walked quietly at his side chewing on a strip of boar meat.

They had not gone far when Skreee lifted his bow and asked in a hopeful tone, "Can I kill the Evil One now?"

Kisa began to choke on the bite she was chewing. Joachim pulled out his knife, but Shorty shook his head and stepped before the boy with a big grin on his face. "Bug no bery smart. Boy gots friend." Joachim's protest died in his throat as he looked up at the ogre in surprise.

Skreee buzzed his wings and flew up before Shorty's face. "Not bug. I am Mighty Warrior. I am not afraid."

Shorty waved his hand at the small flying figure. Skreee was forced to back away. "Must show bees warrior little bug. Must show den me beliebe."

Skreee buzzed angrily back to take his place on Kisa's shoulder. The group hurried to catch up with the retreating figure of the dwarf. Shorty hung back reclaiming his position as rear guard. Kisa whispered as she walked, "Friends are a good thing, Skreee. They watch out for each other. They could be your friends too." The sprite had no answer.

Kisa followed Thorn as he dodged through the trees. The dwarf's small stature made it easier for him to avoid many of the branches along their path. Kisa had to be more careful. She did not mind though. There was a nice breeze that rustled the leaves and kept her cool. As she pushed the smaller branches aside, Kisa noticed that some of the leaves here were beginning to change color. She had not thought about the time of year since leaving home. She wondered where would she be when winter came and brought the snow. Adventuring in the snow did not seem that appealing. She enjoyed being out in the mountains, but knew in her heart that she was still a town girl at heart.

After about twenty minutes of dodging trees, the group came out of the trees onto the bank of a dried-up stream bed. The ground before them was hard packed clay with rocks sticking up in various places. It was obvious that water had not flowed here in a long time. On the far side of the old stream was a high ridge. The face of the ridge was nearly vertical as it stretched as far as they could see in both directions. The height of the ridge varies from about fifteen feet up to around thirty feet. The changes in elevation seemed to follow the rolling hills on the far side of the ridge.

Joachim looked at the old waterway and asked, "Why no water with all the rain we had?"

Thorn pointed above ridge to the mountains not far beyond. "Those are mostly old rock, but they still shift from time to time. Sometimes when the mountains shake, the water finds an easier path to follow. Then streams like this dry up. My guess is that this one now flows into Long Lake instead of going south and west to join the Trade River."

Thorn took a moment to study the streambed both north and south. He stared up at the nearby peaks and turned north. He moved out into the middle of the stream bed and began a brisk trot along the mostly smooth path. The ridge line to their left steadily shrank as they headed north. By the time they reached a sharp turn in the streambed, the ridge was barely a dozen feet over their heads.

As they came around the curve, the path ahead was covered in rubble where the ridge wall had collapsed down into and halfway across the old waterway. The collapse created a steep ramp leading upwards that ended just short of the top of the ridge. Thorn pointed to the rubble strewn path. "It is mostly rock, loose dirt and dead trees. It is climbable, but I had a nasty time getting to the top. It does not take much to start it sliding down. It is not easy to climb even if there is not someone at the top trying to kill you."

The group stood examining the battleground and H'aor finally nodded. "Nice choice. It should do as long as they want us bad enough to come up after us."

Thorn pointed up to the top of the ridge. "There are two large boulders up there that we can move forward. They will make a good barrier and maybe a bit more. The trees to the side are close enough to use for cover but not so close as to help them climb up with us up there to defend it."

H'aor nodded and said, "Okay, we will see what we can do with it."

Joachim studied the ramp. "I would rather not climb that mess and risk it sliding on us. Especially Shorty. His weight might bring it all down. I can climb up over to the left near that tree and lower a rope. Might be easier than the ramp."

Shorty shook his head. "No climb. Do easy."

They all looked at him questioningly. Shorty walked over to the base of the ridge below the tree Joachim had indicated. He turned his back to the ridge and bent low. Shorty cupped his hands and motioned to Joachim. "Come." As Shorty lowered his hands further, Joachim approached and placed his right food in Shorty's hands. Without warning Shorty surged up, easily tossing Joachim to the top of the embankment. There was the sound of a crash as Joachim disappeared over the edge.

Joachim peeked back over the side. He had leaves in his hair and a dirt smudge on his forehead. "You were supposed to count to three then throw. Nobody just throws."

Shorty just stared up at him. "Not knowed tree. Bees bigger den four?"

Joachim groaned and then looked over at Thorn. "You were right, I did not want to find out how strong he was." Joachim's head disappeared back over the ridge and soon a rope dropped from above. Shorty grabbed the rope and quickly pulled himself to the top.

Skreee took to the air as Kisa stepped towards the ridge. She looked to H'aor as she grabbed the rope. "Never tried to climb in armor before."

H'aor motioned for her to take off her pack, but Thorn stepped forward shaking his head. "Smart people just do not think sometimes." Thorn tied a loop in the rope and slipped it over the toe of Kisa's boot. "Hold on tight, Priestess." Kisa grabbed the rope as Thorn stepped back and whistled. A smiling face looked over the edge and then the rope began to move swiftly up. Shorty easily lifted Kisa over the edge and set her down. Skreee followed her up and settled onto a tree branch above her.

The rope came down twice more and soon the group stood looking down the ramp.

Thorn pointed out a couple of medium-sized boulders not far back from the ridge line. Together with Shorty, he positioned them near the edge of the ramp. Thorn and Joachim began cutting saplings and sharpening them. Kisa leaned out and pressed them into the loose soil of the ramp.

As the group stood back, studying their defenses, H'aor slapped Thorn on the shoulder. "This should do nicely. We just need to encourage them to come after us."

Shorty turned from the ramp and began dropping most of his gear back behind the two boulders. He stared at his shield and then dropped it as well. H'aor studied him. "What do you have in mind, Shorty?"

Shorty turned his head back into the woods. "Scout."

H'aor stared thoughtfully at him. "You are good in the woods my friend, but why take such a risk?"

Shorty checked that his swords were both ready and that his waterskin was mostly full. "Maybeso too manys. Runs no fight den. Me finds out."

H'aor nodded in comprehension. "You are probably right, but if you get caught, we will never know. Worse, we lose a fighter and a friend."

Shorty studied H'aor's face. "Friend good. Me likes. Me bees careful."

H'aor indicated the tree branches above Kisa. "Maybe you take someone with you? Someone to let us know if you run into trouble?"

Shorty's eyes followed the elf's gaze. "Bug?"

H'aor smiled. "If you get in trouble, he can bring us word. He does owe you help for sparing him."

A hopeful look crossed Shorty's face. "Den bug go way?"

H'aor smiled. "Maybe so."

Shorty moved to the spot where they had come up the ridge as H'aor crossed to the tree and called the sprite down. The two held a brief discussion and then Skreee flew over to hover before the ogre. "This is the aid you require of me?"

Shorty nodded. "Helps scout." The sprite spun in the air and passed swiftly across the streambed to crouch on a branch above the old stream bank. Shorty's eyes followed him and then he jumped from the ledge. There was a thud and a small cloud of dust as his large frame came down on bent knees. Shorty ran across to join Skreee and they disappeared into the trees. The last sound to echo back as they disappeared was an argument about who was boss.

H'aor stared into the tree line long after the two voices faded away. "I hope it wasn't a mistake to let the two of them go like that."

Thorn clapped him on the back. "Those two will probably end up killing every orc within a day's travel."

H'aor looked unconvinced.

They both turned as Joachim added sarcastically, "More likely the orcs kill themselves just to avoid listening to them insulting each other."

Both elf and dwarf began to laugh as Kisa reached across and slapped Joachim on the back of the head. Then the four sat down to see what was left of Leaky's food.

Chapter 8
Intrepid Explorers

Shorty followed the sprite on a somewhat direct path back to their old camp. They had argued briefly as Skreee had wanted to head back along the path the dwarf had taken to get here. But Shorty did not want to run into the orcs, he just wanted to watch them. Skreee had eventually understood. That had started the second argument. Skreee wanted to prove he was a warrior by slaying all the orcs. The sprite had not given up his plan until Shorty had left him to find the camp on his own.

Skreee had flown in front of him and asked. "Are you afraid to fight them? I am not afraid."

Shorty had stared him down. "Posed protect friend. Sees how muches orc. Dat bees all."

Skreee had hung there for a moment before nodding, "Protect Pretty One." Then he had turned and pointed a little left of the path Shorty had taken before flying ahead to take the lead.

Shorty was pleasantly surprised at how easy it was to work with the sprite after that. They moved quickly through the forest area with little sound. They took turns ranging ahead as both stayed well within the cover of the trees. Shorty paused frequently to try to catch the smell of wolf or orc. The sprite would move to the top of the trees near clearing to look ahead while he waited.

There were many clearings as they moved through the trees. The constant change in lighting meant that Shorty could not see as well as he liked. He began to depend more on his sense of smell. There was a steady breeze coming from the south, so Shorty angled more to the northeast so he could approach their old camp with the wind in his face.

As they prepared to turn south, Shorty detected a new smell. He paused, but it was not the smell of the orcs or their wolves. It smelled almost like bad meat. Shorty began to move forward cautiously. The smell came and went, but seemed to be growing stronger. He signaled a halt and waited for the sprite to join him.

Skreee settled on a branch just above Shorty's head. Skreee pointed ahead. "That is the way you want to go. Why stop here?"

Shorty rubbed at his nose. "Stink bad. Dead ting smell."

Skreee let out a high, squeaky laugh. He pointed to some bushes around the base of a nearby tree.

Shorty wandered closer and the smell grew much stronger. The odor definitely came from the bush. Shorty had never seen a bush that smelled like long dead animals. It had bright green leaves in clusters of three. Shorty picked a leaf and stared at it. He could see lines running through the leaves. He rubbed his nose again and realized the smell was now on his fingers too. He turned back towards the sprite. "Many dem?"

Skreee pushed himself off the branch and rose into the air turning a cartwheel before continuing along their path. He laughed as he replied. "Oh, so many. Just wait, you will see."

Shorty allowed Skreee to take the lead. This was like when he was young and had left the cavern of his family where Mama's forever light glowed. He would always be blind until his eyes could adjust to the darkness of the tunnels. These bushes made him nose blind. Worse, Skreee was right, the bushes grew in number going from single bushes to whole patches of them. Shorty knew he would have no warning of danger.

They had traveled through the trees and bushes for half a mile when Skreee came to a stop at the edge of a clearing. Shorty found the sprite hovering near a large tree right on the edge, staring ahead intently.

Shorty moved up beside him to look around. Standing on the far side of the clearing was a large male deer.

Shorty's stomach began to growl as he watched it graze. The sunlight in the clearing made its pelt glow with reflected light. Shorty knew he was in the perfect position to catch dinner for himself and his friends. The wind would not betray his presence. And the stink of the bushes made detecting his scent even harder.

His fingers itched to pull out one of his throwing rocks, but he realized there was no time for a hunt and no easy way to carry the meat while he scouted. In frustration, he bent down and picked up a dry stick. Skreee watched suspiciously, but Shorty only snapped the stick in two with a loud crack. The head of the deer shot up as it scanned for danger. Shorty tossed the broken stick into the clearing and the deer bolted away down the length of the clearing to disappear into the trees.

Shorty watched it go then motioned Skreee to lead again. He watched the sprite fly quickly across the clearing and dart into the trees ahead. Shorty waited a few breathes and then followed. He noted a large patch of the smelly bushes on the far side of the clearing.

Shorty crossed the open space at a run and left the bright sunlight once again for the dimness of the canopy. As he slipped beneath the trees, he paused to let his eyes adjust. There was the sound of a large body moving in the bushes to his right. Shorty spun towards the noise to see a large male wolf rising from among the leaves. Its head rose to nearly the height of his chest. Its lips curled back to reveal a set of sharp teeth as it snarled.

Shorty had time to realize the wolf had probably been stalking the deer and he was now its intended replacement meal before the beast sprang. Shorty did not waste time reaching for a weapon. Instead, his arms came up as the wolf hit him full in the chest. He stumbled back into the clearing, landing on his back with the wolf on top of him.

Shorty tried to roll to the side, but he could not use his arms to get any leverage to roll the huge beast over. His hands and arms were too busy trying to keep the snapping jaws from his face and throat. Both of Shorty's hands were locked in the fur of the wolf's neck working to shove it away. The beast was strong and the sharp teeth were moving slowly closer.

Shorty realized that the wolf's neck muscles were stronger than his arms were. This was almost as bad as wrestling with the larger ogre youth when he was much younger. Strength was not the key here, leverage was. He would lose this fight if he did not find a way to get the wolf off its feet. He wondered where the bug was and why it was not helping him.

The wolf pulled back slightly in preparation for a lunge at Shorty's throat. Its jaws opened wide and its saliva began to drip in Shorty's face. Shorty released his hold with his left hand and balled it into a fist. As the wolf lunged forward, Shorty drove his fist into its open maw. The wolf reacted in surprise and began to bite down on his hand. Shorty felt the sharp teeth pierce his skin and his wrist begin to drip blood. But the force of his blow combined with the wolf's own lunge had driven his fist in deep so it could not fully close its jaws.

The wolf began to whine and tried to pull its head back. Shorty understood the danger of allowing the beast to come at him again. He slid his long right arm around its neck pulled the wolf in closer. He tried to force his fist further down its throat.

The wolf began to struggle harder. Its front legs pressed into Shorty's chest and began to rake at him. Its sharp claws slid harmlessly over his chainmail doing little damage. The wolf was not stupid and managed to plant its front paws to either side of Shorty's body. Then it brought its rear paws up to rake instead. Shorty felt them shred the leather that protected his upper legs. Sharp claws dug into his thigh.

With the weight of the huge creature off his chest, Shorty managed to twist to the side toppling the wolf. While keeping the pressure on with both arms, Shorty brought his bleeding legs up and wrapped them around the body of the wolf. He began to squeeze. The breathing of the wolf became more labored. Between the fist in its mouth and his legs constricting his chest, Shorty was sure he could win this fight.

That was until the orc stepped out from beneath the trees and into the light. It was not large as orcs went. But it carried a spear that it handled with skill. Its hair was greasy and had many feathers and bones

braided into it. Shorty realized it was the beast's trainer. He figured
he was about to die. Hopefully the fool bug would warn his friends.
Shorty tightened the grip of his legs hoping to eliminate one danger to
those same friends.

Shorty squeezed with all his might as he watched as the orc step
forward and raise its spear. Then it let go with one hand and began to
swat at something near its face.

Skreee flew slowly through the trees, looking for trouble. He had gone
several hundred yards in when he spotted the orc sitting beneath a tree.
It was eating something bloody. There was a large spear lying on the
ground beside it. He spun in the air and shot back towards the clearing
to warn the ogre. He was almost there when he heard a growl and then
the crash of bodies.

Skreee flew up among the tree branches as he moved closer to the
sound of combat. Better to find out what was happening before he got
involved. As he came to the edge of the clearing, he stopped, hanging
in the air watching the ogre fighting with a really, really big wolf. The
stupid ogre was not even using either of the two very large swords he
carried.

The crazy ogre had one hand deep in the wolf's mouth and the other
was wrapped around its head like he was hugging it. Skreee stared
in fascination. He knew he should help, but his arrows would not
penetrate the wolf's fur. He could not shoot it in the face since the ogre
was wrapped around its head. So, he watched this most unusual fight.

Skreee saw the wolf begin to rake the ogre just before they rolled to the
side. Somehow, the ogre managed to wrap his legs around the wolf's
body. He swore he could hear the wolf's ribs creak as the ogre began to
squeeze. Skreee had totally forgotten about the orc until it stepped out
from into the sunlight clearing.

Skreee darted towards the orc and flew at its eyes in an attempt to
distract it from the ogre. The orc began to swing one of its hands
at Skreee, so the sprite flew backwards and pulled out an arrow. He
launched the first one and saw it strike the orc in the cheek. It grabbed

the spear with both hands again so Skreee fired a second arrow and
then a third.

Skreee watched the orc slump to the ground and then spun back
towards the other fight. He was just in time to hear a large pop
followed by the sound of cracking bone. The wolf whimpered and
its rear legs went limp. The ogre pulled a bloody fist from its mouth.
There were teeth marks and gashes along the side of his huge hand and
on his wrist.

Shorty lost sight of the orc in his struggle with the wolf. He could not
understand why the spear had not entered his body yet. Then he felt
something give in the wolf's back. The ribs shifted out of place and a
heartbeat later, he heard them crack. The animal whimpered and lay
still, breathing in shallow pants.

Shorty pulled his hand from its mouth. It was bleeding and it hurt a
lot. He would not be able to hold a sword in that hand for a while. He
stared around him and saw the orc on the ground a few feet away. It
appeared to be sleeping. Shorty looked up to see Skreee motionless in
the air except for his swiftly beating wings.

Shorty rose slowly to his feet and grabbed the spear from the ground
in his right hand. He casually shoved the point into the orc's throat.
He pulled it out, turning towards the wolf. Shorty stared down at it
and then drove the spear deep into its chest where the ribs had broken.
Shorty stood and just breathed.

Skreee flew up before him. "I saved you. See I am a warrior."

Shorty just nodded while he studied the orc and wolf. After a second,
he bent down and grabbed the wolf by the scruff with his right hand.
He dragged its body over beside the dead orc. He rolled the orc fully to
his back and studied it for a moment before reaching down and pulling
a pouch from its belt. "For boy to play wid."

Skreee looked at him strangely. "What are you doing? Are you insane?
We need to go. You made a lot of noise playing with that wolf. We
should go."

Shorty grinned up at the sprite. "Surprise fer orcs." Then he again grabbed the wolf by the head. He pulled with his one good hand until the wolf's body lay across that of the orc. Shorty struggled with his one good hand but managed to maneuver the wolf's distended jaws over the puncture wound in the orc's throat. Then with a bit of pain, he used both hands to squeeze the wolf's jaws closed on the orcs neck.

Skreee suddenly understood the game and flew down to pull his three small arrows from the orc's face. "This should be fun."

Shorty and Skreee moved back across the clearing and hid in the trees near the place they had watched the deer. Shorty noticed that he had left blood traces along the way. But there was not much he could do about it. He used some fresh green leaves to pack the wounds on his legs while they waited. It was almost midday when the first orc arrived.

Shorty and Skreee watched as the orcs found the two corpses. It was not long before the yelling began. They pointed at the scout and the dead wolf. There was a great deal of arguing and even shoving as the orcs tried to figure out what had happened. The argument was close to breaking out in a fight when a robbed figure entered the clearing. The argument died almost immediately.

Shorty began counting the orcs with his fingers as the orcs clustered across the clearing. He started over several times and then gave up. Skreee noticed the effort and began a count of his own.

The robed figure barked a command that Shorty could not make out.

The orcs spread out and to search around the bodies. One of the orcs soon found the place where Shorty had fought the wolf. The arguments began again, but once more the robbed figure barked a command and it stopped.

Shorty pointed backwards and he and Skreee faded back into the trees. Skreee led the way back along their trail. Skreee began to fly faster but he noticed that the ogre was not keeping up anymore. The ogre waved him to go ahead, but Skreee slipped into the canopy of the trees and waited until he heard the ogre go pass.

Skreee dropped back down behind the large warrior and watched him hobble along on his injured legs. Skreee decided he liked this ogre.

He would keep him. He continued along behind Shorty watching their back trail. The orcs would not get his ogre. Skreee the Mighty Warrior would not let them have him.

———————————

Kisa and H'aor pulled the last of the hard biscuit and cheese from their packs. The small amount of jerky that was left was set aside for Shorty on his return. The four ate in silence as each contemplated the coming battle. When he finished his share, Thorn moved back to the two boulders. He studied them for a bit and then began to shift them slightly closer to the edge.

H'aor watched him. "They are fine, Thorn. They should provide enough cover."

Thorn grunted as he shifted the larger of the two rocks. "They are not just cover. Sending these down the slope will break their advance. Might even take one or two out of the fight." Thorn returned to the group and sat down. "What can your magic do, H'aor?"

H'aor shrugged. "As I said last night, I only have a few spells available to me, that I think will be useful. I can use my magic missiles twice today. I plan to save them for any spell wielders we face. They are fast and will disrupt any spells cast at us. I also have one stinking cloud spell. If we can get some of them bunched up, I may be able to disable most of them." He grinned before adding, "Assuming bad smells bother orcs."

Thorn nodded and looked to Kisa. "And you?"

Kisa looked down at her Holy Symbol. "I have more spells, but they are not as useful in combat. I can heal four times today and I can use Spiritual Hammer twice. I also have the scroll to hold several of them immobile. I cannot use both my mace and the magical hammer at the same time though." She pulled out the mace from the orc treasure. The dirt and grime had all been cleaned off it. Somehow, it seemed more menacing now.

Joachim grinned at Kisa. "Do not take offense, but I kind of hope we do not need your healing magic. But I suspect we will before this is done."

The four waited restlessly through the remainder of the morning. They grew more and more concerned as time went by. Joachim began to fidget with his knife. He went from spinning it on the ground to idling tossing it up into the air. It would flip several times as it traveled up and then back down to land with the hilt in the palm of his hand.

Thorn looked at him and grinned. "So much for all the tales about the patience of thieves."

Joachim's face showed his frustration. "Where are they? Our scouts are missing and there is no sign of the orcs either. Watching a mark is one thing, feeling like the mark is another. I do not enjoy waiting to be attacked."

No one answered as they continued to watch the area below the ridge. About an hour after midday, the sound of buzzing wings could be heard in the distance. It closed rapidly on their position. The sprite appeared and shot directly to Kisa's shoulder. Skreee sat silent and still as he caught his breath.

H'aor studied the small figure carefully as he gave him a few moments. "Did you find the orcs?"

Skreee nodded his head yes and pointed back the way he had come. "Found and fought. My ogre is hurt. He is coming, but not very fast."

Kisa asked softly, "How bad is Shorty hurt?"

The sprite held out his left hand. "This hand is not good. Both legs are cut up too. One is bad, I think. He is not going to be able to climb the rope."

Joachim moved quickly to his rope and untied it. He moved to a tree directly behind the ramp and retied it there. Kisa moved to the ramp and began to remove the stakes she had shoved into the soil as Joachim tossed the now coiled rope down the ramp.

Something large could be heard moving slowly through the trees across the dry streambed. Shorty stepped out into the open. He looked tired and worn. His left hand was held against his chest. It was covered in dried blood. His leather leggings were both shredded and splattered with Shorty's blood.

The big ogre moved to the bottom of the ramp and studied it. He picked up the rope lying at his feet and carefully began to make his way to the top. About midway, the loose earth began to slide. Shorty stood still and braced against the rope. When the ground at his feet settled again, he carefully made it to the top.

Shorty moved carefully over to sit beside his gear. He dropped to the ground with a groan. Thorn handed him a fresh waterskin and Shorty lifted it one handed to his lips. He drank deeply. Kisa pulled her own waterskin out and began to rinse the blood from Shorty's left hand. "These are teeth marks!" She exclaimed. "What bit you so badly?"

Shorty met H'aor and Thorn's eyes before responding. "Wolf. Bery big wolf."

Kisa began to fuss over the hand as she lifted her Holy Symbol above it. "What did you do, stick your hand in its mouth?"

The sprite began to giggle and Shorty looked at her with a very serious expression on his face. "Yes, Kisa Lady. Bery far."

The sprite's giggle changed to almost hysterical laughter. It leaned too far to the side and rolled down Kisa's arm, landing on the ground. Kisa glared at both of them before focusing once more on Shorty's injuries. She began casting her spell.

Shorty sighed in relief as the emerald light began to drip down into his wounds. They began to close up. He flexed the hand several times and tried made a fist. It would do to hold a shield, but he was not sure about using a sword yet. Shorty just watched as the green light faded away.

Kisa moved down to his legs and began to pull out the leaves that Shorty had stuffed inside the armor as padding. Kisa began muttering about bandages and keeping wounds clean. She stared up at Shorty. "I supposed you rolled around on the ground with it too." Shorty started to open his mouth but shut it at the warning look Thorn gave him.

The laughter from the sprite abruptly ceased. There was awe in his voice as he said, "You should have seen the fight. It was incredible."

Kisa again raised her Holy Symbol and cast another healing spell targeting the leg wounds. As the glow of the healing dripped into Shorty's legs, he groaned in relief.

H'aor knelt before Shorty and handed him the jerky they had set aside. Shorty began to eat ravenously.

Thorn turned to the sprite that had climbed back to its feet. "If you can get past the humor of it all, care to tell us what happened?"

Skreee took a breath. "Well, this really big wolf surprised him after he chased away the deer it planned to eat. It leapt on him before he could pull out one of those big swords."

H'aor cocked one eyebrow up. "And neither of you noticed a really big wolf that close to you?"

Skreee looked indignant. "It was hiding in the bushes while it snuck up on a deer. Even the deer did not see it."

Shorty added through a mouth full of jerky. "Bush smell bery, bery bad. Dead ting smell. No could smells wolf."

Joachim quipped from the back as he recoiled his rope, "I think I am getting a headache. Do we really have to hear this?"

Thorn shot Joachim an angry look then turned back to the two scouts. "And Shorty just stuck his hand in its mouth."

Shorty merely nodded but then Skreee got a strange look of admiration on his face. "He stuck his whole fist in there. I think he was trying to rip its tongue out. He kept pulling it closer. Then he wrapped his legs around it and started to squeeze. It was amazing to watch."

Joachim snorted as H'aor sputtered, "You just watched?"

Skreee met his gaze. "Arrows will not go through its fur. Only target for my bow was its nose and it was under the ogre's arm. So, I watched the show. Until I saved him from the orc with the spear. It was gonna stick him good with that spear."

Thorn looked even more confused. "What orc?"

Shorty again mumbled through his food. "Scout. Him wolf boss."

Thorn looked back at Skreee. "And you saved him?"

Skreee stood up proudly. "Shot him three times. Put him to sleep before he used that spear."

Thorn shook his head. "And then what?"

Skreee pointed to Shorty. "He broke the wolf with his legs. I never heard ribs crack like that before. Then he used the spear to stab them both. Then he made it look like they killed each other. It was a great joke." Then we hid and watched the other orcs fight about it until the one in robes came. Then we ran away."

Thorn and H'aor stared at each other while Kisa and Joachim began to laugh. Joachim looked over at Thorn. "How did you put it; I know. You do not want to know how they did it."

Skreee walked over to stand before Shorty. "I saved you. Not a bug, now I am Mighty Warrior."

Shorty coked his head to the side as he stared at the sprite. "Not bug. Small Warrior."

Skreee thought for a second and then he nodded. "We are even now ogre. Since I saved you last, you are now my ogre."

Shorty smiled down at him. "Youse do good. No owe. Now bees friend."

Skreee locked gazes with him and then nodded. "Friends."

H'aor stepped between the two. "Fine, you two had fun playing with the orc scout. But how many of them are there and how far behind you are they?"

Shorty looked up proudly. "Lots. Bees soon."

H'aor shook his head. "All that and your answer is lots? Not sure what is dumber, the answer or the fool who expected more.

Skreee started to laugh so hard he had to sit down again, clutching his stomach. "Wait…. Wait…." The Sprite had to gasp a deep breath through his laughter. "Ask him to count for you." Skreee clutched his belly as his laughter continued.

H'aor turns a perplexed look at Shorty. "Please count for me, Shorty."

Shorty held his hand up and spread his fingers. He began to count. "One, two, four, lots." Shorty looked at his last finger. "No know next. Maybeso more lots."

Thorn winked at H'aor. "Pretty good counting for an ogre." Then he turns his gaze to Skreee. "How many did you count or were you too busy laughing then too?"

Skreee stopped laughing and wiped tiny tears from his eyes. "There were eleven orcs in the group."

Shorty added, "Nudder wolf. Female."

Skreee began to argue, "I did not see another wolf."

Shorty shrugged. "Smelled on male dat me kilt. Him mate come."

H'aor sighed. "Not good. Anyone else got any more bad news?"

Shorty nodded. "One wid robe gots magic stick."

Skreee piped up as well. "They are not far behind us. My ogre could not move fast"

Thorn grunted and moved back to his position by the boulders. "Did you have to ask for bad news elf? Everyone get something to drink and take care of your other needs. It is time to kill us some vermin."

Skreee rose slowly into the air and flew back towards the approaching enemy and disappeared into the trees again.

Shorty finished eating and moved to stand beside Thorn. Shorty took his place behind the larger boulder but even crouching, it did not provide him much cover. Thorn began to whisper instructions to Shorty and mimed shoving the large boulder forward. "But not till I tell ya, got it?"

Shorty nodded and Thorn moved behind the smaller boulder with H'aor behind him. Kisa positioned herself behind the tree they had used to climb up. Joachim stayed way back from the ridge line unsure of how to help. Skreee had flown off into the trees across the dry bed checking on the movement of their enemies.

About a quarter hour later, Skreee returned and landed in the tree above Kisa. "They are here."

Part 2
Becoming More

"Do good hurt sometime, do bad hurt ebry times."

Chapter 9
Ambush or Trap

Kisa turned her head from the tree line to study her companions. They all stood ready for the coming battle even if some, like Joachim, seemed less than eager for it. She thought back to the fight at the inn. The odds there had been better, especially with the distraction provided by all the other patrons. Then again, what did she really know about combat? This was only her second battle and the first ever in the wild. But she knew she felt confident. Maybe it was because this time they fought together and not as a bunch of individuals in the middle of a brawl. This time, she had people she trusted and that was something strange and new to her.

Kisa heard a noise from the tree line and turned back to see a lone orc slip out from among the trees. It glanced furtively along the ridge until its eyes came to rest on the three warriors standing at the top of the ramp. Then it slipped back into the trees and was gone.

Moments later, the orc reappeared striding boldly out to stand in the middle of the dry steam bed. This time Kisa could see that it wore leather armor and carried a spear with a broad metal head that flashed in the sunlight. Close behind it came three more orcs. These also wore leather armor but carried loaded crossbows. They moved onto the streambed to stand about twenty feet to the right of the spear wielder.

The shrubs at the edge of the wood were trampled down as another group of orcs marched into view. These appeared to be wearing ragged chainmail armor. Two carried large axes and the three remaining orcs were armed with swords and large oval shields. This group moved into the gap between the spear wielder and the crossbows. The final orc to emerge from the trees was wearing robes. It came to a stop close to the tree line directly behind the spear-wielder.

The orc in robes began to shout commands in orcish while gesturing towards the ramp and those at its crest. The language seemed harsh to Kisa. The jarring tones seemed to agitate her. Kisa gripped her mace tightly to calm herself.

The orcs in chainmail shifted forward to the base of the ramp and glared upwards. As Kisa watched them maneuver into place, she cursed as she realized that the stakes had not been replaced after helping Shorty to reach the top. The path up would be much easier now for their foes.

Shorty stared down at the orcs standing near the base of the ramp. He wanted them to attack and get the fight started. He did not like waiting. The orcs seemed to be studying the ramp looking for a way up. Shorty did not want them thinking. Thinking was bad. They might find a way to hurt his new friends. Shorty fidgeted for a couple of heartbeats and then decided he had had enough of waiting. He reached down and picked up a hand-sized rock from the ground. The orcs with the axes seemed to be the easiest targets. He quickly stood up and hurled the rock at the axe bearing orc on his right.

One of the orcs with a sword took a step forward and raised his shield. The rock sparked as it deflected off the shield. The orc grunted and stepped back at the impact. He regained his balance and returned to his place in the line. The orc with the axe pointed his weapon at Shorty and yelled in orcish. Shorty did not understand orcish, but he guessed he had just been called a not nice name.

Thorn cleared his throat and spit in the direction of the orcs. "It was a nice throw, Shorty. Too bad it did not hit. The good news is, I think you made them mad. Maybe they will stop standing around wasting my time."

The robed orc raised its voice again and stabbed it finger towards the ramp. The warrior orcs raised their weapons, but held their positions.

The robed orc raised his other arm. As the arm came up, the long sleeve slid back to reveal a thin white wand. He aimed it at the top of the ridge. H'aor managed to yell a warning as a pale white light flashed towards the ridge.

The light was quickly followed by the two axe-wielding orcs charging up the slope. Their progress was slowed as the rocks and lose soil began to sift under their combined weight. Another sharp command came from the robed orc, the three orcs to the side raised their crossbows and fired. The bolts streaked over the heads of the two orcs climbing the ramp. All three targeted the larger boulder at the top of the ramp.

––––––––––––––––––––

At H'aor's shout of warning, Joachim faded back into the trees. He found a deep shadow behind a large tree trunk and huddled behind. There was a flash of light that eliminated the shadows and Joachim felt a wave of cold air wash over him.

Joachim peeked out from behind the trunk of his tree to discover a smooth semi-clear wall before him stretching in both directions. The wall seemed to sparkle in the sunlight. Joachim slowly reached out a hand to touch the glistening surface. It was a solid barrier of ice. Joachim looked up. The wall was nearly twice his height. He might be able to climb it, but it would be slippery and difficult. Probably easier to scamper up a tree and drop down on it from above. Then again, the top of the wall was probably slippery too.

Joachim decided to see if he could make his way around the wall. He turned south and began to run alongside the wall dodging trees as necessary. After a few steps, Joachim realized the wall curved. It arced towards the edge of the ridge. He hurried on, running his left hand lightly across the ice.

––––––––––––––––––––

Kisa tensed as the wand emitted its pale flash of light. She blinked in confusion when nothing appeared to happen. She checked quickly to make sure her companions were all okay. The three at the ramp were fine other than the orcs moving up to attack them. She glanced backward to check on Joachim. In the place where she had last seen the young man, there now rested a large glistening wall that curved around them. They were trapped against the ridge line. Their enemies were not going to let them flee.

Kisa turned back to her friends defending the ramp. "We are trapped. The wand created some kind of wall behind us. It may have gotten Joachim. I do not see any sign of him."

Thorn's voice grumbled from the ramp. "Except for the boy, the wall changes nothing. We were not planning to run anyway. Focus on making them pay for the boy's life."

Joachim's loss hurt. Kisa looked up into the tree above her. "Skreee, please look for Joachim. I need to know if he is still alive."

The sprite rose into the air with a stubborn look on his small face. "You are safer if the Evil One is dead."

Kisa stared up at him with sadness in her eyes. "Please." The sprite shook his head and flew over the wall. Kisa focused her attention back on the orc who had killed her friend. The mage was a threat and she intended to deal with him. She picked up the parchment from the orc shaman. It was not a spell she had used before, but if she could immobilize the mage and his guard, it would keep her friends safer.

Kisa began to read the spell. Casting from the parchment seemed simpler than using her own Goddess-granted magic. There were no gestures or need to gather her power. She simply had to read and focus on a target. She felt the power peak and she reached out towards the mage and spear wielder.

There was instant resistance as Kisa brought the magic of the scroll to bear on the two orcs. She had never tried to impose her will on another being in this fashion before. She had to concentrate as her targets fought against the spell. She felt the spell enfold the spear wielder, but the mage refused to give in. For a moment, she thought she had him as well. The orc mage froze for a fraction of a heartbeat before recovering. He looked up at her and cackled at her failure. Then he turned to his unmoving guardian and began to chant what Kisa assumed to be a spell.

At the flash of light, Shorty raised his shield and lowered his head. He had no desire to be hit by whatever bad magic was coming his way. His shield jarred into his head as he felt two hard impacts on it. Shorty felt fine. He was surprised the shield had somehow stopped the bad magic from hurting him. He raised his head and tipped the shield to see what had happened to it. To his surprise, there was a single crossbow bolt stuck in it near its center. The bolt had penetrated the steel but had failed to go through the thick wooden core.

Shorty heard Thorn complain from beside him but ignored it. Kisa's outcry was more of a concern, but he was more worried about the three orcs with crossbows. They appeared to be reloading the bows. He decided that he really did not like crossbows very much. He should have thrown the rock at them. But before he could deal with the crossbows, he had to take care of the two orcs with their large axes that were slowly climbing up the ramp.

Shorty placed the shield on the ground beside his sword and placed both his hands against the boulder the way Thorn had showed him. He glanced to the dwarf and Thorn gave him a quick nod. Shorty bent his knees and heaved against the boulder with all his might. He dropped to a crouch and grabbed his sword and shield before looking up.

H'aor went down to his knees when he saw the wand come up. He was expecting a fireball or lightning bolt. When neither hit, he raised his head. At Kisa's yell, he glanced back to see a wall of ice encircling the group. The orcs did not intend for them to get away. Time to teach them how dangerous a trapped animal really was.

H'aor examined his options quickly. He had to trust Thorn and Shorty to control the slope. That left the mage or the crossbows. He chose to deal with the archers first. He reached down to the spell components he had laid out before him and selected the small ball of Sulphur he needed to cast his stinking cloud spell. He wondered briefly if there was anything that orcs truly considered to be a bad smell. Then his mind fastened on the Arcane words of his spell.

Thorn was angry with the orcs. It stung his pride that all three orcs had fired at Shorty. One had hit the shield dead center, the second glanced off the edge of it, and the final bold had shattered on the rock before the ogre. What kind of orc did not hate dwarves? He was going to teach them to show more respect.

He nodded to Shorty and watched as the ogre shoved his boulder down the slope. Except, it did not roll down the slope as it was supposed to. The muscle-bound fool had launched it into the air.

The two orcs already on the ramp simply threw themselves flat and watched the boulder fly over their heads. It bounced once before the next three orcs who danced out of its way. Thorn could only shake his head at the ogre's apologetic "Oops."

While all five orcs had their attention on the first boulder, Thorn set his shoulder to the one in front of him. It slowly slid over the edge and began to roll downhill. The orc lying below him tried to roll to the side, but the boulder rolled over its leg, settling on top of it. There was a sharp crack as the boulder sank into the loose soil. The pain-filled cry of the orc echoed across the battlefield.

Thorn glanced nervously at the three orcs with crossbows, a little concerned that he had given up his only cover. Then H'aor's voice came from Thorn's rear, "BOsh-AW awB." As Thorn watched, a yellowish green cloud formed in the air above them. As it began to settle over them, Thorn heard the sound of choking and gagging from within the cloud.

"Nice work, elf." Thorn muttered to himself.

Joachim followed the ice as it curved back to the ridge. He peaked around the edge of the wall to find he was about thirty yards south of the orcs. It was clear that they were all focused on the battle at the ramp. He looked down to see the ridge was about twenty-five feet high at this point. Joachim smiled at the many roots and other handholds available to him. Much easier than climbing ice. Joachim lowered himself over the edge and quickly descended to the base of the ridge.

He checked again to make sure the orcs were occupied and darted silently across to the tree line. He sighed in relief as the shadows closed around him. He paused behind a tree as the vague beginnings of a plan began to form in his mind. He shifted a little deeper into the trees and began moving parallel to the tree line towards the orcs.

When Joachim reached a point that he believed was behind the orc leader, he began looking into the trees above him. It only took a second to find a tree that met his needs. He leapt up, catching the branch he had selected then pulled himself up. He climbed rapidly until he was about halfway up the tree, then he settled on a wide branch to catch his breath.

Joachim took a long drink of water as he worked out a plan to take out the orc mage. He was about to stand when he heard bodies coming through the underbrush from deeper in the trees. Joachim lay down on his branch and began to watch. A large wolf came into view, moving through the shadows towards his trail. Joachim almost panicked at the thought of the wolf picking up his scent. He needed a plan. Being trapped in this tree would not help him get to the orc mage.

Joachim had no experience with wolves. But they were just really big dogs, right? He knew about guard dogs and the dogs that the town watch used to track people like him. He should be able to use the same tricks with the wolf that he did with the dogs of the watch. Joachim slowly reached down to his left boots and slipped two fingers inside. He pulled out a vial filled with a black powder. He pulled the cork out and sprinkled a bit into the air below him. He thought for a second and sprinkled about half of the vial into the air below him. "Pepper is such a useful tool," he muttered quietly to himself.

He watched ats the wolf continued forward and crossed his trail. It lowered its head and sniffed in one direction and then the other. Joachim mentally urged it to go the other way. But it ignored his silent plea and turned towards him. It was below the next tree over when it suddenly snorted as if trying to expel something from its nose. Its front paw came up and it rubbed at its face and it began to back away. An orc with a large spear came out of the trees behind the wolf and began to watch it with a puzzled expression.

Joachim was beginning to sweat. This was not going to work. Suddenly, there was the sound of a tree limb falling back along his trail towards the ridge. The orc turned and began to jog towards the sound. It gave a thin whistle and the wolf turned with a growl and ran after the orc.

Joachim was still lying on his branch, thanking the gods and trying to figure out what had just happened, when he heard a light buzzing noise and Skreee dropped to the branch before him with a grin on his face.

Joachim blinked in surprise. "If you made that noise, thank you. But why are you here?"

Skreee gave him a look of disdain. "Pretty One thinks you might be dead. She asked me to find you and save you. I tried to tell her it was better if you died, but she said please. Now Evil One owes Skreee his life."

Joachim shook his head but decided it was not a good time to argue. He whispered his reply. "I think I can help our friends, but you must remain very quiet." Joachim thought for a moment and then added, "Please." The sprite did not reply, he just stared at him. Joachim stood carefully on the branch, peering through the trees towards the ridge. Then he slid quietly down the tree and angled towards the place where he had seen the orcs.

———————————

Shorty watched intently as Thorn's boulder came to rest on top of an orc's leg. As soon as it stopped, the remaining three orcs began to scramble up the incline using the boulder and the pinned orc for hand and footholds. Shorty's attention shifted to the remaining axe wielder who was crawling upwards. As it neared the top, it rose to its knees and sank the axe head into the soil at the top of the ramp.

The axe head bit deep and the orc grasped the haft with both hands and began to pull itself forward. Shorty stepped forward and drove his long blade into the junction of its neck and shoulder before it could reach the top. The orc sank face down onto the rubble, its axe haft jutting out over its head.

Thorn stepped to his side as Shorty saw the fastest of the three orcs crawled over its dead companion's body. Shorty chopped down at the leading orc, but it pulled its shield over its head. Shorty's sword rebounded from the shield. From its position below him, the orc slashed at Shorty's ankles trying to drive Shorty back from the edge. Shorty's heavy boot came down hard on the blade pinning it to the ground. Shorty brought his blade down again slicing deep into the orc's sword arm. The blade did not stop till it hit bone. The orc cried out as blood began to spurt from its arm. It slid slowly back down the ramp.

Shorty had just stepped back beside Thorn to wait for the next orc when there was a thud in his left shoulder and his arm went numb. Shorty staggered backwards as the two remaining orcs swarmed across the two bodies and gained the top of the ridge.

Thorn stepped protectively in front of Shorty. It was finally his turn to play with the orcs.

H'aor watched in admiration as Thorn and Shorty controlled the ramp. There really was no room for a third blade. The look on Shorty's face when the boulder flew through the air instead of rolling would have been funny in other circumstances. But Thorn's boulder and Shorty's sword thrust had eliminated the threat of the axes. H'aor smiled in satisfaction as Shorty took down another of the orc warriors.

His smile evaporated when the crossbow bolt penetrated Shorty's shoulder above his shield. H'aor cursed himself for not paying attention and assuming his spell had eliminated the threat of the crossbows. Watching his friends in battle was a good way to get them killed. H'aor turned his gaze back to the cloud that he had cast. It was beginning to dissipate in the light breeze. Two of the orcs were face down on the ground. They did not appear to be conscious. The third was on his knees. A recently fired crossbow lay before him and he was reaching for one that appeared to already be spanned. The second crossbow was lying near one of the other two orcs.

H'aor's anger at himself fueled his next spell. As he spoke the Arcane words, "shEH laKH," two sapphire bolts flew from his hand towards the orc below. Just as it fitted a bolt into the crossbow, the two missiles impacted the center of its body. It looked up in confusion as the crossbow fell from its grasp. It toppled backwards to the ground.

––––––––––––––––––––

Joachim slipped from shadow to shadow as he made his way to the tree line. He came to the edge about seven feet to the side of the orc mage. He grimaced at the extra space he would have to travel in the open. He quickly examined the ground between this tree and the one right behind the mage. He did not think he could get through the underbrush quietly. He would have to try to close on the mage from here.

Joachim took a moment to study his friends to see how they were doing. He glanced up to see two blueish bolts shoot from the ridge towards one of the orcs below. The mage laughed and began casting. Joachim broke from the trees hoping to somehow disrupt the spell before it could hurt his friends.

Joachim has almost reached the mage when the orc spun towards him lifting a hand in his direction. Joachim slashed wildly with his trusted knife. The blade caught the side of the extended hand leaving a thin line of blood. It must have been enough as the mage jerked the hand back and stopped chanting.

The mage reached behind its back and pulled out a curved dagger half again the size of Joachim's knife. Joachim was no fan of knife fights, but he moved closer knowing he could not turn his back on the spell caster. They began to shift back and forth, thrusting and slashing, trying to find an opening. Joachim quickly realized that the mage was not very good with but the orc's longer reach and the unusual shape of the blade were causing Joachim problems.

The orc mage began to mutter as Joachim searched for a way past its treacherous blade, "mAh-ar-tsAW aw-khAZ." The odd-sounding syllables made no sense to Joachim. Was it speaking orcish? He didn't know, but its strange utterings slipped from his mind as the orc suddenly went on the offensive.

After blocking several clumsy attacks, Joachim saw an opening. He stepped in close, preparing to thrust his knife into the mage's stomach when the mage's bloody hand grasped his shoulder. The moment the hand clutched his shoulder, raw energy course through Joachim's body. His jaw clamped shut and his muscles seemed to lock. The mage released his grip and Joachim fell backwards hitting the ground hard. His limbs began to spasm uncontrollably.

The mage laughed and stepped forward with his wicked dagger raised. A small form suddenly darted before the mage's face screaming, "Skreeeeee!" The mage flinched, but reacted quickly by swinging his bloody hand at the sprite. Skreee tried to duck beneath the swing. It was not enough and the sprite was knocked to the ground at the mage's feet. The mage raised its booted foot over the tiny form.

———————————

Kisa's failed spell had cost her more than a little confidence in herself. She was even more disappointed when the mage seemed able to dispel her magic on the spear wielder. She continued watch the robed one carefully. She had only one spell that could hurt him at a distance and she was determined to make it count.

Then Joachim had stepped out of the trees. Kisa had been so sure he was dead. She wondered if Skreee had found him or if her friend was down there alone. Skreee had not returned so there was hope.

Kisa held her breath as the young thief snuck up behind the mage. But somehow, he had been detected. The fight had been short. She had no idea what the mage had done to Joachim, but her friend was lying on the ground and at the mage's mercy. She completed the spell she had held ready and called her spiritual hammer into existence near the mage. As he stepped towards her friend, she brought it down in desperation.

———————————

Joachim could only watch the helpless sprite. He wanted to do something quickly before the little pest would be flattened. Joachim came slowly to his knees. The orc hesitated with his boot over the sprite as if taunting Joachim's inability to prevent the fall of his boot.

Then Joachim saw a glowing white hammer come down out of the air to strike the mage. The mage stumbled to the side. Joachim realized that Kisa must be trying to save them. He could not waste the chance she had given him.

The mage spun to look at the hammer floating in the air. The orc began to chant another spell. Joachim carefully rotated the knife in his hand so that he held the blade between thumb and index finger. He raised the arm over his head and waited until the next time his muscles relaxed. Joachim's arm shot forward. The mage arched his back as the blade sank into the area above his kidney. The knife went in up to its hilt.

The mage fell to his knees but turned an angry gaze at the young thief. He began to raise his hand once more when the hammer descended a second time. The mage fell forward to the ground. Skreee stood up and stared at Joachim. Joachim slid back to a seated position and whispered, "Now we are even."

Thorn faced the two orcs and raised his axe and shield. "Where did they find the ugly mold used to forge you vermin? I cannot believe even an orc mother would not have screamed in horror at the first sight of either of you."

The orcs growled in anger and took turns taking swings at the dwarf. Thorn stayed on the defensive, biding his time and using his axe to slap away strike after strike as he continued taunting them. "Tell me you were not twins. No mother deserves that much ugly in a single litter."

The orc swings began coming a little harder but with less accuracy. Thorn continued to bait the two orcs. "My baby sister, bless her cute little beard, can hit harder than either of you." He kept his shield low at his side, not moving it much, his axe remained his primary defense.

Finally, one wild slash made it partially past the blocking axe to slice off a tiny piece of the dwarf's beard. All three watched as the tiny fluff of red hair floated to the ground. Thorn pointed down at the strands of hair with his axe. "Do you see that? Do you realize what you did?" The orc to Thorn's left actually bent over to take a better look. Thorn lashed out with his shield catching the orc in the face. There was a small spurt of something red from its nose and it flew back over the embankment.

The second orc spun to watch his companion slide down the ramp. It seemed to realize its mistake and it spun back towards the dwarf just in time for Thorn to bury his axe head in its chest. Thorn pulled the orc down to eye level and whispered, "Never, ever, trim a dwarf's beard without permission. Really makes us angry. Stupid orc."

Thorn jerked the axe free. The orc fell to the ground at his feet. The angry dwarf stomped on it as he stepped across it to get to the ramp.

Thorn dropped to his seat and slid down the ramp to the orc he had knocked over the edge. Well, knocked out. He stood over it and glared down. He waited until its eyes fluttered open and seem to focus on him. "Dwarven rule number one. A shield bash really, really hurts. Do not forget it." Thorn struck hard with his axe. Then he shook his head. "Too late. Forgot already I bet."

Shorty stumbled, back releasing the shield from his injured arm. He pressed the blade of his sword into the ground and reached up to snap the bolt a short distance from where it penetrated his armor. He tried to move that arm, but it was too painful to use with either sword or shield. He pulled the sword back out of the ground with his good hand and looked to see where he could help.

Shorty heard something moving behind him. He spun around searching for the new threat to his friends. He was surprised to see an orc with a long spear and a wolf standing on top of the wall. Shorty stepped forward to place himself between these new enemies and his friends.

The orc on the wall waited for Shorty to get closer and then leapt at him with his spear extended. He clutched the shaft in both hands so as to put his entire body weight into the thrust. Shorty brought his sword across his body catching the spear just behind the spearhead. The force of the blow knocked the spear to the side and spun the orc sideways as it fell. Its body slammed into the ogre's chest with bruising force.

Shorty hissed in pain as the force of the orc's landing jarred his injured shoulder. But the big ogre barely moved with the impact. The orc rebounded as if it had hit a rock wall. It landed flat on its back. It tried to sit up and bring the spear back into line, but the great sword had a longer reach. Shorty's sword sank deep into the orc's chest. The spear clattered to the ground as the orc's hands came up to grasp the long blade that had killed it.

Joachim slumped as he continued to stare at the dead mage. He lived and that was all that counted. Well, maybe not all as he again glanced towards sprite standing a few feet away. He was not sure what the mage had done to him, but he vowed not to get that close to one the next time. Better yet, he was going to do his best to make sure there was not a next time.

Joachim began to slide closer to the dead orc. He wanted his knife back. He looked up to see how the others fared. What grabbed his attention, though, was the spear wielder watching him with its head cocked to one side. It raised the spear and began to walk towards him.

Joachim tried to move faster to get his knife, but nothing was working right. Why did all the orcs seem to want to kill him? Then again, why was he the only one stupid enough to be down here with the orcs anyway? Skreee pulled out his tiny bow, but the quiver was empty when he reached for an arrow. Joachim finally got his hand on the knife but realize it would not help much against a seven-foot spear. Joachim could only stare as the orc raised it spear to strike. Two more blue bolts flew through the air to take the orc in the back. Its eyes shot open wide as they struck and it sank to the ground.

Kisa spun around as Shorty hissed in pain. She could not figure out where the orc on the ground or the wolf on the wall had come from. How had they gotten behind her? She had no time to watch the orc as the wolf dropped from the wall and began to stalk towards her.

The animal's speed had caught her off guard. Its sudden lunge at her legs had almost got through. She barely managed to bring her shield down to block. She tried to keep the shield between them but the wolf's jaws clamped onto the lower edge of the shield. The wolf began to snarl and tug on the shield. Kisa was forced to one knee to keep her balance. The wolf was low to the ground as it backed away. Kisa knew she was losing the battle for control of the shield.

Kisa was considering letting the shield go before she was pulled further off balance when there was another growl from her right. This growl was louder and much deeper. It made the hair on the back of her neck rise. The wolf suddenly released her shield as it spun to face the source of the growl. Kisa fell backwards as the pressure was suddenly gone from the shield. She turned her head to see what the wolf was so afraid of.

To her surprise, Shorty crouched not far away. The ominous growl was emanating from him. His lips were peeled back exposing small but functional ogre tusks. Kisa's gaze snapped back to the wolf, but it was also staring at Shorty. It began to back away. When it had distanced itself from her, it turned and darted past her using her body to protect it from Shorty. It reached the ridge and leapt down. Kisa turned just in time to see it disappear into the trees at a full run.

Chapter 10
The Road Ahead

Kisa continued to stare at the place where the wolf had disappeared into the trees. It had been frightening the way the wolf had pulled her to her knees. The beast had been so close that she could smell rotting meat on its breath. She could almost belief it was more than just a mere animal. The wolf had controlled the fight. She wanted to understand why had it turned and run off that way. She was sure it could have savaged her before Shorty could have intervened. Kisa put her sense of dread from her mind and looked to see how her friends were doing.

H'aor came and stood beside Shorty. "That shoulder looks bad, my friend. I should have paid more attention to those crossbows. I am sorry"

Shorty looked down at the wound. "No youse fault. Me make dem mad wid rock. No hurts bery muches."

The sound of sliding rock and dirt came from the ramp. All eyes turned as Thorn scrambled noisily back onto the ridge. "Took care of the orcs below. Those two in your cloud were still face down in their own mess. You know elf, orcs smell bad enough without you adding to it that way. Enough to turn a dwarf's stomach. Must have been pretty bad in that cloud of yours. Oh, and Joachim is moving around now. Actually, crawling around is probably more accurate."

Kisa walked over and began to examine Shorty's shoulder. She made him sit down so she could clean the wound. "You know, Shorty, one of these days you should try not to get hurt. You use up most of my healing every time we get into trouble."

Shorty smiled at her. "Ogre bees big. All likes ta hits."

Kisa laughed softly as she moved around to stand behind him. She reached over his shoulder to grip the small piece of the bolt that protruded from his armor. Kisa lifted her Holy Symbol and began her healing as she slowly pulled the bolt free. Shorty relaxed as the glow disappeared into his armor.

Kisa moved back around to stand in front of Shorty. She stared up into his eyes. "Shorty, the wolf. Why did it run? It could have hurt me. All you did was growl at it."

Shorty turned his eyes to where the wolf had stood. "Maybeso it tinks us bees mate. Fight mate same time bees bad."

Surprise and confusion battled for control of Kisa's face. "What? Say that again?"

Shorty shrugged. "Wolf tinks youse bees me mate. No wants fights both us same time. Bees smart. Runs way."

Kisa's face went red with embarrassment. Then outrage washed over her. Her hand shot forward as if to slap Shorty, but she stopped herself. "Mates? We are definitely not mates! You had no right to tell it..."

Shorty interrupted her, "Me no tell. No ken wolf talks."

Kisa continued to glare. "Then why did it..."

Thorn's laughter interrupted her. "Go easy on him, Kisa. You are thinking like a human and not like an animal."

H'aor made a calming gesture. "Among wolves, a fight between two females would be over dominance. No other wolf would interfere except a mate or the pack leader. Shorty came to your defense so the wolf believed you were mated."

Kisa shook her head. "Fine, but no one chooses for me. Not my parents and not some guy that thinks I need protecting." She stared at the Holy Symbol she still held in her hand, then turned back to Shorty. "I am sorry, my friend. You tried to help and I took it wrong."

Shorty looked relieved. "Kisa Lady no bees mad me?"

Kisa placed patted his uninjured shoulder. "No, I am not mad at you. I am mad at my parents. Thank you, Shorty."

Shorty smiled happily at her.

Thorn looked to Kisa and said, "Make sure you understand girl. Shorty probably saved your life again. If you had gone down, that wolf would have ripped out your throat. We won this fight because we looked out for each other."

Kisa met the dwarf's gaze. "I know that now. The mate thing caught me by surprise is all."

Thorn smiled at her. "Everyone has problems they haul around with them. And just so you know, you did good today. Your spells made a difference. Now, how about checking out the boy. That mage did something to him. He might need your last healing spell."

Thorn watched Joachim moving slowly towards the ramp and wondered what trouble the boy had gotten into with the orc mage. Since there was nothing that he could do about it, he turned to Shorty. "You let the wolf go. Is it going to lead more trouble our way?"

Shorty shook his head. "No needs kill. Mate dead. Orc dead. It outcast. No go back eber."

Thorn nodded then pointed down at the large boulder. "Next time roll it my, powerful friend."

Shorty ducked his head. "Oops."

Joachim came slowly up the ramp. The sprite sat on his shoulder. They seemed to be arguing again, but the tone was very different from before.

Joachim tapped the hilt of his knife. "My throw saved you from being squished."

The small figure on Joachim's shoulder waved a tiny finger before his nose. "No, Pretty One's spell saved me."

Thorn turned in resignation and headed for the ramp. "I think I liked it better when they wanted to kill each other. They argued less then. I am going to check the bodies. Please check out the mage once you are done up here, H'aor." Thorn stepped onto the ramp and did a controlled slide to the first body.

Kisa stared at her two friends. "Stop arguing please. No one owes anyone. We are all friends now. What happened, Joachim?"

The two gave each other mock glares, but then both focused on Kisa. Joachim described what the mage did to him. H'aor listened in. "Shocking grasp. Nasty spell. But a general healing should take care of most of the damage."

H'aor turned then and followed Thorn down the ramp while Kisa raised her Holy Symbol and began to heal Joachim. The lines of pain eased from Joachim's face as the healing glow washed over his body. The small tremors in his hands disappeared.

Joachim turned to look back towards the dead orcs but he shook his head and walked over to sit beside Shorty. "I think that mage did something to my brain too. I am not even in the mood to collect pouches. Thorn and H'aor can have all the fun."

Shorty's head popped up as if remembering something important. He reached down to his own belt and untied a bloody pouch. He reached over and placed it in Joachim's hand. Joachim gave him a puzzled look. "What is this for Shorty?"

Shorty reached out a large hand and tapped his index finger on the young thief's chest. "Fer youse."

Joachim's hand closed about the pouch. "Why Shorty? Where did it come from?"

Shorty pointed over at Skreee who was now flitting around Kisa. "From scout. Bees from orc bug put sleep. Gibs ta youse. Boy like little metal tings."

Joachim started to protest at being called boy, but then simply smiled. "I guess I do like them. Thank you, Shorty."

———————————

It was well after dark when the companions moved about a mile north and west of the site of the battle. The ice wall had disappeared, but the area still felt damp and cold. Worse, some of the smaller scavengers were already nosing around the bodies of the dead orcs.

H'aor and Joachim brought in a supply of wood while Thorn built a small fire pit. Shorty stretched and flexed his shoulder trying to loosen it up.

Kisa looked on and said, "Go easy on it, Shorty. It is not fully healed. I can cast another healing on it tomorrow. You did almost as much damage snapping off part of the bolt as when it went in. And no more putting leaves on your wounds. I had to get them all out and clean the leg wounds. Do not make my job harder."

Shorty stretched it one more time and replied without thinking, "Yes Mama"

Thorn began to snicker. "You had that coming, Girl." Shorty looked confused as his friends all began to laugh.

H'aor's grin faded as he cast a worried look at Kisa. "Be careful, I am not so sure he meant that as a joke."

Kisa studied Shorty. "I think you are right; he does not even realize what he said." Kisa reached up to rub her temples. "Oh, dear Goddess, is nothing simple anymore?"

Skreee buzzed up and looked at Kisa carefully. She nodded once and he settled on her shoulder. He looked around and asked. "What do we have to eat?"

Kisa reached into her pack with both hands and pulled out a double handful of nuts and piled them on the ground. "This is all we have left, Skreee, until we have time to hunt or search for more." Kisa reached out and took two of the nuts, cracked them and began to eat.

Skreee shook his head. "I am not a squirrel."

Shorty nodded. "Squirrel bees funner."

Skreee flew off in a huff as the group broke out in laughter once more.

H'aor pulled out a familiar sack and began tossing a pile of pouches in front of Joachim. Joachim stared down at the pile in front of him.

H'aor grinned. "Open them up and then have some fun playing with the coins. You took a big risk today. Time to do something you enjoy."

Joachim laughed softly and began pulling them open like a small child with a bag of new toys.

H'aor then pulled out the wand and a small book. He lay them in the firelight. "The first is a traveling spell book. Mages use them for more risky adventures. Our normal spell books are too large to tote around and too difficult to replace if they are damaged. This is not everything their mage knew, but it contains the spells he was most likely to need in battle. I carry a similar one."

Kisa looked at the book. "Anything you can use in it?"

H'aor touched it softly. "I am not sure. Learning new spells is different for a mage. Your Goddess grants you magic to use. I must study and understand each spell. I need to learn its wording and its gestures. This will take more time to study than we have right now."

H'aor ran his fingers over the book. "This is a treasure to me. There are spells here that are not in either of my books. Several are of the Third Circle. I would very much like to keep this."

Kisa gestured for him to take the scroll. "No one else here can even read it. Take it, H'aor. It might help us all."

H'aor nodded his thanks and tucked the small book inside his cloak. "My thanks. As for the wand, it is pretty obvious that it is a wand of ice wall. I have no clue where they got it, but it is of Elven make. I can guess at the activation word. There is nothing about it to indicate it is special in any way. Based on the power I sense in it; I would guess it has no more than four or five charges left. I would hate to waste one experimenting with it."

Thorn grunted. "So, it has no value at the moment. It is too risky to count on unless we are in a real bind. Which is something I would prefer to avoid. Hang on to it and use your best judgement, H'aor."

Thorn paused for a moment and asked, "If its nearly depleted, why did they risk using up a powerful magic item on the likes of us?"

H'aor shrugged. "I would suggest we only use it as a last resort. And as for why? That is very good question. One bar fight should not have stirred things up that much."

Kisa looked up from her nut snack. "Maybe we are the first to fight back. We set an example they do not want repeated."

Joachim looked up from his counting. "The innkeeper said the one Shorty killed was important. Somebody might want payback."

H'aor slid the wand inside his boot. "Whatever the reason, we may not be out of trouble yet. Did this group have anything else worth looking at, Thorn?"

Thorn reached back into his sack and pulled out a vial of green liquid and a parchment that was rolled on both ends so as to open in the center.

Thorn pointed to the vial. "This was on the scouts down below. Equal bet as to whether it is poison or healing. As for the other, I want to save this for last. What did you find, Joachim?"

Joachim looked up from the coins piled in front of him and shook his head. "Orcs are poorer than street urchins. I could do better with one good purse from an old widow back in Island Town. This was not worth the risk."

Kisa looked over. "It is more than you had. More than we had. So, what did you find?"

Joachim waved his hands over the pile. "There are only three gold pieces, five silver pieces, and thirteen copper. There is also a gem, but it is badly flawed. Might get a gold or two if we can find a blind man to buy it."

Shorty leaned over to examine the pile. "Metal tings bees bad. Bees no fun. Gots pretty marble. Me likes ta plays wid marbles. Bery fun game."

Joachim's eyes sparkled. "Well, my large friend. That could be your share. But that would be all you get...."

Shorty grinned. "Me happy" and grabbed up the small gem.

Kisa cleared her throat. "Not so fast, Joachim."

Joachim tried to look innocent. "Well, he is happy and it makes the rest easier to split. Only four shares now."

Kisa frowned. "The gem will count towards Shorty's share. I will hold the rest of his share. He may need money eventually."

"Fine," Joachim muttered with a grin and he began to divide the loot into five piles.

Joachim stopped and snapped his fingers. "Forgot one." He reached into his backpack and pulled out a bloody pouch and lay it beside the pile.

H'aor looked at it. "Where did you get that, Joachim? That is not an orcish pouch."

Joachim pointed to Shorty. "Shorty gave it to me. He brought it back from his scouting trip. I think it is from that orc they killed." Joachim untied the leather straps holding it closed and looked inside. He dropped the pouch and backed away from it. His face was pale and he looked as if he was about to be sick.

H'aor reached over and upended the pouch. Several copper pieces tumbled out stained with something reddish black. H'aor gave the bag a shake and a finger fell out to land among the coins. There was a silver ring on the finger just above the second knuckle. The ring had a large front face embossed with the image of a single oak tree.

H'aor lifted the finger and gently slid the ring free. He placed the finger back in the pouch and set it before him. "This probably answers the question of where the wand came from. I will return the finger to the land and to the trees later tonight."

Joachim slowly returned to the fire. "You know what that is? Or who that was? That was kind of creepy."

H'aor held the ring near the fire. The light reflected off its surfaces. "This is an Elven House Ring. They are worn by members of the council and their families. Mine has a lake embossed on it instead of a tree. The elf who wore this was from Forest Home."

Kisa looked at the ring. "Why are you not wearing your ring?"

H'aor grinned at her. "It is hard to pretend to be a vagabond elf if you wear a ring that proclaims you to be of high rank. It is safe at home waiting for me."

H'aor held the ring out to Joachim. "Shorty gave it to you as was his right. He recovered it. It is yours now."

Joachim did not reach for the ring. H'aor gestured for him to take it. "Joachim, House Rings are magical. They are not powerful, but they are rings of protection. It will aid you in battle and it will help protect you against spells meant to harm you."

Joachim slowly reached out and took the ring. "Is it safe?" H'aor nodded and Joachim reached out and took the ring. At the elf's urging, he slipped it on his left ring finger. At first it seemed a little lose, but as he settled it into place it seemed to shrink to fit his finger.

H'aor took the vial and placed it carefully in his pack. "We have several other items we do not understand. I will try to identify them when we have time." He turned to Thorn and pointed at the parchment. "What has you nervous, Thorn? Something valuable?"

Thorn picked up the rolled parchment carefully. "Not valuable so much as peculiar and maybe disturbing. Something the orcs should not have."

Thorn backed a little further from the fire and unrolled the parchment in both directions. He places a small stone on each side to hold it open.

Thorn leaned back. "It is a map. And a pretty damn good one."

Thorn gave everyone a few moments to study the map and then went on. "It does not show all of the small villages or inhabited areas, but it does show all of the major towns where you might expect troops to be available." He pointed to three points on the map. "Boat Town,

Island Town, and my own Deephole. It also shows most of the major waterways that are used for trade and travel." Thorn leaned back with a deep frown. Then he pointed towards a lake to the north on the map. "Not sure why this lake is also named."

H'aor touched the map and ran his finger from the lake to the mountains east of the lake. "It is another place of strong defenses. That is near where our large friend comes from. The valley east of Long Lake is protected by the Druids. Their leader is pretty powerful. And he has the ranger Sademäärä there as well."

Joachim looksed puzzled, "Who?"

Shorty smiled happily. "Big Drud wid Elf Lard. Me home."

H'aor chuckled and interpreted. "Sademäärä is a powerful Ranger Lord originally from Forest Home. He has an unusual past. He is rumored to be one of Mielikki's chosen warriors. But he left the Elven lands after his son defied the Elven Council. He and the druid are powerful foes."

Kisa pointed to the map. "Where are your lands, H'aor?"

H'aor gestures to the northern parts of the map. "The elves are scattered across the northern plains on the far side of the river that flows out to the Great Salt Sea. There are five Homes. Forest Home is here at the top of this map. Sea Home is to the east along the Great Salt Sea. Ice Home is far to the north and protects the lands along the Northern Ice Sea. Mountain Home is far to the west among the great mountain peaks there. My family is Lake Home. We protect the land along the series of lakes that divide the Human and Eleven nations. You can see pieces of two of the lakes here on the map."

Thorn looked down at the map and tapped its center. "Geography lessons aside, the big question is, why does an orc raiding party have a map like this? The orcs are a recent problem that came out of the western mountains. They should not know that much about these lands. And orcs do not make pretty maps like this. This map does not make sense."

H'aor met Thorn's gaze. "It is not a puzzle we are going to solve any time soon. I agree though. Someone must be supplying the orcs with information. It would be nice to know who and why?" Then he looked down and tapped to a spot about an inch below the Long Lake. "Leeky's place is about here. Not far from the river. We have been running roughly north west." He shifted his finger over slightly. "Near as I can figure, the Bard was sending us to this smaller lake up in the mountains. There are many small lakes in this region. They aren't shown. Why this one up in the mountains? Why is it important?"

Thorn removed the rocks and rolled up the map. "Too many questions. Guess we will know when we get there. Now we sleep. I will take first watch. Kisa has second watch. She can pray to her Goddess before I go to sleep. Get some rest, the next couple days will be long run."

H'aor nodded to Thorn. Then he picked up the pouch with the finger in it and walked out into the darkness. Kisa, Shorty, and Joachim pulled out their bed rolls. Thorn waited till they were settled and then headed into the darkness as well.

Chapter 11
Trouble in the wind

The first part of the night passed without problems. Kisa woke as Thorn whispered her name. She moved out into the darkness and stared up at the canopy of stars. There were so many of them. They were much brighter and clearer here than back in Boat Town. The air smelled cleaner here in the foothills as well. The peace she felt here strengthened her connection to Akka. Kisa bowed her head and basked in the love of her Goddess.

Kisa began to pray silently for her spells to be renewed. As she felt her powers restored, she looked up at the sky. "My thanks, Akka, Earth Mother. Please, help me find the path that best serves our world. You have given me some interesting companions. I am not sure if I am to teach them or they are here to teach me. Watch over them, Goddess, as they heal our world."

Kisa returned to the firelight and Thorn settled in to sleep. The next few hours were uneventful. Kisa found she did not mind the silence. It gave her time to think about the past few days. The sky to the east was just turning pink when Shorty got up. He moved quietly for one so large.

He looked at Kisa and whispered, "Finds sumtin ta eats." Then he disappeared into the trees. Kisa wandered around the campfire occasionally adding wood to chase away the chill of the early morning hours. She noted with interest that Skreee did not sleep in the camp. She wondered where or even if he rested.

125

H'aor rose next and pulled out his spellbook. He turned his back to the fire and sat studying it in the light of the flames. Soon after, Thorn and Joachim began to pack their gear. Skreee finally returned and flitted around Kisa happily.

Kisa finally shooed the sprite away so she could pack and Skreee flew around checking out everything as the companions packed up. Suddenly, the sprite shot up above the bustle and spun around. "Where is my ogre?"

Kisa started to reply when the sound of something large moving through the trees was heard by everyone. The noise headed directly for the camp. Thorn stood ready, but relaxed when he heard muttering coming through the trees. "Lots friend. No so manys fish. Maybeso bees nuf."

Shorty emerged from the trees with a sharpened branch over his shoulder. Speared onto it were four large trout. Shorty held his catch out happily. "Nuf fish?"

Joachim's mouth opened, then closed. He shook his head. "It will be enough Shorty. Thanks."

Kisa grinned at him. "You are learning."

Thorn took the fish and quickly cleaned them and got the fish over the fire. After a short time, the hot fish came off the fire and was shared amongst the small crowd of hungry people.

After muttered thank-yous, Shorty watched happily as H'aor banked the fire and buried the coals. Shorty looked at his new friends. "What way go?"

Thorn rose and slipped his pack on. He pointed north along the foothills. "You take the lead, Shorty, but keep the pace down. Some of us have short legs."

Shorty grinned. "Me sees dat."

The group set off at a good pace and Skreee spent much of the day flying here and there around them as they traveled. The only stops were to occasionally gather fruit that Skreee found in his wanderings.

Towards noon, Shorty came to a halt and began to pace from side to side. The group caught up quickly but there was no obvious sign of trouble.

Kisa placed her hand on his arm and asked, "What troubles you, Shorty?"

Shorty sucked a deep breath in through his nose. "Fire smell. Dead ting. No bery far."

Kisa shook her head. "I do not smell anything, Shorty."

Shorty touched his nose. "Big nose. Smell lots."

H'aor moved to the front of the group and up to the top of a nearby rise. He stood there taking in the scents. "It is faint, but I think Shorty is right. It is a way ahead, but we need to be ready for trouble."

Kisa looked to Skreee. "Will you scout for us please Skreee? Do not take any chances, but please try to see what trouble lies ahead?"

Skreee did a cartwheel again in the air. "Yes, Pretty One. Skreee is a good scout." The excited sprite shot off ahead.

Shorty pulled his shield into place on his left arm and drew his old blade into his right hand. He followed Skreee at a more careful pace, moving from one cluster of trees to the next. Shorty paused frequently to sniff and peer ahead. The rest of the group stayed together about a hundred yards behind the ogre.

Their cautious pace continued for nearly an hour as Kisa scanned the canopy more and more nervously. Finally, a small shape darted from the trees to land on her shoulder. Thorn hissed for Shorty to stop and the group gathered together once more.

"What did you find?" demanded H'aor.

Skreee looked at him then slumped more heavily on Kisa's shoulder. "Tired. Flew far and fast. There is or was a human dwelling not far ahead. Small one. But it and something else were burned down. Not much is left. There is a dead man on the ground out in front."

Thorn studied the trees around them. "Any sign of who did it?"

Skreee shook his small head. "That is why I am so tired. I circled for quite a way. Whoever attacked it left before the buildings finished burning. There are tracks of a large force headed to the North. There are other tracks too, but I saw nothing."

H'aor looked unhappy. "We need to check it out. Please show us, Skreee."

The sprite pointed to a little to the left of the path they had been following.

Thorn held up a hand. "We do not serve your Elven Council. I am willing to get involved. But maybe you should clue everyone in before you get us caught up in something that is not our business."

H'aor started to object but then stopped. "If we had more information, I would not be running around out here trying to get myself killed. I don't have much to tell."

Kisa looked at him solemnly. "Then tell us what you do know."

H'aor shrugged. "Something is up far into the mountains. Maybe even on the far side near the lakes. The orc's have been coming down from the mountains in large numbers. We are not sure if they are invading or fleeing. But we suspect this is all being orchestrated."

Joachim shrugged. "Raiding parties have come before. Why is this one different?"

H'aor's tone grew more serious. "They are bringing their women and children. Raiding parties are always just males. Most of those are warriors. And there are more of them than normal. They also have a new leader."

Shorty interrupted. "Me say go looks."

Everyone nodded and H'aor turned in the direction indicated by the sprite. "Skreee, please show us the way."

————————————————

The group eased to the edge of a large area of cleared land. Furrows were clearly visible on much of the land, but whatever crop had grown here was now ash. The flames appeared to be recent. Tendrils of smoke and ash drifted in the steady breeze. Two small buildings were little more than burnt timbers. Even the heavy support beams of the buildings were reduced to ash. The only thing left was a wooden post fence around the remains of the two buildings.

Thorn whispered, "Fire is at least a day old to have burned the logs so fully. I think Skreee is right. Whoever did this is long gone."

H'aor did not look convinced. "This is a home for more than one. If they did not get them all, they may be watching the place for survivors."

Thorns studied him. "Lot of trouble to kill a couple more people."

H'aor met the dwarf's gaze. "The bard said something about captives and slaves."

Thorn nodded. "Then we best stay alert."

H'aor led them out of the woods and headed to the fence surrounding the burned-out husks. The smell of the smoke was strong, but there was another fouler smell in the air. As they got closer to the gate the sound of flies and other insects could be heard over the breeze.

A shape could be seen lying near the remains of a gate in the fence. On the ground near the body was a woodsman's axe. One that probably felled the trees used to build this homestead.

Shorty reached out and rolled the body over on its back. Two crossbow bolts stuck out of the body. One in the leg and another from the man's neck.

Kisa waved away the flies and studied the man. He appeared to be about sixty years of age. His face was weathered and he had a full beard of long grey hair. His hands were heavily callused. He had the arms and shoulders of a man used to hard work.

Thorn looked down at him. "He was ready to fight."

Joachim looked troubled. "They cut him down with crossbows. He was murdered just like the bard."

Thorn nodded thoughtfully. "He did not have to be out here in the open. What was he so willing to die to protect?"

H'aor moved towards the burned buildings. "Farmhouse and barn are my guess. We should make a quick search for more bodies."

Shorty moved forward to check out the small building to the right. Kisa and H'aor circled the main building.

Thorn sighed and picked up the dead man's axe. He began to chop at the sod inside the gate. The axe head sank deep into the grassy soil and Thorn began to cut a rectangle slightly larger than the body of the old man. He muttered as he worked. "Terrible way to treat a fine blade, but I did not think I would need a shovel or a pick to go adventuring. Besides, I really hate digging."

Joachim smiled as the dwarf continued to fuss while he worked. Joachim began to wander the yard and study how the farm was laid out.

Thorn began to roll up the sod he had cut and placed it to the side. Shorty came back and began to help Thorn dig. "Pig an birds dead. Only head left. Meat gone. Horsy gone. Bery sad. Me hungry."

Thorn laughed softly. "Dwarves are not fans of horses. But eating one is not my idea of a meal."

Kisa and H'aor return as Shorty took his shield and began to scoop dirt from the hole. He began to sing a silly nursery rhyme as he dug. Everyone was smiling as they watched when a voice interrupted them. As one, they all spun to face the voice.

Three orcs stood just outside the fence. The one closest to the fence was large and carried a longsword and shield. He smiled at them. "We figured there was more of you around here somewhere. Now where is the woman and her whelps?" Shorty stood ankle deep in the hole he had dug. He growled at the orcs and reached for his sword.

The orc shook a finger at Shorty. "That would be a bad idea, ogre." He pointed behind the group. Coming around the side of the burned-out farmhouse were two more orcs. One held a loaded crossbow pointed at the companions. The orc across the fence laughed. "So many easy targets. Who is he going to shoot ogre? The elf? The boy? Or maybe the woman with the bug on her shoulder?"

Shorty's hand dropped back to his side. He gave Kisa a worried look.

The two orcs moved closer but stopped about fifteen feet back. Their leader moved to stand in the ruined gate.

Thorn lowered the head of the woodsman's axe to the ground and muttered. "Forgot to post a guard. Getting stupid I am."

The orc laughed. "All dwarves are stupid. Comes from breaking rocks with your heads. Now tell me where the family that lived here is hiding."

H'aor slowly raised his hands. "We just got here. Smelled the smoke and came to see if someone needed help. We know nothing. Just thought we would bury the old man."

The orc laughed. "Well, if you like digging so much, I think we have just the work for you. Our Chief is looking for people to dig for him. And I bet an ogre and a dwarf can do a lot of it before they starve to death."

The other orcs began to laugh as well. Their leader turned to appraise Kisa. "But our Chief does have a thing for human women. I bet he will give me a bonus for you. Then again, you might be worth keeping for our own use."

Kisa's face grew red with anger. She pulled the mace from her belt and stepped forward. "You would not survive trying."

The orc leaned his sword and shield against the fence. Joachim whispered, "Careful, Kisa. This is not a game."

The orc motioned her forward. "Human women are weak. Come, show me what you can do against one unarmed orc. I smell your fear."

Kisa brushed the sprite from her shoulder and moved forward. She stepped before the orc and raised her mace. But the orc was unarmed and Kisa hesitated. Without warning, the orc's hand flashed forward and struck Kisa across the face. She went to her knees before the orc.

Shorty began to growl and stepped from the grave. The orc raised his hand and pointed back at the crossbow. "I can have her killed at any time, ogre. Calm yourself."

The next growl came from the ground before the orc leader. Kisa brought her mace up with both hands. She drove it upwards between the orc's legs. As it hit, the orcs hands dropped down to cover its injury. It staggered and dropped to its knees facing Kisa.

The other orcs stared at their leader in surprise. H'aor spun and barked one word in the language of the Arcane. Two magic missiles slammed into the orc carrying the crossbow followed an instant later by Joachim's knife. Thorn spun to face the remaining orc behind them.

Shorty's swords seemed to leap into his hands as he crashed through the fence. Before the wood of the fence had hit the ground, Shorty buried his Papa's sword in the gut of the orc on the right. The orc to his left died a heartbeat later when his new sword cut deep into its neck.

Thorn raised the woodsman's axe over his head and brought it down hard burying it in the forehead of the second orc that had come up behind them. He watched the orc fall to the ground with the axe haft pointed towards the sky. "That is the way to treat a good blade. Old man might have done it himself if you cowards had not shot him down." Thorn spit on the orc before turning back to watch Kisa.

Kisa stared into the eyes of the orc before her. "I choose. No one chooses for me." She raised the mace again, but could not bring herself to kill the unarmed orc.

The leader whispered to her through his pain. "Weaklings."

Kisa bit her lip in frustration, but before she could do anything the orcs body leaped into the air. Shorty held the orc before him in the air with only his left hand. Both of his swords were still in the bodies of the orcs behind him. Shorty gave the orc a tremendous shake. "No hits Lady. Bad orc. No hurts me friends." Shorty drew back his right fist and drove it into the orc's face. There was the sound of something breaking inside the orc. Shorty dropped the body to the ground and bent to help Kisa up.

As she rose to her feet, Kisa stared down at the orc. The bone over its left eye was shattered. She guessed that fragments of the bone had been driven into its brain. Kisa heard Skreee's voice from behind her. "Do not make my ogre mad." Kisa just closed her eyes. She suddenly felt cold, but she was very glad that Shorty was on her side of this battle. She knew that she had much to learn still.

The bodies of the orcs were stripped and drug off into the woods. Joachim was placed on watch while Shorty finished digging the hole and then helped Thorn move the old man's body into it. Kisa said a prayer to Akka over the body and then the dirt and sod were replaced over it.

Before he walked from the grave, Thorn knelt and drove the axe haft into the soil near where the old man's head rested. The bloody blade stood like a flag over the grave. "Let this speak to your bravery old man. Let orc blood on your axe mark your resting place."

H'aor stared at the dwarf as he rose from the crave. "That sounds kind of personal."

Thorn looked at H'aor. "I do not like orcs much. Especially these days. Do we move on?"

Shorty interrupted. "No go. Finds kids. Makes safe."

H'aor smiled at Shorty and then replied. "I was going to suggest that, but I would not want to make Skreee's ogre mad."

Chapter 12
Burden of Honor

The companions spread out looking for signs of the woman and children the orcs had wanted.

Joachim wandered around the charred remains the farmhouse and stared at what had been the backyard. He had a puzzled look on his face. "I feel like I am missing something back here. Something does not make sense."

Shorty and Kisa followed him around the ashes of the home. Shorty began poking around but Kisa came to stand beside Joachim. "Relax, Joachim. The best way to remember is to think about other things. It will come to you."

Joachim nodded and then asked softly. "You okay, Kisa?"

Kisa's hand went up to the bruise on her cheek. "This is going to hurt for a bit, but yes. I think I am okay now."

Joachim grinned at her. "That was a sweet uppercut with the mace. I think you made your point."

Kisa smiled shyly. "Maybe. I guess Shorty is not the only one with anger issues. I could not kill him. He was helpless."

Joachim looked away. "Killing isn't easy. It changes you. And not in a good way. I am glad you could not do it."

Kisa turned to watch Shorty's search. "But I just made it someone else's burden to bear."

Joachim followed her gaze. "I do not think Shorty views it as a burden. There is a gentle side to him, but not for people who hurt others."

Joachim watched the ogre searching the ground in the back yard of the ruined farmhouse. "You know, I am not afraid of him anymore. He only gets scary when someone tries to hurt one of us. Maybe he is my ogre now too."

Kisa smiled and leaned over to give Joachim a quick hug before turning back to Shorty. "Can you smell anything?"

Shorty shook his head. He picked up a handful of dirt and studied it before dropping it. "All ken smells bees smoke."

Thorn and H'aor returned from the remains of the barn. "Nothing over there. Where is Skreee?"

Kisa waved towards the woods. "He is searching back in there. Maybe they have a hideout or a hole in the ground where they are hiding."

Shorty turned a pleading look on H'aor. "Needs ta find kid."

H'aor nodded. "We are trying, Shorty. We just need to figure out where they are hiding."

Kisa pointed to a small rocked off area to one side of what was the back door. This looks like an herb garden. Nothing survived the fire though. I am not sure why she did not grow on both sides of the door. There was plenty of room on the other side."

Joachim snapped his fingers suddenly. "Of course."

They all looked at him questioningly. Kisa stared at the small garden area. "The garden is what was bothering you?"

Joachim smiled with growing confidence. "No, it's the place she did not grow anything. Something else is missing from that spot."

Thorn shook his head. "I am not following you, not that I know much about human homes."

Joachim tapped his chest. "Believe it or not, I have actually worked a time or two when I was hungry enough. Most farmers will feed you a meal if you work hard for a day. They might even let you sleep in the barn on a cold night if they do not have any young daughters."

Thorn snorted. "I am having a little trouble swallowing the work part, but what is your point?"

Joachim pointed to the woodsman's axe that stood over the old man's grave. "One of the chores I usually had to do was chop wood."

Thorn pointed to the wood pile out in the middle of the yard. "They got wood."

Joachim smirked at the dwarf. "Would you put the fuel for your fire way out there when winters are so cold? Would you make your wife go that far to get wood to cook your dinner?" Joachim pointed to the empty spot across from the herb garden. "Or would you stack it by the door so she could get it when she needed it? And there are no ashes there so it did not burn in the fire,"

Thorn and H'aor turned towards the pile of cut wood sitting across the yard from where the door would have been. H'aor chuckled. "I think he's on to something. No wood chips there so it is not where they split the logs. Why would you stack your wood way out there?"

Thorn began to walk forward. "Because there is something under the wood? The ground is too flat there. I should have seen it."

Thorn began to walk around the wood pile. He stopped on the far side and reached down to place a hand on the dirt. He stood back up and stomps his right foot once and then again.

Kisa asked, "What is it?"

Thorn turned and grinned at her. "My guess, root cellar back near the tree line where its cooler. Those logs are there to hide the entrance."

Shorty started to rush forward to help clear the logs. Kisa grabbed his arm. "No, my friend. You should wait here with me."

Short looked down at her in confusion. "Me bery strong. Ken mob log."

Kisa smiled up at him sadly. "I know, Shorty. But they are probably very afraid right now and you are… well…"

Shorty seemed to deflate. "Me bees scary. All tinks ogre eats peoples."

Kisa held on to his arm protectively. "I know better now. You taught me, my friend." Shorty nodded and stood watching.

H'aor motioned Joachim forward. "You are the least threatening looking person among us. See what you can do."

Joachim grimaced as he moved forward. "And the most expendable if it is trapped. Thanks a lot."

H'aor chuckled. "Who would trap a root cellar in the middle of the wilderness?"

Thorn began to toss the cut logs to the side. As the area was cleared, a trap door became visible. The door was propped open about an inch on one side.

Kisa let go of Shorty and moved closer to the open side of the door. She looked at Thorn and asked, "Air hole?"

Thorn shrugged and Kisa called out quietly. "If you are down there, we are not here to hurt you. Only to help." There is a small sound from below and Joachim leaned closer to the door. He gave a nod and Thorn flipped the trap door open. There was a sharp crack from below and Joachim dropped to the ground. A crossbow bolt flew out and disappeared into the foliage above his head. Joachim turned his headed and gave H'aor a dirty look.

Joachim raised his head to peek inside, but he pulled back quickly and coughed as the strong odor of unwashed bodies and human waste rose from within.

Kisa walked over to stand beside the young thief. She looked down to see a woman in her mid-twenties clutching a small girl of about six. In front of them was a small boy of about eight holding a crossbow in his hands.

Shorty could no restrain himself and came forward to look down into the hole. He bent over and said, "Hullo." The woman screamed in terror and Shorty fell backwards with hurt expression on his face.

Kisa motioned Shorty back. She looked at the rest. "They are frightened. We need to give them some space."

H'aor and Thorn nodded and headed back to the gate. Shorty followed slowly with his head hanging low.

Kisa squatted down and showed her empty hands to the woman. "It is alright. I serve Akka, the Earth Mother. I just want to help."

Fear was obvious on the woman's face, but she stepped forward between her children and the opening. She stared at Kisa but finally managed to ask, "What was that thing? Surely it was not an orc."

Kisa sighed. "It is kind of complicated. He is a friend. I assure you; he only wants to protect the children. The orcs are not very fond of him."

The young boy started to move around the woman towards the opening. She grabbed the boy's shoulder and pulled him back. The boy shook her off and began to slowly span the crossbow.

Joachim pushed Kisa a little to the side and sat on the edge of the trap door. He lowered his feet into the opening and let them dangle there. He eyed the boy and winked. "Nice shot there. Any closer and I would be looking for a guide to the afterlife. Do me a favor and try not to kill me yet. I got big plans. Who taught you to shoot like that?"

The boy grinned proudly for a moment and then his smile faded. He looked at his mother nervously. "My grandpa taught me but he stayed outside to fight the orcs. Did you see him or Pa?"

Joachim's banter seemed to ease the tension and the boy rambled on. "What was that big thing? It did not look like no orc. Does it work for you?"

Joachim chuckled at the boy's questions. "He tells us he is half ogre and half human. He protects us all. I got him to do it for free cause I am smart. He is very safe, just be nice to him."

Kisa gave Joachim a light slap on the back of the head. Joachim grinned at the boy showing no repentance. The boy whispered to Joachim. "Ma does that to me sometimes too."

Kisa just shook her head and looked to the woman. "Please excuse my friend here. He sometimes thinks the world revolves around him."

The woman smiled tentatively. "Most boys do. Young ones and old ones too."

Kisa laughed. "My name is Kisa. My friends and I have been dealing with orc problems for several days now. They keep turning up everywhere we go. I assume that your family had a problem with the orcs too?"

The boy nodded and started to answer, but the woman placed her hand gently on the back of his head. "Hush, Will. Let me talk now." She looked up and focused on Kisa. "Yes, there were orcs. A lot of them. My father spotted them in the woods north of here. He had us hide down here with the harvest. He and my William stayed up there to defend our home."

The woman's eyes drop and she whispers fearfully, "Are they…. Are they safe?"

Kisa stared down at her Holy Symbol as she answered. "I am sorry. The old man… er… your father is dead. We buried him near the gate. There was no sign of anyone else. But the fire took everything. He may have been inside."

The woman began to cry silently. "Then they have my William. Death would have been better."

Joachim looked down curiously. "Have him?"

The woman nodded. "Our last neighbor left about a month back. Rumors about the orcs have been circulating since spring. The word is that they have been taking slaves since they arrived. No one knows why though."

The boy turned to face her. "Ma, can we get out of here? I am tired of being in the cellar and it smells bad now."

The little girl piped in. "And I need to look for Sussi. Papa would not let me bring her down here. I want my Sussi back."

The woman hugged the little girl. "If anything survived Moira, I am sure that cat did." Then she looked up at Kisa and Joachim. "Please, could you mind moving back? Forgive me but strangers make me nervous right now."

Kisa nodded. "Of course." She and Joachim stepped back near the remains of the cabin.

Kisa watched as the woman climbed out and moved protectively before the entrance to the root cellar. Her eyes filled with tears again as she stared at the remains of her home. The young boy, Will, came up next holding the empty crossbow defensively like a club. Kisa could see a small quiver at the back of his belt. Lastly, the young girl crawled out and ran immediately back into the edge of the woods calling softly. "Sussi. Sussi. Where are you?"

Her mother said sternly, "No further, girl. I will not lose you now over some fool cat."

Without moving, Kisa pointed to herself and then to Joachim. "As I said, I am Kisa. I am a Priestess of Akka. If any of you are hurt. I will happily heal you. And my friend here is Joachim. He is an …. Um… adventurer. May I ask your name?"

The woman studies them carefully. "I am Dorna. And them others?" She points towards the three near the fence.

Kisa gestures back. "The dwarf is Thorn. He is from Deephole. They are a goodly people. The elf is H'aor. He was sent this way by the Elven Council to see what needs to be done. The last, well, his name is Shorty and he saved my life from orcs at an inn a few days from here."

Will laughed. "Shorty? He is bigger than our horse." He looked with sorrow at the other burned-out building. "Guess we do not have a horse no more."

Dorna waved a finger at him. "Hush, boy." She looked back at Kisa. "Strange group to be traveling together. Why are you all heading this way?"

Joachim started to answer but Kisa places a hand on his arm. "Let me, you are less of a problem when you cannot exaggerate." Joachim blushed and Kisa continued. "We were all getting out of the rain at a place called the Leaky Bucket. Orcs there killed someone, an old bard that was singing there. They hurt some other folks too. We sort of interfered and now we are on the run."

Dorna nodded. "I know Leaky. And that bard has been all around this region asking questions and stirring up trouble." She looked at the group by the gate again. "So, you stuck your noses in and now the orcs want you too. If you are trying to get away from the orcs, why are you heading closer to their main camp?"

Kisa sucked in a breath. "We did not know their camp was this way. I could not save the Bard. But he asked us to do something before he died. He wanted us to deliver something to his daughter. He indicated we could find her at the lake a day or so north west of here."

Dorna nodded again. "She will be there. She is not hard to find. But know this, the orcs are not more than a day north of her. They have a big camp from what I have heard."

Kisa bowed her head. Thank you for the warning."

Joachim raised a hand. "Excuse me, ma'am. But, is there any food down there? We have had nothing but a couple fish and some fruit and nuts for the last day."

Dorna pointed to the cellar. "Only crop we harvested so far is the potatoes. There is also a little cheese left down there. The rest was still in the fields. I suspect it is gone now too. Show him what to take, Will."

Joachim followed Will and began to talk about the crossbow as they climbed down inside.

A faint buzzing noise came from the trees behind the cellar and Dorna turned to face the approaching sound. Moira pointed at a small shape darting through the trees. "What a funny bird, Mama."

Dorna shook her head. "That is no bird child."

The shape approached rapidly and a small voice yelled out. "No, not a bird. It is I, Skreee. Mighty Warrior and defender of Pretty One!"

Skreee flew around Kisa twice before landing on her shoulder. "No humans in the woods. Where did you find these?"

Dorna began to laugh. Tears rolled from the corners of her eyes. "Oh, Priestess. Did no one ever teach you not to mess with the little folk? They are worse than the sniffles. At least you can get rid of the sniffles. You might be stuck with that one forever."

Skreee looked indignant and Kisa began to giggle. Moira joined in. Joachim and Will just looked puzzled as the climbed out of the cellar. Joachim had a bag of potatoes in his arms and Will had half a wheel of cheese.

Thorn sat leaning against the fence chewing on a raw potato. Kisa and H'aor rested on the grass nearby. He raised the potato to his mouth. "Never much cared for them raw, but beats going hungry or attracting orcs with a new fire." Thorn took a large bite and began to chew.

The three watched the activities on the side yard in silence. Joachim and Will practiced attacking a piece of firewood they had set up on an old stump. Will fired his crossbow, sinking the bolt into the log.

Joachim nodded appreciatively and then his hands flashed and a pair of small throwing knives sank into the log beside the bolt.

The two boys wandered over to the log and pulled their weapons from the wood. Joachim handed his knives to Will and appeared to be demonstrating how to throw them.

On the other side of the yard, Shorty sat on the ground about a dozen feet from Moira. They were bouncing a small ball back and forth between them. Shorty was grinning happily while the young girl at least seemed to be relaxing from her ordeal.

Dorna was kneeling in the grass a short distance away. She was packing up what few possessions were hidden in the cellar with them.

H'aor glanced over at Thorn as the dwarf popped the rest of the potato into his mouth. "You know we cannot protect them if we run into any more orcs. We could get them killed."

Thorn shrugged. "Where is it safe around here? Might be they could make it to Leeky's place. We killed a bunch of the orcs back that way."

H'aor shook his head. "No good answer. There might be more on our trail."

Kisa grinned and looks at them both. "And which of you two is going to tell them that they should not bring the children along?" Kisa raised a finger to point at Shorty and Joachim. "Either of you brave enough?" Kisa jumped as a large gray and black tom cat landed between Shorty and Moira. The cat pounced on the ball with a mock growl.

Thorn began to chuckle and soon it grew into a hearty belly laugh.

H'aor frowned. "What do you find so amusing?"

Thorn looked at them both. "Well, here we are, a Priestess of Akka, a dwarf of Deephole, and the representative of the Elven Council. We sit here debating right and wrong choices. In the end, we take lessons in honor from a thief and an ogre."

Kisa laughed and H'aor groaned, but a small grin was on his lips. "Then I guess we need to put this lesson into practice." He got up and headed over to help Dorna get her things ready.

Shorty bounced the ball carefully to the little girl. He smiled again hoping she would smile back.

The girl caught the ball and bounced it back. She looked at Shorty with anger in her eyes. "I hate orcs."

Shorty watched as the ball dropped into his large hand. He held it for a moment. Then he rolled it back to her. "No hates. Bad."

The ball rolled between her knees and stopped. She glared down at it. "Why? They took Papa and Grampa. They burned our house. They are evil."

Shorty looked sad but stared her in the eyes. "Hate make youse like dem. Makes youse no bery nice." He pointed to her mother and brother. "How lubs dem ifn hate so muches."

Moira sat for a moment and then picked up the ball. "What do I do then?" She rolled the ball back to Shorty. It was still between them when a large gray and black cat, near two feet in height, leapt from the bushes to land on the ball.

The girl sucked in her breath and squealed, "Sussi!"

Shorty stretched out a hand slowly and wiggled his index finger in front of the cat. It reached out a paw and batted the finger away. Shorty whispered softly, "Hullo, night warrior." The cat turned from him and wandered over to rub up against the girl.

Shorty looked up at the young girl as she clutched the cat to her. "Lub bestus. Fix ifn ken. Ifn no ken fix, let go it."

The girl looked at him with sad eyes but the beginnings of a true smile on her face. "How do I know which ones I can fix?"

Shorty shrugged. "Bees mo smarts den Shorty."

Moira wiped a tear from her eye and began to pet the cat. It sat near her purring happily. Moira whispered, "What if it needs fixing and I am too small?"

Shorty stared deep into her eyes. "Asks fer help."

The young girl returned his stare and asked, "Will you help me find Papa?"

Shorty sighed and nodded. "Try bery hard."

Moira nodded again, then she picked up the cat and ran towards her mother. "Mama! Mama! Sussi is back!"

Chapter 13
Shared Destinations

The morning dawned cool and overcast. The clouds were white with streaks of grey running through them. There was a steady wind from the north. Shorty stood tall sniffing at the fresh breeze.

Joachim faced into the wind and asked, "Danger?"

Shorty shook his head. "No, Jus smell muches good. No smoke in nose."

Dorna gathered her children close and asked, "Still going on your fool's quest to the mountain lake?"

H'aor nodded. "I need more information and the Bard's daughter is the best source I know of right now. Besides, we promised to take something to her."

Dorna sighed. "We will not make it back to Leeky's place on our own. I have nothing left to start over with here. I had hoped you would change your minds. I do not want to get closer to the orcs." She stared down at the small potato sack that held all of their remaining possessions. "Maybe we can find someplace to stay in the old village near the lake. It was abandoned a long time ago. One way or another, we need someplace that will keep us warm through the coming winter."

She shuffled her feat nervously and was about to speak when Shorty picked up her small bag. "Youse comes wid us."

Dorna scowled at Shorty. "Do I really have a choice?"

Shorty looked confused by her response, but Moira and Will grinned happily. Their mother still looked uncertain. She glanced at Kisa. "Priestess?"

Kisa winked at Thorn. "We cannot guarantee your safety, but we will do all that is in our power to get you to the lake. I think you are better off with us than alone. Besides, I think a couple of us would protest any other decision."

Dorna relaxed. "I guess that will have to do. I think there is a better way to get there though. There is a trail due west of here that heads up into the mountains. Once in the canyon beyond the first pass, you can head north to another pass. The second one leads into the valley you seek. It might be safer than heading through the foothills. If we are lucky, maybe we can avoid the orcs that way."

Thorn grunted. "If not, then I would rather fight in the mountains than out here in the open. Solid rock at my back would be a comfort."

Joachim looked over at Will. "Since it looks like we will travel together, see if you can use that bow to get us something to eat. Potatoes are gonna get old, cooked or raw."

Will nodded. "But no swans. The Lady at the lake will not be happy if we hurt one."

Joachim pointed to Shorty and whispered back. "No squirrels either. My big friend thinks they are his best friends. Kind of strange." Will and Moira giggled at his accusing tone.

H'aor raised an eyebrow as he looked at Will. "Why? Swan does not taste as good as duck, but it is not bad especially when you are hungry."

Will's face went very hard. "Grampa's rule. Never hurt a swan."

H'aor raised his hands in surrender. "Okay then. Grandpa's rule it is then."

They traveled through the morning, finding the trail with Will's help. The trail ran through veins of old rock. They passed numerous large boulders and at other times the trail seemed to move through the remains of old cliffs. Thorn stopped from time-to-time to study the rock. In places, the trail seemed to have been carved through the mountain itself. There were no signs of tools that Thorn could find. It was more like entire sections of the rock had simply been removed. The face of the rock walls glistened with water seeping down from above.

Thorn ran his hands over one of the smooth walls. "Almost looks like an old road had been cut through the mountains. But if so, it was so old that the rock has been worn smooth. It is like a clean cut on both sides."

Towards midday as they approached the first pass, Will held up a hand. He placed a finger to his lips and moved off to the left. He cautiously crawled onto a medium sized boulder jutting up from the ground. He leaned against it and peeked over the top.

On the far side of the rock was a pheasant wandering aimlessly around in the grass. It was upwind from Will and focused on something in the grass. Will placed his foot on a nob at the front of the stock of his crossbow and quietly pulled the string back until it locked. He set the safety and then loaded a bolt.

The group watched as the boy lay partially across the boulder and aimed at a point that seemed to be in the air above the bird. There was the sharp crack as the arms of the crossbow shot forward. The bolt leapt out as the pheasant took wing. The bolt and bird met about three feet above the ground and both tumbled to the grass.

Joachim whistled. "Nice shot. How did you know which way it would go?"

Will grinned back at him. "Practice. And hours spent searching for bolts that missed. Grandpa always made me find my misses."

Joachim wandered over and picked up the bird by the bolt. He carried it back to the trail walking beside Will. "Now what? Never eaten one with feathers on it before."

The others laughed but Dorna just sighed and pulled it from him. "Fool boy, you never had to hunt for your own food before, did you?"

Joachim shook his head. "Where I grew up, the only thing to hunt were the rats. You gotta be really hungry to eat them. Not as bad tasting as they look though."

Moira stuck out her tongue. "Ewww! Nobody eats rats. They are dirty."

Joachim's face went a little red and he just nodded silently. Then he turned away to help Thorn clear a small space near the boulder. Kisa and Moira gathered wood and Thorn started a small fire. Dorna looked around the group. "I am guessing none of you has a small pot? The feathers come out much easier if you dip the bird in boiling water."

Shorty came over and gently took the bird from her. He grabbed several feathers and ripped them out. He smiled down at Dorna. "Bery strong finners." Dorna watched carefully as he pulled feathers from the bird. Once Shorty had removed most of the feathers, Dorna took the bird and gutted it. While she was doing that, Moira and Will gathered some sticks to spit the bird upon. Kisa watched it all. "You all work well together."

Dorna smiled ruefully. "You have to out here in the wilderness. Our nearest neighbor was half days walk. You learn to depend on each other for everything."

Dorna slid a couple large rocks into the fire with Thorn's help. As Moira turned the bird on the spit, Dorna sliced potatoes in half and lay the cut edges down on the now hot rocks.

In half an hour the bird was done and everyone's stomachs were growling at the smell. The potatoes were sizzling. Kisa bowed her head and thanked Akka for their bounty and then it was time to eat. The bird and potatoes were quickly devoured. Even the large tomcat feasted on pieces of meat from the bones.

Thorn studied the pass ahead. The slope grew steeper near the top. The old trail was still visible, but it was obvious that portions had washed away over time. There was loose stone visible, but there were also bushes and plants growing from cracks in the rock that could be used as handholds.

Thorn seemed satisfied as he turned to face the group. "This one will not be too bad. But some of the rock is loose. I want to go up first. I would like to tie off Joachim's rope to make the climb easier."

Joachim pulled out the rope and tossed it to him. Thorn looked over to Shorty. "You come up next, my powerful friend. We can use those arms of yours to pull up people and packs if anyone has trouble."

Thorn began to climb. He swore softly as Skreee flew up past him grinning and taunting him. "So slow." the small sprite yelled as he turned several cartwheels in the air as he rose up and disappeared from sight.

Thorn continued at his own pace, touching the rock frequently and placing his feet with care. He eventually disappeared over the top. Moments later, the rope flew out over the trail and uncoiled as it fell along the slope. It reached about two thirds of the way to where everyone waited.

Shorty began to scramble up the slope next. In addition to his own pack, he had Kisa's pack and Dorna's small bag tied to his back. His large frame lumbered upward rapidly. His longer reach made the climb go faster, but his greater weight caused several rocks to tumble down the slope. Once Shorty reached the top, Thorn waved the group forward. H'aor and Joachim moved up to the rope and pulled it tight. They kept careful watch as the women and children slowly made their way up the slope.

Joachim motioned H'aor to go next. "I think I climb a little better than you do." Joachim watched as H'aor made his way up with easy grace. As he watched the elf move effortlessly up, he muttered. "Or maybe I do not." Joachim was about to begin his climb when rocks began to clatter down the slope. He looked up to see Shorty rushing back his way.

Joachim cocked his head to one side. "What are you up to?"

Shorty shook his head. "No up. Dis bees down." Joachim groaned.

Shorty pointed behind Joachim. "Fergetted."

Joachim turned to see the tomcat pacing back and forth staring up the slope unhappily. Shorty wiggled a finger in front of the cat and it came up and began to rub against his leg. Shorty scooped it up and stood to full height. He placed the cat over his head onto his backpack. The cat's claws came out and dug into the leather of the pack. It yowled its displeasure as Shorty scampered back up the slope with his passenger complaining bitterly.

Joachim could not repress a smile as he began his climb. He realized how many strange tales he could tell if he lived long enough to grow old.

Joachim reached the top not too far behind Shorty. Shorty knelt and the indignant cat leapt free and turned to hiss at him. Shorty grinned and the cat turned and headed after the young girl. Joachim paused to examine the view ahead.

The backside of the pass faced into a long, narrow valley. The valley ran roughly southeast to northwest. It appeared to be several miles long. There was a stream running down the center of the valley ending in a small pool at the base of the rise that he stood upon.

The valley was dotted with pine and few smaller maple trees. There appeared to be heavier vegetation at the far end of the valley but it was hard to see from this distance.

The slope down this side of the pass was not as steep and most of the group was already well on their way to the pool.

Shorty scurried after the cat while Joachim untied and coiled his rope. As Joachim walked slowly down to join his friends, he realized how nice it was to have real friends. People who would put themselves between him and danger were something he had never expected to find. There were shocked screams from below. Joachim's head snapped up to see that Shorty had jumped into the pool splashing everyone. Joachim smiled as Shorty began to splash the children. Their yells of delight were a welcome change from the fear of the last few days. He hurried to catch up.

The games did not last long as the water in the pool was very cold. Everyone refilled their water bags. They began the trek to the far end of the valley. Most of the afternoon was spent in quiet conversation as they hiked up the valley. They reached the far end with several hours of daylight left. Again, they faced a steep rise into the next pass. This pass was different though. There were brown vines, bushes and small stunted trees that choked off most of the path up unto the pass.

H'aor approached the growth carefully. He drew his slender sword and used it to push aside some of the leaves. He could see a mass of sharp thorns within the thicket. Despite the water in the area, the growth seemed dry and brittle. H'aor let the leaves fall back into place as he backed away.

He turned to face the group. "I do not know what that is. It does not seem to be native to this region. There are some rather nasty looking thorns inside. We will not be able to push our way through it."

Dorna looked up into the pass. "I have never seen anything like that and we have lived here for a while. William came this way from time to time. He never mentioned anything like them."

Thorn slipped off his pack and set it on the ground. He moved up and carefully reached into the thicket to break off a piece. He stared at the sharp, black thorns along the branch. "I recognize it. Damn nuisance plant. It is called buckthorn. We see it from time to time near Deephole. Hard to root it all out once it gets a foothold. It has a nasty bite. Very painful."

Joachim smirked. "Like some dwarves I know. But where did it come from?"

Thorn grinned then looked up the slope. "Birds eat the berries and spread the seeds in their droppings. Like I said, nasty stuff. I do not think we want to tackle this in the dark."

Joachim gave Will a nudge. "We should go get some firewood before they find other work for us." The sharp two headed back into the valley to search for wood.

The group began making camp. Shorty wander off with his snares in hand. He was not gone for long when he returned with a plump rabbit dangling from his leather strips. "Many big bunny. None hunt dem muches."

Dorna took the rabbit and began to prepare a meal. Joachim watched for a moment and then pulled out a knife and began cutting the potatoes for her. "Thank you, Lady, for cooking. I have never eaten so well before." A chorus of thank-yous drifted in from others.

After the meal was done, Dorna sat and began to sing softly to the children as the shadows from the peaks began to darken the campsite. Her words were soft and soothing.

'Long, long ago in times of ol'
lived a rich and wicked old troll
His home lay along the edge of the bay
He grew more evil each passing day.
Across the bay lived a decent old man,
who worked hard to farm the land.
His pride was not in the tilling he had done,
But in the raising of three strong sons.
The old farmer warned of trouble some day
If the wicked troll was allowed to prey
The oldest boys thought his words were folly
But not the youngest boy named Ollie.

Kisa recognized the ancient hero tale. Dorna had a beautiful voice that carried the tune well. Even Shorty seemed entranced by the tale. Suddenly, the melody was interrupted as the cat began to hiss and yowl. It paced back and forth between the fire and the tangled growth. It faced the buckthorn making its displeasure known.

Moira cried, "Sussi," and began to move towards the cat, but her mother grabbed her arm and pulled he back behind the fire. The cat's yowls grew painfully loud and the fur along its nape stood straight up. Dorna clutched the children to her and began backing away. The cat turned and raced to Moira and it sprang into her arms.

Thorn and Shorty stood first, and Thorn raised his axe and shield. Shorty pulled his old sword from its sheath. Thorn looked over. "Why not the magic blade?"

Shorty glanced lovingly down at the blade. "Papa's sword. Keep me safe."

H'aor moved up beside them with his slender blade in hand. Kisa and Joachim stood a few feet behind them with weapons drawn as well. Dorna continued to back away with Moira in her arms. Will had twisted free to grab his crossbow which he quickly loaded.

The sound of breaking branches drifted from the thicket. Multiple bodies could be heard forcing their way through the growth. The rustle of the branches was clear now that the cat had ceased its battle cry. Joachim looked back at Thorn. "How is anything moving through that stuff?"

Before Thorn could answer, a white shape forced its way through the thorny growth. The shape was humanoid, but that was all Joachim could be sure of. There was no flesh left on the frame and he could not identify what race the skeleton had been when it lived.

The skeleton stood nearly six feet tall. It wore rusted chainmail and carried a broken sword in its right hand. The shattered blade seemed somehow more ominous for its broken edge. Hanging from various places on its body were pieces of buckthorn leaves. It finally turned its head to face the companions arrayed before it. There was a single strand of buckthorn protruding from its right eye socket. A thorn seemed to point backward into the socket. A dull red glow emanated from both of its eyes. It stepped forward and there was a clattering noise as it moved.

Chapter 14
Facing Death

The companions froze as several more pale forms began to push through the buckthorn. The crack of a crossbow broke their trance. The bolt struck the chest of the first skeleton and slipped between its ribs to rattle uselessly. A heartbeat later, a fist-sized rock struck the skeleton in the ribs as well. Several of the ribs shattered, but the skeleton did not seem to notice.

Shorty's voice sounded confused. "Bones bees dead. How mob?"

Kisa gasped in shock as the second and third skeletons broke free from the tangle of the buckthorn. The second skeleton was somewhat shorter. It wore rusted plate armor and held a large axe handle in its hands. The blade of the axe was missing. It also wore a helm that showed no signs of rust or decay. The third skeleton had no weapons or armor. Kisa realized it had been a woman once. She whispered to her friends, "Undead. But how? We are in the middle of nowhere."

Thorn's laugh was a little strained as he replied. "Too late to be whispering, they found us already. And that one in the plate armor used to be a dwarf." As he spoke, the three skeletons turned their stares towards him. All three had glowing red eyes.

The three figures began to move forward. More rustling could be heard coming from the tangle of buckthorn. The plants did not seem to be damaged by the undead forcing their way through.

Thorn moved forward towards the plate-mailed skeleton. Its movements were slow but powerful as it swung the axe haft at Thorn.

Thorn's shield came up and the haft rang off it. Thorn swung his own axe in a viscous cut that caught the skeleton in the knee. The lower leg came off and it crashed to the ground. It continued to crawl towards Thorn swing the haft at his legs.

Shorty also attacked. He used the longer reach of his great sword to strike at the skeleton with the broken sword. His swing caught the skeleton in the neck. Its head flew to the side, bouncing several times before coming to rest, still facing Shorty. The glow from its eyes stayed hauntingly bright. The body of the skeleton continued to press forward, swinging the broken blade. Shorty barely managed to get his shield up in time to block.

The final skeleton came after H'aor. H'aor's elven blade darted forward, sliding harmlessly between the skeleton's ribs. The skeleton forced itself further up the blade as it reached for the defenseless elf. H'aor tried to rip his sword free, but the blade was wedged in place. As H'aor struggled, the skeleton raked its talon-like fingers down his sword arm. Blood ran freely from several deep scratches as H'aor stumbled away. The skeleton was oblivious to the sword protruding from its chest.

Kisa stepped forward quickly and brought her mace down on the skeleton's shoulder. The entire shoulder and half the chest came apart at the blow. Despite the damage, the skeleton turned on Kisa. Its movements were clumsy as its head now hung sideway from its right shoulder.

Kisa struck again and the skeleton collapsed into a pile of loose bones. "Blades and weapons with an edge are not effective against them. Blunt weapons will shatter them. If you can hold them, Akka may be able to aid us. I am not powerful enough to destroy them but I might be able to turn them away."

Thorn scowled and brought his axe down hard removing one of the arms of the skeleton. "Bah. Stupid dead thing. What can you do with no arms or legs?"

Shorty swung again at the headless skeleton and caught it in the chest. His blow knocked the body backwards and crushed the left side of its chest. The arm on that side hung useless, but the broken blade struck against Shorty's shield. Shorty muttered, "Uh oh" and he began to back up as four more skeletons emerged from the tangle. Two of these were much larger than the first three.

Kisa stepped forward behind Shorty and raised her Holy Symbol so that it hung above her head. "Akka, Earth Mother, protect your faithful from this evil!" As she called upon her Goddess, the Holy Symbol took on a golden glow. The glow intensified and spread out forming a globe around the entire group including Dorna and the children.

As the golden light touched the skeletons, most of them began to back away. The headless body facing shorty stumbled back into the thicket and retreated inside. Three of the new skeletons also backed into the tangle. The final skeleton, one of the larger ones, struggled forward.

Thorn drove his axe once more into the skeleton removing its last arm. He backed away and dropped the axe. He reached to the back of his belt and pulled out a hammer. Shorty started to move forward to block the larger skeleton, but Thorn called for him to wait. Thorn studied the undead and then threw his hammer. It slammed into the skull and crushed it. The skeleton's body rotated towards the dwarf who smiled. As it took another step towards him, Thorn stepped in close and slammed his shield into its right hip. There was a clatter of bone and the skeleton collapsed.

H'aor grabbed his sword from the pile of bones on the ground. "How long can you hold them, Kisa?"

Kisa looked worried. "Not long. There is something more powerful coming."

Thorn stared into the tangle before him. "There are more. But they have flesh."

As he spoke, two more forms struggled to pull themselves from the buckthorn. These did have flesh that the thorns of the tangle had been ripping and tearing. The flesh seemed to be knitting itself closed again as they watched.

The was a cry of a frightened little girl behind them. Kisa held her Holy Symbol high, but the new threat did not seem to notice. "Zombies. I cannot stop them. Shorty. The fire. They will burn."

Shorty stabbed his sword into the ground and darted back to the fire. He grabbed the unburnt end of one of the logs and moved forward. He began to wave the burning brand at the zombies. They backed towards the tangle. Joachim grabbed another brand and began to force the second zombie back as well.

When the undead were fully within the thicket, Shorty threw the burning log at them and rushed back to the fire. He grabbed another log and spun back to see the dry tangle had caught fire where the flaming log had fallen to the ground.

The fire spread rapidly through the buckthorn. It began to spread up the tangle towards the pass. The forms of the undead could be seen moving within the flames. The zombies burned like torches within the tangle spreading the flames further. The skeletal forms blacken and fall apart.

Within moments, the flames traveled all the way up to the top of the pass. Clouds of foul-smelling smoke rose above the mountain. None of the figures cried out or tried to flee the flames. As the last figure collapsed in the flames, the golden glow of Kisa's Holy Symbol faded away.

The flames continued well into the night. No one slept that night, not even the children. Shorty took most of the bones and equipment from the skeletons they had fought and threw them into the flames. Shorty kicked the skull which still stared at them into the fire as well. Thorn stopped Shorty from throwing the helm from the undead dwarf into the fire. Thorn sat it on the ground and studied it.

Kisa cleaned and healed the bloody scratches on H'aor's arm. The flames burned hot that night, but they did not chase away the cold they all felt at their brush with death.

Morning dawned and found them all tired and hungry. The trail up to the pass was filled with ash. A haze of smoke and ash still filled the air. H'aor and Thorn studied the way forward. Thorn moved upwards on the edge of the ash. "I suggest we do this quickly and stay to the edge. It does not look like anything survived the blaze."

H'aor nodded and turned to the group. "I know everyone is tired, but we can rest in the valley beyond."

Dorna stared down at her children. "I am not sure they can make it that far. They are exhausted."

Will glared at his mother. "I am not a baby, Ma. I can make it." He punctuated his complaint with a large yawn.

Little Moira just sat holding tight to her cat. She stared at the ash trail with fear. Shorty walked over and crouched before her. "Ifn no bees fraid up high. Me ken gives ride."

Moira let go of her cat. "You promise not to let me fall?" She pointed to the ash. "I do not want to touch it."

Shorty smiled. "Youse bees bery safe." The little girl nodded and Shorty lifted her to his left shoulder. She wrapped a tiny arm around his neck and squeezed tight. Then he scooped up the cat in his right hand and slowly rose to his feet. Moira's eyes darted around as she studied things from this new height. Shorty began a slow hike to the top of the rise. Thorn waited until Dorna made it to his side and walked up beside her. Will and Joachim followed next.

The last to climb up were Kisa and H'aor. H'aor was studying the helm that Thorn had saved from the skeleton. Kisa asked, "What are you going to do with that?"

H'aor hung it from his belt. "Thorn thinks it is magic. He asked me to examine it when I check out the other pieces we picked up."

Kisa frowned. "Be careful. It came from the undead."

H'aor smiled. "Always try to be careful."

Kisa glanced up the hill to see Thorn and Joachim standing about a dozen yards from the crest of the pass beside Dorna and her son. She and H'aor sped up to join them. The four seemed to be staring up at the top of the pass. Kisa shielded her eyes from the bright morning sun and looked up to see what everyone was staring at.

Shorty stood at the top of the pass framed by blue sky and a few wispy white clouds. One foot rested on a small rock. His right hand cradled the large tomcat as the other scratched its ear gently. The little girl with curly brown hair sat on his left shoulder still. She was chattering happily and pointing down into the valley before them. The ogre had a contented smile on his face.

Dorna whispered softly. "Somehow, I think things will be okay now. How can my daughter in an ogre's arms make me suddenly feel safe? Does he realize?"

Thorn laughed. "He does not have a clue. He just is. And if we are all lucky, that will be enough." Thorn took Dorna's arm and helped her climb the last few yards to the top. Moira turned on Shorty's shoulder to smile at her mother. "Mama, it is very pretty. Can we play in the lake?"

Dorna smiled back. "We will see when we get there, child. No promises."

The tired group crested the pass and stared down into a small valley of green and blue. Trees covered the slopes and the valley floor except for the center that was dominated by an almost rectangular lake. On the northern side there was a small river that flowed down into the lake. A larger pass could be seen on the eastern edge of the valley. On the north eastern corner of the lake, nestled in the angle between the river and the lake shore, was a small village.

Moira let out a peal of excitement and pointed to the left where two large white birds were drifting down towards the lake. "Swans!"

Thorn began to move down the gentle slope into the valley. "Birds have the right idea. We need to get to the bottom where we can rest for a while."

Shorty let the cat down to explore on its own. The little girl slid down into his arms. She yawned and he held her close as he followed the dwarf. The little girl was asleep in moments.

H'aor waived the rest ahead. "Refuge of a kind awaits us." They began a slow descent into the valley.

Part 3
Friends and Foes

"Bestus friend maybeso no bees peoples dat youse tinks."

Chapter 15
The Valley of the Swans

Thorn led his friends down into the valley. The slope down to
the valley floor was not steep. The path they followed once again
suggested to Thorn that this might have been a road in the distant past.
Thorn studied his surroundings as he walked, something about the
valley just did not feel right. It was like an itch that grew more intense
the closer he got to the valley floor. He even watched the trees and
undergrowth. The plants all seemed healthier and more vibrant the
closer they got to the valley floor.

There was a faint trumpeting sound somewhere above him. Thorn
paused and examined the mostly blue sky. He spotted two swans high
above and to the right of his group. Thorn could not tell if they were
the same two birds that they had seen at the top of the pass, but how
many swans could there be in this place?

Thorn moved on but he knew he was missing something important.
Something warning that he should have noticed. Thorn paused
again and turned to study his friends and the small family they were
protecting. They all seemed relaxed and had smiles on their faces.
They did not look like a group that had just fought for their lives
against a bunch of undead.

It was like they were all at peace right now. Thorn felt that same sense
of peace, but it was not coming from within him. The feeling emanated
from the valley and it grew stronger the further in they went. Magic.
The itch he felt was his subconscious trying to keep him alert. The
magic might want him to believe he was safe, but he did not trust it.
And he definitely did not like it.

Thorn signaled to H'aor and slowed until the elf had caught up with him. "Do you feel it, elf?"

H'aor nodded slowly. "The magic? Yes, I was wondering if it would affect you or not."

Thorn spat to the side. "I do not like magic being used on me, especially without my consent. This magic wants to convince me things are alright when I know they are not. Even Shorty is walking into the valley like a sheep to slaughter."

H'aor laughed softly. "I guess that is one way to interpret it. What you are feeling are very weak wards. This valley had powerful magic protecting it at one time. What you are feeling is a pale echo of what once was."

Thorn's scowl did not lessen. "What do you know about this place?"

H'aor looked around the valley. "My people have no legends or tales of anything this far south. But there have always been places of power in this land, some for good and some evil. I judge this place to be of the light. I suspect it is why the refugees are all drawn here."

Thorn grumbled. "I do not have to like it. I also do not care for the durn birds that seem to be watching us."

H'aor glanced up. "I had not noticed those. Are they the same swans?"

Thorn shrugged. "Not sure, but makes you wonder what the boy's grandpa knew."

H'aor nodded. "Do not shoot a swan or the lady will be angry. This could be an interesting meeting."

The two continued on in silence. By mid-morning they had reached the south eastern corner of the lake. The water was clear and clean. They paused briefly to drink and refresh themselves. The waters of the lake were surprisingly warm for a small mountain lake. When everyone had drank except little Moira who was still sleeping in Shorty's arms, the group continued along the eastern edge of the lake.

Thorn and H'aor took the lead again. Thorn stared out at the waters of the lake as they walked. There dozens of pairs of swans swam circling in the water. He also spotted many more nesting along the shore. He guessed that answered his question about just how many there could be. A damn lot of the fool birds. Thorn jutted his chin towards the water. "Too many big birds out there. Does not seem natural."

H'aor's eyes swept the lake. "I noticed. But I have seen more ducks in the lakes near my home."

Thorn looked troubled. "This late in the season? Snow cannot be far off here in the mountains. No more than a month before it gets cold here. If you look at the ones on the shoreline, they have nests. These birds do not appear to be heading south for the winter."

H'aor looked thoughtful. "I cannot explain it. Maybe the waters here stay warmer for some reason."

Thorn motioned towards the buildings that were clearly visibly across the waters of the lake. "Notice anything about them?"

H'aor stared across the corner of the lake as they walked. "The buildings seem to be in good condition. I can see a few people moving around. Something about them bother you?"

Thorn glared at the buildings for a moment and then shrugged. "The design is older than the buildings appear to be. Dorna said this place was abandoned a long time ago. I would expect them to be a lot more run down than they seem to be."

H'aor had no response as they continued to travel beside the lake. Just before noon, the lake shore turned sharply to the west. As they rounded the corner, the trees were mostly cleared away and the village was clearly visibly before them. They stopped to examine their destination.

The outskirts of the small village were mostly small buildings that appeared to be homes. The buildings became larger the further towards the center of town which was situated in the junction of the small river and the lake. The buildings appeared to be a mixture of stone and wood construction. None of it seemed to be in need of repairs. All of the buildings were painted a white that was reminiscent of the swans they had been watching most of the morning. The paint showed no signs of dirt or age. Smoke rose from the chimneys of a few of the buildings, but many appeared unoccupied.

They traveled down a central road of crushed stone. The road appeared to run straight towards the center of the village near the shore of the lake. Streets seemed to cross the main road every three to four buildings. There were few chimneys with smoke rising from them on the edge of the village. Thorn again took the lead and headed towards the lake. There were no people in sight but as they moved closer to the water, they could hear the sound of voices ahead.

They all watched the buildings closely as they followed the dwarf. Joachim pointed to one window where the cloth coverings were moving. "We are being watched. I feel like a target moving up the street this way."

Kisa smiled at him. "They are probably more afraid of us. A band of warriors entering their small village would be unnerving even if they were not worried about orcs."

The voices grew louder as the waters of the lake became visible through the buildings. The voices were growing louder. Thorn pulled his axe into his hands as the volume of the angry voices got closer. As they entered the last intersection before the lake shore the companions saw a group of five people standing before a small home on the street to their left.

A young woman, who looked to be no more than seventeen, stood facing an older man who was very agitated. His arms and hands were moving rapidly as he spoke. Several yards behind the man stood another man in the robes of a mage. Two other men stood more to the side as if observing the conflict.

Thorn turned the corner and began to approach. The older man who was doing most of the yelling had his back to them and did not notice his new audience. The young girl glanced their way but kept her attention on the man before her. The man in robes also noticed them and moved over next to the small building keeping everyone in front of him.

The older man raised an arm and pointed to the south. "You saw the glow last night above the southern pass. That was a large fire. If the orcs cut us off in that direction too, then we will be trapped in this valley. You need to let those of us with more experience help you with the important decisions."

The young woman met the man's gaze without backing down. "Councilor Typerys, I have kept this valley safe since the orcs came out of the mountains to the west. I have not allowed anyone within the valley to be harmed by them. I have a better understanding of the dangers than you do."

The older man slammed a fist into his open palm. "You are young. You do not have a clue about the real dangers. The activity at the southern pass is proof of that. You need lo let me help you run this village."

The girl shook her head. "You mean let you make all the decisions. I think not."

The man started to raise his voice again, but Thorn coughed loudly. The man spun to stare at the group that had appeared behind him. His anger seemed to fade quickly and a broad welcoming smile took its place.

Thorn raised an eyebrow as he studied the man before him. Thorn waved a hand towards the southern pass. "If it makes you feel any safer, the fire in the pass was not the orcs. We are sort of responsible. Had a bit of trouble with a patch of buckthorn among other things. The buckthorn tangle is gone, so your pass is open."

The man stepped forward. "I see. We thank you for your help then. I am Typerys. The people here asked me to speak for them."

Shorty stepped forward with his eyes on the young woman. The man looked up at him and smiled. "Greetings, warrior. I hope that you…"

Shorty brushed past the man without noticing him. The man crossed his arms and turned an angry gaze at Shorty's back. The young woman turned her gaze from Shorty to the man. "Perhaps we should save Council business for the meeting tonight. Allow me to great our new arrivals."

Typerys gave her a sour look, but he turned and walked away. The mage hurried after him. The remaining two men offered their welcome and walked away in quiet conversation.

Shorty smiled down at the young woman. "Hullo, Bird Lady."

The girl looked up at him in surprise. "How do you know about..."

Shorty studied her face. "Youse smells like dem big bird."

The young girl nodded and reached a hand out to touch Moira's head. She ran her fingers through the girl's hair. "Will you help me protect the people here like you protect this child?"

Shorty nodded. "Shorty ken dos dat."

She patted his arm. "Thank you, Shorty." Then she turned her gaze back to Thorn. "So, good dwarf. Welcome to you and your friends. I am Essabeth Sunderin. This is my valley and I offer what protection I can to all who seek refuge here. Would you be so kind as to mind introduce yourself and your companions?"

Thorn bowed his head. "Before I introduce my friends, I would first like to introduce the family that we rescued just south of here." Thorn turned and motioned Dorna forward. "This is Dorna. She and her husband and father ran a farm to the southeast. It was burnt to the ground by the orcs. Her father died in the attack and her husband is missing. Dorna and her son Will and daughter Moira need a place to stay."

The young woman stepped forward and hugged Dorna. "I am sorry for your loss. We have homes to spare here in the village. But everything else we must work together for."

Dorna looked relieved. "Thank you. I am not afraid of work. Neither are the children."

Will stepped up beside his mother with his crossbow in hand. "I can hunt, Lady. I am good with the crossbow. But no swans. Grandpa taught me that."

The young woman smiled at him. "Your Grandpa was a wise man." She raised her hand to her chest. "Call me Essabeth please, all of you. Or if you must be formal, most just call me Swanmay. And your help will be greatly appreciated, young Will." Essabeth pointed back behind the group. "Is the furred hunter part of your family as well?"

Dorna turned to see the large tomcat sitting in the road with a mouse under its paw. She sighed. "Pardon Essabeth. Sussi is Moira's. The cat does have its uses. Especially if you have a mouse problem."

Essabeth smiled. "There are not many, but we cannot afford to share our food with them. I think your Sussi will be a welcome addition."

Thorn stepped forward and bowed. "I am Thorn, late of Deephole. The rest of us recently met during a disagreement with the orcs. But I think I will leave that story to the elf."

H'aor waved Kisa forward next. "I am Kisa, Priestess of Akka. I travel with my friends and serve the will of the Earth Mother. If I can be of assistance, please let me know."

Essabeth stepped forward and hugged Kisa too. The sudden move was unexpected and Kisa felt confused as she awkwardly returned the hug. Essabeth backed away. "I am sorry. There have not been many women to join us here. The orcs take great pleasure in taking them captive. Other than the ranger and Old Mara, there is no one I can talk to. I hope we can be friends."

Kisa smiled at her. "It is alright. It just caught me off guard. Hugging was not a part of my childhood. I would like us to be friends. Is there a place where I can stay? I do not see a Temple here in town."

Essabeth pointed to a large building down the street that sat on the water's edge. "That is the Hall of Healing. It has rooms and a kitchen. Old Mara is the only cleric staying there right now. She is a Priestess of Ilmatar. She is powerful, but does not move around well due to her age. I am sure she would appreciate the company and your help in the Hall."

Kisa thanked her and stepped back. She turned and motion Joachim forward. But he did not seem to see her. His eyes were locked on the young woman before him.

He did not seem to notice the smiles and grins of his friends or the fact that his mouth was hanging open. Shorty whispered rather loudly. "Posed ta say hullo now. She no hurts youse." Thorn began to chuckle and Joachim's face went red.

He stepped forward and bowed to Essabeth. "I am… umm.. My name is Joachim. I am, well, an adventurer. I help as I can."

Essabeth smiled as she studied him. "It is nice to meet you, Joachim. I imagine the life of an adventurer is very interesting. You must tell me about your adventures one of these days." Essabeth started to turn towards H'aor, but then looked back and asked. Tehel mon oe Ural?"

Joachim shook his head. "I do not have a master." Then he stopped and stared at Essabeth in surprise. "I mean. Oh, never mind. Where did you learn to speak that language?"

Essabeth laughed. "Thieves' Cant? My father taught me. A good bard does not just sing. They must be able to fight and to spy or steal. A true Bard must have many skills if they are to serve both kings and paupers."

Joachim voice faltered. "You are the Bard's daughter?"

Essabeth's face lit up. "You know of my father?"

Joachim stammered and looked to H'aor and the Thorn for help.

H'aor stepped forward. "I am H'aor. There are things that I wish to discuss with you at another time. But I bring a final message from your father."

Essabeth's face lost all expression. "Final? Then he is dead?"

H'aor looked down at his feet. "I am sorry. He angered the orcs at an Inn several days from here. Their leader ordered his death. We tried to save him but the crossbow bolts they used were poisoned."

Essabeth's eyes grew hard. "Crossbows?"

Kisa replied. "They gave him no chance. It was little more than an execution."

Essabeth stared directly into the elf's eyes. "And the orcs that killed him?"

H'aor's face took on a satisfied expression. "Most of them died in the Inn. The two with the crossbows were definitely killed."

Essabeth nodded in satisfaction. "And their leader?"

H'aor gestured towards Shorty. "Our large friend snapped his neck."

Essabeth turned to Shorty. "My thanks again, Shorty."

Shorty shook his head. "Me posed protect Music Man. No dos bery good job."

Essabeth stood on tiptoes to lay a hand against Shorty's cheek. "He chose his own path, Shorty. All you could have done was avenge him." Then she turned back to H'aor. "You said there was a message."

H'aor slid his backpack off and set it at his feet. "He told me that I was to tell you that he found it. Despite all odds he said."

Essabeth's eyes seemed to burn with inner fire. "Did he send it with you?"

H'aor reached into his pack and brought out the bracer. The sunlight gleamed off its bright surface. Essabeth drew in a breath and reached out her hand. H'aor hesitated for a moment. "Lady. Essabeth. I must warn you. This is dangerous. It has powerful magic. We detected magic on the items we got from the orcs. But this, it outshone everything. You must be careful."

Essabeth closed her eyes for a moment and nodded. "I know, H'aor. I know what it is and what price it demands." She reached out and took the bracer and slid it inside the shirt she wore. "I owe you all an explanation. But it is a story for tomorrow. You must all be tired. There are two homes on the street where I live. My home is across from the Council Building. Perhaps Dorna and her children can take one of those houses and you gentlemen can take the other. That way Shorty can protect his young friend. We will meet in the morning and I will explain what I can of the situation here."

At their nods, Essabeth turned and led the way past the Hall of Healing to two small homes where she left them to rest.

Chapter 16
Rebirth

The next morning, the four men were awakened just after sunrise to a pounding on their door and the sound of two women talking just outside. Kisa's voice called out loudly, "Time to get a move on! We have some walking to do this morning. No more lying around in bed."

Shorty called back to her. "No fits in dis bed. Bees muches too small."

The two young women began to laugh. The men grabbed their gear as Joachim complained. "Does the walking ever end?"

Shorty was out the door first with a happy smile on his face. "Hullo, Kisa Lady an Bird Lady. Bery nice day fer walkin."

Thorn and H'aor came out moments later. Kisa nodded to them and yelled through the door, "Guess we know who is not interested in fresh bread and cheese for breakfast."

Joachim popped out moments later. "Fresh bread? This better not be a joke or I will…" His threat faded out as his eyes came to rest on Essabeth. "Oh, umm, good morning."

Essabeth smiled at him and then lifted a sack and began to pull out small loaves with cheese baked into the middle. She handed one to each of them except for Shorty who got two.

As they ate, Essabeth pointed down the street to the west. "The place I must go is on the western edge of the lake. It is not a long walk to where Father and I began the process of awakening this valley. I must return there to finish what we started. As we go, I can explain some of the history of this place."

They finished their meal and Essabeth led the way through the village. On the far side they came to the edge of the river they had seen from the southern pass. The meeting of the river and lake was broad and shallow. The river flowed gently into the lake as the water trickled around and over rocks of various sizes. Essabeth looked across to the far bank. "Sorry, it does not flow fast at this time of year but the river is still really cold." With that warning, she dashed across the river followed closely by Shorty who seemed to take great joy in splashing as he ran. The others followed in a more dignified manner.

On the far side, Essabeth moved onto the rocky shoreline of the lake as she headed west. The northwestern corner of the lake was clearly visible ahead of them. Essabeth paused and turned to face them. "There is much that I should explain before we get to the pool. It will be easier for me if you save your questions until I am done. Please, be patient."

At their nods, she turned and continued walking. Her voice gained strength and took on a practiced cadence as she began her tale.

> "This village is named Swanton. And yes, its name does relate to the swans that inhabit the valley. Swanton has existed for hundreds of years. Father believes it has been here much longer than that, but we can find no records to prove his theory. It may have been here for a thousand years or more. The buildings here have not aged in all that time. There was great magic in this valley. Some of you must have felt when you entered the valley.
>
> The wards here tend to repel evil and they bring peace to those who favor goodness and light. The wards were much stronger before the Swanmays disappeared. If I am successful today, they will be strong once again.
>
> This valley was the home of a race known as the Swanmays. The Swanmays were very close in form to humans and elves. They had a great affinity for nature and had abilities very similar to those of the druids and

rangers of our world. The two biggest differences were that the Swanmays were all female. They had the power to transform into swans such as you see in this valley.

As we understand the legends, they bore very few male children and those males did not have the power to transform. Swanmays tended to marry humans and elves that caught their fancy. They were drawn to those who shared their love of the wild. Legends indicate they also liked warriors of some renown. Rangers and elves were popular mates.

Tales of Swan Wives or Bird Maidens exist across our land. Father believes that the Swanmays spread from this valley to many places across the land where swans nested and thrived. Father is sure that they could communicate somehow with the great birds.

Father and I have never been able to determine what happened to their race, but it began to die out. When only a handful remained, they returned here and worked a great spell with the help of the Gods. They created an artifact that would allow their race to be reborn. The artifact was responsible for the preservation of this valley and the village itself. Father and I have spent most of the last two years searching for clues as to how to bring the Swanmays back. His efforts were interrupted by the arrival of the orcs. He suspected that some power wished to prevent the return of the Swanmays. Today, I hope to complete his quest and turn his dream into reality."

They were heading south along the edge of the lake as Essabeth finished talking. H'aor asked quietly, "I suspect the completion of his quest has a price, Essabeth. Is it one that you really want to pay?"

Essabeth shrugged. "It was a discussion that Father and I had many nights before we began the process. I think it is too late to choose another path."

Kisa placed a hand on Essabeth's shoulder and pulled her to a stop. "How can it be too late? You do not have to do this."

Essabeth turned to look at Kisa. Her right hand slid into her shirt and withdrew the bracer she had taken the day before. Her left hand went to the right sleeve of her shirt which hung down past her wrist. She quickly pushed it up to reveal a matching bracer on her forearm. "Because I chose to wear this over a year ago. Right before the orcs came. When I put this on, the wards you feel now came to life. It has already changed me. I am stuck between. I want... No, I need to be whole again. I believe that I can only go forward."

H'aor's breath hissed out in frustration. "I hope you do not regret this, Essabeth. We will stand with you when you do this. I only hope your sacrifice is not too great."

Essabeth stood silent for a moment before she asked. "Tell me, H'aor. Is the salvation of many not worth a sacrifice by one or even a few? Especially if the sacrifice is a willing one?"

H'aor went silent and Essabeth turned from him. She began to move forward. "The pool is just ahead on the far side of those trees." She gestured to a thick stand of white birch trees. The stand grew right up to the edge of the lake and was so thick that they could not see through the trees.

She led them into the warm waters of the lake to move around the trees. As they came around the trees, they paused in the water's edge to stare. The waters of the lake curled inland to form a pool. The pool was a perfect half circle of calm water. The bottom of the pool was covered in a pure white sand that extended into the lake to complete the circle. The sand came up onto the shore to form a second circle. The only disruption to the smooth stand was a series of circular pink stepping stones that lead from the farthest point from the lake to the center of the pool.

Essabeth pointed to a trail that led along the edge of the white birch trees. "Please stay off the sand. It does not like to be disturbed." Thorn raised an eyebrow at that, but they all followed Essabeth along the trail to where it ended in a grassy area just behind the first pink stone. "You must observe from here. Even Father was not allowed to come closer last time."

H'aor studied the scene before him. "What happened last time?"

Essabeth stared into the pool. "Nothing spectacular. I do not think they intended that anyone to put only one of the bracers on. There was the feeling that the valley stirred, but then it was like everything held its breath. I think it is still waiting for me to finish what I started. I do not expect this time to be as uneventful."

Kisa came forward and hugged Essabeth. "You will not be alone. We will wait for you."

Joachim stepped forward but could not meet Essabeth's eyes. "Try not to lose yourself. I, well, I want to see you again."

Some of the tension left Essabeth's face. "Thank you both for that."

Essabeth turned from them and began to unbutton her shirt. She took it off to reveal a plain linen shift of white. It had short sleeves that left the bracer on her right arm visible in the sunlight shinning from the east. She bent and removed her boots and socks and set them beside her shirt. Finally, she removed her pants and set them down as well. The white shift hung to her knees.

Essabeth walked across the pink stones to the water's edge. She paused there and held the second bracer above her head. The sound of trumpeting began to echo from around the lake. Several of the large white birds could be seen taking wing above the waters of the lake.

Essabeth lowered the bracer and stepped into the water on the next of the pink stones. The water came to her ankles. She again raised the bracer over her head. A warm breeze stirred the water of the pool. More swans began to take to the air. Their calls grew louder and carried a note of longing within them. Essabeth moved to the second submerged stone and lowered the bracer.

She stood for a moment on the second stone as if gathering her courage. Then she advanced to the third submerged stone. The water was now above her knees. Again, she raised the bracer to the heavens. Bubbles began to rise in the water around her. The surface of the pool appeared to be covered in a thin white foam. There were now dozens of swans in the air. The large birds seemed to be circling the pool as if waiting for something. Their cries became more urgent.

Essabeth stepped to the fourth submerged stone and lowered the bracer so that it was just above the water. The water was now at mid-thigh. The young woman turned back to face her friends. She smiled sadly and then closed her eyes. She took one final step backwards to the final stone. The foaming water rose above her waist. The birds went suddenly silent.

Essabeth raised the bracer arms above her head. Her right hand placed the bracer across her left wrist. She fumbled for a moment and then there was a snapping sound as the clasp closed on her arm. As she lifted both bracer clad arms towards the sky. Great geysers of water shot up across the pool. Within moments, Essabeth was hidden by the rising and falling water. Joachim began to move forward to rescue her, but Shorty's large hand locked onto his shoulder. "Must hab trust. Bery potent." Joachim tried to twist free, but the ogre's fingers held him firmly.

The breeze suddenly stopped and a loud trumpet call came from within the curtain of water. As its last notes died away, the wall of water fell and a large female swan rose from the pool on effortless beats of its wings. As it rose, there was a chorus of trumpeted cries as the birds above the pool welcomed the swan rising to meet them. The female quickly rose above the bevy of birds and began to circle the lake.

The companions watched at the birds flew south around the lake. When they came around and reached the Village, they turned north and left the valley. The sound of their cries faded across the mountains. A silence they had not heard since coming to the valley reigned. Shorty released Joachim and turned back to find a seat in the grass. He was joined by Kisa, Thorn, and H'aor. Joachim continued to pace back and forth across the grass. He watched the mountains to the north for the return of the birds.

H'aor looked over at Thorn. "Did you feel the wards when she transformed?"

Thorn head turned as he scanned the valley. "Yeah. Damn strong ones now."

The sun crawled slowly across the sky as midday came and went. Eventually even Joachim came and sat while the other talked quietly. Joachim rose in expectation each time a white shape drifted back towards the lake. He grumbled each time it was a pair of birds returning to their nests around the lake. Late in the afternoon, a single large form came across the eastern pass and circled over the village. Then it turned west and approached the pool. They all stood in anticipation.

The form resolved into a single large swan that drifted slowly down towards the pool. When it was a dozen yards over the pool, it drew in its wings and dove beneath the water. Kisa let out a cry of surprise. Before they could move, Essabeth rose to stand upon the last stone within the pool. She began to walk towards them.

She still wore the plain white shift, but the white seemed brighter and yet softer than before. The bracers gleamed upon her arms as the water dripped from them. She now wore a white shawl about her neck and shoulders. There was a fluttering motion at the edges of the shawl as if feathers were moving in the breeze.

Shorty smiled and whispered, "Bird Lady."

H'aor corrected him softly, "No. Swanmay."

Joachim glared at them both. "That is still Essabeth."

Essabeth walked slowly out of the water. There was a smile on her lips and joy seemed to radiate from her. Her eyes had changed from the deep blue they had been that morning to a pale hazel color. Those hazel eyes now shone with excitement.

Kisa pulled her new friend into a fierce hug as she left the sand. "Are you well?"

Essabeth returned her hug then pushed her back to stare into her eyes. "I flew. It was so incredible. The air is so alive. I am not sure that I can explain it. You need not worry. I am myself still and yet I am more." She looked into the worried eyes of her new friends. "It truly was a gift and not a curse. Can we rest for a bit? I am tired."

Essabeth moved to her clothing and put back on the pants and boots. She stared at the shirt and shook her head. She left it where it lay and sat down upon it. "I have more to tell now."

H'aor studied her for a moment. "Before you speak, I need to tell you some things. I was sent here, well, south at least, to meet with your father. I am here as an agent of the Elven Council. I am supposed to be learning about the orcs."

Essabeth smiled at him. "I suspected as much. Not many elves visit these lands. Father told me the Council had approached him. He used your business as a pretext while he searched for the second bracer. I wish I knew where and how he found it."

She fiddled for a moment with the shawl on her shoulders then continued. "The orcs came east across the mountains as soon as the passes opened up. They were forced this way. I do not know what could chase an entire nation of orcs out of their homes. Worse, their old chief was challenged and defeated. The new chief is an evil monster. But I think even he is being manipulated by someone or something very powerful. He is searching for something in the foothills north of here. It's the only reason they have not moved deeper into the eastern lands."

Thorn looked at H'aor. "Your people wait much longer to make a decision and things down here are going to get bad."

H'aor nodded. "I will see if I can get word to my father, but I am not ready to walk away from this yet. If I carry word myself, I might be ordered to stay home."

Thorn chuckled. "Sounds like you are planning to beg forgiveness instead of permission."

H'aor stared at the grass before him. "Maybe the druids had the right of it. They sent Shorty to fix what he could. That sounds like a better plan that asking questions and running home."

Essabeth smiled at them all. "I need your help. All of you."

Thorn sighed. "What help do you need?"

Essabeth laughed. "I need a general. Someone to command my troops. The wards can defend us from magical attacks, but I know nothing of battle or defense. I think a good solid dwarf would make a fine commander."

Thorn stared at her. "Not like I have much experience. How big is this army of yours?"

Essabeth laughed. "There are five rangers in a camp outside the village. And I think I have an ogre in my army these days."

Shorty gave her a happy smile but Thorn had a pained expression on his face. "You want me to defend this entire valley with five rangers?"

Shorty reached over and patted him on the shoulder. "Gots bestus ogre too."

Thorn grumbled. "That makes things so much better. I think we will both regret this girl, but I will do what I can. Best head out to meet the rangers tomorrow. You coming, elf?"

H'aor shook his head. "No, I have some Arcane work to do here. You can brag about your army when you get back."

Essabeth rose then. "We should head back before dark and see if there is anything left to eat."

Chapter 17
No Fall Down

Kisa carried two bowls of stew to the large table that occupied most of the room. The table could easily seat a score of people instead of the two who were sitting down for lunch. The dining area in the Hall of Healing was meant to feed the clerics in residence as well as those who came to the Hall seeking healing.

Today, it was just Kisa and Essabeth. Kisa had already taken a bowl of the day-old stew out to Old Mara who was sitting on the porch. She and Essabeth were taking advantage of the quiet space to plan for the next Council meeting. Kisa slid a bowl in front of Essabeth before taking a seat on the far side of the table.

Essabeth dipped a spoon into the bowl and stirred the vegetables around. "There are some, shall we say, concerns, being raised about the lack of meat since Thorn headed out to the ranger camp. Seems he is keeping them too busy scouting to hunt. Little Will brings in a rabbit or two every day, but it is not enough to feed all the people now living in the village. We need to figure something out especially if we get many more refugees."

Kisa swallowed the carrot she had been chewing. "Joachim went out to the camp this morning to check on things. I suspect he will be by for his free meal soon. Hopefully he can tell us what is up."

A young male voice echoed from the kitchen. "Two beautiful women anticipating my return. This is my lucky day. I must say though, this meatless stew is not the best way to draw me back from my adventures."

Joachim wandered out from the kitchen with a large bowl of stew in one hand and a spoon in the other. He sat down next to Kisa and gave a shy smile to Essabeth. "Hopefully your desire for my return is not just for the news I bear."

The two women began to laugh. Kisa gave him a nudge with her elbow. "Since when did you get so bold?"

Joachim stared down at his stew. "A certain lady ranger told me I was too timid. Needed to be more sure of myself."

Essabeth shook her head. "She just has not figured you out yet."

Kisa lifted a bite of stew and blew on it. "What is up with Thorn and Shorty?" Then she placed the bite in her mouth.

Joachim shrugged. "Shorty is just having a good time. He is playing tracker games with the rangers. They are teaching him to do more than sniff out a trail. He is catching on fairly well. They also tried to teach him to hide his own tracks. That lesson is not going well at all. Hard to hide footprints that size I guess."

Joachim began to eat. After a couple bites, Essabeth prompted him. "And Thorn? They have been out there for three days now."

"Thorn is grumpier than ever. He is frustrated."

Essabeth stared at the young man. "By what? The rangers are a really good team."

Joachim chuckled. "He is frustrated because they are rangers. They can track just about anything. They are incredible at setting up an ambush or a raid. According to Thorn, they just do not get fighting on defense. I think the word he used was clueless."

Kisa reached out a hand and placed it on Essabeth's arm at the look of concern on the young woman's face. Kisa glanced over at Joachim. "What is his plan then?"

Joachim held up a finger as he shoved another large bite into his mouth. "He says we need to get more people into the village. Build a militia."

Essabeth shook her head. "How? The orcs are not letting many get through to us. I am not sure how we can solve that problem."

Joachim winked at her. "Thorn said that was the easy part. Says he not only has rangers, but he has himself an ogre. He said to tell you he will explain it to you in the morning. He and Shorty will be back then."

Essabeth smiled at him. "Thank you, Joachim. Even knowing that much will keep Typerys at bay for a bit."

Joachim looked up from his bowl and met her eyes. He stared at their hazel color unsure if he liked them better this way or not. Kisa reached across with her spoon and stole a carrot from his bowl. Joachim jumped and scowled at her. "Hey! I walked a long way today. I need all the food I can get."

Kisa laughed and stuck her tongue out at him. "Stop staring and pay attention before you lose everything to a craftier thief." Joachim chuckled as he turned his attention to finishing off his meal.

Kisa's face turned serious. "Joachim, do you know where H'aor is? I have not seen him since Thorn and Shorty left. I am a little worried about him."

Joachim shook his head. "Something to do with his magic. He spends half the day hiding in his room and the other half tramping across the river where he can be alone. He seems obsessed by something. I am not sure he has eaten much lately. He will not talk to me, maybe the two of you can get him to open up."

Essabeth slid her empty bowl over beside Joachim. "I think we will. Thanks for volunteering to clean the dishes for us." She winked at Kisa who slid her bowl over beside Joachim as well.

Joachim glared at them as the two laughing women got up and walked out of the room. "So, this is my reward for walking all the way out there and back. Maybe I will eat the rest of your stew as payment."

Essabeth led the way to the small home the four men has been sleeping in. They waved to Dorna and Moira as they walked up to the door.

Kisa raised a fist and pounded on the door. When there was no answer, she pounded on it a second time.

H'aor's voice came from somewhere inside. "I am busy. Thorn can help you when he gets back."

Essabeth glanced at Kisa in surprise. Kisa turned and banged on the door one more time. "We are not leaving until you come talk to us. You might as well let us in."

His voice could be heard muttering from within. "Stubborn women." Kisa smiled as he opened the door. H'aor stood there blinking in the midday sun. His clothing was disheveled and he had the odor of a man who had not bathed recently. When his eyes adjusted to the light, he looked at them. "I am a bit busy. What can I do for you ladies?"

Kisa shouldered her way into the house and waived for Essabeth to follow her. "You can start by explaining what has turned you into a hermit. You look bad enough, but the smell is not something I would recommend."

H'aor blinked at her in confusion. Then he sniffed carefully. His nose wrinkled in mild disgust. "Maybe I have been a little absorbed in my work. I think I have earned the smell if it is any consolation."

Both women gave him a dubious look. Kisa asked, "How?"

He waved for them to follow and entered his room. His sleeping blankets lay crumpled in the corner of the room. There was a small table and chair in front of the window. On the table sat two vials, a helm, a silver ring, and a wand. Also sitting on the table right before the chair was a small book that Kisa recognized from their fight on the ridge line with the orcs.

H'aor sat down in the chair. "One of the first spells I learned was a spell to identify the properties of magic items. It is an exhausting spell and one that takes a lot of time. But I am rather good at it. I have been working to understand the items we found on our way here."

Kisa stared at the items spread across the table. "I am impressed. Is any of this useful?"

H'aor looked at the items before him and nodded. "The two vials are both potions of extra healing. I suspect they will be needed in our fight with the orcs."

Essabeth studied the two vials. "What will you do with them?"

H'aor nodded towards Kisa. "Turn them over to the Hall of Healing and trust our clerics to use them wisely."

Essabeth looked grateful. "The village thanks you for your generosity. Sorry if I am being nosey, but what about the rest?"

H'aor touched the wand next. "This we knew was a wand of ice wall. I now know the activation word for certain and I know it has five charges remaining. Not a lot but it is something that might help our defenses."

Kisa pointed to the helm. "That came from the undead. Is it cursed?"

H'aor chuckled. "Only if you like magic." Kisa gave him a puzzled look. H'aor reached out and picked up the helm. "This one was the hardest to understand as its basic nature tended to disrupt my spell. It is a powerful helm. The magic crafted into it enhances the protection it gives from physical attacks. It also provides magic resistance against spells. I think Thorn is going to be very happy to wear it. Might even make him smile."

H'aor placed the helm back on the table and picked up the ring. "This is useful, but not really. It is a ring of feather fall. The person that wears it can jump off a cliff without fear of being hurt. They will simply float slowly from any height."

Kisa reached out to touch the ring. "What should we do with it?"

H'aor placed it back on the table. "I think we should give it to our impetuous ogre. If anyone is going to go over a cliff it will be him. The question is if I can teach him to trust it."

Kisa chuckled. "That should be fun to watch. Is that what you have been doing across the river? Jumping off cliffs?"

H'aor grimaced. "That thief has a big mouth. No, I have been working on this." H'aor reached out to touch the small spell book. "This has been my other obsession of late. I have almost mastered one of the orc's spells."

Kisa looked intrigued. "What spell?"

H'aor's hand caressed the book. "Lightning bolt. It is the first spell of the Third Circle that I have ever attempted. It is safer to practice it away from the village. I can cast it out over the water where it cannot hurt anyone."

Kisa patted his shoulder. "That is wonderful news. But how about you bathe, get some rest, and join us for dinner. We have some vegetable stew simmering at the Hall. Assuming Joachim does not eat it all."

H'aor nodded. Kisa picked up the two vials as she and Essabeth left the room. H'aor heard her voice as she closed the front door. "Bathe. Please." He chuckled and went to his pack to dig out some soap.

H'aor rose the next morning to the sounds of Thorn and Shorty coming through the door. He stepped out into the main room of the house. "Kind of early."

Thorn shook his head. "Them rangers are up before dawn every day. They like moving around before anything else wakes up. I am looking forward to sleeping till after the sun is up tomorrow."

H'aor retrieved the helm from his room and tossed it to Thorn.

Thorn caught it with a hopeful look. "Is it safe?"

H'aor nodded. "Better than safe. Magical armor with a lot of magic resistance thrown in. It will protect your head and deflect spells."

Thorn popped it on his head. "The dwarf that forged this was a genius."

H'aor smiled. "Just take it off before you ask Kisa to heal you. She will not be happy if you disrupt her healing spell."

Thorn laughed and gave the helm a solid rap.

H'aor turned to Shorty. "I have a surprise for you as well, my friend. It is a new toy of sorts."

Shorty looked at him with a broad smile. "Me like prises. What bees it?"

H'aor pulled out the silver ring. Shorty's smile faded. "No ken play fun game wid dat. Marbles no eben fit dat hole."

H'aor held the ring up as he explained. "This is a ring of feather fall Shorty. When you wear it, it will keep you from being hurt when you fall."

Shorty held up his hand. "Finners bees too big. No fits. Me no falls down. Walks bery good."

Thorn laughed and headed out the door. "I would stay to watch this, but laughing that much is not good for my grumpy reputation."

H'aor groaned in frustration. "Shorty, how about you come with me and we can see if you can learn a new trick to show, Kisa."

Shorty nodded and smiled. H'aor led him out the door and down the street to the Hall of Healing. H'aor led the way inside. Kisa was busy cleaning the scraped-up knee of a young girl. Shorty waived to the child. The little girl waved back. Kisa looked up and asked, "How is it going with the ring?"

Kisa got a good look at H'aor's face and giggled. "Never mind."

H'aor pointed to the stairs. "We are going up onto the roof for a bit."

Kisa smiled and turned back to the little girl. "Good luck with your project."

H'aor led Shorty up on the roof and over to the knee-high wall on that ran around its perimeter. H'aor held up the ring and slid it on his finger. Then he stepped up to the edge of the wall. "Shorty. I am going to jump now. I want you to watch what happens."

Shorty placed a restraining hand on the elf's shoulder. "No bery smart. Kisa Lady gonna bees mad ifn youse make her fix ouches."

H'aor shook his head and slid from Shorty's grasp. "I will not get hurt. The ring is magic."

Shorty bent over and looked at the ground two below. The drop was at least three times his height. "Bery big jump. Break leg. Kisa Lady make sad face youse."

H'aor began to mutter to himself. Then he stepped onto the short wall and jumped off. Shorty leaned over to watch his friend bounce. He was surprised to see H'aor floating slowly down to the ground. He yelled down to H'aor, "Youse makes magics? Bery fun."

H'aor landed softly on the ground and hurried back into the Hall. Kisa looked up again and H'aor raised his hand. "Do not say anything. "

H'aor reached the roof to find Shorty bouncing his rubber ball and counting to two. He held out the finger with the ring. "See, the ring works."

Shorty shook his head. "Youse makes magic. Bery good trick."

H'aor shook his head. "Watch again, Shorty. It is the ring, not my magic."

Shorty caught his ball and moved to the edge of the roof. He said nothing this time as H'aor jumped from the roof and floated down. H'aor hurried back inside. He glared at Kisa when she began to laugh.

When he reached the top, he found Shorty again bouncing his ball. He slid the ring off his finger and held it out to shorty. "It is the magic ring, Shorty. I want you to try it now."

Shorty shook his head. "No ken dos."

H'aor sighed. "Why not?"

Shorty held up his hand. "Finners too big."

H'aor stepped forward and took hold of Shorty's hand. He held the ring to Shorty's finger and began to push. The ring did not go on at first and Shorty gave him a knowing look. The ogre's grin turned to one of curiosity as the ring began to stretch. Shorty watched in amazement as the ring slid up his finger and settle above the second knuckle.

H'aor tapped the ring with his index finger. "Magic."

Shorty smiled at the ring. "Bery good trick. But me nos gonna marry youse."

H'aor's mouth fell open then his face turned red as he heard two women laughing behind him. He turned to see Kisa and Essabeth standing by the stairs watching the show.

H'aor groaned "Is there nothing important you need to be doing right now?" Both women shook their heads and wandered closer. He turned back to Shorty. "The ring fits now. Will you try to jump?"

Shorty shook his head and H'aor asked, "Now why not?"

Shorty came and stood next to H'aor. "Dat bees no bery smart. Youse be bery littles. Ring ken makes youse no fall down. Shorty bery big. It maybeso drops Shorty."

H'aor turned to Kisa. "I have no argument for that."

Kisa smiled and walked over. "Sometimes in life you only learn by doing."

H'aor shrugged. "But he will not try."

Kisa winked at him. "Sometimes you have to use a little bit of persuasive shove to get things moving in the right direction. You need to help him to learn."

Kisa moved over to stand beside Shorty. "How about we try a new game with your ball, Shorty?"

Shorty held out the ball to her. "Funner game?"

She smiled at him. "It could be. But it is a hard game. Are you good at bouncing your ball?"

Shorty bounced the ball on the roof and caught it with one hand. "Me berry good."

Kisa tapped her lip. "Bouncing on the roof is too easy then. You should try something harder. Do you think you can bounce it off the ground below and catch it when it comes back up?"

Shorty thought about it. "Maybeso. Hab to throw bery hard."

Kisa led him over to the short wall. "Here is what we do. You bend over and hold onto the wall with one hand. Throw the ball down with the other hand and try to catch it when it bounces back up. Do you understand?"

Shorty stared down at the ground below. "No bery safe."

Kisa patted him on the arm. "I think you can do it, Shorty. Hold on to the wall."

Shorty bent over and grabbed onto the small wall. Kisa spoke loudly. "Be ready to help him."

Shorty threw the ball at the ground. The bounce was well short of returning to his hand. Shorty leaned forward to reach for it and something hit him from behind. Shorty went forward over the wall with a yell of surprise. But instead of falling, he floated slowly down. Shorty rolled over in the air and stared up to see H'aor leaning over the wall to watch him. Shorty wagged a finger at him. "No bery nice. Bees mean."

H'aor yelled back down at him, "You are not falling, Shorty!"

Moments later, Shorty landed softly on his back. He scrambled up and found his ball. Then he headed back into the Hall and to the roof where he had left his backpack. When he reached the top of the stairs, he gave H'aor a look of betrayal. "No bees me friend."

Kisa came over and held his hand. "He is your friend, Shorty. He gave you some of his magic to use. It is in the ring."

Shorty stared down at the ring. "Works all da times?"

Kisa squeezed the hand. "As long as you wear that ring, it will always work. You will not fall down no matter how high up your go."

Shorty spun the ring on his finger. "Ring fer no falls down? Kisa Lady bery sure?"

Kisa nodded and Shorty moved back to the edge of the roof. He stepped off the edge and tensed to fall. Again, he floated down slowly.

Kisa watched as Shorty came running back up the stairs. He waved to her and ran to stand before H'aor. "Muches tanks. No fall down bery funner game." Shorty ran to the edge of the roof and jumped again.

Kisa stared at H'aor. "You might as well come in and sit down. I do not think he will tire of this soon."

Kisa, Essabeth, and H'aor stood and waited until Shorty ran up the stairs again. As he headed for the edge of the roof, they hurried down the stairs to avoid being trampled.

Eventually they got Shorty to take a break for lunch. As he sat eating the leftover stew, he announced to everyone, "Bestus day eber. No fall down muches fun."

Chapter 18
Rescue from On High

Thorn stared down into the valley stretching to the east before him. The midday sun glittered off the waters of Long Lake. He had to admit it was a pretty place. Would be downright peaceful if not for the orc vermin that overran everything outside their small valley. He shook his head at that one. How had it become his valley?

He and his friends had arrived in the small village of Swanton barely a tenday ago. Now they were its official protectors. Worse, somehow he had ended up in charge of its small fighting force. He was no military genius. He was not sure how that scrap of a girl talked him into it. She was a sneaky one. One minute he was telling her how sorry he was about the death of her father and the next he was agreeing to protect her valley and the band of refugees that were streaming into it.

How was he supposed to defend the entire valley with only five rangers and an ogre?

Well, the non-magical defenses at least. If H'aor was right, the Swanmay now had the ability to shield the small valley from hostile magic and possibly even creatures from other planes. But she had paid a price for that protection. Even that was partially he and his friend's fault.

The bracer that they had promised to deliver for the Bard was half of an ancient artifact. She was already wearing the first bracer when they arrived in the village. It had provided some protection to the people there. But once she placed the second one on her left wrist, Essabeth Sunderin has been transformed into Essabeth the Swanmay. Thorn was not so sure that becoming the living host for a holy relic was such a good idea. Within the Valley of the Swans, she had great power. But she could never leave it. "Bah, fool girl!" He muttered quietly to himself.

Besides, the magical protection did not stop raiders from slipping into the valley. It also did not help the people outside the valley who were trying to reach it before the orcs captured or killed them. Those were his two big jobs. Essabeth had gifted him with command of the village's small militia to help him out. All five of them. He had his work cut out for him even with Shorty's help.

He had to admit that the rangers were not a bad group. Their leader, Anjelique, was pretty good with a blade and her bow was downright deadly. Thorn was not sure, but he suspected there was elf blood in her. Her eyesight was far better than any human he had ever met. The four male rangers were a descent lot too. The problem was that they were rangers. They made great scouts and could set up one hell of an ambush, but they just did not do pitched battles. They would not survive if he asked them to hold a defensive position. At least he had the ogre.

Thorn glanced to his right. Anjelique was stretched out on the bluff staring through that strange contraption she called a spyglass. She was checking out the small band of refugees they had spotted earlier that day. Thorn grew impatient and stomped over to stand beside her. "How many in this group?"

The ranger looked up at him. "Patience, Thorn. There are at least a dozen of them down there headed our way with several horses carrying their possessions."

Shorty's deep voice came from behind Thorn where the ogre still crouched on the edge of the bluff. "Bees mo kid?"

Anjelique smiled in Shorty's direction. "Yes. I see at least three children in the group." Then she gave Thorn a peculiar look. "Never thought I would ever be working with an ogre to save folks. Ogres were the ones I was trained to save people from."

Thorn chuckled. "My family would disown me if they knew I was friends with one. But I have given up trying to understand all the strange twists in life. Just make the best of them. Where is your team?"

She pointed them to a clump of ash trees down in the valley about a half mile ahead. I saw them move into position there a while back."

Shorty pointed down at the same cluster. "Pretty light. What dat be?"

Thorn and the ranger turned back to study the mirror signals flashing from the trees below. Angelique swore and turned her spyglass towards a small ravine much closer to the refugees.

Thorn was frustrated that he had not been able to learn their signals yet. The mirrors were a great idea above ground. They would have been useless back in the tunnels. "What is it?"

Angelique pointed at the ravine she had been studying. "Orcs. Waiting to ambush those people. Don't the orcs have enough slaves already?"

Thorn sighed. "The ones they have keep dying from being overworked and underfed. How many orcs?"

Anjelique studied the ravine again and cursed again. "At least ten, maybe as many as fifteen. I cannot be sure. Too many for my team to take out. What do you want to do, Thorn? It will take the three of us longer than we have just to get down from this bluff."

Thorn turned to stare at the human group that was still over a mile away. "Any way that your team can warn the humans off or distract the orcs without getting themselves killed or captured?"

The ranger shook her head. "Nothing that would work. The refugees are to slow and the orcs would just run them down. The bows might get a few of them, but Ruse and the others do not have a good line of fire into that ravine."

Anjelique suddenly scrambled backwards as a large shadow fell over her. Thorn turned to see that Shorty had risen from where he had been kneeling and was now towering over them both. Thorn smiled over at the ranger. "He moves almost as quietly as you do out here." The ranger just scowled at them both.

Shorty pointed at the refugee party. "No gonna lets orc gets kid!"

Thorn turned to his friend. "I am sorry, Shorty. But there are not enough of us. And unless you can find a way to warn the people or distract the orcs, we cannot get there in time."

Shorty stared down at his friend as he tried to understand Thorn's words. "Makes orcs bee fraid?"

Thorn shrugged. "That might work if we could pull it off. But they know we do not have many fighters."

Shorty tapped himself on the chest. "Me ken do dat."

Angelique stared up at him. "How can you possibly do that from here?"

In answer Shorty turned from her to face the valley floor.

Thorn held up a hand. "Wait, my friend."

Shorty just smiled and raised both hands to his mouth. Thorn tried to grab one arm. "Shorty no…."

But the large ogre ignored him and took in a deep breath. "Aaaaarroooooooooo!" Shorty took another deep breath and again bellowed out, "Aaaaarrooooooo!" At the sound of his third cry, the ranger shuttered and turned her glass to face the ravine that held the orcs.

Mirror signals began to flash from the corps of trees where the other rangers were hiding.

Thorn turned to Anjelique. "What did he just do?"

Anjelique pulled her own mirror out and began to flash a signal back to her team. "No reason to pretend we are not here anymore. That was the battle cry of an ogre tribe going into battle. The orcs are in a blind panic now."

Shorty turned and smiled down at Thorn. "Orcs come fer me now. Leabe kid lone."

Thorn stared up at him. "Damn fool ogre. Not sure whether to kiss you or kick you off the bluff. "

Thorn turned at the ranger's next curse. "What else has gone wrong?"

Anjelique studied the mirror flashes from below. "You want the good news, the bad news or the worst news?"

Thorn wiped his hand down his face. "Start with the worst."

The ranger slid her tube into her backpack and pulled out her bow. "There are at least twenty orcs." Thorn groaned in frustration as she continued. "The bad news is that they already have some captives. There are about eight orcs breaking north with the prize they already have."

Thorn frowned. "And the rest?"

She turned towards the trail down the side of the bluff. "About half are headed towards us and about half are chasing after the people we are trying to save. My team is going to hit the group after the humans from behind. That leaves the three of us to deal with a half-dozen or more orcs on a narrow trail."

Thorn nodded. "Then we had better hurry."

Shorty laughed and stepped to the edge of the bluff. Thorn shook his head. "Wait, you dag blasted ogre."

Shorty held out his hand where a ring shined in the sunlight. "No fall down. Bery muches fun." Shorty jumped over the edge of the bluff and began to slowly drift downward.

Thorn shook his head and ran for the trail down as another "Aaarrooooo!" echoed across the valley floor. Anjelique rushed after Thorn. "Exactly how did your group survive battles with the orcs?"

Thorn glanced at her and grinned. "Wait till you see him fight."

Thorn was breathing heavy as he ran. The ranger passed him before he was a quarter of the way down to the valley floor. He really hoped he would be in time to get at least one orc. He would be a very grumpy dwarf if he ran all that way and missed all the fun.

Shorty floated slowly down the front of the bluff. He landed softly on a ledge about halfway down. He looked below to make sure he was not going to land on a tree and he stepped off again. No fall down was a muches fun. Shorty was glad his elf friend had given him the magic ring. Shorty had not really believed H'aor when he had taught him how to use it. This was almost as much fun as the ball the fuzzface had given him when he was little.

Shorty could see a group of orcs running his way. He was very happy to see that they did not have crossbows. He really did not like crossbows anymore. They hurt lots. Most of the orcs had big clubs. But one had a whip. He had never fought a whip before. This would be fun. Or maybe it would hurt lots. But the kids were safe now.

Shorty turned in the air so see where his friends were. The Bow Lady was almost halfway down the trail. She ran really fast. Thorn had small legs. He was way behind. Shorty thought about saving him an orc, but was not sure if the orcs would be willing to wait for his friend.

Shorty's feet touched the ground and he moved quickly into a group of trees with white trunks. Shorty could not remember what the big drud had called them. They were not much cover, but it was the best he could find at the moment. Shorty placed his shield under the largest of the trees. There were many orcs and he would need to kill them quickly. He drew out both of his swords and stabbed them into the ground. Then he reached into his pouch and pulled out two rocks to throw.

Shorty did not have long to wait before the orcs arrived. They must have been smart orcs because they all came in a group. Shorty was hoping the fast ones would get to him first. The orcs spotted him and began to spread out in a circle around him. Shorty threw his two rocks. The first one missed. The second caught one of the orcs in the shoulder. The orc dropped its club and began to back away. It was not dead, but it was not going to fight either. Shorty reached down and pulled both his large swords from the ground. He was beginning to think this would hurt muches.

There were more orcs than Shorty had numbers for. More than lots. The orcs began to circle around the small cluster of trees that shorty had chosen for his fight. He was hoping the trees would prevent them from all attacking at the same time. But he realized he would have been better off standing with the bluff to his back. "Ooops." Shorty began to spin in place trying to keep the orcs from attacking him from behind.

As Shorty rotated left, the orc with the whip attacked his right side. The end of the whip wrapped itself around his wrist. It had tiny pieces of metal in it that cut at his arm. The orc began to pull on the whip. Shorty realized he would not be able to fight with the orc tugging on his arm that way. Shorty did not like this game. He stabbed the left sword into the ground and reached over to grab the whip. He gave it a sharp tug. It was jerked towards Shorty so hard that the orc forgot to let go of the whip. Shorty turned Papa's sword to the side and it entered the orcs stomach. The orc backed away with its hands clutching at its stomach. Its hands were very bloody.

Shorty released the whip and pulled his sword free again. He was beginning to worry. He could not defend against all the orcs at the same time. One of the orcs barked a command and they all charged at once. The orc to Shorty's right suddenly sprouted an arrow from its neck. He quickly turned his back to that one and began to back towards it.

The three orcs charged in and began to strike at Shorty with their clubs. He blocked one, but took a hit to the ribs and one to the shoulder. Clubs hurt, but they did not cut through his chainmail and make him bleed. The orc to Shorty's right tried to rush him. Shorty simply brought his Papa's sword up and the orc impaled itself on the blade. It twisted as it fell and pulled the sword from Shorty's grasp.

Shorty sensed movement to his left and spun as the orc on that side stepped forward bring its club over its head. Shorty slashed with his new sword. The swing was high. Instead of taking the orc in the neck, it caught the orc in the wrists. The magic blade went through both wrists. The club sailed backwards with the orcs hands still clutching it. The orc brought both arms down as if to strike, spraying blood on Shorty's face and chest.

Shorty spun back to face the last orc wondering why the orc had not hit him yet. The orc lay on the ground with two arrows in its back. Shorty decided that bows were his friends. It was only crossbows that he did not like. The orc that had lost its hands was down on its knees whimpering in pain. Shorty ended its suffering. The orc that had used the whip as already dead.

Shorty looked around for the orc he had hit with the rock, but it had disappeared so he bent and pulled Papa's sword free from the orc's body. He cleaned the blades and then sheathed them.

Anjelique stared at him. "You were going to take on all six by yourself? Even you cannot be that good."

Shorty gave her a confused look. "How manys bees dat? Bees more den lots?"

Anjelique began to chuckle. "Oh, Forest Lady, you cannot count." Her laughter grew at the sound of the dwarf charging down the trail grew louder. His words seemed to echo from the bluff. "You will both regret it if them orcs are all dead when I get there."

Shorty looked at her with a big grin. "Uh oh."

The other four rangers rejoined them just before sunset. They led a frightened band of thirteen humans including a small baby strapped to its mother's chest. There appeared to be three families. Everything they had left in the world was strapped to the back of two horses, both well past their prime.

Anjelique stood eating an apple and staring at the group. She checked in with her team before turning to Thorn. "It took them a while to convince them it was safe to continue on to the valley. Essabeth said you were in charge. What do you want us to do?"

Thorn stared at the group for a moment and then looked north. "Can two of your rangers track the ones with the other prisoners?"

Anjelique nodded. "Sure. But why? We know where the main camp is."

Thorn took off his new helm and scratched the back of his head. "That crew that tried to take the family we brought in. They said something about digging. I think the prisoners are being used somewhere else. Be nice if we can find out where."

The ranger nodded and walked over to talk to an older scout. After a moment, he nodded and tapped another of the rangers on the arm. The two took off at a lope.

Anjelique returned to Thorn's side. She paused to stare in surprise at the ogre sitting on the ground playing ball with two of the kids. "Is that for his enjoyment or theirs?"

Thorn just grinned at her. "Yes. One or both I guess. We need to get these folks back into the valley. They will be safer within the Swanmay's wards."

Chapter 19
Out of Slavery

Thorn sat on a tree stump high in the eastern pass. He had hiked up here alone to think. He studied the valley before him trying to wrap his thoughts around some way to defend it. There were only two large passes into the valley. The southern pass would require days of travel just to get to it. Thorn did not think it was feasible for them to attack from that direction.

The pass he was sitting in was the larger of the two and it was not far from the region that the orcs liked to raid. But the rangers kept a good watch on it. The orcs would take heavy loses to the ranger's bows if they came this way. That left him two directions to be worried about.

The western mountains were fairly high and their slopes were treacherous. The rangers had yet to find a path through them that a mountain goat could climb. Now that there was snow on the western peaks, it was even less likely to be a problem.

Thorn dismissed the western slopes and turned his attention to the northern rim of the valley. This was the real reason he was sitting up here worrying. The two northern peaks were fairly low. The rangers indicated that there were dozens of trails that ran between and around the peaks. The trails might not be well suited to a large attack force, but the orcs could get enough small raiding parties through to make life hard on the refugees. The next valley to the north was just too close to the orc village for his liking.

Thorn continued to stare in hope that a plan would come to him. He cocked his head as a rock shifted somewhere behind him. His hand went to the haft of the axe leaning against the stump he was resting on. He listened a moment longer and then relaxed. "Yer slipping, woman. I thought rangers were supposed to be silent out in the wilderness."

A soft feminine laugh drifted down the slope. "Might just be that rock moved on purpose. I would not want our grumpy commander taking a swing at me with that axe." Thorn smiled without turning his head so she could see it. "I would hate to lose a ranger because you tried sneaking up on me. Do not have enough to spare even one as scrawny as you are."

There was another laugh from behind him. "Also, might just be that I was confident I could take you with my bow before your axe could reach me."

Thorn just grunted and continued to stare at the northern edge of the valley. "Arrows is cheating." He heard her say, "So?" as she stepped closer.

Thorn tugged at his beard in frustration. He needed more fighters to do this right.

Anjelique wandered down the slope and lowered herself to the ground. She crossed her legs and lay her longbow across her lap. She sat in companionable silence until Thorn sighed and turned to her. "There just are not enough of us to keep this place safe."

Anjelique smiled ruefully. "We saved a couple families yesterday. Those men will fight to defend their families. It is a start."

Thorn shook his head. "We stirred the orcs up taking out their raiding party like that. How long before they come looking for payback?"

The ranger turned to study him. "We might be able to add a dozen or so men to your little army. They are in pretty rough shape right now, but they are alive. If your Priestess and Old Mara can heal them up. It would give you a small defensive team."

Thorn studied her. "What do you have for me? There is always a catch."

Anjelique grinned. "No, it is never that easy. You asked us to track the orcs that took off with prisoners yesterday. It is not hard to track ten orcs dragging a half dozen prisoners through the forest. Their trail was pretty easy to follow."

Thorn studied her face. "I take it they did not go to the main encampment?"

Anjelique shrugged. "Well, yes and no. The first stop was at a logging camp. They left a few of the men there. Then they traveled to the village the orcs are building. A woman was left behind there. Another woman and an older child were taken further west. And before you ask, we do not know where they went. There were too many orcs around to try and follow them any further."

Thorn grinned. "And the men you offered me?"

The ranger pointed to the pair of peaks along the northern rim of the valley. "There are some trails we can follow to their logging camp. If we do it right, I think we can free the prisoners there."

Thorn stared at her thoughtfully. "You are better at raids than I am. What are the risks?"

Angelique brushed her hand across the ground in front of her to clear the dirt. She began to draw. "The men are kept in cages at night. There are at least two dozen orcs there to guard them. A lot of crossbows. They have to be careful since the men have axes when they are cutting down trees."

Thorn whistled softly. "That is a lot of orcs to take on."

"Not really," the ranger replied. "We have five rangers who are damn good with longbows. If we hit them at night from outside the firelight, we will kill a lot of them without much risk."

Thorn studied her. He could see that something was eating at her. "What are you worried about then? If it was that easy, you would already have hit them."

Anjelique grimaced. "Orcs can be vindictive. They might turn their crossbows on the prisoners just to make sure we do not get them."

Thorn stared at the drawing she was tracing in the dirt. "What are you thinking?"

Anjelique pointed to a spot behind the cages. "If your team could get to the cages and protect the prisoners, we might get most of them out."

Thorn studied the rough map where she had marked the tree line behind the cages. "It is not that close to the trees, but I think I can make it there."

The ranger began to laugh. "We were thinking the ogre and the thief. They know how to move quietly. You make more noise than a pair of boars mating."

Thorn gave her an injured look. "I am not that bad. Then where do you want me?"

She tapped a spot over to the side. "We thought this would be a good spot."

Thorn turned his gaze to her. "What am I going to do from there?"

Anjelique began to rub out the map. "You are our big distraction. Rumor has it that orcs hate dwarves. It is a vital part of the whole plan."

Thorn rose to his feet. He had a sour expression on his face. "Distraction or target?"

The ranger rose to her feet and turned towards the valley floor. "There is the dwarf we all know and love. Grumpy face and all. At least we know why you are in charge of defense. You are so quick to catch on to the subtle parts of a plan. Besides, we did not want you to feel left out." She began to jog towards the valley floor. "We need to be on our way by sunset. That elf's magic might be useful if he is not too busy casting spells at the lake."

Thorn began to swear under his breath. He grabbed his axe and followed the ranger down the slope. She was already out of sight.

————————————————

Thorn crouched in the underbrush and stared into the large clearing where the orcs had set up their logging operation. The journey through the mountains on the north side of the valley had not been too bad. That had its good and bad points. It made tonight easier, but it also meant the orcs had a ready path into the valley.

They had only run into two sentries on their way into this small valley. The first had been an easy kill for the rangers. The orc had been out in the open and both arrows had hit. It never made a sound. The second orc had been in a stand of trees. There had not been a clean shot. The boy had slipped in unnoticed. He had not hesitated to stab the orc from behind. That too had its good and bad points as well.

Thorn realized that Joachim had changed somewhere along their travels. He had never wanted to be a part of this war. He had only wanted to get away. Thorn was not sure when the boy had committed himself to their cause. Maybe it happened when they saved Dorna and her children. More likely it was meeting the Swanmay. The boy was certainly infatuated with her. Thorn was glad the Joachim was committed to saving the valley. He just was not sure he liked that the boy was more willing to kill. The world had enough people like that already.

Thorn turned his eyes towards the wooden cages where the human prisoners were locked up. The bars were only wood, but the men were too beaten down to put up much resistance. The orcs had starved them too. Damn vermin needed to be taught a lesson.

Anjelique whispered in his ear, "Your two friends are almost in position. Sethrin is with them. Once they are ready, he will fire the first shot. We will start picking off orcs then." She gave him a nudge. "That will be your signal to get the orcs attention."

Thorn shook his head in the dark. "Looking to turn me into a crossbow target. You are a hard woman." Thorn smiled then. "If you had any kind of a beard, I might be forced to propose to you."

She chuckled softly. "I prefer my men to be a taller than my bow, but I appreciate the compliment." At that moment, an orc between the cages and the campfire let out a cry of pain and reached for its back where the feathers of an arrow now protruded. Anjelique disappeared into the darkness. Thorn heard her bow thrum as she began to fire. In the span of a few breaths, Thorn counted six orcs down with arrows in them.

The orcs were not as stupid as he had hoped. They responded to the attack quickly. One orc near the fire turned and raised a crossbow. He fired directly into the center cage. There was a cry of pain from within. Two orcs armed with axes headed towards the cages as well. A large shape stepped from behind the cages and Thorn caught the gleam of a huge sword in the firelight.

Another orc stood and aimed its crossbow at the cages. Before the orc could fire, a voice rang out from the darkness. "shEH- laKH!" Two sapphire bolts slammed into it before it could fire. It fell into the fire and did not move. Thorn smiled, stood, and began to move into the firelight. He began to whistle a happy tune. Five orcs stopped and stared at him. He stopped whistling and called out, "You as stupid as you are ugly? I would think you could recognize a dwarf when you see one. Especially one with a nice shiny axe like mine." Thorn raised his axe overhead so the firelight reflected from its blade.

Several of the orcs hesitated, but two charged Thorn. Neither made it more than three steps before they fell with arrows in their chests. Thorn muttered, "Knock it off, woman. If I have to stand here, at least let me play with a couple of them."

Two of the orcs turned and ran. The final orc began to stomp forward. Thorn suddenly realized this one was big. Not just tall, but very fat. It had a long scar down one side of its face and it appeared to be missing an ear. It carried a two headed battle axe in its hands. Thorn grinned and raised his shield.

Shorty smiled as he stepped protectively in from of the cages. Two of the orcs were coming to fight with him. And one of the orcs with the nasty crossbows was dead. That made him happy.

Joachim whispered from behind him, "What do you want me to do? Knives do not work that well against axes."

Shorty raised his sword and shield as he stepped away from the cages. "Me fights. Youse gets peoples out. No posed bees in dere."

There was a note of relief in Joachim's voice as he replied, "That is something I can do well."

The two orcs began to spread apart. Shorty did not wait for them to bring the fight to him. He darted towards the orc on his right. The orc back peddled, but Shorty spun and used his greater reach to slash at the orc on his left. The orc brought its axe up to block. Shorty's blade glanced off the axe head and cut into the orc's arm. Shorty spun back as the orc to his right stepped in and chopped with his axe. Shorty caught the blow on his shield as he thrust his sword into the orc's thigh.

Shorty stepped back to study his two wounded opponents. The one with the arm wound ducked behind the orc with the injured leg. It turned and ran for the trees. It never made it. It fell with an arrow in its neck. The remaining orc tried to limp forward. Shorty stepped in and thrust again. The orc dropped to the ground.

Shorty turned to see the first cage door hanging open. Joachim was cutting through the ropes that held the second cage closed. Shorty stepped over to the final cage where he struck the door twice with his sword. The wood splintered with each blow. Shorty was about to hit it a third time when Joachim hissed, "Shorty, look out!"

Shorty spun to see an orc standing a few yards away with a crossbow hanging limply from its hands. Two small throwing knives protruded from its stomach. The orc dropped the bow and reached down for the knives. Shorty watched as the orc slipped to the ground. He glanced over at Joachim. "Muches tanks. No likes crossbow bery muches."

———————————————

Thorn waited for the large orc to stomp towards him. Thorn grinned as he looked up at the orc. "You bring all new meaning to the phrase 'pig-faced,' orc. You must spend a lot of time at the feeding trough."

The orc growled and brought its axe down in a two-handed chop. Thorn's shield came up to meet it. The force of the blow drove the dwarf to one knee. Thorn realized with a touch of annoyance that there might be more than just fat in this particular orc. The orc raised its axe for another blow, but Thorn rose and stepped backwards. The second blow missed by a comfortable margin. Thorn darted in as the orc brought its axe to the side for a slash. As the axe came across, Thorn angled his shield to deflect the blow over his head. Before the orc could pull his weapon back, Thorn brought his own axe down on its foot. The blade sank deep into the orc's right boot. Thorn sprang backwards as the orc staggered.

The orc advanced again, but it was moving slower now. Thorn spun to the right, extending his axe as he moved. The blade left a bloody line on the orc's left shin. The orc grunted in pain as it tried to turn and face the dwarf.

Thorn studied the orc. It was not going to be able to keep up with him with both legs injured. He just was not sure which side it was more vulnerable on. Before he could make his decision, a female voice began to chide him. "Are you done fooling around? We have a lot of injured people to get back to the village."

Thorn pointed at the orc with his axe. "It is not dead yet. Big orcs take more chopping."

Thorn heard the thrum of a bowstring and the orc fell backwards with an arrow through its chest.

Anjelique stepped out of the trees. "It is dead now. We have work to do and you were just playing with it."

Thorn looked at her and shrugged. "You take all the fun out of killing the vermin."

The ranger reached out and pulled her arrow from the orc's body. "You worry me sometimes."

Thorn smiled and turned to the men trickling out of the cages. "You are free now. Grab any weapons you want from the dead orcs. I hope to give you the opportunity to pay the vermin back for what they did to you. If you are interested that is."

There was a cheer from most of the men. They all began to scavenge the bodies of the dead orcs. Even the man with the crossbow bolt sticking from his arm grabbed an axe with his uninjured arm. Most took axes and swords from the orcs. Thorn saw two pick up crossbows. Several also grabbed the axes they had used to fell trees.

Anjelique stood beside Thorn. "Why get them worked up about revenge? Most of them can barely walk. Carrying those weapons is going to make the return trip even harder."

Thorn studied the men. "Gives them something to live for and I need a militia. These are a good start."

The ranger frowned. "They are simple woodsmen, Thorn. They do not know much about fighting."

Thorn nodded. "They can learn. Axes can take down orcs as well as trees."

Anjelique gave him a disapproving look. "Orcs do not stand still like trees. Orcs fight back."

Thorn sighed. "I know. But unlike trees, orcs usually only have to be chopped once. And this way, they do not leave this camp feeling like victims."

The journey back that night was hard on the freed prisoners. They all seemed to do better once they passed the wards as they came into the valley. But even with that, Shorty was practically carrying two of them by the time they reached to village.

Thorn and Anjelique were surprised to see that the entire village had turned out to see their return. Shorty lowered the two he helped to the ground and Kisa moved forward to care for their injuries.

Essabeth came to stand beside Thorn. "It went well?"

Thorn nodded. "Till the orcs come to take them back."

Essabeth opened her mouth to ask another question, but a cry of joy rang out across the clearing.

"William! Oh, William! You are alive!"

Thorn looked up to see Dorna and her children running towards a one-handed man with a woodsman's axe. The man dropped the axe and gathered them into his arms. Thorn glanced around to see Shorty standing beside Kisa. The damn ogre was actually had tears on his cheeks. Thorn coughed and turned away.

Anjelique nudged him. "Careful, dwarf. Do not ruin your reputation."

Thorn grumbled and turned to head into the village. "Watch your step. I might be really grumpy after I get some sleep."

Anjelique turned towards the tree line. "I am counting on it." She gave a short whistle and the other rangers followed her into the trees.

The villagers began helping the new arrivals to move towards the Hall of Healing. Everyone seemed happy except for one small group to the edge of the crowd.

The tall man in robes frowned at the bustle of activity. "Their popularity grows with each victory. Are you worried yet Councilor?"

Councilor Typerys shook his head and turned away from the crowd. "They will make a mistake eventually. We will see how popular these new heroes are when someone's death is laid at their feet. We may just have to get creative about it." The mage fell in behind him as he walked into the village.

Shorty was tired. The two men he helped had gotten heavy as they crossed through the mountains. He turned for his new home. He stopped when a small form stepped in front of him. Little Moira stood there with a serious look on her face. Shorty smiled at her.

The little girl held her arms out. Shorty bent and picked her up. He began to walk towards her home. She wrapped her arms around his neck and hugged him. As he bent to put her on the ground in front of her house, she kissed him on the cheek and whispered, "You never scared me. Not ever."

Shorty patted her on the head and watched her go inside. He heard her cry, Papa. Then he turned for home. There was a contended smile on his broad face. He was not really sure how he had done it, but he was pretty sure he had finally not made a mistake.

Chapter 20
Branded a Thief

Shorty stood at the edge of the village. It was a good day because it was his turn to be the guard. It was an important job. His friend Thorn had said there must always be a guard to protect peoples. He liked to protect. Thorn decided they needed a guard after the orcs had attacked the village. That had been… Shorty counted on his fingers. One, two, four. The orcs had attacked in the morning four days ago. There had only been a few orcs, but they had almost taken a family from the village. Shorty and his friends had only managed to stop them because his friend H'aor had used the magic stick. The shiny wall had kept the orcs from taking the family into the woods.

Now Shorty got to have a turn every day and when he was done it would be time to eat. Eating was good too. Moira's Mama let him eat lunch with her. He got to play ball with her and pet the cat. It was fun. Being guard was fun too. He was supposed to watch for orcs, but mostly he watched the people of the village go places. Many were nice. They would even say hullo to him. Sometimes the kids would come to play ball with him while he watched for orcs. That was nice too.

Today was going to be the bestus of all. New peoples were going to come. Shorty really liked that. Maybe there would be new kids for him to meet and say hullo to. There were not many people to watch today and he was getting bored. He was trying to find something interesting to do when he saw the Bow Lady and the other scouts come out of the trees. Behind them was a small group of peoples that Shorty did not know. He stared as they approached. None of the new peoples looked very happy. Shorty knew that they had probably lost their homes to the orcs. That was no bery good.

Bow Lady got the new people together and pointed to the center of the village. After she talked to them, she and the other scouts headed back into the woods. They did not like to stay in the village. They had their own place out in the trees not far away. Shorty visited their tents a couple times. It was a nice place, but he thought it was pretty lonely with only the scouts around.

There were lots of new people and that was good. The first two that walked past his guard place were a man and woman. They were not old, but they did not have any kids. They walked quickly towards the center of the village where Bird Lady was waiting to meet new peoples. There were two other groups that followed more slowly. The first was a man and a woman with two kids. There was a little boy and a girl that was older. The little boy pointed at Shorty but his Mama pushed his arm down. She looked scared. Shorty smiled. He did not want her to be afraid of him.

Walking right behind the family was an old man with an older woman. The old woman stood up very straight and tall. Shorty thought she must be important. Only important people walked like that. He watched closely as they approached in case they needed help. The woman turned to look up and down the street. She did not have a happy look on her face. As she turned sideways, Shorty saw something that sparkled in the sunlight on her chest. It shined like blue fire. He could not take his eyes from the shiny thing.

Shorty began to move closer. He knew he was supposed to stay at the guard place, but he wanted to see what was on her coat. He wondered what could make such a pretty light. He wandered even closer so he could see. Finally, Shorty realized that the woman had a small blue sword stuck to the front of her heavy coat. It looked to be made from a marble. Shorty did not know that marbles could be not round. He took two more steps towards the woman as he stared in fascination.

The woman glanced over at him. She gave him a mad look. "What do you want?" The old man beside her stared up at Shorty and placed a hand on her arm in warning. The old woman slapped at his hand and looked back at Shorty. "Well?"

Shorty lifted a heavy finger to point at the tiny sword. "What bees dat?"

The old woman shook her head and began to walk towards the center of the village. "What business is it of yours?"

Shorty puzzled at her words, not quite understanding. He pointed again at the sword on the woman's coat. "Please? What bees dat?"

The woman's hand rose protectively to cover the sword. "It is a broach. It is my family crest. Why do you care?"

Shorty looked eagerly at her covering hand. "Please to gets dat? Want? Needs fer…"

The woman scowled at Shorty. Her voice became loud and shrill. "So, this is what the rangers call a safe refuge? We have not even made it into town and you want to rob us?"

Shorty grew more confused. He began to shake his head. "No bees bad." The young family began to pull away. Several people from the village had stopped to stare at the exchange. The woman stepped behind her husband and pushed him towards Shorty. The man looked back at his wife who demanded, "Do something." The old man turned back to Shorty. There was a sheen of sweat on his forehead despite the cold of the winter morning. "You have no right to a tribute from us. We were told that this place was a haven for everyone."

Shorty shook his head. "No ken unnerstan. Dis place Bees safe. Me bees bestus guard."

The old man whispered to his wife, "What do you expect me to do against him?"

The woman slapped the back of her husband's head. "Old fool!" Then she turned and began to yell. "Thief! Robber! Monster! Someone help us, please!"

The young couple and their children hurried away, but a small crowd began to gather around. Shorty looked at the woman in confusion. "No bees thief. Hows come need helps?"

The old woman looked at the growing crowd and smiled. She stepped forward and stabbed a finger into Shorty's chest. "I need protection from you. These people can testify that you robbed a defenseless old woman.

Shorty looked around helplessly. He was not sure what he had done wrong. Then he spotted Thorn and Joachim moving through the growing crowd. They were following one of the children that Shorty sometimes played ball with. He waved for them and raised his voice. "Needs muches help."

The old man tried to pull his wife back, but the old woman pushed her husband aside and shook a finger at Shorty. "Does it take more than one of you to rob a helpless old woman?"

Thorn stepped up between Shorty and the woman. Thorn raised his hands to calm her. "Take it easy, Lady. No one here is going to rob you. There must be a misunderstanding."

The old lady placed her hands on her hips. "There most certainly is if that brute thinks he can just take my broach."

Thorn turned to Shorty. "Tell me what is going on, my friend?"

Shorty looked ready to cry as he stared down at Thorn. "Little sword. Needs. Me want ta…". Shorty shook his head sadly. "No gots word."

Thorn turned to stare at the woman. Her hand moved back up to cover the sword broach. Thorn looked back at Shorty. "Why, Shorty?"

Shorty held his fingers apart about the length of the broach. "Gibs ta bug. Him ken bees warrior wid sword."

Thorn suddenly smiled and patted Shorty on the arm. "It is okay. I think I understand now." Thorn turned back to the woman and raised his voice so the entire crowd could hear. "He was not trying to rob you, Lady. He wanted to tradefor it. He just did not know the word."

The woman looked flustered but held her ground. "Then he should have said so. As for trade, this broach is very valuable. What could he possibly have to trade for my broach?"

Thorn turned to Shorty. "Will you give a marble or two for it, Shorty?"

Shorty nodded his head and took his marble bag from his belt and handed it to Thorn. Thorn accepted the bag and opened it.

The woman protested. "This is a diamond broach. I will not trade if for a couple of children's toys."

As he dug though the bag, Thorn continued to speak in a raised voice. "Lady, I am a dwarf. We leave diamonds bigger than that out on the ground as junk. Telling me what is or is not valuable is like telling a hog how to eat slop. It is a waste of your time and the hog's." Thorn handed the bag back to Shorty before turning to face the woman. He held out his hand. On it were two medium sized gemstones that sparkled in the sunlight. One was a brilliant red and the other a deep green. "The two of these are worth nearly double that piece you wear. It's as good an offer as you will get anywhere."

Greed flashed momentarily on the old woman's face. She began to argue and Thorn simply closed his fist over the two stones. The old man nudged his wife. "Do not be a fool, woman. Those two stones are worth more than the lie you tell about it being a family heirloom. Take the gems. We can start over with the gold they will bring."

The old woman gave him a nasty look but then began to unpin the broach from her coat. The crowd was mostly laughing now and had begun to disperse. Joachim looked at the woman as she made the trade with Thorn. "Lady, the 'monster,' as you like to call him, is my friend. He has saved most of the folks in this village at least once. You should treat him better."

The woman turned a haughty glare on all three of the companions before walking away leaving her husband to catch up.

Thorn shook his head and turned to hand the diamond sword to Shorty. Shorty turned it over in Thorns hand. "Ken youse takes metal ting off da sword?"

Thorn studied the piece for a moment. "Easy to do with my tools. Anything else?"

Shorty touched his own scabbard and belt. "Need dis but no ken hurts bug's flyin tings."

Joachim replied. "We have a tanner in the village now. I will see what he can do."

Thorn turned and headed back towards the house they shared. "Meet me before dinner tonight. We will give the bug a sword." Shorty began to follow, but Thorn paused for a second. "Shorty, I believe you have guard duty now. Maybe you should get back to your post."

Thorn heard a softly muttered apology as he continued on. He looked down at the small diamond sword and smiled.

———————————

Joachim and Shorty showed up just before the evening meal and war council. Thorn was still bent over his table working on something. The two watched as the dwarf used a small set of jeweler's snips to finish winding a small wire around the hilt of the tiny sword.

Joachim bent close to stare at his work. "What have you been up to?"

Thorn pointed down at the diamond sword. "The hilt was going to be too smooth to get a good grip on. I tried to shave leather thin enough to wrap it, but it kept fraying. This wire is the best I could come up with to give it a good grip. How does it look?"

Joachim picked it up and studied it. "Nice work. Really nice. How did you manage to tuck the end underneath the coil? I can't feel where you cut the wire."

Thorn chuckled. "Family secret. Only way I can tell you is if you marry my sister. She has a beautiful beard. I can introduce you if you like. Much better catch than that whisp of a Swanmay you have been mooning over."

Joachim blushed but shook his head vigorously. "Thanks, Thorn, but I am not quite ready for a beard on my bride to be." He gave his body a fake shudder and then reached into his belt pouch to bring out a small leather loop. One side of the leather loop was tiny chain loop. Joachim slid the tiny sword into chain loop and then handed it back to Thorn.

Thorn examined the design. "Not a bad idea. I wondered how he was going to make a sheath that small."

Joachim touched the small chain loop. "It would have been too small to stitch. He had a broken chain from a necklace so he snipped off a small section and attached it to the belt."

Shorty just watched the two as they completed the gift. Thorn went to hand it to him, but Shorty shook his head. "Muches small. Me breaks. Youse gibs ta bug."

Thorn laughed. "Alright, Shorty, but I think you just do not want Skreee to know how much you really like him."

The three friends left the small house they shared with H'aor and headed for the council building. As they entered; Kisa, H'aor, and Essabeth were piling food on their plates. Skreee was in his normal spot sitting on Kisa's shoulder. After they all had food and were seated, H'aor pulled out the scouting report.

Thorn held up a hand as he finished his last bite. "Before we start going over your reports and numbers, we have a little business to attend to. Skreee, come here please."

The sprite slid down Kisa's arm to the table and walked over to stand before Thorn. The dwarf pulled out the tiny belt with the diamond sword and handed it to him. Skreee studied it carefully. There was eagerness in his expression as he put a hand to the hilt of the tiny sword. A smile consumed his small face as he pulled the sword from the chain loop. "Why are you giving me such a gift, dwarf?"

Thorn pointed to Shorty. "Ask Shorty. This was all his idea. Damn near caused a riot today. That old woman was downright mean. Wonder if her husband survived telling her to take the trade."

Skreee turned to study Shorty who refused to meet his eyes. "Why did you do this?"

Shorty stared down at his half-eaten plate of food. "No ken bees mighty warrior ifn no gots sword." Thorn cleared his throat and looked to where his axe leaned against the wall. Shorty glanced at him and muttered. "Oops."

Skreee stepped into the leather belt and pulled it up. He pulled at a tiny leather loop and the belt tightened about his waist. He returned the sword to the chain loop. It hung right beside his right hand. He looked up at Shorty. "Thank you, my ogre."

Shorty gestured to Thorn and Joachim. "Dem helps muches."

Skreee bowed to each of them. "Thank you all." Then Skreee quietly returned to Kisa and climbed up to her shoulder. His small hand kept moving to the tiny sword.

The room remained silent for a time until Shorty let out a belch and began to eat again. H'aor grinned and reopened his report.

Chapter 21
Thieves in the Night

Typerys sat in the dining room of the large home he had appropriated when he arrived in the small village. It was the nicest home he had seen and it sat right on the lake. He glanced out the large window in the dining room and watched the moonlight reflecting off the water. It was strange to see snow on the ground and see the swans swimming in the lake. The water never seemed to grow cold. He assumed it was part of the magic of the place. A magic he was determined to possess.

He turned his attention back to the three men sitting at his table eating a late meal with him. Ohrmed the mage was his ace in the hole. The man was powerful. The ways he used his power was not exactly popular with many people. The man needed a powerful sponsor to protect him when he went too far. As long as Typerys covered up his bigger mistakes and provided him some opportunities to indulge himself, the man would do anything Typerys asked. Typerys understood the man was a liability, but he was one that could be sacrificed when his magic was no longer useful.

The second man was Brome. He was a fighter. Not as good as the ogre or the dwarf, but good enough. He also liked to hurt people. Typerys was fairly certain he could meet Brome's desires as well. There would be quite a few people who needed to be dealt with before this venture was complete.

The last one was the wild card. Cord was a thief, or so he claimed. Typerys thought it more likely he was an assassin. He had no idea how good the man was, but he was Typerys' fallback plan for dealing with the village's new heroes. Typerys suspected the man was playing his own game and that was a concern. He did not like not knowing what motivated the man.

Brome was the only one still eating. The man's appetites had no limits. The big man stuffed another large bite in his mouth. The vulgar brute began to speak as he chewed, "Half the town is hungry with the snow and you manage to serve up a feast almost every night. Where do you get the food Councilor?"

Typerys looked away. "I have my sources outside this village. Information and gold can bring many good things. And I share with my loyal friends."

Ohrmed's laughter was like a sharp bark. "Loyal means as long as we stay bought."

Brome waved a fork at him. "Keep me well fed and let me fight. All a man really needs to be happy. Well, maybe a woman. But once those fools are gone, there will be plenty of them available."

Typerys winced as the conversation came back to the Swanmay's heroes again. He looked up to see Ohrmed studying him. Typerys frowned. "No, your plan is too risky."

The mage placed his napkin across his plate. "Are you sure? Four of them in one small house. One fireball would eliminate all of your problems."

Typerys shook his head. "First, you do not even know if the wards will allow you to cast your spell into one of the village's buildings. Second, are you willing to risk destroying the spell books and the wand? And finally, what will you do if the dwarf or the ogre survives the blast?"

Brome grunted. "That damn ogre is bad news."

Ohrmed shrugged. "This would not be the first place I have had to run away from. Probably will not be the last either."

Typerys slammed his palm down on the table. "I am not running from this village. I will control the magic of this place. That girl is too young and foolish to be allowed that much power."

Cord smiled. "So, we steal it. Have you got a plan for that, Typerys?"

Typerys shook his head. "Not yet. But those fools are going to lose their support soon enough. People are getting hungry and they keep bringing more mouths into the valley. When the villagers get hungry enough, they will turn to me. Those fools, as you name them, will not harm the villagers. They are too noble for that."

The thief nodded. "Might work, but how long are you willing to wait? Maybe we can find other ways to sabotage them. Let me think on it for a bit."

Typerys studied the man. "Run your ideas by me first. I do not want any missteps."

Cord smiled again. "I do not make mistakes. Mistakes get you killed. I prefer to see others die for their mistakes. Now, if you will excuse me, I want to check out a possible recruit. Willing or not." Cord stood and glanced out the window. "So many things are seen more clearly in the dark of the night." He turned and left the room.

The mage rose as well. "That one needs to be watched, Councilor. "

Typerys waved him away and turned again to stare out the window.

Ohrmed motioned to Brome and the big man grabbed another piece of meat and followed the mage out.

———————————————

Joachim sat on the roof of the Hall of Healing staring across the village. He liked the tiny place a lot. Well, he had to admit that it was mostly Essabeth that he liked a lot. But the village was not bad either. It was small though. Being a thief here was not going to work out well for him. Getting caught would not improve his standing with Essabeth at all. But being a thief was all he knew. He was a loner that was good for little more than taking care of himself. On the other hand, saving those men the other night had felt really good. He just did not see any way to keep himself fed rescuing prisoners and slaves. Orcs never had many coins, dead or alive.

He stared from his vantage point on the roof towards Essabeth's place. He shook his head. He had to get his head straight. There was little chance that she would find him interesting. But it did not stop him from hoping.

He rose to his feet. It was time to head to bed. He turned towards the stairs when he heard the sound of Skreee's wings beating hard. The sprite seemed to be headed towards him. He scanned the sky, but could not spot the tiny beast with the moon obscured by the clouds.

Joachim jumped as Skreee spoke from the air behind him. "You must come and help me tonight."

Before Joachim could turn around, the sprite landed on his shoulder and sat down. "Long trip to find you. You must help me."

Joachim sat back down on the edge of the roof. "Long trip from where?"

The sprite pointed off to the north. "Camp where orcs keep prisoners that dig."

Joachim pointed to the house he and the others were sleeping in. "Go wake the others. This will take everyone."

Skreee shook his head. "No, just you to help me with this thing."

Joachim shook his head. "What do you expect me to do? Take on a whole camp of orcs?"

Skreee lifted from Joachim's shoulder and spun to face him. "My ogre cannot do this thing. The dwarf cannot do this. Even the Elf and his magic cannot do this."

Joachim was growing curious now. "Why not?"

Skreee pulled out the tiny blue sword at his waist. "They would fight. If we fight, the archer might die."

Joachim held up a hand. "Slow down. What Archer? And what do you need me to do?"

Skreee flew small circles in frustration. "Moon archer. You must open the lock on his cage so he can be free. No fighting. Sneak in, open lock, run away. This is thing you can do that the others cannot."

Joachim's face was thoughtful. "Okay, that sounds reasonable, but why are we saving this archer of yours?"

Skreee pointed with his sword at the sky. "I tell you this already. He is touched by the moon. He must be free of the cage to do what is needed."

Joachim slowly got to his feet. "You want me to spend half the night slipping through snow covered trails to pick a lock so you can free some archer that is whatever 'touched by the moon' means?"

Skreee smiled at him. "Yes. That is my plan."

"I think your plan is kind of crazy."

Skreee flew up to hover before Joachim's face. "I came for you when Pretty One asked. I wanted to let you die. I will ask as Pretty One did. Please."

Joachim signed. "Fine. I just know this is a bad idea. But after this, you will not be able to claim I owe you for the orcs anymore. I will meet you by the north side of the village soon. I have to get ready."

––––––––––––––––––

The trip through the northern peaks was easier that Joachim expected. They followed a different trail on the western side of the two peaks. The snow was deeper than Joachim liked, but it was not icy underneath and he made good time. It was entirely unfair that the sprite got to fly above the mess though. This trail came down into a different valley than the one where they had saved the woodcutters. Joachim could not make out much about this valley in the darkness. Skreee seemed confident about where he was going. Joachim did his best to keep up.

It was well past the middle of the night when Joachim caught sight of a pair of fires ahead. Neither fire was that small. He came to a stop. He called out softly. "How many orcs are out there, Skreee? You said this was not going to be a fight."

Skreee landed on Joachim's shoulder and spoke into his ear. "There are many orcs near the fires. They like to stay warm." He placed his small hand under Joachim's chin and turned the thief's head to the left of the fires. "The cages are that way. The orcs do not care if the diggers are warm or not. Only one guard is there. He is for me."

Joachim nodded and began to work his way to the left, well away from the fires. He took his time and moved slowly through the snow. It was much easier to remain quiet in the snow than it would have been in the underbrush. Skreee disappeared ahead. Joachim could only hope that the sprite knew what he was doing. He was confident he could stay out of sight in the darkness, but come morning his tracks would be easy to follow in the snow.

Joachim was still working his way along the line that he thought the sprite had shown him when he heard the something fall to the ground. Whatever it was, it was fairly large. Then Skreee's voice whispered in his ear. "You go too far. This way."

Joachim adjusted his path a little to the right and hissed at the sprite. "What of the guard?"

Joachim could hear pride in Skreee's voice as he replied. "It sleeps."

Joachim continued to move forward carefully. He sucked in a breath when his hand came down on the stock of a crossbow. His fingers moved lightly up the weapon. It was spanned and loaded. Joachim eased the bolt from the weapon and dropped it to into the snow. His hand slid to the right and felt the shoulder of a warm body. Joachim's hand jerked back quickly as he went for his knife.

A soft almost melodious voice came from the far side of the body. "It sleeps. Your small friend is quite skilled. He had two of his tiny arrows into it before it even realized it was in danger."

Joachim considered the voice. The rhythm of the words was unusual and there was an accent that he had never heard before. "Who are you?"

The voice came again. "I am the one your small friend brought you to save. I am known by some as the Archer. I am called slave and digger by the orcs. But, my name is Roiland. If you can free me from this cage, I would call you friend."

Joachim began to move carefully around the body on the ground. "I do not know anything about you, but no one deserves what the orcs do to people. You are welcome to come to our village. We take in a lot of refugees."

The voice seemed to consider his offer. "I am not sure that your people will want me. But that is something that we can discuss in the light of day. My cage is a few more steps in front of you. That will bring you to the back of the cage. Come around to the left. There is a lock on the door. My feet are chained together as well. Unless that orc has the key, I do not think you can free me. But your small friend seemed to think otherwise."

Joachim grinned into the darkness. "I do not think we need a key."

Joachim moved forward and found the bars of the cage. He followed them around the cage. This cage was much sturdier that the ones used to hold the prisoners in the logging camp. Joachim's fingers found a large lock that held the door closed. It dangled from a chain stretched between the bars of the cage and the cage door. As Joachim's fingers moved lightly over the lock, he recognized the general type of lock he was dealing with. His biggest concern was the rust he felt on the lock. If the mechanism inside was as rusty, he might have trouble forcing it open with his slender wires.

Joachim's hand moved to the back of his belt. He pulled out a small cloth bag and opened it. He reached in with two fingers and pulled out a pinch of fine powder which he dropped into the lock's keyhole. The strangers voice came to him softly as he returned the bag to its hiding place. "What did you just do?"

Joachim answered without looking up. "The powder is very fine. It helps the mechanism to move more freely. Oil is a better solution but it is messy and it affects my grip on the wires." Joachim's fingers slid down to his left boot and came up with two stiff wires. He continued to hold the lock in his left hand as his right guided the two stiff wires into the keyhole.

Joachim alternated wiggling each wire deeper into the lock as he felt for the mechanism. He began to twist the wires, but stopped when something did not feel right. He moved the lower wire one more time and then grinned. The young thief turned the wires counterclockwise and the lock dropped open. The voice came from within the cage once more. "A very useful skill. It might be worth learning if you would be willing to teach it."

Joachim slipped one end of the chain from the lock and slowly unwrapped the chain from the bars of the door. He piled it to one side of the door. He pulled the bag of powder from his belt once more and rubbed some into the hinges before opening the door.

The figure within slid forward until a pair of light boots slid out the open door. A single chain wound around each of the prisoner's ankles. The chain was secured to each ankle with another lock. There were no more than a couple inches of slack between the two legs. Whoever the prisoner was, they were not going to be moving quickly. Joachim used a little more of his powder on the two locks. His fingers moved slowly over the locks. These were simple locks and he had them open quickly.

Joachim stepped back and the figure within stood. From the voice, Joachim knew the prisoner was male. The man was not much taller than Joachim and seemed to be even more slender. Joachim could not make out any other details, the figure seemed to blend perfectly into the night. The voice spoke again. "I owe you a great debt. One which I will pay. Now if you will let me past."

Joachim stepped back a bit uncertain what to do next. "We need to get out of here. We have a long way to go before sunrise. We will be too easy to track in the snow."

The figure moved past Joachim and knelt beside the sleeping orc. He heard the voice speaking to the orc. "Your weapon is in terrible condition. How any creature could so mistreat a bow." Joachim could hear the man removing the quiver from the orc. Joachim sensed it when the figure rose to stand above the orc once more. The man spoke again. "You deserve death for the things you have done. If you were awake, I could give you the justice that you deserve. It saddens me that I must let you live to hurt others once more."

Joachim hissed, "We need to leave."

The figure turned to face him. "I cannot not leave until we open one more cage. This one will be easier."

Joachim shook his head in the darkness. "More people will make us easier to track. Probably slower too."

The voice sounded calm as it responded. "We cannot save the men locked in the mine. But I cannot leave the woman or the four children. If you will not help, then I will do what I can to save them alone."

Joachim hesitated. "Woman? Children? Where are they?

The voice replied. Their cage is close. They are kept separate to force the men to comply."

Joachim stepped forward. "Okay, show me."

The voice hesitated. "Please do not try to touch the woman even to aid her. She has not been treated kindly. She will fear you or any male. And do not shame her by speaking of what I just told you. Her control is fragile and she must be strong for the children."

Joachim cursed at the man's words. He did not like what he had heard nor was he really sure how to help the woman.

The figure spun and began to move. Joachim was impressed. The man moved without sound. Joachim was not sure even he could move that quietly. Skreee flew to Joachim's shoulder from the direction of the fires. He whispered softly. "The orcs have been drinking. They will not interfere. We should still hurry."

Joachim moved to follow the dark figure. As he moved, he heard the soft thrum of a crossbow. He tensed but heard the same voice from in front of him. "The guard will not give us problems anymore."

Joachim moved towards the voice. His foot hit something large on the ground. Joachim's hands reached down to find another body on the ground. He ran his finger over the form. There was a bolt in the orc's throat. His other hand found a small pouch with coins inside. Without thinking, he untied the pouch and slid it in his boot.

Joachim moved forward again and found the second cage. This one was secured with rope instead of chain. Joachim pulled his knife and sliced the layers of tope. He quickly pulled the rope from around the bars and dropped it to the ground. Joachim remembered the warning and backed away from the cage.

There were softly whispered words between the man he had freed earlier and those within the cage. The figure backed up and the cage door opened slowly. The figure whispered to Joachim. "Take the lead and move slowly but steadily towards your people. The woman and children will follow you."

Joachim nodded. "What of you?"

The figure chuckled. "I will guard our rear. If the night is good to me, some of the orcs might just catch up to us."

Joachim shuddered at the menace he heard in that response. He turned and with Skreee's help found his way back to his own trail through the snow. He began to lead the way back up the mountain towards the gap he had crossed through on his way here. Once he was headed in the right direction, Skreee disappeared into the darkness.

The night on the mountain was cold and not nearly long enough as far as Joachim was concerned. The woman and children did not move very quickly. The eastern horizon was turning pink as they reached the top of the rise. He stared down into the valley where he could see the lights of the village far below. He turned back to check on the woman and the children. They were still moving but it was obviously a struggle for them. They were breathing hard. He hoped they could make it.

Joachim spoke softly despite his concern. "We must hurry. Once it is light, they will not be able to miss our trail in the snow."

A calm voice that Joachim now recognized came from somewhere in the darkness behind the woman. "Be at ease noble rescuer. You have time now. There were only four orcs on our trail."

Joachim started to respond but then paused to ponder the stranger's words. "Were?"

The stranger spoke again, "They will not carry word of our passage back to the camp. This bow is a poor tool, but it served its purpose."

Joachim voice trembled a bit. "You took out four of them? At the same time?"

The response faded as the voice moved back towards the orc camp. "I had to chase two of them. This bow does not reload quickly."

Joachim shook his head and turned to continue down into the valley. He was beginning to worry about who he was leading into their home.

The sun was up when Joachim crossed through the wards. It felt good to be safe again. Except, something about the wards felt off this time. Joachim raised a hand to pause those following him. He looked around in the weak morning light. Something was wrong.

A raspy voice came from the trees ahead of him. "I am impressed, young thief. Not many would have noticed me. But the wards on this place do not really like my presence." A scrawny man stepped out onto the trail about a dozen yards ahead of Joachim.

Joachim's hand went to his knife and pulled it from its sheath. "Who are you and what do you want?"

The man smiled. "I go by Cord in this place. But names have little importance. They are but a tool to be used and discarded. As for what I want, there are many things I want. Your pretty knife, that woman cowering behind you and even the lives of your friends in the village. The question is, what are you willing to let me have? And what must I take from you?"

Joachim stared at the man in confusion. "I do not understand."

The man grinned. "Laryn to ukal."

Joachim's expression hardened. He shook his head as he retreated a step. "You are not my master. No man is. I am not guild. I chose to be free."

The man drew out a short sword and stepped forward. "You will swear yourself to me and help me take down your friends, or you can fight me. Either way I will take the woman and your pretty knife as my own. The only question is whether you live or die."

Joachim glanced behind him to see the woman standing very still in front of the four young boys. She stood there despite the fear he could see on her face. Joachim sighed and turned back to the man who called himself Cord. "We fight then. I will not let you have her and I will not betray my friends."

The man's raspy voice came again, "Then come to me, boy. Let us see if that knife can save you."

Joachim began to move forward when he heard a soft melodious voice from behind him. "Hold, friend. He baits you into a fight you cannot win."

Joachim's pride was stung. He did not take his eyes from the man before him but he raised his voice in protest. "I can fight."

Cord froze before him. There was a look of fear in his eyes. From the corner of his eye, Joachim saw the loaded crossbow move up beside him.

The voice spoke calmly. "I do not question your bravery. Your response to his request proved you have honor. Now, look closely at the blade he carries."

Joachim stared as the man named Cord growled out, "Stay out of this, elf. Your kind has no business meddling here."

Joachim finally noticed the wet gleam on the edge of the man's sword blade. He turned his head to thank the ex-prisoner for this warning. Joachim's eyes widened as they took in the dark skin and pointed ears of his new companion. The words Drow and Dark Elf flashed through his mind, but he could nor reconcile them with the man who had insisted on saving the woman and children. Would a Drow actually risk his life to protect their rear? He could simply have disappeared into the darkness and left them to fend for themselves. His thoughts jumped to the village and his friends What have I done? And yet, Skreee sat on the dark elf's shoulder glaring at the human down the trail.

Joachim blinked in confusion as the dark elf continued without taking his eyes from the man before him. "His blade is poisoned. He never intended you to live. This was all a game such as my own kind would play."

Joachim turned to look back at the man before them. Before Joachim even realized the danger, the man dropped his sword and his hands thrust forward. The dark elf shoved Joachim to the side and dropped to one knee. Joachim hit the ground hard but his sharp eyes still caught the flash of steel as two throwing knives fly flew past. One went through the air where he had just been standing while the second flew over the head of the dark elf. Joachim heard the bow thrum. He turned to see the man Cord stumble back with a bolt in his stomach.

The dark elf began to walk forward, easily spanning the crossbow. He reached for the quiver on his belt. "Take up your sword while you can, assassin. Be quick or die."

Despite the bolt, the man moved quickly to snatch up the sword. Before he could raise it, a second bolt sank into his chest. The sword slipped from his fingers to fall on the snow now red with blood. His mouth opened to speak, but he coughed and more blood came from his mouth. The dark elf stood before him as he slid to the ground. "A fitting end for one so evil."

Joachim slowly rose to his feet. He stood behind the dark elf, his hand in a tight grip around the hilt of his knife. The elf before him tensed for a moment and then knelt. He placed the crossbow on the snow and picked up the short sword. He carefully wiped both sides of the blade on the tunic of the dead man. Then he plunged the blade into the snow. "Judge me by my skin or judge me by my actions. The choice is yours. You freed the woman and the children. I will not raise a weapon against you."

Joachim stood confused. "I have only stories of your people to go by. Most are stories meant to scare little children into being good. Nothing that I have heard would explain why you just saved me. Or why the wards did not react to your presence."

Joachim stood watching as the dark elf cleaned the blade a second time on a different spot on the tunic. The dark elf laughed softly as he laid the short sword beside the crossbow. "A Drow that is not evil is even harder to believe in than a thief who is good."

Joachim was still puzzling over what to do when he heard a voice from behind him. One of the young boys stepped forward. "Please do not hurt him. He shared his food with us. He kept us as safe as he could."

Joachim stared down at his knife and then slid it back into its sheath. "I cannot judge you. Too many pieces of my own life I have not figured out. It is Essabeth's valley, let her figure this one out." Joachim continued to stare at the dark elf's back and then sighed. "Thank you. Roiland, was it? Thank you for saving my life just now. I do not know this Cord. I might have seen him in the village, but I am not sure."

Roiland stood slowly and turned around. "That one was evil and has been for a long time. I could sense it in him." He took off the quiver that still held two bolts and dropped it beside the crossbow. "You should keep that sword. It has no magic, but it is good steel. You need something with more reach than that knife."

Joachim glanced down at the sword. "Knives are all I know how to use. I can fight with one or I can throw them. But I have never held a sword before."

Roiland bent down and ran his fingers over the hilt. "Short swords are faster and easier to control. They do not have the reach, but they are less likely to be overextended. If your people do not kill me, then I will teach you how to use it. I owe you that and more for my freedom." Roiland looked up to where Skreee now sat on a branch above them. "I owe you as well mighty warrior."

Roiland moved back from the bow and sword. "Take the weapons, young thief. It is better that I enter your village unarmed and as a prisoner. Keep the bow on me so your friends do not become afraid."

Joachim moved forward and picked up the short sword. "My name is Joachim. I do not think we got around to that back in the orc camp. I agree about no weapons to start. But I will not bring you in looking like you did something wrong. You deserve better than that."

Joachim stepped to the dead man's body and reached for the sword's sheath. Roiland spoke from behind him, "Not that, Joachim. I believe it is where the poison is stored. If you place the sword back in the sheath, you will recoat the blade."

Joachim pulled his hand back from the sheath and stood. He bent and grabbed the crossbow. "I am going ahead to get my friends. Can you follow slowly with the others? I would rather my friends meet you outside of the village."

The dark elf nodded. "As you wish, Joachim. Please make sure at least one woman comes back with you. It will make things easier."

Joachim turned to the trail down into the valley. "Skreee. Go get Kisa and Essabeth. Have them bring our friends to the edge of the village. Hurry please."

Skreee whooped. "Yes, Pretty One. She will be proud of us." The sprite soared above the trees and headed straight towards the village.

Roiland gave Joachim an inquisitive look. "Pretty One?"

Joachim shook his head and headed down the trail with the sword in one hand and the crossbow in the other. "It is complicated. If we live though this, I will tell you the story." With that, Joachim began to jog through the snow heading for the valley floor.

Chapter 22
Hard Choices

Joachim came out of the trees to the west of the small river. The sun was in his eyes as he turned to look for his friends. Five people were walking towards him out of the morning glare. He smiled at the strangeness of the tall ogre walking side by side with the dwarf. The difference in their heights was almost comical. It made as little sense as the story that he was about to tell. He hoped they could find some humor in his tale because he had yet to find words that did not make him sound like a fool. He hardly understood his own reasons for trusting Roiland.

Shorty walked up and "gently" patted Joachim on the shoulder. Joachim felt like his shoulder was being knocked out of its socket. But Shorty was just being friendly. Thorn stood back staring at him. "Any chance you can make more sense than that fool sprite? I could use a good explanation for why you were in the peaks last night. And where did you get a crossbow and sword?"

Joachim looked around the circle of his friends. "Well, it is kind of like this. I mean we were supposed to. You see, Skreee asked me to help him and things just kind of got out of hand."

Thorn looked from Joachim to where Skreee sat of Kisa's shoulder. "So much fir an intelligent answer. More babbling. I should know better than to ask questions with the companions I keep."

Essabeth patted Thorn's shoulder as she walked past him to stand beside Joachim. "The wards woke me this morning. They pulsed

234

twice, Joachim. One was a feeling of welcoming. The second was bad. Do you know what either of those meant?"

Joachim nodded. "Sort of, at least the bad one I do. The other, maybe?"

Thorn muttered, "Bah!" and stomped past Joachim to stare up his back trail.

Kisa interrupted, "Let me try." She stepped up before Joachim and asked, "Where did Skreee lead you last night?"

Joachim pointed to the northwest. "The orcs have more prisoners back that way. They have this lot digging for something. Skreee wanted me to save his friend. He said please so I went along."

Shorty looked at his friend. "Youse go fight orc ta save peoples? Not lets Shorty come too?"

Joachim shook his head. "No, Shorty. That was the whole point. This was not supposed to be a fight. We were going to sneak in and then sneak away afterwards."

Joachim winced at the sarcasm in Thorn's voice. "How did that work out for you?"

H'aor shot an exasperated look at Thorn and motioned to the weapons in Joachim's hands. "And?"

Joachim held up the sword. "This, uh, fight happened after we got back in the valley. I think that was the bad thing that Essabeth felt. The bow. Skreee put one orc to sleep. His friend used it. He, well, he killed a bunch of orcs with it. So really, I was only in the one fight after we came back to the valley and that was not with orcs."

Joachim looked into his friends faces. "Okay, that did not help any."

Kisa pointed to the sword. "Why not start with that. Who did you fight?"

Joachim stared down at the blade. "There was an assassin. He called himself Cord. He wanted me to join him, but not really. He was going to kill me with this sword. It had poison on it."

Kisa looked a little confused but asked, "You defeated him?"

Joachim shook his head again. "Yes. No. I mean, Skreee's archer friend, his name is Roiland, he shot Cord before he could poison me."

Kisa smiled at Joachim. "And where is this archer friend of Skreee's?"

Skreee launched himself into the air. "I go get him, Pretty One." Kisa watched the sprite fly off and then turned her gaze back to Joachim.

Joachim pointed back up the trail. "He is back there with the other folks we rescued." Kisa started to open her mouth again. Joachim smiled. "Sorry. Roiland wanted to save this woman and some kids that were in another cage. He is back there with them. The woman, she does not like men right now. That is why I had Skreee come get you."

Shorty turned and started to move towards the trail. "Kid? Me ken helps."

Kisa raised her voice, "No, Shorty. She does not know you yet. Best to let me meet her first."

Shorty paused with a sad look on his face.

Essabeth asked quietly, "Why did you come down before them? You could have escorted them into the village."

Joachim looked around at his friends. "Well, Skreee's friend is... Well, he is not what you might expect. He is well, different."

Thorn marched back over to stand beside the nervous young thief. "Different how?"

Joachim stepped away from Thorn. "He is sort of a Drow."

All eyes turned to stare at Joachim. Joachim dropped his gaze to stare down at his feet. "You know, like dark elf kind of Drow. But he is really nice and the wards did not reject him. I think that was maybe the good thing the wards felt. He saved all our lives and…" Joachim's voice trailed off at the looks of disbelief on his friends faces. "I should have just let Skreee explain it all."

———————————

Kisa stared down Thorn outside of the locked room. "I am going in to see him. Someone needs to talk to him before the Council meeting."

Thorn shook his head. "That is not going to happen, Priestess. I am not risking you in a room alone with a damn Drow. There has never been one that could be trusted."

A sad voice came from the far side of the room. "Neber bees good ogre neither. All ogre eats peoples."

Thorn spun to face Shorty who was sitting on the floor. "That is…"

Kisa smiled at her friend. "Different?"

Thorn glared at her. "You are not listening. That is a Drow warrior in there."

Shorty spoke up again. "Me talks wid kids. Kids like dark man. Says him share food when dem bees hungry. Him gets hurt protect dem. Maybeso him bees good peoples."

Kisa placed her hand on Thorn's shoulder. "I know you want to keep me safe. But that woman trusts him. She went through hell at the hands of the orcs, but she still trusts him. A dark elf. That says a lot. I am going in."

Thorn glowered at her. "Take out your mace. If he moves towards you hit him with it. And you yell for help. Give me a good excuse to use my axe on him."

Kisa smiled and unlocked the door. "I will be fine, Thorn. You and Shorty are right here." Kisa opened the door and stepped inside.

She stood staring at the elf seated on the floor in the far corner of the small room. He did not look particularly dangerous, but that really did not prove anything. She cleared her throat. "I am Kisa. I am a Priestess of Akka. I serve her and care for the needs of the people of this village. Skree calls you the Archer. Joachim said your name is Roiland?" Kisa saw the look of wariness that came into his eyes as she told him that she was a Priestess.

The man remained where he was sitting. He studied her carefully. "You are the one that the small warrior calls Pretty One?"

Kisa blushed slightly. "Yes, Skree has a somewhat unique view of things." Kisa met his gaze. She felt magic was over her. It was not an attack, but she felt like she was being somehow measured by the elf's gaze. "What did you do?"

The elf appeared to be mesmerized by what he saw. "No, the small one has named you correctly. His sight is true. If anything, he has understated things."

Kisa glared at him more to hide how uncomfortable his words made her. "My looks are not that impressive and you gain nothing with your flattery."

The elf shook his head. "Your looks are indeed nice but that is not of what I speak. Your spirit glows with a goodness I have seldom seen in any save a child."

Kisa stared at him. "My Spirit?"

The elf cocked his head to the side. "Perhaps the word aura would have been a better choice. The magic you felt is an ability that I gained when I became the Archer. The Archer must be able to see the evil within. To recognize evil like that of the assassin, one must also be able to recognize goodness. You truly care about these people you serve. You protect them like a mother does her children."

Kisa was at a loss for words. "Thank you. Sometime I would like to speak to you more about being the Archer. But for now, our leader has asked me to cast a spell upon you. One that can detect evil in you. I want your permission first."

The elf nodded. "You may cast your spell. I promise I will not cry out at the pain."

Kisa looked confused. "There will be no pain. Why would I hurt you?"

The elf shrugged. "Where I come from, all Priestesses serve the Dark Queen. Every spell they cast, even those that heal, come with great pain. It is their way."

Kisa frowned. "It is not the way of Akka. I only wish to detect evil. It will help us to defend you before the council."

He smiled at her. "Cast your spell then, Priestess. I do not think it will matter. Those like your dwarven friend will believe what they will no matter the truth of who I am."

Kisa smiled back at him as she raised her Holy Symbol. "Thorn is a bit touchy these days. He is responsible for protecting all of us. Shorty already put the dwarf in his place. Thorn just needs time to admit it."

The elf looked incredulous. "The ogre? He stood up for me?"

Kisa laughed. "You protected the children. Shorty will not let anyone harm you now."

The elf nodded. "Your ogre is very special indeed. Now cast your spell, Priestess."

Kisa raised her Symbol and began to chant. A glow surrounded the sheath of wheat in her hand. It moved towards the elf sitting on the floor. As it wrapped itself around the dark elf the glow went from its normal golden color to a pure white light that illuminated the room. Kisa lowered her arm. She stared at the man seated before her. "That was not what I expected. The light carried no hint of a shadow. I have never seen the light turn white like that."

The Drow stared up at her. "It was the glow of moonlight. I know it well. But I am far from without shadows. Those of the light have no reason to fear me though. I am Roiland. I am the Archer. Although without Oikea Lakko, that title has little meaning."

Kisa stared at him. "Those words. I do not know them."

He closed his eyes and rested his head against the wall. "Oikea Lakko is the bow of the Archer. Oikea is alive. The bow speaks to me. It chose me as the next Archer. Despite my heritage, the bow chose me to defend the meek. But she was taken from me."

Kisa considered her words carefully. "I cannot help you find the bow, but there are many here who need defending. If we can convince the Council, maybe you can still be the Archer."

He opened his eyes. Kisa realized that they were a pale violet in color. How strange she thought. "Go then, Priestess, and see if your Council will allow me to live and serve."

The Council chamber was full. Voices were raised as people strove to make their opinions heard. Finally, Shorty had his fill of the arguing and the noise. He stood and raised his voice. "Fights too muches. No talks all same time."

Essabeth stood. "I agree. We do not normally have this many in our meeting, but this is an unusual circumstance. Please, take turns and be polite. And yes, Councilor Typerys. I see you. You may speak first."

Typerys stood and turned so that most everyone in the room could see his face. "You and your new commander have brought too many people into this village already. We cannot feed the people we have. People, children, are going hungry. And yet, you keep bringing more. Now, of all the foolish moves, you endanger us all by bringing a Drow into our midst. Do you really expect us to accept him without fear of the evil his kind bring?"

Kisa rose and stood quietly. Essabeth waited until Typerys sat and then turned to her. "Yes, Priestess?"

Kisa fought to control her anger. Her gaze locked on Typerys and she frowned. "Which of the families we brought here would you have turned away, Councilor? Which people would you have condemned to be slaves of the orcs?" She turned to face Essabeth. "As you asked me, Swanmay, I cast a detect evil on Roiland. Akka's spell detected no evil in him. The spell responded in a way that I have never seen before. I spoke with Old Mara. She thinks he may be a paladin."

Typerys laughed and slapped his palm against the table. "Really, Priestess. A Drow paladin that uses a bow? What will you come up with next? Does he ride a unicorn into battle?"

Kisa gave him a harsh look. "He has done more to protect innocents than I have ever seen you do, Councilor."

Typerys rose to his feet to argue the point. Before he could speak, the room erupted with the sound of bickering.

Essabeth raised her voice, "Enough! The wards that protect this valley also welcomed him. Not accepted, but welcomed."

Essabeth motioned to Thorn. "Bring the Drow Roiland in please, commander. I would like to ask him some questions. Maybe we can all learn something here."

Thorn nodded towards the door and two rangers walked the prisoner into the room. Roiland's hands were tied together. He was led to a seat near Essabeth.

Essabeth nodded her head. "I apologize for the bonds, but there are some who fear your presence." Roiland simply nodded and Essabeth continued. "How did you come to be a prisoner of the orcs?"

Roiland met her gaze. "I was the protector of an area to the west of these mountains. It was near where the orcs used to live. I traded my freedom to save the life of a young woman. I was given to the orcs as a slave by the being that chased the orcs from their lands."

Essabeth frowned. "What has the power to chase several orc tribes across the mountains?"

Roiland looked around the room before he responded. "An army of undead and something that is powerful enough to control it. I never found out what was behind the undead. I only know that it is powerful."

H'aor stood. "You are sure of this?"

Essabeth cleared her throat, "Later, my friend. You may ask more when we have finished here."

Thorn leaned forward to glare at the Drow. "You said that they were making the prisoners dig? Dig for what? There has not been gold in the mountains for centuries. Do they seek some treasure? An item of power? Is there another danger to this valley?"

Roiland met Thorn's gaze without blinking. "Nothing that you would deem a treasure. But it has value to someone. They have us digging for bones. Large, ancient bones. I believe they are from a very old dragon."

Voices sprang up from around the room. Thorn slammed his hand down on the table making it jump. The room went silent again as the dwarf stood and glared around the room. Then he turned back to Roiland. "What use have they for a dead dragon?"

Roiland's face turned grim. "The orcs have no use for it. But someone does. I think they hope to trade it. Either to get back into their homeland or for the power they need to survive on this side of the mountains."

Thorn nodded. "If whatever controls the undead across the mountains can also animate the dragon, we could all be in trouble."

Thorned turned to Essabeth. "Swanmay, when we entered your valley, we fought undead in the southern pass. The buckthorn we mentioned was infested with them. We never mentioned them before because we did not see a connection to the orcs."

Essabeth nodded. "My father was right then. There is a much bigger problem that faces our world. Whatever that power is, it did not want this valley revived."

Thorn gestured towards the Drow. "As much as it pains me to admit it, I see no reason not to allow the Elf to remain. He has shown nothing but honor in the camps and since his escape. And I guess if there can be good ogres, why not a dark elf?"

Shorty smiled happily at the dwarf.

Typerys stood, his face red with indignation. "You cannot let an armed Drow run around this village. The people will not stand for it."

Thorn frowned. "Is there anything that you do not like to complain about, Typerys? Only things he has hurt so far are orcs."

Essabeth rapped her knuckles on the table. "Enough, gentlemen. Roiland, would you swear to carry and use no weapon as long as you remain in the valley without my express permission?"

Roiland stood. "You have my word, Lady." Roiland glanced over at Joachim and then asked. "Would you consider a wooden stave about the length of my arm to be a weapon?"

Typerys snapped at him. "What would you use that for?"

Roiland ignored him as he stared at Essabeth. "I promised to teach Joachim to use the short sword. The stave would only be used in his training. He can hold onto it when we are not practicing."

Essabeth's eyes turned to study the young thief. Then she nodded. "You have my permission to train, Joachim." Essabeth rose. "We are finished here tonight."

The snow began to fall in earnest as the meeting ended.

————————————————

The next morning, Joachim met Roiland in a plaza in the south-eastern corner of the village. Joachim stared at the smoothed piece of wood in the dark elf's hands. "Where did that come from?"

Roiland smiled. "Your dwarven friend is quite handy with wood. He fashioned it last night. Apparently, he likes the idea of you learning to use the sword."

Joachim stood in the slowly falling snow thinking. So, what is Thorn up to now? Then he turned to Roiland and said, "Fine, what do we do first? It is cold out here."

Roiland smiled. "First you learn how to hold the sword. It is not a knife. Then, I think you will not be cold for long. Your dwarven friend suggested that you sweat a lot. He also liked the idea of a few bruises to make the lessons stick.

Joachim grumbled. "Some friend."

They began with a series of stretches. Roiland and Joachim worked through the morning as the snow continued to fall. By midday, Joachim was tired, hungry, and more than a little sore. He understood the sore muscles in his arms. He was using them in ways that were new. But the soreness in his legs made little sense to him. He walked and ran way too much for sore leg muscles.

Roiland slapped him on the back. "Three days we work and one you shall rest."

Joachim shook his head. "I will be so stiff tomorrow. I do not think I will be able to move. And Thorn will have the bruises he asked for."

Roiland smiled. "That is something that I can help with. Stand still, Joachim."

Joachim watched in interest as Roiland stood before him. The Dark Elf seemed to relax and a look of peace spread across his face. Roiland reached up and placed his hands against Joachim's chest. Joachim felt warmth enter his body and spread to all of the places that were sore and bruised. His pain faded and was gone.

Joachim blinked in surprise. "You can heal like Kisa?"

Roiland shook his head. "No, Kisa uses spells to invoke the power of her Goddess. I can." He paused in confusion. "My teacher never named this power. I only know that each day I can lay hands on an injured person and provide minor healing. But only twice each day."

Joachim turned to begin gathering up the training equipment. "I am not sure my sore muscles are the best use of your gift. But I do thank you."

They walked back towards the center of the village as the snow continued to drift down.

––––––––––––––––––––

Snow continued to fall as the days past. Roiland spent much of his time training with Joachim and helping in the Hall of Healing. He arrived early one morning as Joachim had a day off from his training. Kisa was cleaning the kitchen when he arrived. He took the cleaning rags and bucket of water from her and began to scrub the stones of the floor.

Kisa stared at him with a wry smile. "You must have more important things to do than help to clean this place."

Roiland chuckled. "Joachim does not train today. I am not allowed to carry a bow to hunt. This work is as good as any other and I enjoy your presence."

Kisa smiled as she turned back to the dirty bowls sitting on the sideboard. She took them to another bucket of water and began to clean them. They worked in silence for a time.

A child's voice came from the main hall. "Priestess? Anyone? Please help."

Kisa left the last bowl in the bucket and dried her hands on her skirt as she moved towards the voice. She felt Roiland's presence at her back. In the main hall, a young boy was holding his arm against his chest with a look of pain on his face.

Kisa moved forward and gently examined the arm. "What happened, my young friend?

The boy sniffed bravely. "I was running and slipped on the ice. I tried to catch myself when I slipped. But now my wrist hurts real bad."

Kisa reached for her Holy Symbol but then she realized it was hanging on a hook in the kitchen. She had placed it there to keep it out of the water as she cleaned. "Give me a second and I will heal this for you. My Holy Symbol is in the kitchen."

Roiland reached out his hand. "Let me, Priestess."

Kisa nodded and watched as his dark features went still. She could sense the profound feelings of peace as he reached out and lay his hands on the boy's arm. The pain vanished from the boy's face. "Thanks, mister. That was great." The boy tugged his arm free and hurried towards the door.

Kisa raised her voice. "Be careful not to slip and fall again." The boy waved and ran out of the Hall.

Kisa stared at Roiland. "Joachim mentioned that you could heal. But I had no idea you had so much power. Might I ask which God or Goddess grants your healing?"

Roiland stared down at his hands. "The one who's power I channel has no name. He just is. He does not speak to me. I know only his intermediary. The Lady of Silences. Even she does not speak to me. I can tell you no more than that. I sense when the Lady of Silences has work for me and that is enough."

Kisa smiles at him. "Faith is usually enough."

———————————

Typerys stood before the dining room window staring out at the waters of the lake. He had an intense frown on his face. Ohrmed's voice came from behind him. "Your schemes are not working, Councilor. The people even accept the Drow now. And the assassin has been missing for weeks now."

Typerys grunted. "Have you found Cord?"

The mage was silent for a moment. "No, but the thief wears his sword now. Perhaps the boy killed him."

"That boy was no match for Cord. It had to be that Drow. He is dangerous and he has allied himself with the Swanmay."

Typerys could hear the excitement in the mage's voice. "I could…"

Typerys turned with a growl. "No fireballs. We discussed this already."

Ohrmed grinned. He liked to bait Typerys. The man was just too easy. "You know what he wants, to help you with your problem."

Typerys frowned and turned back to the window. "Such a waste. She is quite exceptional. Make the deal Mage. And then make sure it happens without anyone pinning it on us."

Typerys heard the mage rise and leave the room. He stared out the window. He was tired of snow falling. At least it seemed to be lighter today.

———————————

Joachim sat on the fence rail outside of Essabeth's home. She came out of her door and stopped to stare at him. "I take it Roiland is not giving you new bruises today?"

Joachim grinned. "He thinks I need a day off from time to time to contemplate the next beating he is going to give me."

At Essabeth's soft laugh, Joachim seemed to relax. He waved his hand through the slowly falling snow. "How much snow does this place get? It does not build up much near the lake, but the passes are all blocked now."

Essabeth watched him for a moment and sighed. "The warmth of the lake keeps the snow from building up here in the valley. The passes will be blocked for another moon or so. Then you can be moving on, Joachim."

Joachim looked up in surprise. "No, it is not that. I was just, well, curious."

Essabeth came and leaned against the fence. "Listen, Joachim. I like you. But you are wasting your time. You will move on and I will not."

Joachim looked hurt and confused. "I do not understand."

Essabeth turned to face him. "You are a thief and a good one from what I can tell. There is nothing for you here. This village is too small for a thief to operate in. You will move on to do what good thieves do. I cannot move on." She held up her arms so the two bracers were visible. "When I accepted these, I bound myself to this valley. I cannot leave it. Ever."

Joachim reached out a finger to touch the bracer on her left arm. "You said that Swanmays lived all across the land."

Essabeth smiled sadly. "Those born Swanmays can move across the land. My daughters, should I have any, will be able to leave this place. But I am bound here. I am the Guardian of this place." She kissed him softly on the cheek before she turned and walked into the village. "I think this place is too small for you Joachim. You would feel trapped. Better to move on as soon as the pass opens and save us both the pain."

Joachim sat and watched her walk away. When she was out of sight he muttered. "Maybe I do not want to go." He sat for a long time on the rail and watched it snow.

The snow continued as the weeks went by and winter settled in.

Chapter 23
Betrayal

Joachim cursed as the short wooden stave smacked him in his ribs again. He grew angry again and began a series of wild cuts with his short word. But he never seemed to be able to hit the Drow warrior dancing before him. Most of the time, he did not even come close. It was embarrassing. The wood stave clipped his hand and the short sword fell to the ground.

Joachim went perfectly still as he felt the stave resting below his chin. The sprite that had been flitting about slashing with a tiny blue sword came to a stop as well. Skreee whispered loudly, "You are not supposed to drop it. That is three times now."

Roiland stepped back. "Anger will get you killed even more quickly with a sword than it will with that knife you love so well."

Joachim sighed in disgust. "I will never be any good with that sword."

Roiland pointed at the short sword with his stave. "You have improved a great deal, Joachim. We have only been working for a few weeks. Be patient. You must not treat the short sword like a knife. You must remember that the longer blade is slower. If you take your swing too wide, you cannot get the sword back fast enough to block. Control is the key. You fight with the sword as much as you do me. Now pick it up. Once you are tired and sore enough, your body will do what your mind cannot."

Joachim retrieved his sword and glared down at it. "Traitor," he muttered to the blade. He raised his eyes to see Roiland grinning at him. "So why are we practicing after sunset tonight? We normally do this in the morning."

Roiland motioned him forward. "You are a thief. You work in the darkness. You need to practice when your vision may not be as sharp."

Joachim stepped forward and raised the shorty sword.

Roiland whispered. "Slow and measured strikes for a bit."

Joachim brought the short sward across in a slow-motion slash.

—————————————

Kisa stepped from the small house. She was tired, but very content. Imerus and her newborn daughter were both doing well thanks to the healing of Akka. Kisa stopped at the bucket of water that Imerus' husband Larson had left for her and began to rinse off the blood and the sweat.

It had been a tough afternoon. The baby had been facing the wrong way. Not ideal at any time let alone for a first child. Kisa had been able to get the baby turned the right way. But it had taken a long time. Hours longer that Kisa had expected. Imerus had been exhausted long before her daughter was born. Mother and daughter had both required Akka's healing afterwards. Now it was done. Imerus would be able to bear more children with Larson and the baby would grow healthy and strong. Praise be to the Earth Mother.

Kisa stared up at the crescent moon. It was after dark and the Council meeting would have started already. She began walking towards the Council building. She should join the meeting if it was still going on. After a dozen steps, she changed her mind and turned towards the Hall of Healing. She had earned a night off. She came to the next intersection and paused. There were three orcs standing there almost as if they were waiting for her. She was about to cry a warning when she heard movement behind her. She spun about to see Councilor Typerys' pet mage standing there with a broad smile on his lips.

Kisa felt her anger begin to rise and she reached for her Holy Symbol. "Traitor! You brought orcs into our home?" Then she shouted, "Guar…"

Before Kisa could grasp her Holy Symbol or finish her warning, the mage uttered an Arcane word and Kisa found herself unable to move.

The mage walked up to stand before her. "They come only to collect the payment their chief was promised."

Kisa tried to respond, but she could no more talk than she could move. The mage smiled at her. He snapped the chain around her neck and dropped her Holy Symbol to the ground. Then he took the mace from her belt and dropped it as well. "Do not worry, Priestess, we do want your friends to figure this out. Typerys has a plan. The good news is that you will live longer than your friends. Once they learn the orcs have you, they will rush to save you. One way or another they will die. You shall live long enough to bear their chief a child or two."

The mage beckoned to someone behind her and Kisa heard the orcs move forward. She was picked up by two of them and they carried her out of the village. Kisa could not tell which direction they took as she was facing down. All she was sure of was that they were moving through snow covered trees heading away from all her friends. She would not be able to warn them before they were betrayed.

Joachim was moving slowly around in a circle. Roiland was counting as they made slow, precise strikes and counterstrikes. Joachim was amazed that the Drow was willing to spar at all with a wooden stave against the sharp steel in Joachim's hand. But Roiland insisted that the only way Joachim would master the blade was to keep using it.

Joachim continued the moves as he was forced to make the same cuts over and over again. Roiland said eventually his muscles would make the moves automatically. Joachim wasn't sure. Picking locks always required thought. His fingers did not do it without his brain.

Joachim glanced to the side as it came time for the next parry. He almost missed the block as the fool sprite shot across the circle stabbing something that was not there. Thankfully Roiland did not reprimand him for losing focus.

Suddenly there was a shout from down the street and Roiland's head spun that way. His stave missed the block and Joachim's sword almost caught him in the shoulder. Joachim paled at the thought that he had almost stabbed his mentor. Before Joachim could ask what happened, Roiland dashed down the street. "That was Kisa."

At those words, Skreee shot ahead. Joachim clutched his sword and followed. He pulled his magic knife into his left hand as he ran to keep up with the swift Drow warrior.

They came to an intersection, but there was nothing visible there. Roiland was crouched on the ground near the entrance to the side street. As Joachim came up beside him, Roiland was picking something up from the ground. Joachim stared in the moonlight. He could barely make out a golden sheath of wheat in the Drow's left hand. Kisa's Holy Symbol. Fear for her shot through Joachim. She would never let that fall to the ground. Roiland dropped his stave and his right hand came up with Kisa's mace. Roiland stared down at the unfamiliar weapon. His hand trembled with the strength of his grip.

Joachim shook his head. "You promised no weapons."

Roiland growled. His grip loosened and he held the mace out to Joachim with a look of pleading in his eyes. "Someone has to save her, Joachim. Speed is her only chance. We must catch them before they get her to their camp. You know what their Chief will do to her."

Joachim's face went pale as he stared at the mace. "The others. Shorty can track them. He found her once before.

Roiland's voice dropped to a harsh whisper. "Maybe your ogre can track her through the snow and the darkness. How long will it take him Joachim? Will it be in time? I was born to the darkness. I am her best chance. Let me do this, please. Once she is safe, I will accept whatever justice your Council wishes to impose on me. You know I can do this."

Joachim was silent for a moment. Then he sighed. "You are not going to save her with just a mace. I do not think even the short sword will be enough. What else do you need to bring her back?"

Roiland rose to his feet. "Get me a bow, any bow. And a few arrows. With that I will bring her back. You have my word."

Joachim nodded and then turned to stare around trying to remember who lived near this intersection. He turned back the way he had come. He pounded on the third door down the street. Joachim opened the door and stepped inside.

Roiland could hear voices from inside but could not make out the words. Joachim returned moments later with a short bow and quiver. There were six arrows in the quiver.

Roiland strapped the quiver on and slipped Kisa's mace and Holy Symbol inside it with the small supply of arrows. He took the bow in hand and smiled. "It is not Oikea Lakko, but it feels good to have a real bow in my hands once more. Go warn your friends, Joachim. The orcs have her. I suspect they had help."

Joachim turned for the Council building. He was not sure what he dreaded most, telling them about Kisa or telling them that he had given Roiland a bow. "Come on, Skreee."

The sprite hovered over Roiland. "I go to help save Pretty One."

Joachim nodded once and then began to run. The Drow bent once more to study the ground before running towards the village's northern edge. He reached the tree line and stared at the tracks in the snow. He turned his gaze upwards, his eyes locking on the thin crescent moon shining above him. "Keep her safe, Lady of Silences. Please, keep her safe."

Roiland began to run. The Sprite shot ahead of him as they both appeared to fly across the snow.

Part 4
A Call to Battle

"Always bees nudder way. Jus gots ta finds it."

Chapter 24
Council for War

Essabeth closed the door to the small house that would probably be her home for the rest of her life. She had never really thought about the future and having a home. Life with her father had been an unending journey of songs, research, and new places. But that part of her life was over. The rest would be spent in this valley or very close to it. Tonight, that did not seem so bad.

The glow of the night sky captured her attention. It was the first time in weeks that the sky was clear. The sky was a tapestry of light and it called to her. She wished she was free to take wing tonight. It would be glorious to soar above the valley surrounded by so many stars and wrapped in their light. The temptation was almost more than she could resist. But not tonight. Her duties as the Swanmay came first.

The thought of leaving the open sky behind to go into another meeting was almost painful. So, she just stood in the tiny front yard. She lifted her arms and let the breeze flow across them. It was the first time in weeks that snow was not falling. A part of her she did not understand told her that spring would be coming soon. A part of her yearned for the change in the season. It was a feeling she had never had before. She suspected that this too was a part of her transformation into the Swanmay. At the same time, she dreaded the coming of spring. The orcs would return with the melting snow and their battles would begin anew.

Essabeth drew in another deep breath as a breeze ruffled the tiny feathers that ran across her shoulder and upper arms. She took the white shawl of the Swanmay and lay it across the signs of her transformation. There was no reason to advertise what she had become something not quite human. Typerys had enough reasons to make her life difficult as it was.

She sighed and headed across the street to the one-room building they used for council meetings. There were lights in the windows and she could see that almost everyone was already there. She braced herself and opened the door.

Essabeth stared around the room. She noted that all three of her battle commanders were present. She had solid support from them. Only two of the village's three councilors were there tonight. Gurdman had left the valley to bring back supplies and would not return for several days if not a week or more. Essabeth had to wonder if that was part of the reason this meeting had been called. The First Councilor probably sensed some advantage in his absence.

The blacksmith, Simeon, was the third councilor. He was the most recent one to be appointed. She liked him. He was as capable of using his head as he was at using a hammer. That left only her First Councilor. Typerys Valistunut was the problem. The self-appointed Councilor was always manipulating people to his own ends. Essabeth had no idea what scheme he was working when he asked for this emergency meeting.

Essabeth closed the door and crossed the room. She glanced at Thorn as she moved around the table, but the dwarf just gave a slight shake of his head. Apparently, he had no idea what this meeting was about either. That was not surprising. Typerys hated the dwarf. Thorn was as immune to Typerys as he seemed to be to magic.

Essabeth pulled out her chair and sat at the head if the table. She immediately picked up a scroll that was waiting there for her. She took her time reading the estimates of food supplies that H'aor had put together. She decided to let Typerys wait for a bit. When she finished the report, she placed it on the table before her. "It has been a very long day, Councilor Typerys. What is so urgent that we needed to meet tonight? Most of us have earned a little time to relax."

Typerys stood and straightened his tunic. "My sources report that a large war party left the main orc camp earlier today."

Essabeth glanced over at Thorn. "Which of the rangers brough the report in?"

Thorn shook his head. "His source is not one of the scouts. This is the first I have heard of it."

Essabeth returned her gaze to Typerys. "What sources do you have that our battle commander does not have access to?"

Typerys smiled at Thorn. His voice rang with mockery as he addressed Essabeth. "Swanmay, your commander does not trust in magic. He has shown little interest in the information that my mage has been able to provide."

Thorn ignored the jibe. "Assuming the mage is correct, it is does not really impact us unless the orcs try to come in this direction. Even if they can get through the snow in the passes, the rangers will alert us in plenty of time to deal with them."

The Councilor turned on Thorn with obvious disdain. "Any military leader with a handful of sense would see the significance of my information. They have few warriors left in their camp. Most of those left are women and children. They are vulnerable. We have nearly twenty men that we can attack with. We can destroy their base if we act now."

Essabeth suppressed her desire to strangle the fool. "Councilor Typerys, conducting a raid and freeing slaves is one thing. You are talking a battle against what amounts to a fortified town. That seems risky at best."

Shorty interrupted a bit loudly. "Bery no smart. Eben me know dat."

Typerys glared at the ogre and then focused his attention on Essabeth. "Swanmay, Essabeth, you are young. This is a tough choice even for more mature people like myself. But this may be our only opportunity to put an end to our problems. Your dwarf only thinks in terms of defense. Sometimes the key to victory is a masterful offensive attack."

H'aor started to rise, but Essabeth held up a hand. "Age is not the only path to maturity, Councilor. I have and will protect this valley and its people. Our strength is here. If we take this battle to them, we sacrifice the protection of the wards. We have no advantages if we take the battle to them. We cannot afford to lose any of our warriors."

Typerys bowed his head. "I meant no disrespect, Swanmay. But your experience in military matters is somewhat limited."

A large dwarven axe thudded on the table before Typerys. Thorn stepped forward to stand beside the councilor. "I wonder how much real battle experience you have Typerys. Seems me and my friends have borne the brunt of the raids so far."

Essabeth stood up. "Enough bickering. My concern is for our people. We cannot keep ourselves safe if we lose many warriors in your attack. As you pointed out, we only have a score of warriors." Essabeth scanned the room. "Where is Kisa? I have questions about what our clerics can handle if we do this."

H'aor rose briefly. "She was called to support a birthing. Imerus went into labor early and asked for her help. Kisa said she would join us when mother and child are safe."

Essabeth sat back down. "What is your plan, Counselor? They have walls around their village. Getting past them is no easy task."

Typerys smiled. "Ohrmed and I have been working on some ideas. He can cast fireball. I provided him with some ink and parchment. He has completed two scrolls. That would give him the ability to cast three fireballs against their village. With some help from the archers, he believes we can burn their village to the ground."

Essabeth grimaced. "You are talking about killing many who are not warriors."

Typerys shrugged. "Better treatment than our women and children received."

A low growl emanated from Shorty. "Youse wants hurt kid?"

Typerys did not take his eyes from Essabeth. "They are only orcs."

Before Essabeth could intervene, the door flew open and Joachim pushed inside. He was out of breath and looked upset. "Thorn. H'aor. They have Kisa."

H'aor moved around the table to stand before the panicked young man. "Who took her, Joachim? What happened?"

Joachim stared around the room meeting the eyes of Shorty and Thorn before locking gazes with H'aor. "Somehow orcs got into the village. I was practicing with Roiland. We heard a yell. But by the time we got there, she was gone. Her Holy Symbol and mace were just lying in the street."

Thorn stepped up beside them and placed a hand on Joachim's shoulder. "Relax. We will get her back. Now, where are Roiland and Skreee?"

Joachim hesitated. "They went after her."

Thorn scowled. "I understand the fool sprite. But that elf is smart enough to know better than to chase after orcs with a practice sword. Going to get himself killed too."

Joachim looked down at his feet. "I sort of gave him Kisa's mace."

Typerys cry of outrage was cut short when Thorn reached over and grabbed his axe from the table in front of the Councilor. "You should have asked first, boy. But even a mace is probably not enough to take on orcs."

Joachim squirmed as he refused to meet the dwarf's gaze. "We sort of thought that getting after her quickly was a good idea. And, well, the bow and arrows I gave him were supposed to help too."

Typerys voice held real anger. "You had no authority to arm him like that. He might kill someone."

Thorn cut him off. "He might kill some orcs. You got a problem with that, Councilor? That seemed to be all you cared about moments ago. Seems you will get what you want out of this. We will attack their village for you. I am not doing this to wipe out the orcs like you want to do but because we are going to get the Priestess back."

Thorn turned and began to giving orders. "Joachim. Get word to the rangers. Tell them to prepare to lead us to the orc camp. H'aor, please spread the word to the rest of the militia. Councilor, get your mage ready. And that bodyguard of yours is going to earn the food he has been eating. I want everyone here as soon as possible."

H'aor nodded and headed for the door with Joachim on his heals. Shorty moved to follow them but Thorn placed a hand on his arm. "Wait, Shorty."

There was concern in the large ogre's eyes. "Wants save Kisa Lady."

Thorn nodded. "We will. But together. No mistakes."

Thorn spun to face Typerys. "What are you waiting for, Councilor. Get your mage moving."

Chapter 25
Running with the Moon

Roiland moved quickly through the trampled snow towards the small northern pass. He was moving faster than was really safe. If the orcs were smart enough to set up an ambush, he was going to run right into it. But he needed to move fast if he was ever going to catch them. That meant depending on the sprite to warn him. Sprites were notoriously undependable. He really hoped the small warrior was as capable as the others thought he was.

Roiland kept his eyes open as he ran. To eyes raised in the darkness of the deep tunnels, the moonlight reflecting off the snow was almost painful. It was more than enough to illuminate the trail of the orcs through the twists and turns of the mountain slope.

Roiland's thoughts raced as fast as his feet. He needed to make sense of what he had observed this night. He was certain that there had been three orcs in the group that had captured Kisa. They had joined up with another group of orcs outside of the village. The group was carrying the Priestess, switching off frequently to stay ahead of pursuit. They did not seem concerned about the trail they were leaving. Did they want to be tracked? If this was intended to be a trap, he had to hope they were not expecting to be detected so quickly.

There were other pieces of this attack that did not make sense. How had the orcs gotten into the village undetected? There was nothing to indicate that Kisa had fought her abductors. That was not like her. The thing that bothered him the most was that the orcs had traveled directly to where they found Kisa. They had passed a dozen occupied homes to attack her in the center of town. Why not find easier victims? It looked like they had come specifically for Kisa. How could they have known where to find her?

Everything he knew about this attack pointed to intrigue and betrayal. This type of scheme would have seemed normal in his homeland. It felt out of place among the humans. But his experience with humans was limited. He only knew that he did not like where his thoughts were headed.

Roiland came through the narrow section at the top of the pass and came to an abrupt halt. The Sprite, Skreee, hovered in the air before him. "Two have stayed behind to deal with any who follow. They hide just ahead."

Roiland lay down in the snow and waited for his body temperature to cool. He did not want the heat of his run to give him away. When the steam of his breath had almost disappeared, Roiland crouched and eased forward. He studied the slope before him. The orc's trail led down a fairly steep descent to the right of a stand of trees. He did not see the orcs in the moonlight. He wanted nothing more than to rush after Kisa, but he knew that course was folly. He had once hunted Drow in the darkness. He would be patient in this hunt for her sake. As he watched and searched the area before him. He cursed himself silently. He could not see anything out of place in the moonlight. Then he cursed his foolishness. He had been above ground so long that he was beginning to rely only on what he could see by the light of the moon.

Roiland closed his eyes and forced his vision to shift into the spectrum he had depended on most of his life. He needed to be looking for heat on this frozen mountainside. He reopened his eyes to view the slope before him. His vision was now dominated by deep blues and a few pale oranges. The snow and ice stretched before him in a consistent cold blue. The trees had a pale orange to them that indicated some heat and life. Then he spotted the first orc behind the third tree in the cluster. Its body was well hidden, but its breath made small clouds of red. As each breath faded, a new one appeared to mark its place. The combination of the run up the mountain and taking turns carrying Kisa had overheated its lungs and betrayed its position. Roiland smiled and moved his eyes on looking for the second orc.

Roiland shifted his gaze to the other side of the trampled snow. There were several boulders resting in the undisturbed snow. Their temperature was just a shade different from that of the snow and ice. Roiland realized that one of the boulders was warmer than the others. He assumed the orc was leaning against the boulder, its body heat slowly transferring into the rock. Now it was time to eliminate these two and get back on Kisa's trail.

Roiland began to slide through the snow to his right. He would crawl forward a step and then pause. Two steps and another pause. He stayed low in the snow as he circled around the rock. It was cold, but he remained low in the snow as he moved into position.

When he could finally see the red glow of the orc's body against the rock, he slowly pulled a single arrow from his quiver. Roiland placed the arrow on the string as he rose into in the darkness. Snow clung to his clothing, helping to mask the heat of his body. The arrow remained by his ear as he studied his target. He slowed his breathing. When his heartbeat slowed, he pushed the bow out and away from his body. The bowstring and arrow did not move. He breathed out. He drew in a slow breath, held it for a heartbeat as his left arm reached full extension. His fingers released the string. The arrow leapt into the darkness as he exhaled.

He had not needed to adjust for wind at this range. The shaft was buried in his target before there was time for the arrow to drift. The orc grunted and slid to the ground. Its partner stepped out from the trees trying to see what had happened. Roiland had another arrow to the string already. He shifted his aim just slightly for the longer shot. Again, he breathed in and held. This arrow caught the second orc in the throat as it stepped back into the trees. It made more noise as it fell to the ground. Roiland heard the sprite move past the ambush site heading into the valley below.

Roiland paused to check his arrows. The one in the first orc had gone through its armor before sinking into its chest. The arrow would not fly true a second time. He left it where it had struck. The one in the second orc's neck was undamaged. He began to clean it on his shirt as he followed after the sprite. He had lost some of the ground he had gained.

As Roiland came down onto the floor of the valley, he saw signs of an old camp. Many trees had been cut here. This was probably the logging camp that Joachim had told him about. The young man had been proud of helping save those men from the orcs.

Roiland continued to follow the trail north. Roiland saw movement ahead and stopped. It was the sprite coming back for him. Skreee landed on Roiland's shoulder so he could speak softly into the Drow's sensitive ears. "They have stopped. I think they tire. Now there are two less to carry Pretty One. She is tied but struggles. She makes it harder for them. One of them slapped her. His nose is very bent. We must hurt him."

Roiland shook his head. "That one we will save for your Pretty One. Tell me where they rest."

Skreee pointed to the trail ahead which led into an area dominated by larger trees that had not been cleared by the orcs or their prisoners. "There is a large clearing near the center of those trees. They rest there."

Roiland thought for a moment. "Can you get past them? Then you would need to give me time to get in place. I need you to make some noise in front of them. I do not want them paying attention to the Priestess."

Skreee smiled and nodded. He lifted into the air and headed along the edge of the wooded area flying just above the tree tops. Roiland ran for the trees. He needed to be in place before the sprite got the orc's attention. Roiland reached the first of the trees and slowed. From here, he would not follow the orc's path. There was a lot less snow on the ground among the trees. The orc's path would be noisier. The orcs had exposed many old leaves and dead branches.

Roiland moved slowly into the trees. He placed each foot with care to ensure he did not warn the orcs of his presence. Their trail was soon hidden by the trees. He hoped their path did not deviate much, as he was forced to move around many of the larger trees. This world presented many challenges that had not existed in his homeland. His sense of direction was less accurate in the world above and obstacles like leaves and branches had not existed there.

Roiland sighed mentally when he heard the voices of the orcs as they argued amongst themselves. He crouched low as he moved forward one handspan at a time. The clearing came into view and Roiland stopped to assess his position. Kisa lay on the far side of the clearing. One orc, the one with the broken nose was sitting not far from her bound form. The others were scattered about the far side of the clearing. Roiland understood little of their language, but he recognized the complaining tone in their voices.

Roiland examined the trees near him and selected one that had a thick trunk and few low branches. He moved slowly behind the tree he had chosen, timing his movements to the complaints of the orcs. From his new position, he could peak around the tree and clearly see all four of the orcs. Roiland took each of his five remaining arrows and set their points into the ground beside him. Then he waited. The orcs talked amongst themselves. Then the sound of snow falling from a tree came to his sharp ears. The orcs stood and drew their weapons.

Normally Roiland would have wanted them facing him as he took them down. But this was a rescue mission and Kisa could not defend herself. Her life depended on his shots. Roiland pulled the first arrow from earth. He wiped soil from the arrowhead on his leg and set it to the string. Roiland began with the orc farthest from Kisa. His bow thrummed and the arrow was on its way. Before the first shot struck, he had the second arrow at his ear. He released a second time and then a third time. Three orcs lay on the ground.

The fourth orc, the one with the broken nose, spun to face him. Roiland stepped out of trees with an arrow notched. The orc held still with a long dagger in its hand. It looked at Kisa. Roiland raised the bow and spoke softly in the human tongue. His voice was filled with menace. "If you so much as lean towards her, I will kill you."

Roiland moved to stand near Kisa. He kept the arrow pointed at the orc. Skreee flew into the clearing and dropped to stand beside Kisa. "Pretty One is safe now." The sprite pulled out his blue sword out and began to cut away the ropes the bound Kisa's hands and feet.

Kisa sat up as soon as the sprite finished cutting the ropes. "Thank you, Skreee." She began to rub her arms and legs to get the circulation moving. Roiland smiled at the orc as its eyes darted nervously between its dagger and the bow. Roiland smiled at him. "My arrow is the least of your concerns."

Kisa rose and came to stand beside Roiland. "My thanks, Archer."

Roiland glanced at her face and hissed in anger. The side of her face was bruised and swollen. Kisa placed a hand on his shoulder. "It will heal. What are you going to do with him?"

Roiland chuckled and it was not a nice sound. "I am not going to do anything, Priestess. Look in the quiver at my back."

Kisa did as he asked and Roiland heard her surprised exclamation. "Akka's Symbol and my mace. But why?"

"Because I knew you would have need of them. Are your prepared?"

Kisa stepped to his side with the mace in her right hand and the Holy Symbol dangling from its broken chain in her left. "Ready for what?"

Roiland stared at her with obvious admiration. "You are a Priestess of power. No man controls you or acts in your stead. This creature offered you insult. His punishment is yours to decide." Roiland stepped back and lowered the bow.

Kisa looked at him and then turned to the orc. It kept its eyes on Roiland. "You will not shoot me down? Even if I win?"

Roiland spoke with confidence. "You will not win. But if you do, I will let you go for today."

The orc grinned at raised its dagger. Kisa thought for a moment and handed her Holy Symbol to Roiland. "No magic." She nodded to Roiland and turned back towards the orc.

The orc struck before she had fully turned to face it. The dagger came forward tearing through the sleeve of Kisa's shirt. She jerked her arm back almost in time. A small finger length cut was visible on her wrist through the rip in her sleeve. Roiland's voice was almost a caress as she turned on the orc. "I placed my trust in you, Priestess. Do not let me down. It will pain me greatly if you allow this creature to hurt you again."

At his words, Kisa realized how much it cost the Drow warrior to let her fight this battle. It was a gift. But more importantly, it showed a level of respect that no one had ever given her before. Her face hardened with determination as she stepped towards the orc. It came at her again with a slash of its dagger. This time, her mace came down and hit the blade. Sparks flew as the dagger's steel slid across the head of her mace.

The orc drew back. It seemed surprised at the speed of her parry. It grew more cautious as it feinted another attack. Kisa barely shifted position. The orc began to weave from side to side. Kisa did not try to match its motions. Then it lunged, driving the dagger point towards her unarmored stomach. Kisa twisted to the side and brought the mace down hard. The orc raised its other arm to block the strike. Kisa's mace connected with its elbow and there was a loud pop.

The orc stumbled back out of Kisa's range. Its arm below its elbow hung at the wrong angle. Kisa realized that she had dislocated the lower arm. She could see the pain on the orcs face. The orc pulled the arm in against its body and turned so the arm was angled away from Kisa. There was a new look in its eyes. Kisa could have sworn it was respect. Kisa hesitated. She was unsure if the fight was over or not.

The orc drove forward again but its slash came to soon and was well short of her body. Kisa brought the mace down again. This time she hit the shoulder of its uninjured arm. The force of the blow drove the orc to its knees. It lost its grip on the dagger. The weapon landed on the ground before Kisa's feet.

Kisa stood over the orc with her mace raised once more. The memory of this orc punching her in the face when she had twisted from its grip flashed through her mind. She felt the anger and the shame of that moment. She had felt helpless then. But she was not helpless now, the orc was. Her mace went up higher to strike down at the orc. The mace stayed above her head as she stared down at it. So much emotion raged in her, but she could not bring the mace down to kill it. It was not in her to strike one who could not fight back.

She felt Roiland's fingers wrap around her hand. He brought her hand gently to her side. She felt him squeeze once, softly. Suddenly the anger left her. "I am sorry, I cannot kill him this way."

Roiland's voice was warm and approving. "Do not apologize. It is as it should be. To kill him after you had defeated him would have darkened the light within you. That would have saddened me greatly."

Kisa turned into him and leaned against his strength. "Thank you, Roiland."

The orc suddenly smiled up at them. "You may get away. But your friends will still die when they reach our village. It was all meant to lure them into our trap. Your friends and all your warriors will be gone soon." The orc lunged for the dagger on the ground.

Kisa tensed, but Roiland suddenly spun her away from him. Kisa saw the orc's fingers wrap around the dagger's hilt as she spun away. Before it could lift the weapon, Roiland's boot came up to smash into its face. The orc landed on its back, unconscious. Its face was already darkening and blood trickled from its rebroken nose. "We will see about your trap."

Kisa took Roiland's hand. "Can we get back to the village in time to stop them?"

Roiland studied the sky and the moon now low on the horizon. "No. I would guess they are well on their way. Maybe we can get to them before they are trapped. If not, we can at least fight beside them."

Kisa nodded. "Skreee, can you lead us to their village?"

The sprite turned without words and flew towards the north. His tiny blue sword was gripped in his hand.

Chapter 26
The Assault

Thorn wandered down the street to the house they had been using and grabbed the rest of his gear. Then he returned to the Council building to wait.

One of the first to join his was Anjelique. Thorn was not surprised. He had seen the ranger run down a narrow trail during their first raid against the orcs. She was fast and graceful. She came and sat beside him at the table. "We going to get her back, Commander? The Priestess has helped a lot of folks. Most of them are going to be angry when they find out she was taken."

Thorn clenched a fist. "Oh, we will get her back, girl. You can count on that." Thorn shifted in his seat and reached down to the backpack sitting near his chair. He pulled out a thick parchment rolled on both sides. Thorn rolled it out to both sides and used his axe to hold one end down. He reached behind his back and brought out a throwing hammer to hold the second side down.

Thorn leaned back to reveal a detailed map of the northern lands. Anjelique scooted closer to study it. She gave a short whistle of appreciation. "This is beautiful work. Where did you get it?"

Thorn kept his face blank as he replied. "From the body of an orc scout out in the middle of nowhere."

Anjelique gave him a rueful glance and then paused. "Wait, you are serious. Where would an orc get a map like this?"

Thorn nodded at her reaction. "If I knew that, we might be able to put an end to this whole business." Thorn waved his hand at the map. "What can you tell me?"

Angelique studied the map a little longer. She pointed to the small lake within the mountain range. "We are here, of course." Her finger moved a short distance to the north. "The orcs have settled and built their village here. It is not much, but considering they have been here less than a year, it is a respectable effort."

Thorn watched as her fingers slid across the map. She placed her finger back near the lake. "There is a trail. It is just on the other side of our pass. It isn't much more than a game trail, but it leads to the valley where the orc village is."

Thorn bent to study the map near her fingers. "Why that route?"

Anjelique tapped the pass near the orc camp. "This pass is steep and it is always guarded. The other route in goes past the site where we rescued the woodcutters. It is fairly narrow in places. If they ambush us, we will not get past them easily." She placed her finger back on the game trail. "Nobody uses this route except deer, moose, and rangers."

Thorn nodded at her reasoning. "Then we go with your plan. You know the area best."

They talked a bit more about the route and then Anjelique got up. "I will be back. I want two of the rangers out ahead of us scouting."

She disappeared out the door. Thorn looked up to see Essabeth smiling at him. "What now, Swanmay? You have that same look Joachim gets when he nabs a purse."

Essabeth chuckled. "That woman works harder than most people. Not many recognize how good Anjelique is. You never question her abilities. Not many men can do that."

Thorn just shrugged. "You never met my little sister. Last dwarf that questioned her abilities needed a cleric so he could walk again. Worrying about whether the person helping you is a woman is like worrying about what color paper a gift is wrapped in. The outside is not nearly as important as what is inside. The inside is what makes you who you are."

"Thanks for the warning about your sister." Essabeth's smile faded. "You know I cannot come with you. I can only leave the valley as a swan. Even then I must return within a few hours. I cannot help you."

Thorn grunted in acknowledgement. "If you want to help us, just keep the wards up and make sure we have a safe place to come back to."

It was nearly midnight before the small army was ready to move out. Thorn made sure each person had food and water. They were already planning to fight on next-to-no sleep, he did not need them hungry or dehydrated as well.

Thorn took the lead as they headed up into the eastern pass. He did his best to break a path through the snow. Anjelique stayed at his side apparently unaffected by the snow and ice. On the far side of the pass, the ranger pointed to a length of ribbon tied to a branch on the left side of the trail. "This is it."

Thorn studied the snow where she stood. "Where is the trail?"

Anjelique untied the ribbon and pointed to a set of tracks in the snow. "This way."

Thorn stared at the ground. "I thought you sent two scouts. I only see one set of footprints."

Anjelique smiled in the light of the crescent moon. "Second scout followed in the first's footsteps. Safer if the orcs think there is only one."

Thorn nodded his understanding. "Lead the way. These are your tunnels not mine."

The trail they followed around the mountain was narrow and they frequently had to push their way past the snow-covered branches of evergreen trees. Anjelique pointed out frequent signs of deer and moose along the way. The winter had been hard on them as well and the trees showed signed of their foraging. The sky was beginning to lighten as one of the forward scouts returned to report that the gates of the orc village were open.

Thorn paused the group well back in the cover of the trees. Anjelique sent the two forward scouts back to watch their rear incase the orc raiding party returned. Shorty and H'aor moved forward to study the orc village. Thorn ordered everyone to eat while he began to organize his people into teams. He matched each of his weaker fighters with stronger ones to protect them.

Thorn knew the people he had brought were dependable. All except the three he really did not want along. Thorn had brought the mage and bodyguard to prevent the Councilor from causing trouble while he was gone. He had not expected Typerys would insist on accompanying them. Thorn realized he had little hope that any of the three would listen to his orders so he did not waste his breathe on them.

Shorty and H'aor returned from the tree line. Thorn called his friends and Anjelique together. "What can you tell me?"

H'aor drew a large rectangle in the snow. He took some dried sticks and made a second rectangle in the middle of the one he had drawn. "They have cleared the trees well back from their village. We will have to cross a lot of open ground to get to the gate."

H'aor pointed to the smaller rectangle inside the one he had drawn. "They have a wooden palisade nearly ten feet high around the whole place. The timber does not seem that old. I am betting some of it is still green. Not sure that fireball plan is going to work."

A sarcastic voice came from behind them. H'aor turned to see the Councilor's mage standing there. "I am Ohrmed. I have been studying this place for some time now. I never intended to use my magic on the walls."

Thorn studied the man from his place beside the map. "Then what is your plan?"

The mage gestured towards the crude map. "They have at least twenty huts and other structures within those walls. Most of those have scavenged limbs and dried grasses for roofs. My plan was always to hit those. They should burn well and force whoever survives into the open. Your rangers can then pick off the dangerous ones with their bows and the other men can slaughter the rest."

A deep rumble came from Shorty. "Youse kills many kid. Mamas too. No bery nice. Bees bad man."

The mage turned and began to walk away. "If you do not like it, speak with Councilor Typerys. I take my orders from him."

Thorn rose to his feet. He reached for his axe, but H'aor placed a hand on his shoulder. "He has a point, Thorn. We need to control Typerys if we are going to control this battle."

The men from the valley had spread out within the tree line. When Thorn and the others finally spotted the Councilor, Typerys was moving among the men giving orders. Thorn noted in disgust that none of the teams he had organized were still together. Thorn marched up before the man and thundered, "What do you think you are doing? Are you trying to get them all killed?"

Typerys glowered at Thorn as if he was an insignificant nuisance. "I am First Councilor. Since the Swanmay cannot leave the valley to lead this attack, I am in charge. I decided to relieve you of command. Brome will manage things for me."

Thorn lifted his axe to his shoulder. "If you want to live through this, Councilor, you will stop interfering or I will personally put you down. And while I deal with you, Shorty will be more than happy to explain things to your bodyguard. Do you understand that?"

Typerys face set in a hard line and he turned and stalked away.

H'aor slapped Thorn on the back. "I doubt that helped our cause in the least, but it sure felt like the right thing to do. What now?"

Thorn gestured at the men milling around among the trees. "H'aor, help me get them back in their original teams. I do not like the mage's plan. We need to find another way to get into that palisade."

The two friends split up and began to move amongst the villagers trying to restore order as the sky began to lighten.

Shorty sat and stared at the map of the orc village. After a few moments, Shorty reached out and wiped the map away in anger. Then he turned and headed back to the edge of the trees where he crouched and watched the gate.

Joachim followed behind him. He studied the ogre as Shorty settled in beside a large tree trunk. Joachim was surprised to see a tear roll down Shorty's cheek. He came and squatted beside Shorty. "What is wrong, my friend?"

Shorty pointed at the open gates. "Muches kid in deer. No posed hurt kid. Me no lets dem bees hurted."

Joachim patted Shorty on the shoulder. "I understand, Shorty. We need to go talk to Thorn and H'aor."

Before either could move, Typerys voice came from behind them. Joachim looked back to see the large bodyguard, Brome, standing beside the Councilor. Typerys had a smile on his face. "They are just orc children. They will eventually grow into orcs. Think of it as an investment in the future."

Shorty turned to stare at Typerys. His face had a dangerous look on it. Brome's hand moved closer to his broadsword, but the big man was clearly nervous.

Shorty looked into the counselor's eyes. "Kids bees kids. Muches to small ta knows what should do. Ifn youse kills, neber know ifn could bees good kid. Only bees dead kid. Den youse be same as orc. Bad peoples."

Typerys paused as he considered the ogre's words. He glanced over at his bodyguard who shook his head no. Typerys looked back at the ogre. "So much fuss over a batch of orc brats. Fine, you save those you can and take them back to the valley. We can raise them like the human children. Will that make you happy?"

Shorty shook his head. "Ifn kills dem Mamas dat hurt kids. Me knows dis." Shorty paused and his brows furrowed as he searched for words. "Ken no teaches kids ta bees people. Dem orc. Always bees orc. No ken changes. Me ogre. Always bees ogre. Bees good ogre. Teach kids bees kid. Hab fun. Play. Lub. Den be bestus kind orc. Bees bery good orc. Unnerstan?"

Typerys shook his head. "This is a stupid discussion. You are incapable of seeing a better way. Come, Brome, we are wasting our time here." The two men walked back into the trees and disappeared from sight.

Shorty turned back to stare at the gates. He spoke softly to himself. "Me no gonna lets kid dies. Me stop."

Joachim moved up to sit beside his friend. "We will think of something, Shorty."

Shorty nodded as his thoughts tumbled though his head. The only clear thing was his memory of Mama. His thoughts calmed as he remembered the important things that Mama had taught him. There was always another way. He just had to find it. He closed his eyes and leaned his head against the tree as he concentrated. Mama and Papa had always found a way. Shorty's eyes flew open as he thought about the stories he had been told of Papa.

Shorty tuned to Joachim with a grin. "Me ken fix."

Joachim stared at him in bewilderment. "Fix what, Shorty?"

Excitement spread over the ogre's face. "Fix all. Save all. Save kids. Makes all bees friend."

Joachim sighed and shook his head. "That might be too big a job for even you, my friend. How can you make everyone be friends?"

Shorty pointed at the gate. "Orc no fight ifn Chief says stop." Shorty began to rise.

Joachim grabbed at his arm. "Shorty, wait. Their Chief wants this war."

Shorty gently pulled his arm from Joachim's grip. He rose to his feet. Shorty smiled as he drew his Papa's sword into his right hand. He picked up his shield in his left. "Den needs new Chief."

Shorty stepped out of the trees and headed for the gate. Joachim ran back into the trees yelling for Thorn and H'aor.

Chapter 27
The Nudder Way

Thorn sat beneath a snow-covered maple tree. Its bare branches sagged beneath the weight of the snow from the last week. Thorn took a drink from his waterskin. The biscuits and jerky he was eating were dry and tasteless. Forcing his way through snow covered trails had burned a lot of energy. His body needed the fuel if he was going to lead the fight against the orcs.

The group from the valley had been lucky so far, the orcs had not noticed his group hiding in the trees near their village. That small break had given his people time to rest before they began their attack. Thorn glanced up at the sun. Things would begin soon enough.

Thorn's attention shifted back to the twelve men preparing their weapons for the assault. He did not want to lose any of them. He hoped that the scheme he and H'aor had cooked up would work. Everything depended on the two of them with Shorty getting to the gate before the orcs could close it. Anjelique was getting her rangers into position. Their archery was supposed to ensure that nothing got between his team at the gate.

The militia was once again organized into teams of three. He wondered if so few men actually counted as a militia. Either way, they were the second wave of his assault. If he and his friends could keep the gate open, the four teams would penetrate the village to look for Kisa. There were risks, but it was better than burning the whole village down with Kisa inside.

Thorn glanced around. H'aor was sitting nearby studying his spell book. But where were Shorty and Joachim? He had not seen either of them for some time now. He needed to make sure Shorty understood his part in the attack and that explanation might require several repetitions. Thorn shoved the rest of the food in to his backpack and looked around one more time for Shorty.

The mage, Ohrmed, was standing nearby unrolling a parchment and scanning it. Thorn assumed it was one of the fireball scrolls. Thorn realized it was past time to explain the change of plans to the mage. Thorn rose to his feet as an angry Typerys stormed back from somewhere up near the tree line. Typerys' bodyguard seemed to be the target of the Councilor's ire. Thorn hurried over as the two men stopped beside the mage.

Typerys turned to face the mage. "Ohrmed, get yourself up there and burn that place out. I am tired of being told what I can and cannot do. It is time to end this."

Thorn cleared his throat as he came up behind Typerys. "We have a new strategy, Councilor. Burning the village down and killing every orc inside it are not a part of the new plan."

Typerys turned his anger on the dwarf. "You are a fool. You know nothing of the true situation here. I do not have time to explain it to you. Let Ohrmed end this before you get all of us killed."

Thorn stared at the Councilor wondering what the man knew and how he knew it. Thorn was about to question the man when he heard Joachim yelling for him and H'aor. The young fool was yelling loud enough to wake the entire orc village. Any hope of getting to an open gate was gone now. Thorn turned to watch Joachim racing through the trees. H'aor stepped up beside him as he waited for the boy.

Joachim seemed in a panic. "Thorn, H'aor. Shorty is headed for the gate. He got some idea in his head. He just walked out there in the open. He is yelling for their Chief. He is going to get himself killed."

Typerys spun back to his mage. "Quick, go cast your spells before that idiot ogre gets them all headed out here to fight us."

H'aor's objected. "You cannot throw that spell without hitting Shorty too."

Ohrmed smiled. "No great loss there. He turned out to be a liability in the end."

Thorn turned on the mage, but Brome stepped between them. Ohrmed laughed. "Discuss it with Brome while I follow my orders."

Ohrmed began to walk towards the orc village. A female voice came from behind him. "Commander said no fireballs. Unless you can move faster than an arrow, I would suggest you listen to him."

The mage froze in place. Thorn glanced over to see Anjelique standing with an arrow drawn. He smiled when he saw she was not aiming at the mage. Her shot was lined up on Councilor Typerys. Thorn began to chuckle as Typerys became aware that he was her target.

Typerys turned to Thorn. "You will regret this insult. I think you will regret not taking my help even more. But for now, I concede leadership to you. We will be leaving now. Brome, Ohrmed. Back to the valley."

The three men headed back towards the trail they had followed in. They all paused as two short whistles came from Anjelique.

Typerys turned his head towards her. She smiled at him. "You will be watched. Try to interfere and my men will shoot. First Councilor or not."

Typerys nodded and motioned for Brome to continue.

Thorn spun to his men. "Move up to the tree line and stay in your teams. Be ready for anything. I have no idea what the ogre is up to." Thorn followed H'aor and Joachim back to the edge of the trees. The ranger followed more slowly as she watched Typerys and his men head down the trail.

They knelt behind the last few trees and looked out to see Shorty standing a dozen yards from the open gate. Shorty was yelling loud enough to be heard inside the camp. "Talks. Talks wid Chief."

An orc with the crossbow was watching the big ogre from the cover of the open gate. A second orc spun around and disappeared into the village. As Thorn and the others watched, eight more armed orcs lined up in the entrance to the palisade. The orcs carried a variety of weapons. There appeared to be having an animated discussion about the warrior yelling to speak to their Chief.

Shorty finally stopped his yelling and stood with his sword resting on his shoulder. Anjelique pointed past the line of orc warriors. "There are many more of them gathering back there. I do not think they are all fighters."

Thorn watched intently. "What is he doing?"

Joachim sounded bewildered as he replied. "Shorty said he knew how to make them stop fighting. He was going to make everyone be friends. He was talking crazy."

Anjelique leaned in closer to Joachim. "Think, Joachim. Did he say anything else??"

Joachim tuned to stare at her. "Nothing that made sense. How is he going to get them to pick a new Chief?"

The ranger smiled. "That ogre just might be smarter than all of us. The question is if he is good enough to take over."

Thorn raised a hand to point at two figures coming into view within the walls. The orcs milling around behind the line of warriors parted to let them through. "Smarter? That is a scary thought, girl, but Shorty looks like he has a plan. Wish I knew what it was."

As the two figures stepped past the line of warriors guarding the open gate, H'aor whispered softly, "By all the Gods."

The first orc to exit through the gates was huge. It stood slightly taller than Shorty, but was not quite as muscular. Its features were definitely orcish, but much larger than orc should be. Its skin had a strange greenish tint to it and there were numerous warts and large bumps visible on its face and arms. A large hammer hung at its side. By comparison, the second figure was almost comically small. The second orc was old and its back was bent with age. In one hand it carried a large feathered rattle and in the other was a set of prayer beads.

The huge orc pointed a finger at Shorty. "What do you want, ogre? Are you here to pledge yourself to my tribe? Is this your cowardly way to survive the war?"

Shorty raised his sword and pointed it at the Chief. "No. Bees here ta fights youse. Ends war. Protects all."

The Chief began to laugh in a deep raspy tone. "Your simple words show you are as stupid as most of your kind. You actually believe that I would allow this war to be decided by a fight between us. I am enjoying the chaos and suffering that I have caused. You wasted your life on a fool's gambit. The war will go on and you will die this day." The huge Chief gestured to the orc with the crossbow. "Shoot him and be done with it."

Thorn cursed. Then he asked softly. "Anjelique, can you take the one with the crossbow?"

Her reply was quick. 'Wait Thorn. He is not done."

Thorn shook his head. "What do you know?"

The crossbow began to come up when Shorty yelled loudly once more. "No fight fer war. Fights fer bees Chief."

The shaman raised the feathered rattle and began to shake it. The orc with the crossbow hesitated and then lowered his weapon. The Chief spun around and stared at Shorty. "What did you say, ogre?"

Shorty again raised his voice for all to hear. "Me challenge! Challenge Chief!"

The Chief laughed again. "I have no reason to fight you for Chief. You may not challenge me. You are not of the tribe." He turned to look at the orc with the crossbow again. "I said kill him."

The shaman began to shake his feathered rattle as he slowly walked around the Chief, then he spoke in a surprisingly strong voice. "Our treaty with the ogre kin has existed for generations. He has as much right to challenge as a half orc from the swamp did a handful of seasons ago. He may challenge."

The Chief's face turned dark with menace. He stepped towards the tiny Shaman and clenched his fist. The old orc did not flinch. "Grumush acknowledges the challenge and the challenger. You must fight or flee."

The Chief turned to face Shorty. "I will hurt you and then I will kill you. After that it will be your friends turn to die. Tell the cowards to step out of the trees so they can see me crush your skull."

Shorty nodded and returned to the tree line to see his friends. Shorty's face was calm as he motioned for his friends to come out.

Anjelique was the first one out of the trees. She moved close to Shorty and gave him a quick hug. "Brave move, my friend. Be careful though. There is something odd about that big orc." Then she winked at him. "And do not die on us."

Thorn led the rest of Shorty's friends out of the trees. The valley fighters followed after. Thorn stared up into Shorty's eyes for a long moment. "Are you sure about this, Shorty?"

The ogre shook his head. "No wants bees Chief. Dis way nobodys get hurted."

Thorn nodded. "No one except you. So be it."

Shorty was about to reply when the Shaman began to shake the rattle again. Shorty studied his friends a little longer and then turned back towards the gate. The Shaman had moved to a point halfway between the tree line and the gate. Many more orcs including some of the women and children had exited the village. They all watched in relative silence.

Shorty came to a stop a few yards from the Shaman. The Orc Chief came to stand facing him on the other side of the Shaman. He now had a wooden shield on his left arm. The Shaman again began to shake the rattle as he circled the two combatants. He began to invoke Grumush as he continued to walk a circle around the two fighters.

As the shaman chanted, Thorn heard the sound of wings behind him. He saw the sprite moving through the trees towards him. Skreee stopped to watch what was happening. "What is my ogre doing? Is he going to fight that monster?"

Thorn snarled up at him, "Skreee! Forget that fight for a moment. Where have you been? What of Kisa and that Drow?"

Skreee turned his attention to the dwarf. "Pretty One is safe. The Archer brings her here to warn you."

Thorn looked frustrated. "Warn me about what?"

Skreee stared around as if looking for someone. He whispered. "Betrayal. The one you call Councilor helped the orcs to take Pretty One."

H'aor spun to face Anjelique. "And we let him just walk back to an undefended village. We need to go after him."

Anjelique shook her head. "If we all leave, it will hurt the ogre's standing with the tribe. They must not think we run because we fear he will lose. They only respect strength. We must wait till the fight is done."

Thorn stared at her and then he sighed. "Fine. We stay, but I am going to kill that traitor. Maybe Shorty's orcs can teach me how to skin him."

Joachim heard the words, but the thought of leaving Essabeth to face Typerys, Brome, and the mage made him feel sick. It was wrong. As his friends turned back to watch the fight, Joachim slid back between the trees. He was going to help Essabeth. Once out of sight, he turned and ran.

The Shaman stopped his circling and the rattle went silent. "The circle is complete. Two have entered. One may leave. Let Grumush decide who is fit to rule the Orc." As the Shaman finished speaking, the circle he had walked began to glow a dull red. All traces of snow and ice along his path melted away.

Chapter 28
Grumush's Choice

The Orc Chief began to walk around the circle the Shaman had marked with his magic. The huge orc seemed to be measuring Shorty with each step. Shorty stood still and patient, his only movement was to open his stance in preparation for the orc's eventual attack. Shorty's face remained calm. He had spent most of his life facing larger, more intimidating foes. He had Papa's sword. He was not afraid.

The orc stopped directly behind Shorty and began to chuckle. "You do not even realize that you were betrayed, do you? Do you think we could have made it inside your defenses without help? One of your own moved the guards so we could capture your precious Priestess. When this is done, my warriors will bring her here so I can claim her as one of my females."

Shorty's lips thinned and his tusks began to show. "No happen ifn me kills youse. What people helps youse takes Kisa Lady?"

Shorty heard the footsteps continue as the orc resumed walking the circle. When it once more stood in front of Shorty, the massive hammer was in its right hand. It smiled and pointed the hammer towards him. "You are either very brave or too stupid to understand the danger you are in. It is too bad you did not join my tribe. I could have done much with a tool like you."

Shorty met the Chief's gaze. "What peoples helps youse?"

The Orc Chief laughed again. "The same fool that led you here to kill me. He thought to betray us both for his own gain. But he was also betrayed. My warriors did not go on a raid. They are up in the pass waiting for my signal to destroy your pitiful army. You and your friends never had a chance. But do not worry, I will get the one that betrayed us both. He will die too."

Shorty's head started to turn towards his friends and the orc leapt forward bringing the hammer down. Shorty was prepared for the attack and rotated his right foot back and around. As his body pivoted, he brought the shield up to knock the hammer away. Shorty continued to rotate as the orc drove past him. Shorty now faced his friend. He raised his voice and yelled to them, "Bees trap!"

The orc spun back to face Shorty. Shorty brought his sword down in from right to left in an arc that brought all of his strength to bear. The orc lifted its wooden shield. The sword struck and sheared away the upper third of the shield. The orc looked down at the large piece of wood lying on the ground. "Very nice. I will add that blade to my collection when you are dead."

Thorn glanced over at H'aor. "What does he mean 'trap'?"

H'aor grimaced. "No clue, but we better figure it out."

Thorn swore. "Anjelique, we need to check all three of the paths into this place. We may be in trouble."

"On it, Commander." There was a pause and her voice continued. "Joachim is gone."

Thorn turned and sighed. "He is going to have to fend for himself. Just find out if that raiding party is really gone, please."

The ranger nodded and disappeared.

Thorn and H'aor turned back to the battle that might mean life or death for them all.

Joachim was well down the trail when he finally slowed to a walk. The path was easier to follow in the daylight, but he was getting tired. He had not slept in over a day now and this was his second forced march in that the last day. He could not help Essabeth if he did not make it safely back to the valley.

———————————

The Orc Chief advanced once more. This time Shorty went on the offensive. His blade slashed and darted in again and again. Shorty used every attack he knew and still the orc moved the shield to intercept each strike. Chips and chunks of wood flew away with each strike of the sword. Shorty was a bit surprised when the orc stepped back with a smile on its face.

The orc lowered his left arm and the remains of the shield fell to the ground. "You at least make this an entertaining fight, ogre. I would never have expected one of your race to actually have much skill with the sword. You are strong, but you fight with more than brute force. Shall we see if you are any good when I actually try to hit you?"

The orc stepped forward again and Shorty brought his sword in for a slash at the orc's now unprotected left arm. The large hammer came across with surprising speed to bat the sword out to the side. Before Shorty could bring his sword back to center, the large hammer punched forward at Shorty's chest. Shorty smoothly moved his large metal plated shield into the path of the hammer. The blow numbed Shorty's hand and arm. Shorty was the one to step back this time. The orc grinned and did not pursue. Shorty looked down at the shield in puzzlement. There was a dent in the metal in the exact shape of the head of the hammer.

Shorty realized the shield was of little use against the powerful weapon. The hammer would just buckle the shield if there was another solid hit. More importantly, the dent had changed the balance of the shield. It was more of a hinderance than it was protection. The orc began to laugh as Shorty slowly lowered the shield. "Your toy will not protect you from my strikes, ogre."

Shorty did not reply with words. Instead, he threw the shield at the orc's face. The hammer came up to swat away the shield. The great sword came in right behind it to cut a long slash along the Orc Chief's weapon arm. A bloody line ran from the orc's wrist to its elbow. Shorty watched in satisfaction as a greenish blood oozed from the wound.

––––––––––––––––––––

H'aor nudged Thorn and an excited "Yes!" slipped out of his lips. "That should slow him down. How long can he swing that hammer bleeding like that?"

Thorn's response held concern, not excitement. "Its blood is green."

They both stared in amazement as the orc lifted the arm before its face and licked away the blood. They could see the wound was already closing. Within a few heartbeats, there was no sign that Shorty had even cut the arm.

Thorn swore, "How could we have missed it? The damn thing is half troll. Apparently, it can regenerate as well. Shorty is in trouble."

––––––––––––––––––––

Shorty watched as the Orc Chief licked his own blood away to heal his wound. He had had never seen magic like that before. Shorty realized that this fight had just gotten much harder. The Orc Chief drove forward once more, bringing the hammer down in an overhead blow aimed at Shorty's head. Shorty wrenched his body to the side as he brought his sword across to block the strike. Sparks flew from the blade as it struck the head of the hammer and deflected it to the side.

Shorty knew he could not let the Chief go back on the offensive, so he stepped in close. Shorty drove his left hand in a hard jab at the face of his foe. It never came close. The orc's empty hand came up and closed around Shorty's fist. Shorty's hand came to an abrupt halt. He tried to jerk it free, but the Chief was strong. Much stronger than Shorty. He could not pull free. The Orc Chief laughed. "Who is stronger, ogre? Not you it seems." Shorty had no answer. The Chief spun and pulled hard. Shorty felt himself go flying through the air. He felt pain as he hit the ground hard.

––––––––––––––––––––

There were cries of astonishment from several members of the militia as Shorty flew away from the Orc Chief. The ogre rolled over one shoulder before coming back to his feet. There was a look of surprise on Shorty's face as he oriented on his opponent.

Skreee's voice came from above Thorn and H'aor. "How did it do that? My ogre is very strong."

H'aor's voice held astonishment, "I do not know, Skreee. I did not think a rock wall could just stop his punch like that."

Thorn watched as Shorty's blade began to move in a dizzying pattern of chops and slashes. "Apparently the Chief is stronger. We need to start thinking about a plan if the big guy loses. The Chief's troll heritage may be too much for Shorty."

H'aor grunted as the great sword sank into the orc's shoulder. There was a spray of blood, but the flow stopped almost immediately and the orc barely seemed to notice. "That should not be possible."

A female voice came from the trees behind them, "What should not be possible?"

Both dwarf and elf spun to see Kisa coming out of the trees to Skreee's happy cry of "Hello again, Pretty One."

Kisa's turned her eyes towards the duel as the hammer and blade crashed together once more. "Earth Mother protect us. What is Shorty doing?"

Thorn gave Kisa a sad look. "He challenged their Chief to save us all. Problem is, that thing is half troll. It heals as fast as he can hurt it. Shorty is beginning to tire. Unless your Akka can intervene, it is only a matter of time." Thorn turned from her and moved over to begin speaking to the militia teams.

As Thorn moved away, H'aor asked, "Where is Roiland?"

Kisa turned to watch Shorty. "The scouts said Typerys is headed back to the Valley. Roiland went after him. It is the Archer's duty to deliver justice."

Shorty backed a few steps away. His lungs were heaving and his arm burned from swinging the sword. This was harder that the lessons the Elf Lard had made him do. He was beginning to lose hope. He had hit the orc several times now. Both of the blows should have ended any fight he had ever been in. No matter how he cut the Chief, the ouch just went away. Somehow, he needed to hit it hard enough to kill it in a single swing.

The Orc Chief moved in with a smile and the two resumed trading blows. The hammer was coming closer now. Shorty could not move like he had earlier in the fight. Shorty ducked a wild swing and the hammer went over his head. He straightened and stepped quickly forward. Before the orc could bring the massive hammer back around, Shorty lashed out with his booted foot. He put all of his strength into a kick to the side of the Orc Chief's knee. There was a popping noise and the leg buckled, dropping the orc to one knee.

Shorty did not hesitate. He brought his sword over his head, grasping the hilt with both hands. He brought it down at the Orc Chief's neck. Shorty was certain that it could not grow a new head. Before the swing had covered a quarter of its arc, the Orc Chief surged to its feet as if the leg was never hurt. Then the orc stepped back.

The great sword missed completely and buried half of the blade in the ground. Before Shorty could pull it free, a booted foot stepped forward to pin his sword to the ground. The hammer quickly followed, striking the side of the blade just below the hilt. The blade shattered and Shorty stumbled back with the hilt still clutched in his fist.

The orc began to laugh. "Well maybe it will not end up in my collection. Not good for much anymore."

Shorty stared down at the hilt of Papa's sword. He did not understand what had happened. The sword was strong like Papa had been. Now he had lost it just like he had lost Papa. Then Shorty's world erupted in pain. He did not even see the blow that stuck his right arm. The hilt dropped to the ground and Shorty flew through the air to land at the feet of the Shaman with the feathered rattle.

Kisa cried out as Shorty's sword shattered. "Shorty!" She could only watch in horror as the hammer caught Shorty in his right arm and side. Her friend flew through the air to land at the feet of a frail-looking orc. The Shaman seemed to stare at Shorty for a long time before he nodded and looked to the large orc still standing near the center of the glowing circle.

Kisa started to push her way past Thorn and H'aor. She had to get to Shorty and help him. H'aor's hand clamped down on her arm. "No, Priestess. They will not let you near him."

Kisa was not the only one to dart forward. No one stopped the small sprite who shot through the air above them. Skreee howled as he flew straight at the large orc. Before the orc had even realized the sprite was there, Skreee stabbed out with the blue diamond sword. The small blade sank deep into the Orc Chief's left eye. Skreee released the hilt of his sword and drifted back to stare at the orc. His voice was angry as he yelled, "Evil One! You should not have hurt my ogre. Skreee, Mighty Warrior, has slain you."

The Orc Chief began to laugh. It reached up and pulled the small sword from its eye. Skreee watched as the blood stopped and the eye turned milky white. Then even that began to clear. Skreee reached for his bow. The Orc Chief slapped out with his left hand hitting the sprite hard. Skreee's broken body landed to the right of his friends and did not move.

Grief consumed Kisa as she examined the monster standing before them. Tears began to streak her cheeks. "Oh Goddess, I have lost them both." Thorn and H'aor moved protectively in front of her. They both looked at their weapons without much hope.

The Orc Chief raised his hammer overhead and released a bestial roar of triumph. As he began to move closer, he boasted, "Your warriors will all die as your foolish champion did. When they are gone, little Priestess, I will claim you as my own. You will bear me many strong brats to inherit my kingdom."

Kisa raised her mace. "You will have to kill me first. I will fight you with everything that I am."

The Orc laughed harder. "So be it. There is always the Bird Woman that rules your village. Once this puny army is gone, there will be no one to prevent us from sacking it and taking all that remain as slaves for the mine. I will restore the dragon and my Master will reward me with even more power."

Kisa pointed her mace at him. "We will stop your master after we destroy you."

The Orc examined Kisa from head to foot. "Big words, little woman. Your champion could not defeat me. He could not even hurt me. I doubt the dwarf or elf can do any better. Let us see which one dies first, shall we?"

Neither the dwarf nor the elf replied. They were beginning to lose hope and it showed in their faces.

Chapter 29
Unfinished Business

Thorn stepped forward to meet the Orc Chief's advance. It had a look of happy anticipation on its face as it eyed the dwarf. Thorn hissed at his friends, "Run! Get back within the wards. I will hold it as long as I can."

H'aor moved up beside him. "No, my friend. Side by side."

Kisa raised her Holy Symbol. "We began this journey together; we will end it that way."

Thorn shook his head and smiled ruefully. "Damn fools, both of you.

The Orc Chief strode towards the still glowing circle. As his boot reached the edge of the circle, it flashed a brilliant red and the big orc was thrown backwards.

A deep booming voice filled with pain called from across the circle. "Hows come youse runs way? Fight no bees done. Youse gibs up?"

The massive orc spun back towards the open gate and grunted in surprise. The three companions could now see the tall form of an ogre standing inside the circle near the Shaman. The ogre's right arm hung limply at his side. It had an unnatural bend between the shoulder and elbow. In his left hand was a great sword that caught and reflected the morning light. Kisa whispered, "Shorty? How is he still alive?"

The Orc Chief began to stalk toward Shorty. "How many times must I break you? Do you really think another sword is going to make a difference? You were not much challenge with your good hand."

Shorty raised the sword and gave it a few tentative swings. "Dis arm no bees bad. It work bery good. No care ifn one hand or udder. Eben ken fights wid dem both same times."

The Orc Chief raised his hammer. "Then it is time to end this so I can claim your Priestess."

Shorty peered up at the orc. "Youse talks too muches."

Shorty began to walk slowly forward. His face had regained its earlier calm expression. The Orc Chief growled in anger and charged. As it closed, Shorty lifted his sword. The Orc swung the hammer in an arc as it came in range. Shorty dropped to one knee and sliced the side of the orc's knee as it thundered past. Shorty rose and turned to face the Orc Chief who now stood before the Shaman.

The Orc Chief stared down at its leg in with a curious expression. It reached down and wiped away the green blood seeping from the shallow cut. "You cannot do any permanent damage with your toys. Why not let me end your pain?"

Shorty glanced at the leg and pointed with his sword. "Still bees hurted. Ouch no goes way. Maybeso need lick it." Shorty lifted the sword and examined it. "Good sword. Me keeps."

The orc stared down at the cut still bleeding on the side of his leg. "It burns. Like poison. But poison does not harm me." It raised its eyes to stare at the blade in Shorty's hand. "Where did you get that blade, ogre?"

Shorty lowered the blade and met the Orc Chief's gaze. "Kills big orc. Him hurts me friend. Me protect. Me breaks him. No bees nice hurt Shorty friend."

The orc nodded. "You were the one that killed my son. Did me a favor there. He was ambitious and he had that sword. I sent him away to die. That sword was not supposed to come back."

Shorty backed to the center of the circle and waited. "Talks to muches agin."

The orc glanced towards the Shaman but the old orc just looked at him expectantly. The Chief turned and to meet Shorty. "Even with that blade, you cannot win. You are broken." The orc glanced at its leg. "You will not get lucky again."

The big hammer darted forward. Shorty's sword came up and deflected the blow. The tip of the sword reached well past the hammer and sliced into the orc's cheek. Blood began to run down its neck. Shorty raised his blade between them. "Udder hand works bery muches good. Two sword be bestus."

Shorty slashed again and the orc blocked with the hammer. As it turned, it punched out with its left hand to strike the ogre's wounded arm. Shorty hissed in pain but did not drop the sword. He took several steps though and watched the orc carefully.

The Orc Chief nodded and smiled at the response to his punch. It began to circle to its left trying to take advantage of Shorty's broken arm. The ogre simply shifted his right leg backwards and waited. The orc darted in once again. Shorty spun and used the longer reach of the sword to slash at the Orc Chief's uninjured knee. This time the blade bit deep and the orc staggered. It tried to reverse directions and back away. The leg buckled beneath its bulk. It landed hard on the injured knee. The greenish blood began staining the trampled snow.

Shorty stared down at the orc with sadness in his eyes. "Good Chief protect tribe like Papa do afor. No takes care of Chief. You bad Chief. Papa not wants bees Chief. Me no wants. Me gots ta do. Me protect friends."

The orc raised its hammer to throw it. "Stupid ogre. Even if you win this fight, you will still lose. My Master has many servants. He will keep sending them. They will take your friends away from you, one by one. There are so few of you and soon there will be only you. No one can stop him."

The orc blinked in surprise at the look of determination that came over Shorty's face. "Me stop. Me protect all friend. No gonna lets bad tings win. Friends no bees hurted."

The Orc Chief laughed and tried to rise to its feet. "What can one ogre do?"

Shorty bared his tusks in a snarl. "Me ken fight. Me neber stop." Before the Orc Chief could bring its arm forward to throw the hammer, the great sword in Shorty's hand shot forward and buried itself in the orc's chest. Shorty stared into his foe's eyes. "No bery smart." Then he stepped back and pulled the sword free. "Stops youse, den stops war." The Orc Chief's body teetered for a moment then fell backwards to the ground. The dull red glow of the circle went out.

Shorty lifted the sword in his left hand over his head as he turned to face the old Shaman. Shorty released all of his anger and sorrow in a roar of challenge to his new tribe.

The Shaman smiled and turned to face the open gate. A large crowd of orcs had gathered to witness the challenge. The Shaman did not seem to raise his voice, and yet, it echoed from within the walls of the village. "Grumush has chosen a new Chief. The will of Grumush is law. The Chief is Grumush's Chosen. The Chief's word is law until he is defeated in challenge."

The Shaman raised the rattle over his head and began to shake it. The ancient orc then turned and walked to Shorty. He circled Shorty three times before stopping before him. Shorty stared at the small figure. The Shaman bowed before smiling up at Shorty. "What do you command, my Chief?"

Shorty lowered his sword. He suddenly felt very tired. "No mo fights. No bees war. Finds nudder way."

The Shaman turned and barked an order towards the open gate. A few heartbeats later, two horns began to call out across the valley. The first gave a long warbling note and the second gave three short high notes. The pattern repeated several times.

The Shaman turned to Shorty. "Your orders have been passed on to the warriors, Chief." The Shaman stared across at the those who had accompanied his new Chief into the valley. "Invite those who would be our allies to come forward. We must speak of the peace you command. We must also speak of the future of the Tribe and the will of Grumush."

Shorty slowly slid his sword into the sheath on his back. Then he motioned his friends forward. The Shaman turned to the two guards. "Bring rugs that we might sit and meet with our new allies." The two guards started to protest, but Shorty turned and reached for his sword. Their protests died as they saw the look on their new Chief's face. They ran into the village to do the Shaman's bidding.

Kisa was the first to reach Shorty and she immediately examined his arm. "This is badly broken. I can help the pain, but I do not have a powerful enough spell left to fully heal it right now." Kisa turned to the Shaman. "Can you help him?"

The Shaman stared at her with a look of sadness in his eyes. "Grumush, God of the Orc, does not grant such spells. We cannot heal our wounded or cure our sick. We only know of battle and pain. Our warriors accept their pain. If they do not recover on their own, then they die. If they are too crippled to be of use to the tribe, they are put down."

Kisa shuddered. "Your God is harsh."

The Shaman studied Kisa closely. "Our lives are harsh. We only know Grumush. He is all that the Orc have. By your standards, he is evil. But he follows the rule of law. Evil and order coexist under Grumush." The Shaman motioned towards the body of the dead Chief where H'aor and Thorn now stood. "The Orc have been without law since that one came to us. But even such as he could not defeat the will of Grumush."

Kisa nodded. "Am I forbidden to heal your Chief?"

The Shaman shrugged. "Why does Grumush care about how you use your magic?"

Kisa held up her Holy Symbol and began to cast a minor healing spell on Shorty's arm. The Shaman watched in fascination as glow of her spell sank into the ogre's flesh and the swelling began to go down.

Kisa looked over at the shaman. "There are other Gods and other ways. Would it offend Grumush if those were shared with his people?"

The shaman smiled. "Grumush demands much of our warriors. He would not allow any other God or Goddess to come between him and those he claims. But there are those among the Orc that Grumush deems below his notice. Perhaps you might find some among them that desire another way." The Shaman nodded his head towards where the women of the tribe were gathered with the smaller orc children."

Kisa nodded in understanding. "You are wise in the ways of your God."

The Shaman nodded his acceptance of her compliment. "Speak to our women. I think many would be interested if it saved their young."

H'aor stood over the body of the dead orc-troll as Thorn came up to join him. Thorn had a sour look on his face. "Anjelique is back. She tells me there were close to a hundred orcs up in the main pass into this valley. They began to break camp when those horns went off."

H'aor did not turn from studying the body lying before him. "What about Skreee?"

Thorn's voice was filled with regret. "Kisa checked on him before she went out to help Shorty. He is dead. That thing broke just about every bone in his body. Anjelique took the body. She knows of a faerie circle. She will give him to the faerie folk there. She will tell of his deeds."

H'aor reaching into a pouch on his belt and pulled out some sand.

Thorn watched closely. "What are you thinking?"

H'aor gestured towards the body. "I do not think its great strength was its own."

Thorn sucked in a breath. "Magic? The hammer?"

H'aor shook his head. "No, the hammer is powerful, but I do not think that it is the answer. I think there is something else hidden here."

H'aor positioned himself between the body and the gate. "Stand on this side, Thorn. Maybe no one else will notice what I do next."

Thorn moved to stand beside H'aor. "What are you up to?"

The elf reached out and began to sprinkle the sand across the body. He uttered several Arcane words as he released the grains, "beNE chARbar." The hammer began to glow first. Its glow was bright, even in the morning sun. As the sand reached the center of the orcs body, there was an almost blinding flash of light. Thorn turned his head away. H'aor continued to stare for a moment and then abruptly stopped chanting. The light faded away.

Thorn turned back as the light suddenly disappeared. "What in the Nine Hells was that?"

H'aor slid out his dagger and lifted the chain mail shirt that the orc wore. Then he cut away the cloth padding below it. As he cut, a finely crafted leather belt came into view. It was about five inches wide. There was no buckle visible in the front. Instead, there were runes etched in silver surrounding the image of clouds resting on a mountain top.

Thorn leaned over to look at the image. "Pretty belt, but what is it?"

H'aor squatted on his haunches and stared. "It is not a belt. It is technically called a girdle. Specifically, a girdle of strength." He pointed his dagger at the image in the middle of the runes. "My guess would be cloud giant strength. This will make our large friend something to be feared."

Thorn whistled. "That explains a lot. Shorty is gonna need an edge if he is to lead this crew. Cover it up. It should be safe for now. The new Chief should get everything from his kill."

———————————————

Five soft rugs were laid out on the ground. Three of the rugs were set side by side and the other two sat a short distance away. H'aor, Thorn, and Kisa were directed to sit to one side. The Shaman and Shorty sat on the other.

As the five took their seats, H'aor looked to the Shaman. "Before we start, may I ask a question?" The Shaman nodded once. H'aor continued. "Why were you digging up the bones of the ancient wyrm?"

The Shaman glanced towards the body still lying out on the snow.
"That one made a bargain with a human of great magic. The human
wished to create an undead dragon. When the bones were all found,
they were to be exchanged for something that one desired greatly."

H'aor nodded. "Thank you for that information."

Thorn gave the Shaman a hesitant look. "I am not really sure how
to go about this. I think the Swanmay should be sitting here instead
of me. She is the ruler of the valley. I am not even sure what we are
negotiating for."

The Shaman laid the rattle on the ground in front of his rug. He began
to slowly spin the beads in his hands. When he raised his eyes from
the beads, his features were hopeful. "We could talk of many things as
people of power often do. It would take much time and provide each
of us many opportunities to betray the other. But we are not people
of power. We are those who do the things that must be done for the
survival of our people."

As Thorn nodded his understanding, he continued. "In the end our
needs are both simple. You wish for a land free of my kind. Or at
least free of orcs that wish to do battle. The Orc need one thing above
all others. We wish to return to the lands we once ruled. This is the
will of Grumush. Long ago, those lands were promised to Grumush
in exchange for his service. That one broke his pact with Grumush.
Grumush desires that his people return to the lands that he bargained
for."

H'aor cocked his head to one side. "And how do we each get what we
desire?"

The Shaman turned to look at Shorty. "This one must act on his
beliefs. He must do what a good Chief is expected to do and work for
the good of the Tribe. He will reclaim our lands from that which took it
from us."

Thorn looked a bit surprised. "What exactly are you asking of our
friend?"

The Shaman gestured towards the west. "When the passes to our
homeland open up, our new Chief must journey there. He must make

his way past the undead to the lair of the black wyrm. After he defeats it, he must claim the stone of power that it uses to control the undead. The stone has the power to destroy the undead. The Orc can then return to the land of our ancestors. When this happens, Grumush shall abide by the deal he made long ago."

Thorn saw the look of resignation on Shorty's face. He understood that Shorty would attempt this quest no matter what it cost him. "That is a tall order even for Shorty."

The Shaman just shrugged. "It is the will of Grumush. It is the reason why Grumush allowed the ogre to win. We will provide a guide. A seasoned warrior of great prowess. We will send the oldest son of he who the troll-kin defeated. When the wyrm is defeated, the Orc will return to the lands of Grumush. There may be a few who desire to stay here, but those will live by human laws and will no longer be part of the Orc."

Kisa glared at the Shaman. "You would send two warriors to fight an army of undead by themselves? An army that chased away your Tribes. And if they get past the undead, those two must defeat a dragon? You send them to their deaths."

The Shaman smiled at her. "The dragon is young. Its only real power is the stone that allows it to control the undead. And I am only sending the two. Perhaps the Swanmay will send others to help our Chief. Or... maybe he has friends that will aid him."

The Shaman looked down at the beads in his hands. His fingers caressed one that was larger than the others. It had the visage of a one-eyed orc carved into it. His head tilted to one side as if he was listening to something they could not hear. "Grumush says that sometimes two or perhaps a handful can go where no army might venture. If these heroes truly believe in what they do, they can accomplish many great things. Things some would believe impossible."

Kisa wanted to argue, but how could she. She and a handful of friends had averted a war. She could only watch as the Shaman picked up his rattle and shook it twice. He rose and gestured to Shorty. "Come, my Chief. Your Tribe awaits you."

Chapter 30
Typerys' Return

Essabeth stared out of the window of the Council building into the growing darkness. The sun was setting on one of the longest days of her life. She had welcomed the transformation into the Swanmay. Trading life in the valley for the freedom to soar across the vast expanse of the sky had been an easy decision. It was a choice she had not regretted, until today. Now, she felt trapped because her human form could not leave the valley or the wards.

Her people… or, her friends, were out there fighting the orcs and all she could do was sit and wait to see if they returned. Her friends had left the valley just before midnight the night before and she still knew nothing of their fate. She had tried to sleep after their small force had set out on its rescue mission. But sleep had not come. She had risen in frustration to read supply and scouting reports. Unable to focus on them, she had given that up too after reading the same report several times.

Essabeth had finally walked out and sat on the edge of the lake staring up into the night sky. Thoughts of flying among the stars had tempted her. Time had little meaning to her swan form. It was guilt that kept her in her human form. How could she reach for such pleasure when her friends might be injured or even dying in battle? As dawn came to the valley, Essabeth rose to see to the needs of the people she was supposed to be protecting.

Essabeth returned to her home and dressed for the day. The full orb of the sun was visible as she began her rounds. Essabeth spent the morning checking on each of the families of the men in the militia. She expected to find at least some resentment about the rescue mission. But everyone wanted the Priestess back. Kisa had made her mark on the hearts of these people.

So, Essabeth had done her best be useful at each home she visited. She had not really been needed at any of the homes, but they let her help anyway. The women must have sensed her need for something to do. They had humored her with small tasks. She only hoped that she had not been too big a burden.

She had eaten lunch with Old Mara. Mara had soon tired of her pacing. The old cleric had sent her off to find someone else to pester. Essabeth had returned home. She had entered her home to see her rapier hanging on the wall beside the door. She took the familiar hilt into her hand. She had not truly practiced with it since her father had left on his last trip. He had drilled her daily when they were together. Why had she stopped the daily routine? Father would not be pleased.

Essabeth had changed into a soft tunic and pants before heading outside to the street. There, she had begun with stretches. Once her body was warmed up, she began with the simple drills that her father had taught her. By the time she had finished, her body was calm even if her mind still raced. Had they managed to save the priestess? How many of her friends were hurt or dead? She had no answer, so she returned to the Council building to wait for word from Thorn.

As the room grew dark, Essabeth turned away from the window. She began to light the lanterns around the room. The darkness of the room did not really bother her, but she wanted it to be lit where she was waiting if a messenger made it back to the valley. Essabeth rearranged the shawl she always wore to cover her neck as well as her shoulders. The room was getting colder, so she built a fire in the fireplace to chase away the chill.

With nothing else to do, she sat in her seat at the head of the table. She lay the rapier across her lap and her fingers ran up and down its hilt. The feel of the leather wrappings soothed her. Essabeth stared into the flickering fire. In the dancing flames, she saw her friends battling for their lives. Her thoughts dwelt on all the things that might have gone wrong that day.

Essabeth was startled by the sound of the latch lifting on the door. She must have dozed off. It was very dark outside. Her hopes began to rise as the door swung open.

Essabeth's eyes narrowed when she saw Brome standing in the doorway with an almost hungry look on his face. She started to ask what he was doing here when she heard Typerys voice from behind the big man. "Get inside you idiot. Gawk at her later. I am tired and I want this over with."

Essabeth sat up straighter in her chair as Brome came in to stand beside the door. She slid her rapier under the table where it could not be seen by either of the men who were invading her sanctuary.

Typerys came into the room and paused to stomp the snow from his boots. He did not have the look of a man fresh from battle. He radiated confidence as he turned towards the council table. Typerys took the chair directly across from her and sat. He steepled his fingers before him as he examined her. Essabeth understood that Typerys was very dangerous at this moment. The man thought he had her at a disadvantage.

Essabeth decided not to play whatever game Typerys had in mind. She would not let him make the opening move. Essabeth leaned forward, pretending not to have any concern about the two men facing her. "What do you have to report, Councilor Typerys?"

Typerys seemed to consider his answer. "Not very much, if the truth be told. Your dwarf was stubborn and refused my guidance. So, I decided to leave them all to their fate."

Essabeth struggled to remain calm. "You just left them?"

Typerys leaned back in his chair. "Of course. You see, the orc chieftain is a rather dangerous individual. I am not sure it is entirely sane. Its only real vulnerability is fire. Your dwarf refused to let me burn down the village. So, I decided not to die with your foolish friends."

Essabeth's hand clenched around the hilt of her rapier. "And how is it, Councilor, that you know so much about the orc chieftain?"

Typerys gave her a patronizing smile. "Because I have been dealing with it for months now. It was my edge while I looked for a way to relieve you of the burden of ruling this valley. I had hoped to kill the orc chieftain in the same battle that killed all your allies, but they are so uncooperative."

Essabeth's anger finally showed on her face. "You betrayed us all. All those lives lost for power you can never have."

Typerys eyes grew hard. "Of course, I can have it child. Everyone knows those bracers are the key to the magic of the valley. You can give them to me or Brome can take them from you. Either way, I will control them and the magic of the valley."

Essabeth began to laugh. "There are so many things that you have miscalculated Typerys. Let us start with this. Why would I give the bracers to you? Do you truly think me so helpless that I would just hand over such power without a fight?"

Typerys brought a finger up to his chin and began to tap it. Then his smile broadened. "No, I realized you might need some, shall we say, motivation. That is why Ohrmed stands just down the street in front of the home of the one-handed woodsman and his family. You remember the little girl that came into the valley with your foolish friends?"

Essabeth glanced towards the window into the darkness. Except it was not just darkness. She could make out the figure of a tall man standing within a pale magical light. Her eyes returning to Typerys. "And what business does he have with Dorna and her family?"

Joachim caught sight of Typerys' group just after nightfall. They were still making their way down from the pass to the valley floor. The three men were illuminated by a globe of wizard light. Joachim's first instinct was to attack them and try to take them out before they could hurt anyone. Shorty could probably pull that off, but that kind of battle was not his strength. Somehow, he needed to get them to split up. He might be able to take them one at a time. Brome would be a problem even alone. Joachim knew he had to get this right. He was not much use if he was dead.

Joachim followed them into the village. The men were talking. Typerys seemed to be doing most of the talking. From what Joachim could make out, it was one long complaint about how his friends had ruined the Councilor's plan. Joachim used the noise they were making to slip unnoticed into the shadows of the buildings. He followed them as closely as he dared. He needed some idea of what they had planned.

Typerys led the way directly towards the lake's edge. Instead of heading towards his own home, he turned directly towards the Council building. Joachim had expected them to get some rest after a night and a day on the trail. He had really hoped to catch them sleeping.

As the trio came to the home of little Will and Moira, Typerys stopped and turned to face the mage. Joachim was not close enough to hear what Typerys said, but the mage began to smile. Ohrmed moved to take up a position not far from the door to the children's home. The pale globe of light stayed with the mage, eliminating any useful shadows near him.

Typerys and his bodyguard continued on towards the Council building. The light from the windows illuminated the street. Joachim stayed where he was hidden behind a small cart. He watched Brome and Typerys enter the building. Joachim was torn. He knew Essabeth was in there. They were only two doors down on his side of the street. He wanted to be close by to help her. At the same time, he knew that she would never forgive him if he let anything happen to the children or their parents. Truth be told, he was not sure he could live with himself either.

Typerys gave Essabeth a knowing smile. "Since Ohrmed did not burn down the orc village, he still has all three fireball spells at his disposal. He has been very curious about how the spell will interact with the magic that protects the buildings. I thought that maybe the first family to experiment on should be a family you really care about. Then I think, the home of Imerus and her newborn. I asked him to save the last spell to thin out the local bird population. A few less swans would improve things." Typerys paused to watch her reaction. "Unless, of course, you wish to cooperate."

Essabeth looked down and closed her eyes. In her mind, she reached for the wards of the village. But she could not see any way to use them against something that was already within the village. There had to be a way, but she did not have time to figure it out now. She saw no way out of Typerys' trap. The bracers would not come off unless she was dead. If she died, the wards would weaken and no one would be safe in the valley. She had no choice but to save as many people as she could.

Typerys voice came as a soothing balm to his threats. "I know it is hard for one so young. But it will be over soon. Just give me the bracers and walk away. Then all those you care about will be safe. I will care for them all. Well, except for those facing the orcs. Some sacrifices have to be made."

Essabeth opened her eyes as she raised her head to meet the Councilor's victorious gaze. She wanted to scream at him. Instead, her voice came out cold and accusing. "You have caused the death of many good people. You may kill even more. In the end, you cannot have what you seek. Even if I could take off the bracers to give them to you, you cannot use them."

A look of confusion crossed Typerys face at her words. Then it was gone. "And why is that, girl? If you can master the magic of the valley, what will prevent me from doing so?"

Essabeth brought her emotions back under control. She had to make him see the truth of her explanation. "Because, Councilor Typerys, you are a man. The magic of the valley can only be controlled by a Swanmay. There never has been, and cannot be, a male Swanmay. Our race is entirely female."

Typerys shook his head. "That is nonsense. You are human. You simply wear a magical artifact.

Essabeth brought up her left hand and slowly removed the white shawl from around her neck and shoulders. The movement of the soft covering ruffled the feathers along her neck and shoulders. She reached up and smoothed the feathers back down.

Typerys stared at her in shock. "What are you?"

Essabeth laid her left arm on the table and rolled over to show where the bracers had merged with the flesh on the underside of her arm. "I am the Swanmay. I am the last of my kind. I am one with the bracers and with the valley."

Typerys face went dark with anger. Essabeth glanced once more out the window. Her thoughts filled with regret. I am sorry, Dorna, that I could not save your family. Then she noticed that the magical light was gone. She could no longer see the mage anymore.

Joachim moved to the front of the cart and studied the mage standing across the street. There was nothing to use for cover to get any closer to the man. He might be able to go back down the street and cross over, but it would take a long time to move that far without any sound. He did not think he had the time. If stealth would not work, it only left him boldness.

Joachim drew the short sword into his right hand and palmed his magic knife in his left. Then he stood and walked casually out into the street. As he came out of the shadows, Ohrmed turned to face him. The mage smiled.

Joachim walked closer as the mage studied him. Ohrmed gave his head a slight bow. "Typerys did not expect any of you to survive the encounter with the orcs. I congratulate you on being smart enough to cut and run. Perhaps Typerys can find a use for you." The mage gestured towards the sword. "We are short a thief at the moment as I am sure you know."

Joachim shook his head. "I am not too fond of your boss. I think I will pass. Why are you out here in the cold instead of in the nice warm Council building?"

The mage stepped closer and gestured towards the home of Joachim's two young friends. "Typerys thought your Swanmay might need an incentive to relinquish her power. Besides, I want to see if my magic can actually destroy one of these buildings. So, it is a duty that serves both my curiosity and Typerys needs."

Joachim stopped before the mage. "I cannot allow you to harm the children or their parents."

Ohrmed reached out an open palm. "I do understand your concern. This is nothing personal. Mah-ar-tsAW AW-KHaz." The mage grabbed for Joachim.

Joachim felt a sudden tightness on the finger with the elven ring. He stepped back two steps out of the reach of the mage. His eyes flared with anger. "I was grabbed once before by a mage. It was not a pleasant experience. I vowed not to let it happen again."

The mage smiled sadly. "It would have been easier if you were just a bit more gullible. But I assume that is why you carry Cord's sword. Do not worry. I intend to be a little more thorough than he was."

Joachim lunged as soon as the mage raised his hand again. Ohrmed spoke a harsh phrase that Joachim did not understand, "shEH laKH." Three balls of black energy erupted from his hand to impact Joachim in the chest and stomach. Joachim's only satisfaction was the feel of the short sword sinking into flesh. Pain washed over him and Joachim lost his grip on the sword. Without its support, he dropped to his knees.

Ohrmed looked down at the half of the sword protruding from just below his ribs. He was fairly certain that some of it had come out the other side. He looked down at Joachim crouched before him. "Impressive reflexes." Ohrmed coughed. It left a coppery taste in his mouth. He raised a hand to wipe at his mouth, but he could not see what came away. For some reason his light spell had gone out. He mumbled to himself, "Most unexpected." Then the mage toppled sideways to the ground.

Joachim began to crawl towards the house where the children lived. Every breath seemed to burn as he drew it in. He could smell burnt cloth and leather. He was not sure why that smell bothered him so much. Joachim made it to the corner of the house. He leaned against it. He was just going to rest for a moment. Then he would get help. Joachim closed his eyes.

———————————————

Typerys rose from his chair. "I do not believe you, girl. A race of only women indeed. Such a race would be doomed to extinction." Typerys moved towards the door. "It is time to let Ohrmed have his fun. Maybe after you listen to the screams of the first family, you will be more amenable."

Essabeth gestured towards the window. "Your mage seems to be gone. Did he desert you like you left my friends?"

Typerys stared out the window and then he turned to point at her. "Brome, take them from her. Give them to me before you indulge yourself."

The big man stepped forward with a grin. Essabeth pulled the rapier from under the table as she rose to her feet. "You may find me to be difficult to convince."

The big man studied the rapier as he drew his broadsword with his left hand. "That tiny blade might be useful in a fancy duel, but it is not going to help you." Brome licked his lips. "I have waited a long time for this."

Typerys snarled from behind Brome, "Hurry up. I do not want any witnesses."

Brome stepped forward and grabbed the table with his right hand. He flipped it over sideways clearing his path to Essabeth. Essabeth did not hesitate. As the table flew to the side, she darted forward. The tip of the rapier seemed to blur as she slashed from left to right before stepping back.

Brome stopped. A look of puzzlement and pain crossed his face. There was a whistling sound as he drew in each breath. He turned to face Typerys.

The Councilor could only stare at the perfectly straight line that crossed the big man's throat. The line of blood seemed to bubble as Brome exhaled. Typerys lifted the latch of the door. He was running into the street as the big man fell behind him.

Typerys looked to where he had left Ohrmed. The only thing he could see was a dark shadow lying on the ground. Typerys ran for his home.

There were things he would need to start over outside the valley. It was time to leave this place.

———————————

Joachim woke to the smell of garlic and boiled cabbage. Someone was standing over him, cackling. Her breath was making him nauseous. There was a pleasant feeling of cold in his chest and stomach. The pain was mostly gone now. It felt good to breathe again, even if the smell of burnt leather was still noticeable over the other smells.

As the figure leaned back, Joachim noticed the light of a small lantern sitting on the ground near his left leg. Joachim tilted he head up to see whose breathe he had been forced to endure. The form standing over him. It was a woman. A really old woman and she was grinning down at him toothlessly.

Old Mara cackled again. "You are a lot of trouble, boy. Make an old woman come out in the cold like this to save your worthless hide. Lucky for you that Ilmatar and the Swanmay both like you. Now get up and help an old woman get back to her bed. And do not get fresh with me."

———————————

Typerys came out of his room with several small bags. He did not have time to try and pack up the gold. The jewelry and gems would have to do. They should be worth enough to get himself settled someplace new. He walked down the stairs and turned towards the kitchen. He needed to pack some food for the journey south.

There was a sword lying on the dining room table. Typerys recognized it as one of the ones from his study. How had it gotten here? There was a soft sound from behind him. He turned to see a dark figure step from the shadows. It was the Drow and he carried a bow in his hands.

Typerys backed up to the table.

The Drow spoke softly, "Take the blade. Defend yourself."

Typerys shook his head. "What good is a sword against a bow? Then again, murder is the way of your kind."

Roiland looked down at the bow he carried. "The souls of those you have betrayed call for justice. But if you fear the bow of the Archer, I do understand. This once, I consent to deliver justice another way."

Roiland stepped back and leaned the bow against the wall. He pulled a dagger from his boot. "Would this do? Your sword against a dagger I took from the body of an orc?"

A smile crossed Typerys face as he reached behind him to pick up the long sword. He brought it forward and charged before the Drow could change his mind. The Drow stood still, waiting. As Typerys raised the sword to strike, the Drow's hand flashed forward. Typerys felt something strike his chest. The Drow's hands were empty now. He looked down to see the hilt of the dagger protruding from his chest.

The last thing Typerys ever heard was a soft voice of the Drow whispering, "Blessed are they who hunger for justice, for they shall be filled with righteousness."

Chapter 31
Epilog

Essabeth crossed the shallow river and began to stroll west along the lakeshore. The sun was bright as it reflected off the waters of the lake. Several of the larger male swans were swimming alongside her as she walked. The ripples from their bodies made the water sparkle in the sunlight. Peace had returned to her valley and spring had come close on its heels.

Essabeth looked up as lightning flashed across the surface of the lake not far ahead. It was followed moments later by the crackle of the discharge. H'aor was practicing again. She had hoped to find the elf out here this morning. She wanted to know how her friends were doing. They had not been around much since the battle in at the orc village. Essabeth hurried towards the corner of the lake that H'aor had claimed as his practice area. The two swans warbled their protest at her path. Neither bird would approach the source of the lightning.

Essabeth moved away from the water's edge to skirt several large pine trees. She saw the elf sitting on the ground studying a small book intently. Essabeth called out to him. "Would you mind some company? I do not want to interrupt your studies."

H'aor put down the book. "Hello, Essabeth. Please, join me. I was just rechecking a gesture. I cannot cast again today so your company would be welcome."

Essabeth wandered over and took a seat on the ground near him. "How are you, my friend?"

H'aor shrugged. "I am good. All Thorn and I did was a lot of hiking. Others took on the responsibility of fighting for our lives. Other than writing a summary for my father, I have had little to occupy myself except my magic. Now that I understand the orc's spell book, I have been free to do what I love."

Essabeth nodded. "I am glad. I see all of you so seldom now. I miss all my friends."

H'aor winked at her. "All of them?"

Essabeth blushed. "Okay, Joachim is around a lot. But it is hard to have much of a conversation with him. He tends to ramble on whenever we talk."

H'aor chuckled. "He will figure it out eventually. He is not used to caring about someone else. He will find the words in time."

Essabeth shook her head. "Maybe. First, he has to decide what he wants in this life. How is Kisa?"

H'aor gazed out over the water. "She took the loss of Skreee hard. But her Goddess has given her new work to occupy her mind."

"New Work?" Essabeth asked.

H'aor nodded. "She has introduced the Tribe's women to the Goddess Akka. There was a lot of interest. She has two new acolytes to train. Kisa says they are learning very fast. When she is not teaching, she has Roiland. He follows her everywhere. He sits and works on a new longbow while she heals and teaches. I do not know what happened the night Kisa was captured, but things have changed between the two of them."

Essabeth felt her worry for her friend slip away. "I am happy for them. What about Thorn?"

H'aor gestured to the east. "He seems to spend most of his time at the ranger camp these days. He and Anjelique spend a lot of time together. I swear, if she had a beard, I think he would have married her already."

Essabeth began to laugh, but it did not last. "What of Shorty?"

H'aor's look was grave. "We are worried about him. He blames himself for the sprite's death. Says he did not protect his little friend."

Essabeth sighed. "The sprite chose his own path. From what I have heard, it was a brave and selfless act."

H'aor nodded. "It was. But convincing Shorty is another story. He has spent the last couple weeks going out to the orc mines with his bodyguard. He has been using that new hammer to crush every one of the dragon bones that were dug up. The mage that wanted them is going to be very disappointed."

Essabeth raised an eyebrow. "Shorty has a bodyguard?"

H'aor laughed softly. "Oh yes, Bruhurst the Spear Striker. He was the son of the Chief that the troll-orc challenged for leadership. Bruhurst probably would have been Chief himself one day if the troll-kin and then Shorty had not come along."

Essabeth looked puzzled. "Why does Shorty need or want a bodyguard?"

"He does not know he has one. The old Shaman told him Bruhurst was his guide through the mountains. He is also Shorty's interpreter since the ogre does not understand orc. The Shaman told Kisa that not all of the orcs are happy about an ogre as Chief. Bruhurst is making sure no one stabs Shorty in the back."

Essabeth sat thoughtfully. "How does this Spear Striker feel about Shorty being Chief?"

H'aor began to pack his things into his backpack as he answered. "Bruhurst has a sort of hero worship thing going on. He wanted revenge for his father. Shorty did what Bruhurst could not. Shorty is just adding to it the way he treats Bruhurst."

Essabeth looked puzzled as she rose to her feet. "What is Shorty doing?"

H'aor smiled and rose to his feet. He slid his backpack on. "He treats him like a friend. I am not sure Bruhurst has ever had many friends. Shorty makes the young warrior practice with him every day. He is teaching him. Shorty says he must be 'bery good' if he is going to travel with him to the dragon's lair. Bruhurst is eating that 'protect all who bees smaller' stuff up."

Essabeth nodded her understanding as they turned back towards the village. They walked without talking for a while until H'aor finally asked. "Are you going to ask what you really wanted to know?"

Essabeth grumbled. "Was there a mind reading spell in that orc's spellbook?" The elf laughed softly and then she continued. "When are you all leaving?"

"The orc scouts indicate that the main trail should be passable in about a week. The Shaman tells us that Shorty intends to sneak out with Bruhurst as soon as possible."

"But why?" She asked. "Why leave behind people who can help him? It does not make any sense."

H'aor's face was solemn. "It makes perfect sense if you are an overprotective ogre that wants to keep all his friends safe. But that is just his plan. Thorn, Kisa, Roiland and I are going to be waiting for him on the trail. He needs us whether he likes it or not."

Essabeth paused to stare out over the lake. "He must learn to trust, to let others choose their own path. That will be very hard for him. Will it be just the four of you? No one else?"

H'aor came to stand beside her on the water's edge. "Joachim has not decided. He never wanted to be part of a war. He does not like killing. Anjelique wanted to come as well, but Thorn put his foot down. He told her she was going to be the new commander whether she like it or not. That was an interesting argument."

Essabeth turned to face him. "I bet it was." She hesitated for a moment. "There is another you should know of. A druid named Karhu. He came to see me before you arrived in the valley. He went west to fight whatever is out there. I do not know if he survived. But he and that big dog of his might be able to help you."

H'aor nodded and they turned and walked back to the village. Joachim was waiting outside of Essabeth's home as they approached.

H'aor turned to her. "He may have found the words he needs sooner than I expected. Be well Swanmay. I will be joining the others this afternoon."

Essabeth leaned in to give him a brief hug. "Goodbye, my friend and thank you. Please tell the others that I wish them well."

H'aor smiled and turned back towards the house that had been his temporary home. Essabeth turned to stare at the young man who was trying so hard to act casual. She sighed and headed to meet him. "Hello Joachim. What can I do for you?"

Joachim did not look up at her. "I wanted to talk. I need to tell you some things."

"Joachim, I do not have the time or the patience for this today. If you have something to tell me, please get to the point."

Joachim sighed. "This is not easy for me. I do not want to mess this up. I came to tell you before I let the other know. I am going with Shorty to face the dragon."

Essabeth felt disappointed. She had hoped he might stay. She had hoped there was more to him than just being a thief. So, he was moving on to new adventures and she would remain here in the valley. She put aside her regret and met his gaze. "We spoke of this once before Joachim. I told you then that I knew the thief would move on. I wish you well." She began to turn away.

Joachim's eyes widened in shock and then grew angry. "Wait Essabeth. That is not fair. This is not about me or what I want. Or at least not entirely about what I want."

Essabeth spun back to face him. "Then what is it about, Joachim?"

Joachim took a deep breath. "It is about this place. This valley will never be safe until the undead and the dragon are dealt with."

Essabeth frowned. "The undead cannot pass the wards. We do not need your protection."

Joachim stared down at his hands. "They cannot come here but the people here will not be able to get out. My friends that live here cannot survive that way. This is important to the people here and to me."

Essabeth suddenly saw something different in him. "How is it important to you?"

Joachim looked down at his hands. "I need to know that I am more than just the boy thief. If that is all I ever am, then there really is no place for me here."

"And then what, Joachim?"

His face took on a hopeful expression. "I want to come back if you will have me. I want to have a home."

She smiled and stepped forward. She linked her arm in his and turned him towards the water's edge. "Walk with me, Joachim. I am interested in hearing more."

Author Bio

Major Ursa's love of fantasy and science fiction began as a child lost in the worlds created by Andre Norton. Her characters were true heroes. They walked the paths of honor even when it came at a price. That lesson became a part of Ursa's own life.

Major Ursa made his first forays into fantasy gaming in 1980. Soon, he was creating worlds and adventures to entertain friends and family. The games became stories to entertain his children and grandchildren. Somewhere along the way, entertainment turned into teaching about honor and sacrifice and ways to persevere when things were hard. Now, the old bear is putting his favorite tales in print. The world needs heroes, even fictional ones, that are willing to put the needs of others before their own desires.

To find out more about Major Ursa and his stories please visit his website at www.ursabooks.com.

Previous works: Tapestry of the World, a collection of short stories